Anne Goring was b
there until she marri
band to Singapore v
before returning to the UK to live in South Devon. She has previously had published a number of articles, short stories and novels. Her two previous West Country sagas, also available from Headline, are A TURNING SHADOW and A SONG ONCE HEARD.

Also by Anne Goring

A Turning Shadow
A Song Once Heard

Return to Moondance

Anne Goring

KNIGHT

First published in 1996
by HEADLINE BOOK PUBLISHING

First published in paperback in 1997
by HEADLINE BOOK PUBLISHING

This edition published 2002 by
Knight an imprint of The Caxton Publishing Group

10 9 8 7 6 5 4 3 2 1

ISBN 1 84067 518 7

Typeset by Palimpsest Book Production Limited,
Polmont, Stirlingshire

Printed and bound in Great Britain by
Mackays of Chatham plc, Chatham, Kent

Caxton Publishing Group
20 Bloomsbury Street
London WC1B 3JH

For Elizabeth and John

Chapter One

The dream was always the same. It began soft and comforting, drawing me in with the familiarity of a warm, longed-for embrace, and even though I knew it would run its inevitable and harrowing course and I should wake with an extra weight of misery to carry with me through the day, I found its initial allure far too powerful to resist. I wanted to believe this dream landscape was real. I wanted to believe that I was truly back at Moondance, running wild and carefree up the hill behind the house on the golden September morning of my birthday, with no thought in my head beyond the special treats that Meg would have set out for Jed and me when we returned. And as with the way of dreams, Meg was no longer bent and evil-tempered with the rheumatics that twisted her hands to clumsy claws and swelled her joints so that her once-brisk walk was now a painful hobble, but young and smiling as she was when Aunt Hettie, too, was young, calling cheerfully to us from the lodge gate not to be late.

'Slow-coach!' Jed hurtled past me, long brown bare legs scissoring through the dry grasses, torn breeches flapping round his knees. 'I'll be at the top first!'

'Not fair!' I yelled. 'You didn't count to ten! You always cheat!'

But he only laughed and I threw myself after him to catch his ankles and pull him down so that we rolled together in a panting, giggling heap until I recollected that I had on my one decent dress and Meg had sworn to take her ash stick to my backside if I sullied its pristine starchiness before my special birthday tea.

Then Jed and I were lying on the hill top, parting the long dry grasses to look back the way we had come. Down, down, the sweep of the hill under the gentle autumn sun, to the house across the valley with the lake spreading at its feet like a length of pale silk carelessly dropped.

I felt the familiar shudder of delight, of pride . . . of possession. Not that I could lay any claim to a stick or stone of it, Papa and Aunt Hettie between them had seen to that. No, it was Moondance that possessed me. As I lay there it seemed that I could feel myself change: my bones the granite of the rock that had been hewn out of the hill to build the house, my blood the water that seeped through hidden springs to feed the lake, my flesh the rich earth from which the shrubs and trees in the neglected parkland grew to smothering excess. And all the people who had ever lived there, loved there, died there, seemed to flow about me, through me, like a continuing stream, drifting in patterns of light and colour as they played out their particular fate . . .

Strange feelings, though in my dream I did not think them strange at all. It was only when I was awake that such weird sensations were troubling and must never be spoken of. Aunt Hettie had made that clear. 'I will not have it, Miranda! It is the sort of nonsense the foreign woman talked which brought no happiness to her or your poor dear father!' Yet her eyes were frightened, for the foreign woman, my mother, had spoken too often of disturbing things that would have been better left unsaid, and had even foretold her own death.

But now they were all gone: Papa, Mama, Aunt Hettie. Only old Meg was left, and young Jed, and they had no power to guard Moondance or me from the incomer.

Even as the thought formed in my mind, I felt the atmosphere darkening. This was the moment when I often tried to escape from the dream, to will myself awake. But I never could. I had to look where Jed pointed, to the thread of earth burrowing between the steeply banked hedgerows that marked the road from Ashburton. And I saw the cloud of dust rising in the wake of the carriage. Dust that cast a spreading shadow, like a cold blight, reaching towards me, pulling me back from the warm sunlight on the hill until I stood once more at the lodge where the carriage had drawn up.

Then the carriage door was opening and the man in the black coat and the tall black hat was reaching out a bony hand to drag me inside. Try as I might to twist and turn away from that seeking claw, I was helpless to move. My body had become leaden, my legs mired in clay, and Meg held tight to Jed to stop him helping me. 'Best you should go, my lover,' she cried. 'Naught left here for 'ee now.' 'No,' I screamed. 'No! I want to stay with you!' But the door was closing on me. I was trapped. And as I looked into the cadaverous face of the stranger, I saw that it was not a man at all but a great black bird with glittering eyes. It sprang across to knock me screaming to the floor and spread its smothering wings across my face. 'Theophilus Crowe,' it cackled. 'I am Theophilus Crowe. I own Moondance now and you never shall . . .'

'Mary! Shut your noise! You'll have Ma Hatcher on us.'

I blinked awake. Biddie's face swam into focus. It was her hand that dug into my shoulder, her sharp knee that jabbed into my side. The familiar smells and sounds of the apprentice house flooded in. Snores and coughs and whimpers, the smell of fifty-odd underfed, dirt-grimed children cramped into an airless room that might comfortably have held half that number; of brimming chamberpots and dank straw pallets. The smell of servitude and exhaustion and despair.

'Oh, Biddie . . . thank heaven it's you . . . I was dreaming.'

'You was twitchin' and skrikin' so bad I thought you'd taken a fit.' It was already dawn. In the cool light filtering through the high barred windows Biddie's thin face was a pallid grey against the strident red straggles of her hair, her eyes huge with relief that I was properly awake and myself again. 'I was frighted you'd wake Ma Hatcher and put her in a temper. Wouldn't take much for 'er to stop you going to Miss Ida's teaparty.'

'Teaparty?' I struggled to gather my scattered wits. The dream – the nightmare – had been so sharp, so intense, that my heart still pounded with the horror of those smothering black feathers, the stabbing of talons and yellow beak against my helpless flesh.

'You can't have *forgot*!'

''Course not,' I said stoutly. ''Course I hadn't forgotten.'

But I had and it took a full minute before I could push away the clinging horror of the dream and turn my thoughts thankfully to the excitements that lay ahead.

This was the day that we had yearned for, talked about, for weeks. Miss Ida Loveridge, our employer's cosseted daughter, would be sixteen this week. I had been chosen as one of six apprentices to take tea with her and the new Mrs Loveridge, Miss Ida's step-mama, this very afternoon, it being Sunday and the one day when the powerful waterwheel turning in its slimy green pit was allowed to rest and the mill to stay silent. And even those not selected for this particular honour would have the chance to fill their bellies at dinner with the unaccustomed richness of gravy-laden roast beef and potatoes and parsnips with a spiced currant pudding to follow, instead of the usual Sunday potato hash sparsely scattered with strips of fat bacon. Ma Hatcher had been bad-tempered for days about the amount of trouble the extra cooking would put her to, while we optimistically dreamed that in view of the double celebration of the master's return to Derbyshire with his new bride and Miss Ida's birthday, we might also expect an equally lavish supper such as we usually had at Christmas, of white bread so fine in texture that it near melted on the tongue, along with a slab of good cheese and a slice of plum cake instead of onion gruel and coarse oatcake. Or that there might be some other unexpected treat in store. Perhaps we would be allowed out beyond the high walls that bordered the mill to fish or paddle in the river or to walk up the hillside to gather flowers or blackberries, this being so special a day like the Wakes or when the fair came to the village a few miles up the valley and we were given the fourpences due to us twice a year to spend as we pleased. Anything was possible with Mr Loveridge in the unexpectedly cordial mood he had displayed last evening.

'Mr Hatcher has not had too many problems with you in my absence,' he had said, pacing slowly past us. 'And such as have come to my notice, I have a mind to overlook for once.'

His voice had a sibilant, carrying quality that hissed into the black shadows cast by the weak candlelight from the lanthorns into the far corners of the room where – boys seated at one long wooden table, girls at the other – we ate our supper. The moment he had walked in we had scrambled to our feet, and though with a curt nod he had indicated we should be seated once again on the narrow benches and resume our meal, not one of us – not even the eldest, best-grown lad – had the nerve to finish the rapidly cooling onion gruel lest the rattle of spoon against tin bowl should draw Mr Loveridge's chilling blue eye and therefore his displeasure. Instead we watched his measured progress around the tables with more than usual apprehension. His narrow smile might hold a hint of good humour rather than the sourness that betokened some sarcastic comment or meting out of punishment, but it could not be entirely trusted. The treat, so long dangled before us like a carrot before a starving donkey, might yet be withdrawn if he fancied some evidence of misbehaviour or slackness at work.

But to our growing astonishment he had even looked tolerantly upon poor Maggie Armitage who had been half choking in her attempts to suppress her rattling cough. She huddled against me and I could feel the tremors that shuddered through her slight body as she fought to contain the spasm. I found myself willing her to hold on and I groped for her hand, wanting to pour some of my own strength into her frail little body, even though I knew that it was quite hopeless.

Yet when the lung-tearing bark burst out Mr Loveridge scarcely faltered in his stride. His face darkened momentarily to a frown at the interruption, but all he growled was, 'The place is plagued with coughs and colds. I shall speak to my wife about a suitable black draught. You must all be dosed against the spread of these inconvenient infections. It is fortunate for you all that your new mistress has expressed an interest in the welfare of my employees, though I have informed her I will not stand for spoiling and coddling so do not think you may take advantage.'

Take advantage? Small chance! I thought grimly of the accidents and illnesses I had witnessed in the five years I had been at Crossbank Mill. The times when some feverish complaint had swept through the apprentice house but we had still been forced from bed and into the mill to tend our machines; the times when I'd seen those with limbs strained or broken from some entanglement with the machinery – or bruised from one of Mr Hatcher's thrashings – dragged to their work, for the drawing frames must not be allowed to stop during the appointed hours or production of the fine cotton, for which Crossbank had a high reputation, would fall behind.

I could not see that the new Mrs Loveridge, however kind, would be able to make much impression on the harshness of the regimen we were forced to submit to in the interests of Mr Loveridge's profits. As for Maggie's cough, that was not likely to be eased by any black draught. It was too deep-seated, and persistently worsening from the effects of labouring from six in the morning to nine at night in the close atmosphere of the carding room, where the air was so clouded with drifting cotton fibres that they constantly clogged in the nose and throat and clung to hair and eyebrows and clothing like flakes of snow. But at least, tonight, she was spared a tongue-lashing from Mr Loveridge or a cuff round the ear from Mrs Hatcher by way of teaching her to know her place. Mr Loveridge, indeed, seemed disinclined for once to dawdle long in the apprentice house. Once he had made his inspection he did not linger, even omitting to call our numbers, as he usually did, to make sure nobody was missing. He hastened off and only when he had gone did we fall thankfully to finishing our supper while, from the boys' table, ribald suggestions spread down the benches as to Mr Loveridge's reasons for wishing to be home to his bride in such a hurry, which set the older girls spluttering into their bowls.

'Stop this racket, else you'll feel my fist,' Ma Hatcher bawled. 'Get to your beds, you young buggers, or there'll be no roast beef for any of you tomorrow.'

But it was not Mrs Hatcher's threats made us scurry to rinse our bowls in the buckets of water set out for the purpose before replacing them on the table, then make for the stairs – it was the sudden appearance of her husband in the kitchen doorway. Slatternly as Ma Hatcher was, and free with her fists and curses, she had been known to display a rough kindliness to tearful newcomers or to a sick child. If Mr Hatcher had any such compassionate streak, I for one had never seen any evidence of it. He was Crossbank's overlooker and master of apprentices and it was his business to see that production at the mill ran smoothly and that no apprentice flagged during the appointed working hours or misbehaved out of them. He carried out all his duties with ruthless efficiency.

He lounged against the doorpost picking slivers of meat out of his yellow teeth with one black fingernail. The short stick he habitually carried rose and fell against his greasy leather breeches with a sharp tapping noise. Mr Hatcher did not like to be disturbed at his supper and his small curranty eyes were sour with spite that boded ill for somebody.

It was Maggie he picked on.

We had to pass him to get to the stairs. Struck silent now. The only sound the patter of bare feet or the shuffle of slipshod boots on the boards to make a counterpoint to the rhythm of Mr Hatcher's tapping stick. I still had Maggie by the hand. Biddie was on her other side, the two of us involuntarily closing up to shield her from Mr Hatcher's gaze, all three of us keeping our eyes down and quickening our pace until we should be well past him.

The stick barred our way and I heard Maggie's frightened whimper as she cowered against me. Mr Hatcher thrust himself from the doorpost and stood before us, a big black bull of a man, the powerful waft of the strong ale he'd just been drinking vying with the reek of rancid sweat from his jacket.

'So, you're the one as is causing trouble,' he said softly. He reached out his stick and stuck it under Maggie's chin, forcing her to look up at him. 'I've had near enough of you today, my girl. Lingering in bed this morning, then found asleep behind the skips when there was a full hour to go before work was finished for the day, and to cap it all you've been larking at table . . .'

'Maggie's poorly today, master.' The words burst out, too sharp, too bold, before I could stop them. I did not want to say them. Did not mean to, but the thought of Maggie in the state she was in having to endure further torment filled me with such pain and anger that there was no containing it. I caught Biddie's warning glance and took a calming breath before I added, more meekly, 'It weren't her larking and laughing, honest. It's just her cough's bad and she couldn't hold it back.'

'Who asked you, Mary Bray?' The stick darted out and jabbed me painfully in the ribs.

'It's the truth, master,' I persisted, in a low, hurried voice. 'She's been badly all week. Some days her's been hardly able to get her breath. Mrs Hatcher knows. She's rubbed goose grease on Maggie's chest every night, but it don't give her no ease . . . Oh, please, master, don't punish her for not being able to stop coughing. She can't help it and a beating'll only make her worse.'

'Oh, dearie me, what a pitiful, sad tale to be sure.' His teeth were bared in a mocking grin. 'Fair tugs at me heartstrings, it does. Ah, but if I had a ha'penny for every such tale I've heard from the slackers and idlers I'm forced to deal with, why, I'd be a rich man and able to buy a mill of me very own!'

'Maggie's not slacking! She's poorly. Look how she's shivering. She can barely keep on her feet. It'd be cruel and wrong to punish her for summat she hasn't done.'

I was shaking myself with distress and fear, on my own behalf as well as Maggie's. I was doing myself no service bringing myself to Mr Hatcher's notice. It was always best to keep quiet, do your work, endure punishment with as much stoicism as you could muster and never make a fuss about anything. Give him no cause to pick you out. I had learned that quickly enough when I first came to Crossbank. I had seen how those who complained and answered back or rebelled against the harsh discipline were always the ones selected whenever there was need of a scapegoat. Far better to lie low, to do as you were told. Neither thinking ahead to impossible dreams of escape into a world that neither knew nor cared what happened to you, nor letting yourself drift into despairing remembrance of a previous life that was lost forever. For there was danger in dreaming, too. The clattering machines which dominated the long hours of our day had no regard for human error. A moment's inattention could mean lost fingers or broken bones or worse. Endurance, that was the thing. Grit your teeth and get on with what you were told to do until you'd served the years of your apprenticeship and could walk out of the mill to freedom, with the law on your side and no one with the power to fetch you back on the strength of a piece of paper you had been made to sign when you were too helpless, too scared, too young, to know you were signing away your childhood.

'So that's the way it is, Mary Bray.' Mr Hatcher's attention was all on me now. 'You've set yourself up as judge and jury over him as is your master. And what gives you leave to think you can tell me what's right and what's wrong, eh?'

I swallowed. 'I . . . I meant no offence, master. P'raps . . . you've such a lot to look to, you mightn't have noticed how badly Maggie was, her being little and not wishing to make trouble. She's a good girl and very quick and willing when her's in good health.'

'Is she indeed?' Something had altered in his expression. Something that deepened my fear and made me wish I was a hundred miles from this shadowy room with the big man standing over me, his red tongue creeping out to lick slowly around his lips, and the tip of the stick which had so recently jabbed me in the ribs, now sliding over my waist and hip and down my thigh. 'And how about you, eh? Are you willing, Mary?'

The stick reached my calf where the hem of my ragged, too-short skirt ended.

'Well? Lost your tongue all of a sudden?' I felt the draught of air up my bare legs as he lifted my skirt. His glance slithered slowly over me. 'Quite a grown wench, aren't you? Can't say I've taken much note before, but I see you're fair bursting out of that dress . . . And so much ankle on show. Dear, dear. Mind, pretty ankles like that deserve to be on public display. Pity to hide 'em. And those fine shapely legs . . . Let's see, how old will you be now?'

'Fourteen,' I whispered, feeling my face burning with shame and indignation and terror.

'A good age, fourteen,' he said, softly, raising his glistening black eyes once more to my face. 'Especially for a *willing* girl.'

'Master . . . Maggie's near dead on her feet.' I wanted to keep my voice calm and steady, and failed. 'Can . . . can we go up now?'

He was suddenly in a good mood.

'I reckon I'll be lenient this once,' he said. 'But think on this, Mary Bray, I'll be watching you carefully from now on. I reckon you and me have got a bit of unfinished business as must be settled.' He paused, then said with slow emphasis, 'Girls with too much to say for themselves must learn to be more humble, and I've a mind to give you a little learnin' in private on that very subject.'

His laughter followed us as we fled up the dark stairs to the sanctuary of the girls' bedchamber.

Looking back, it is possible to interpret the recurrence of the dream on that particular night as holding some significance. But, unlike those other moments of awareness, of prescience, that troubled me deeply whenever they occurred, I noticed nothing different – nothing prophetic – about the dream save its extraordinary clarity. I thought it was worry that had caused me to suffer a nightmare, for even through bone-deep exhaustion my mind would not let me fall instantly to sleep. Mr Hatcher's words wove round and round in my head, dark and menacing. I knew very well what that threat of 'learning' meant though I'd previously thought myself safe from his attentions, being so scrawny and ill favoured. It was the pretty ones he usually pestered with pawings and whisperings when they were at their work. They were the girls whom he would send on errands in order to waylay them in some quiet corner. There they would be obliged to let him thrust his squeezing, pinching fingers up their skirts or down their bodices, none of them daring to resist. I knew of only two who had. To one he had afterwards given so severe a beating on a trumped-up charge of theft that she was never right in the head afterwards and had to be taken off her frame and put to the simplest work of picking out the dirt and seeds from the raw cotton to prepare it for carding. The other, who took her complaints to Mr Loveridge, was met with cold indifference.

'Pray do not come snivelling to me with such lying accusations. I am perfectly aware of the low morals of you and your kind. So many come here steeped in the whorish tricks of the streets, having known no other way. But by God, I will not have such baseness here! You have been brought to a respectable trade . . . you are fed and housed and clothed at no little expense to myself. And what do I get in return? Whining attempts to discredit the honest man set above you in order that you shall learn the ways of obedience and discipline. Let me assure you, I have every confidence in Mr Hatcher who has served me well and faithfully for many years. Your sly words mean nothing against his, so do not try ever again to spread such tales. But perhaps if an example is made it might warn others to desist from inventing lies . . .'

So before we were allowed supper that night Mr Loveridge called her out and himself administered six strokes of the strap kept in the dining chamber for that purpose. Then he took a pair of scissors and cropped off her long yellow curls, her only vanity, so that her hair was reduced to ugly, uneven spikes. She did not complain ever again, though Mr Hatcher tormented her relentlessly in the following weeks – seeming to take extra pleasure in her humiliation – before he grew tired of her and diverted his lustful attention elsewhere.

And now, it seemed, he had turned that attention to me. I shuddered and huddled closer to Biddie, wanting her to distract my thoughts by whispering about the treats in store for us today, but she had drifted back to sleep. Even though sleep was a commodity none of us ever had enough of, I was too restless to settle. I was haunted both by the dream and the evil pictures conjured up by Mr Hatcher's threat. His hands crawling about my body, his wet lips slobbering on my skin, being forced to touch him in return . . . Even the thought of it made me feel sick. I slid from under the grubby sheet that covered us. Better to be up and about than lie here brooding, and I must see if Maggie was better this morning.

My heart sank when I saw that she clearly was not.

Only the biggest girls had the luxury of two to a bed. The rest of us must manage as best we might with three sharing. Biddie and I had been well contented when the older girl who had taken up most of the sleeping space had moved on and little Maggie from the new batch of apprentices had been apportioned to us. She was small for her eight years and, lying with her head to the foot of the bed, seemed to take up no room at all.

Now there seemed even less of her, barely a handful of sparrow bones under the covers, and the sound of her hoarse, ragged breathing frightened me even more than the two unnatural spots of colour on her cheekbones that stood out like fiery beacons against the ashen pallor of her face.

'Maggie . . . Maggie, love,' I whispered urgently.

But she did not stir and when I smoothed the dirty tangle of limp hair from her forehead I felt her skin searing hot and dry under my fingertips. She was burning up with fever!

What should I do? What should I do? I looked around wildly then, with a dim memory of Aunt Hettie, once when I was ill, bathing my forehead with comforting, sweet-smelling lavender water, I snatched up my Sunday pinafore from its hook beside the bed and ran to the pitcher of water that stood on the table at the end of the room. I soaked the coarse cambric and flew back to Maggie to press the wet cloth as gently as I could against her cheeks until she moved her head restlessly on the lumpy bolster. But still she did not wake and the words that came from her dry, cracked lips were the disconnected mutterings of delirium.

I stared at her in despair. It was hard to believe that I was looking at the same lively, eager child who had arrived six months since with a head full of impossible expectations.

'We walked all the way from Gloucester, me an' Ma,' she had announced proudly. 'We come right away when we 'eard there was work to be got 'ere, and that the 'prentices was given good food and learnin' and plenty of free time out in the country. Master thought I looked a bit small, but Ma promised I was a hard worker . . . 'er was that pleased when master said I could make my mark on the paper – an' he give me a whole shilling when I done as he showed me. 'Course, I give it to Ma, an' 'er cried 'er was that happy, for times 'as been mortal bad since Pa was took, an' there's three more younger'n me at home.'

Most of us had heard the self-same tales of fine country living and easy work in the mills. Glossy lies. Put about by agents whose business it was to make sure there were plenty of willing recruits to serve the needs of the mill masters. Lies conveniently accepted by those who had charge of the poorhouses and by those whose best interests lay in encouraging the poorest families to send their children away before they became an extra burden on the parish.

I wondered what Mrs Armitage would say if she could see her daughter now. Not that there was any likelihood of that. She was far off in Gloucester with her own troubles and Maggie might as well be orphaned as Biddie and I and many of the others were.

For once I was relieved to hear the clanging of keys as Mrs

Hatcher unlocked the bedchamber door. Almost before she had time to waddle two steps into the room, I was on her, dragging her, protesting, to our bed.

'What're you about, you young varmint?' she cried, swinging her massive fist so that I had to dodge under her arm to avoid a buffet to my ear. 'I been up half the night 'tending to the beef that's a-roasting for your dinner an' I'm in no mood for daft tricks.'

'Oh, please, Mrs Hatcher . . . it's Maggie. Her's real bad.'

She leaned her bulk over the bed and peered shortsightedly into Maggie's face, at the same time roughly shaking her shoulder. Maggie's eyes fluttered open, but there was little comprehension in their sunken depths.

'Well? What's amiss with 'ee then? Chest still bein' a trouble? You're a bit 'ot, that's for sure, though no spots come out as I can see. Hope you're not sickening for 'owt catchin' for I couldn't be doin' wi' all of you skrikin' about being sick.' She straightened up. 'Well, I 'en't got time to bother with you today.'

'But she needs medicine . . . a doctor.'

'Hold your noise, Mary Bray. Your tongue's too busy by 'alf an' you know well enough master don't 'old wi' sending for doctors unnecessary. What I was about to say when you interrupted me was as you can come wi' me to the kitchen and I'll show you how to make up an 'ot mustard plaster for her chest. Nowt so good as 'ot mustard for a feverish cough. Fetch me your bolster.' She doubled the bolster up behind Maggie's shoulders and propped her against it. 'Her'll breathe easier like that. And best put plenty o' weight on her.' She snatched the covers off the girls curled together like puppies in the next bed and piled them over Maggie's slight form. 'You can bring an 'ot brick up an' all. Put it to 'er feet. Fever'll break in no time wi' that amount of coddlin', so no need to give me that sulky look. Her'll be up and about afore you know it. Now, I got more important things to see to.' She raised her voice to a bellow. 'Out o' bed, you lazy lummocks, or there'll be no breakfast, never mind a beef dinner, if you're not downstairs in two shakes o' the cow's tail.' Which set those who had taken the opportunity to snatch an extra few moments of sleep tumbling hurriedly from their bed.

Biddie, as frightened as I was at Maggie's state, helped me to apply the rag spread with the mustard poultice on to Maggie's narrow, bony chest, moving her limp limbs about as though she were nothing more than a rag doll. We put the hot brick to her feet, which were icy despite her fever, and tucked her up as tight as we could before we ran down to snatch breakfast.

As we gulped down the last of our watery porridge, Mr Hatcher came into the room to inform us, sourly, that Mr Loveridge had ordered, as we'd hoped, the yard gates to be opened and kept open until sunset and we might come and go as we pleased. He quelled the ripple of excited whispers by slamming down his stick on the table to set the tin plates and mugs nervously dancing. 'But if one of you is late for dinner, or strays further than the river bank, then you'll regret the day you was born,' he snarled.

Even his threats were not enough to quench the excitement in the apprentice house today. Once he gave the word, there was a rush for the door. Only Biddie and I were left to trudge back upstairs and stare at each other across the sickbed in the deserted bedchamber.

'We can't leave 'er,' Biddie said after a minute, her voice sounding over-loud in the silence. 'Ma Hatcher'll not bother comin' up to see 'ow she does. Nor anybody else, for that matter.' A long-drawn out pause then, flatly, 'Nobody cares. Not for 'er. Not for us.'

I felt the same bitterness that laced Biddie's words well like bile into my own throat. I saw the same anger that rose, treacherously, in my mind reflected in her narrowed eyes. Dangerous emotions, both, to nurture or to express at Crossbank Mill.

Nobody cares.

And it was more than helplessness in the face of Maggie's illness that made me answer, coldly sarcastic, 'P'raps Miss Ida

Loveridge would come down and sit wi' Maggie for an hour or two. After all, 'er 'as a holiday every day. Her wouldn't miss a nice walk in the country for once.' It was the accumulated hopelessness of the years we had been confined here and the years that lay ahead. The injustice that ruled us, the unending drudgery of harsh, unceasing toil. It was Mr Loveridge cutting off a girl's hair for speaking out the truth. It was barred windows and the sound of Ma Hatcher's key turning the great lock that sealed us in at night. It was Mr Hatcher's arm raised to bring down his stick on bruised shoulders and his black-nailed hand lying heavy on a girl's thin arm.

There was a moment when I wanted to scream and rage and beat my fists in frustration, but Biddie saved me. She laughed. A forced, poor mockery of her usual robust giggle, but a laugh, nevertheless, to jerk me back from the knife edge of perilous impulse.

'Eh, I wouldn't trust our Maggie wi' Miss Dainty-arse. 'Er'd swoon right away sooner than mucky 'er fingers by touching any of us. I heard tell 'er once had a stable lad beaten for brushin' against 'er when he'd been clearing 'oss shit off the cobbles.'

What we knew of our employer's daughter came from rumour and gossip. Glimpses of her were restricted to the two occasions in the year, Christmas and Easter, when we were marched to the church in the village instead of having the usual Bible reading and prayers from a faded cousin, a dependant of Mr Loveridge's, Miss Groom, who on Sunday afternoon performed this duty before she did her best with the thankless task of instilling a little book-learning into the heads of children who were mostly too tired, too listless or too disinterested to take much notice.

From the gallery at the back of St Peter's we could only catch a glimpse of Miss Loveridge's bonnet amid a sea of plumes and ribbons. Then, as we were not allowed to leave after the service until the congregation in the nave of the church had dispersed, we could follow her progress through the throng moving towards the west door.

She was always beautifully dressed in silk or velvet according to the season. Pale, pretty shades that enhanced her delicate pink-and-white colouring and fair hair. She smiled charmingly as she and her papa paused to speak to friends and only once had I ever seen her look up towards the gallery. But it was the briefest of frowning, fastidious glances before she moved on, as though the sight of such a rough, ragged bunch of children was an affront to her refined nature. It was clear that Miss Loveridge did not know – or did not care – that her beautiful clothes, her privileged way of life, were in no small measure due to us.

'Wouldn't be 'er idea, would it? Inviting some of us up to tea to the 'ouse,' Biddie said, as if she had followed my train of thought. 'Not Miss Dainty-arse.'

'The new missus's, I suppose,' I said. 'But I don't see as how I can go now.'

'But you can't not go!' Biddie cried, sounding as disappointed as I felt. 'You got a new dress an' cap. It'll be given to Sal Smith if you don't. You know 'ow her's been green as grass because you was chose instead of her. Her reckons 'erself near as good a scholar as you. Her's properly grieved Miss Groom didn't pick 'er.'

'But Maggie . . .'

'Turn and turn about,' Biddie said stoutly. 'No reason we should both lose our 'oliday altogether. Won't be another till Christmas Day. You sit with 'er this mornin'. I'll stay while you get off to your teaparty.'

'Well, if her's no worse . . .'

But, thankfully, by the time Biddie returned, her tattered skirt sodden from the knees down, her feet and legs unnaccustomedly clean from the hours spent paddling in the river and her eyes bright from the fresh air, Maggie did seem a little improved.

'The fever seems to have broke,' I said, with relief. 'She's started to sweat like Mrs Hatcher said she would. And just now she opened her eyes and smiled at me proper . . . But if only 'er wasn't so weak! I tried to give her a sip o' water just now but 'er barely seems to have the strength to swallow. Tryin' brought on a terrible fit of coughing and that seems to tire 'er even more.'

'P'raps 'er strength'll come back when she's 'ad a good sleep,' Biddie said hopefully. 'By tomorrow 'er'll likely be properly herself again if her can rest up today.'

Wishful thinking, we both knew that. It was clear that it would take more than a day in bed to make Maggie well. Even if the fever had eased, that painful, tearing cough would not be shifted quickly, nor her strength brought back. She needed many long days – weeks perhaps – of rest and care and warmth with a doctor in attendance to order medicines to cure her cough and nourishing food to put flesh on her bones. Instead of which she would be put back to work in the carding room just as soon as her legs could support her. It was so wrong! So cruel! But who was there to listen to, or sympathise with, the likes of us? Certainly neither of the Hatchers nor Mr Loveridge. I clutched at the one faint hope. The new Mrs Loveridge, who had expressed an interest in us, Mr Loveridge had said. Who might turn out to be sympathetic and might, just might, be appealed to on Maggie's behalf. And, in turn, could bring whatever influence she had to bear on an ardent new husband anxious to please her . . .

Biddie was right. I should go to the teaparty. That way lay our only hope of relief for Maggie's suffering.

Miss Groom came promptly at three-thirty, as promised, to escort us to the big house.

She was a faded, elderly woman who once might have been pretty and lively, but her years as a companion to the first Mrs Loveridge – by all accounts a cantankerous and demanding invalid, who had died this past spring – had drained the heart out of her and the odour of lost hopes clung to her as strongly as the musky aroma of the dried herbs she scattered amongst her mouse-grey garments against the moth. She fussed about us with an air of nervous distraction while we stood in the yard, well scrubbed as ordered, to be inspected in our scratchy new clothes and the shiny shoes that felt uncompromisingly rigid to feet that were mostly accustomed to downtrodden old boots, or no boots at all.

'Tom, your hands are still grimy. Rinse them once more under the pump . . . Alice, tuck your hair under your cap. It will not do at all to have it tumbling about your face – and how have you managed to get mud already on the hem of your skirt? No, leave it! You will only make it worse. It will brush off better when it is dry . . . Now, all of you, remember, do not speak unless you are spoken to. You will be shown where to sit, but on no account seat yourselves until Mrs Loveridge and Miss Loveridge do so. You will be offered bread and butter and cake, but do not take more than one piece of each, and for heaven's sake, take care with your plate and cup. Bear in mind that any breakages will earn you a caning. Now, walk briskly else we shall be late.'

She continued her monologue of advice and instruction all the way to the house, but once she had chivvied us across the mill yard, through the big iron gates and on to the road, I did not listen. I did not care how we ought to comport ourselves at Crossbank Grange. Nothing mattered save that we were beyond our imprisoning walls and I must gather every sensation of this free, beautiful world and hoard it against the weeks when there was nothing but ugliness about me.

Once outside the gate we turned from the more familiar way that wound along the wooded valley bottom past the two raw stone terraces built by Mr Loveridge to house some of his waged workers and then to the village two or three miles distant. We took the road that led in the opposite direction, quickly diverting from it on to a narrow footpath that made a more direct, if steeper, approach to the substantial house from where the Loveridges might gaze down upon the source of their wealth while remaining conveniently remote from it.

I felt the silky breeze against my face, heard the bleating of the sheep, inhaled the rich, sweet scents of sun-warmed grass and earth. This was hard, high country and on a less benevolent day the hills that pressed close about the narrow dale looked dark and forbidding. Today, the warm golden light blunted the severity of these sentinel hills so that even the jagged outcrops of craggy limestone seemed less severe.

I looked up at the untroubled blue of the September sky and down at the grasses that brushed against my skirt to leave a feathery trail of seedheads clinging to the coarse grey cotton. I wanted to linger; to have time to touch a leaf, a flower, the perfect whorl of a snail shell gleaming with the lustre of garnet and pearl, but already we were through a wicket gate in the low drystone wall that divided Loveridge land from the rough sheep-grazed moorland grasses. No need here to build walls twice the height of a grown man in order to make prisoners of those within.

The footpath skirted a stand of beech trees and crossed a gravelled carriage drive that swept in a broad, rising S-shape to the front porch then through an arch to the back of the house where I thought we should be directed. But Miss Groom led us up a flight of stone-flagged steps that climbed between regimented, terraced beds of yellow and red roses and marched us straight to the front door. This *honour*, she informed us, had been bestowed by Mrs Loveridge herself. I clutched eagerly at this good omen. Surely a lady who could treat her husband's lowliest employees with such respect would be willing to speak up in favour of a sick child?

The door was unlocked. Miss Groom turned the shiny brass door knob and pushed it wide. The others had whispered excitedly all the way, but now they fell to an awed silence as they saw the richness within. Dancing prisms of light reflected from the cut-glass chandelier on to gleaming oak panelling weighty with paintings in carved and gilded frames, on the sweep of the polished staircase, on the starched and frilled apron of the parlour maid bustling towards us.

I was the last to enter and at the precise moment when I should have followed Alice across the threshold, I stopped dead. Someone was calling me. Not from inside the house but from outside. I turned sharply. A man's voice. I looked round. The terraces of roses were empty of gardeners and nobody else was about. I looked farther off. From this elevated spot I could clearly see the huddle of mill buildings and the road following the meanders of the river until both plunged round the wooded bluff that hid the village from view. I could see the small figures of my workmates idling on the banks and hear, very faintly, their shouts and laughter. Being Sunday there were no wagons trundling to and from the mill. Nothing moved on the road . . . No, I was wrong. A horse and rider coming round the bluff at a brisk canter. I caught the thump of hoofbeats. I saw how the thudding hooves ate up the distance that divided us and sent spurts of white dust rising in their wake like little puffs of summer cloud.

There was no reason for me to believe that the rider was coming here. No reason for the curious sense of expectancy that possessed me. He was merely a traveller who would pass by on the valley road. But as I stood there, the rider looked up towards the house, raising his hand to shield his eyes from the sun almost as though he sensed me watching him. Which was ridiculous. Almost as ridiculous as the fancy that he had been the one to call my name . . . I shook my head, puzzled. The voice had been so clear, so urgent . . . Miranda.

Miranda?

But I was Mary now. Had been for nearly five long years. Nobody knew me as Miranda. Even my name had been taken from me when I entered Crossbank Mill as being too fancy and, as my protests only earned me blows and curses, I had thought miserably that I must learn to accept my new name along with this dreadful new situation. After all, Miranda Brehault – that carefree, innocent child – belonged heart and soul to Moondance. Perhaps it was best that she remained there, untainted, undiminished, while plain Mary Bray bore the servitude thrust upon her.

So who . . . ? Why . . . ?

I was suddenly chilled despite the sun. How could he call out my name, my real name, this stranger? How could I have heard him – if I had – from such a distance? Gooseflesh shuddered up my arms. There was an explanation, I knew that, feared it, had hoped to have grown away from it . . .

No! I would not believe it was something fey and extraordinary. It had been . . . the calling of a bird. Yes, of course. A curlew, perhaps, or a peewit. There were plenty out there on the hillside.

Miranda . . .

Different now, sighing, throaty with longing, with desire . . . And my own heartbeat quickening, the sense of anticipation, excitement, rising in waves to swamp the fear . . .

Yet nobody in sight save the man in a blue coat riding a bay horse. And as I looked – as I had known he would from that first instant when he had rounded the bluff – the rider was slowing his horse, turning it towards the gates of Crossbank Grange.

'Mary!'

I jumped.

'What are you doing gawking on the doorstep?' Miss Groom's fretful voice – human, real – was both an intrusion and a relief. 'Come inside at once!'

'Yes, miss,' I whispered. And did not know whether I was glad or sorry to do as I was bidden.

The first sight of the new Mrs Loveridge was something of a shock. I had expected a matronly person. Someone of middle years, greying and sedate, who would make a suitable step-mama for a sixteen-year-old girl. Instead, in the middle of the parlour carpet, briskly directing the maids in the business of removing chairs through glass doors at the far end of the room to the terrace outside, stood a slender, brown-haired and elegant young woman. Very young. She looked scarcely older than Ida Loveridge herself. Indeed, I later learned she was barely nineteen. But she lacked nothing in self-assurance, that was straight away apparent in her manner and her tone of voice. And in that shaded, severe room, ponderous with large pieces of furniture, she seemed to cast an aura of brilliance like an exotic creature transposed from some tropical place.

It was an effect heightened, of course, by the shimmering coral silk of her fashionable dress, the green ribbons woven into the smooth coils of her hair and the gloss of jade at her ears and throat.

But it was more than that. Some inner quality of animation drew the eye and dazzled the mind into believing her extraordinarily vivid and handsome. If, on closer scrutiny, it was evident that her nose and chin were actually too sharp and determined, her mouth too full, her eyes too narrow and deep-set for true beauty, these imperfections seemed unimportant when set against the overall effect. Mr Loveridge himself, judging from his doting expression, was completely indifferent to her imperfections. He was clearly besotted with his stylish, colourful, vigorous young bride which perhaps was scarcely surprising when for so long he had been tied to a fretful invalid.

'Why, Florence, you have returned so quickly you have caught us wrong-footed,' she cried gaily to Miss Groom. 'I decided it was too fine a day to remain mouldering indoors. We shall take tea *al fresco* . . . and no, Ida dear, I shall not listen to another protest about wasps and cool breezes and the deleterious effects of sunlight on the parlour chairs. It is delightfully sheltered on the terrace and it behoves us to make the most of this sunny weather when next week we might be confined to the house willy-nilly by gales and rain. What say you, Charles?' She held out one graceful white hand to her husband, laughing as she did so. 'Will you agree with me? Or forbid my happy little scheme for fear that the furniture will fade away before our eyes?'

'Oh, you must by all means do as you think fit, dearest,' he said, stepping hastily from where he had been standing by the window. 'Whatever pleases you will give me pleasure also.'

His face was foolish with smiles and his hand as it reached for hers seemed to tremble just a little. But the instant before their fingertips touched her eye was caught by some disarrangement in the ruffle decorating her sleeve. She withdrew her hand, frowning, in order to smooth the ruffle, at the same time remarking with a teasing hint of reproach, 'Ah, but we are forgetting our manners, are we not? Our guests have arrived and we neglect them shamefully while we concern ourselves with this trifling domestic matter. Come, Ida! Florence, will you perform the introductions?' And left him standing there, hand still outstretched, so that this stern, authoritarian figure who could render the apprentice house silent with one chilling glance seemed for a moment strangely uncertain and diminished.

He quickly recovered and moved to stand at his wife's elbow, a sombre, watchful guardian. No smiles for us. On the contrary, his presence was clearly intended to remind us that we were there on sufferance. Miss Ida Loveridge, looking sullen – perhaps aware that against bold coral silk and a sophisticated arrangement of glossy brown locks, pink-spotted muslin appeared insipid and frizzy ringlets excessively girlish – stood on her step-mama's other side. Neither father nor daughter seemed to take much pleasure in the sight of six apprentices lined up in their parlour. Our visit might have been arranged in honour of Miss Loveridge's birthday but I strongly suspected that we would never have been allowed anywhere near had she had any say in the matter. Nor did I think her papa would have dreamt up such a scheme on his own account. Which left Mrs Loveridge as the person solely responsible. Though such a new bride, she already seemed to have the managing of her husband well in hand. I found the thought encouraging.

Mrs Loveridge spoke to each of us in turn and was patient with the stumbling answers to her questions. Questions put to us without a trace of condescension but as if she were genuinely interested to learn what we had to say. But though her manner was gentle, I saw how very sharp her eyes were, missing nothing. When Miss Groom spoke my name and I had bobbed a nervous curtsey, I looked up to find that clear, hazel gaze raking me.

'So, Mary,' she said, her quiet voice belying the intense and uncompromising quality of her scrutiny. 'Do you come from the Clerkenwell workhouse like Alice and Joan?'

'No, ma'am. From . . . from Devonshire.'

'Devonshire! From which part?'

'Ashburton, ma'am,' I said, automatically, as I had drilled myself to say, not wishing to speak of Moondance even to a woman who seemed possessed of kindly intentions.

'Then we have something in common.' Her smile was warm but there was a trace of sadness in her voice. 'I was born in the county town of Exeter and lived my happiest years thereabouts before I was compelled to go to London. We must talk again of Devonshire before you leave. Such green and rolling hills I never saw anywhere else, nor such spectacular panoramas along the coast where the cliffs are made of rock as red as fire. Did you ever go to Exmouth, Mary? Or to Dawlish? Or Teignmouth?'

I shook my head. 'Never saw the sea close up, ma'am.' Only a distant, beckoning shimmer seen from the top of the tor. The sea that had carried my mother, the foreign bride, to the cool, damp climate of England and to her death. The sea that had borne my father off again, never to return.

A maid swished in to announce that tea was ready whenever we wished to move outside and Mrs Loveridge became animated once more, sweeping us to the doors, disposing us about the table set upon the sun-warmed flags of the terrace where steps led down to a stretch of formal garden, a splash of bright, cultivated colour against the backdrop of the wild hillside.

Mr Loveridge favoured us with a cautioning, purse-lipped frown then smiled indulgently at his wife. 'I shall leave you to your teaparty, my dear, and retire to the library to attend to the urgent correspondence I told you of.'

'Such a bore for you, Charles,' Mrs Loveridge said, with a sigh and a shrug. 'And tiresome for us to be deprived of your company. But if you must . . .'

'Business matters, you understand. Everything is behindhand with my absence this last week.' He paused, with a knowing smile, as though expecting further flattering protests from his bride or even a blushing look hinting at the intimacy they now shared, but Mrs Loveridge had already turned away to say something to Alice and he was obliged to make his exit unremarked. He went back into the house where he could be heard calling sharply to the maid to fetch tea to the library. 'And tea only! I do not care to distress my digestion with heavy pastries at this hour.'

Mrs Loveridge apparently had no qualms at all about distressing the digestion of the rest of us.

'Being unaware of your preferences,' she said, 'I bespoke a good selection of savoury and sweet items. I hope you will find something to your liking. Now sit down, do, and help yourselves to whatever you wish. Our excellent cook has worked hard to please me and I do not wish to hurt her feelings. I shall expect nothing to be left but crumbs or I shall be quite unable to face her tomorrow.'

It was food I had almost believed I should never see again. Raised savoury pies sliced open to reveal the close-packed meat and herb-rich jelly within, chicken patties, fruit tarts – apple and golden plum and purple damson – flanked with jugs of cream, fruit cakes, a magnificent sponge decorated with pink icing, maids-of-honour, shortbread . . . it was a far cry from our expectations of bread and butter and a slice of plain cake. Miss Groom was as wide-eyed as we were and though her nostrils flared in disapproval she was too timid to make any formal protest beyond a murmured, 'How very . . . lavish . . . Quite overfacing,' which was lost in the scraping of chairs and settling of skirts.

'Come along, now,' Mrs Loveridge said, seeing us constrained by shyness. 'Let me pass you the chicken patties, Tom. Take two at least. They are but a mouthful each . . . and you as well, Mary – or is it that you overindulged at dinnertime? I am told by my husband that you are *lavishly* fed.'

Though Mrs Loveridge's tone was dry, Ida Loveridge seemed unaware of any irony.

'Indeed they are,' she put in proudly. 'Papa is noted for his charity towards his employees.'

'Is he now? How very agreeable for him. Florence, Alice's plate is still empty. Be so good as to help her to a slice of pie.'

'Oh, yes, he has a reputation in the district as a great benefactor, as you will find, Step-mama, once you are acquainted with society here. In fact, I have heard it said more than once by his friends that the apprentices who serve their time at Crossbank must be the luckiest in the whole of North Derbyshire. For there are few masters who are as lenient and generous as Papa.'

'Really?' Mrs Loveridge's fine eyebrows rose a fraction as she turned her full attention to her step-daughter. 'I had no idea your papa was so . . . distinguished a philanthropist. Why, to look at these six pale and undernourished rabbits, one would never guess how well they lived. How good of you to save me from such a sad misjudgement.'

Miss Loveridge hesitated, blinked uncertainly, then apparently reassured by the polite and attentive expression on her step-mother's face went on, 'You see, the apprentices he brings in from the towns to learn a good trade are from the very poorest orders of society. They are paupers and orphans and other low sorts of waifs and strays. If Papa did not employ them they would remain a dreadful drain on their parishes, or even sink into depravity. Indeed, Papa says half of them would probably have ended up as thieves and footpads and a threat to respectable society had he not rescued them.' She shuddered delicately. 'As it is, there are few among them who know anything of morals or manners when they come here. And with so many being of a lazy and idle nature and unused to regular hours, they will not settle to a fair day's work to earn their keep, which annoys Papa exceedingly.'

I bit hard into a chicken patty. For a moment the melting brown crust tasted like ashes in my mouth. How dare she! How dare this spoiled ignorant miss sit there in her fine clothes and parrot such judgements. What did she know who had never set foot through the mill gate? Who sat there like a little princess, looking down her nose at us and not even bothering to lower her voice as she mouthed this mess of half-truths and downright lies. I felt the treacherous stir of bitter and useless emotions. I must not protest! I fixed my eyes on the plate in front of me. White china with a border of blue flowers. Such a plate as Miss Ida Loveridge ate off every day, while we . . . no, I would not think of that. I would not make comparisons. It was no use. I should not do myself any good. Better to eat this feast as the others did, keeping my eyes down, accepting that today we were lucky and giving no thought to tomorrow.

'So, Ida dear, you believe the apprentices should be grateful to your papa for being given an opportunity to work?' Mrs Loveridge spoke almost lazily. 'But surely it is we who should be grateful to them?'

'Step-mama?'

'If there was no one to spin the cotton – and spin it so cheaply – why, your papa's business would soon falter.'

'No, no, you misunderstand.' Miss Loveridge gave a trill of condescending laughter. 'There are plenty more where these apprentices came from. New children continue to be recruited regularly from workhouses about the country to replace those who have served their time and left. You must not worry about Papa's business. It thrives exceedingly.'

'I am afraid it is you who misunderstand, Ida,' Mrs Loveridge said, her voice no longer lazy but clear and definite. 'My meaning was that without the labour – the long and hard labour – of those less fortunate than ourselves, we none of us could live in the considerable style and comfort that we do. And it behoves us to acknowledge our gratitude to . . .' She broke off, staring along the terrace, the colour draining from her face. 'God in heaven,' she whispered.

'I'm sorry, ma'am.' The maid came fluttering out of the parlour at the stranger's heels. 'The gentleman would not wait.'

'No . . . no. Thank you, Jane. It is perfectly . . . in order.' Then, the colour flooding back into her face, she sprang to her

through our Devonshire friends. I was fortunate enough to be offered the opportunity of travelling north, to Buxton, on a private commission for an acquaintance. It would have been discourteous to pass so close to Crossbank without making an effort to call upon you to present my . . . felicitations upon your marriage.'

'So that we might have another event to celebrate besides a marriage and a birthday? How very gratifying. For they say that happenings – good or bad – go in threes, do they not? Though, of course, we have yet to discover if your return is a good thing or a bad. Ida's birthday, my marriage . . . well, of course, they can be nothing but most heartening events, can they not?' A small, smiling pause, then she lifted her slender white arm to encompass with a gesture the rest of the table. 'But it is most impolite of us to be discussing these private family matters when we have other guests . . . We were speaking of Devonshire earlier, my dear. You said you were from Ashburton. Is it a pleasant town?'

I was so caught up in the little drama, by the hidden emotions that both linked and separated Mrs Loveridge and her cousin, emotions that I sensed swirling underneath their words like violent currents under the calm surface of a river, that it was a second or two before I realised Mrs Loveridge was addressing me. I jumped, instantly plunging back into reality from some place where I had been the absorbed observer of an event that seemed to hold some mysterious significance for me. Though for the life of me I could not think what on earth it was. In my confusion I spoke without thinking.

'Very likely, ma'am. I was only there a few times.'

'But were you not born in Ashburton?'

'No, ma'am. A . . . a very small village a few miles off.'

'And what was its name?'

'I . . . I was only little, ma'am, when I was there and I don't rightly remember. We . . . travelled about.' The lies slid uncomfortably from my tongue. Her gaze was too acute. I stared down at my plate, not wishing to meet her eyes.

'I see. But what of your family?'

'I was orphaned, ma'am,' I muttered.

'How sad for you. I too know the pain of losing dear parents. Do you have no brothers and sisters? Or grandparents?'

'None.'

'And what was your father's trade when he was alive?'

I shrugged and was mercifully saved from further interrogation by Ida Loveridge suddenly pointing her finger at Tom and crying indignantly, 'That boy! He is stuffing his pockets with food! And you, girl! What is that bulging out of your sleeve? Why, I believe it is shortbread biscuits!'

An appalled stillness fell over the apprentices. Miss Groom gave a gasp of horror. 'Such behaviour! And I warned you . . .'

'And what use is warning such creatures? How could they ever hope to understand? They are as ignorant as pigs!'

'Ida! That is enough!'

But her step-daughter, more sure of her ground now and out for revenge for her earlier humiliation, said defiantly, 'It is as Papa told you. It is optimistic to suppose that any of them could possibly benefit from mixing in civilised company.'

'Nonsense! I will not have you parroting such prejudices.'

'All you have done, Step-mama, is to invite thieves to our table! Papa will be appalled! I insist you make them empty their pockets.'

'I shall do no such thing.'

Ida Loveridge tossed her curls. 'It would not surprise me in the least if they had not put away a few silver spoons and knives along with the shortbread.'

'No, miss, no,' Alice whimpered, her cheeks draining of colour. She shook the biscuits from her sleeve. 'It were just to share wi' the others later. Them as didn't come. We'd not take owt else. Honest.'

Impulsively, both frightened for her and fearful for the consequences, I turned and reached out my hand to take hers, meaning to offer what little comfort I could.

It was my undoing. My elbow caught my teacup, sending it spinning across the width of the table to spill its contents across the pristine cloth and shower warm liquid into Miss Ida Loveridge's lap.

With a shriek she jumped to her feet. 'My dress! It is ruined! You . . . you stupid *guttersnipe*! And look at the mess on the table!' She was near hopping with temper. 'You see! You see! This is what happens when ignorant common people mix with their betters. They have no business here! They have no decency, no manners, no more *intelligence* than savages. Oh, I should never have been made to sit to table with such . . . such clumsy, thieving *scum*!'

The anger came up in my head like a red, roaring fire. I could no longer contain it. I had struggled so hard to keep it banked down through all the hurts and repressions and degradations of the last four years, but Ida Loveridge's words were flaming faggots thrust into the heart of coals that had been kept smothered too long. I was on my feet, facing her across the table, the words shouted out in a blaze of pain and rage. 'How dare you speak of us so!'

Since I had been at Crossbank I had fallen into the rough speech of the other apprentices as I had once easily slipped into the Devonshire dialect when I was playing with Jed, though I would no more dare to speak so in Aunt Hettie's presence than I would sit with my elbows on the dining table or slump in a chair instead of sitting upright or be anything other than polite in my manner, even to the lowliest bootboy or scullery maid.

'We Brehaults may no longer have money, Miranda,' Aunt Hettie had said, 'but we must not forget our heritage. It behoves us to keep up standards against the time when your papa returns with his fortune made and we may live again in the style I knew in my own youth.'

Papa had never returned and Aunt Hettie had died from a melancholy brought on by her dashed hopes, but all the pride in our ancestry that she had instilled in me since I was able to understand (even conceding that my mother had added a certain interesting and exotic twig to our family tree, though Eastern aristocracy where princes were two a penny scarcely ranked on a par with a line that could claim descent on the distaff side from the House of Wessex) now came to my aid.

I felt my back stiffen, my chin go up, my memory reach back through the sludge laid over it from the Crossbank years. When Ida Loveridge cried, 'You impertinent hussy! I shall have you whipped,' I looked her up and down in Aunt Hettie's most quelling manner and answered clearly, 'Did your mama never teach you that a well-bred person is always considerate of the feelings of those less fortunately placed?'

'What?' she spluttered.

'No, I can see that she did not. But then, I had heard that she was no more than a poor Manchester weaver's daughter and your papa brought up in the seediest part of Derby. New money is often said to have an unfortunate tendency to put on airs and remain impervious to the finer points of social intercourse.'

She seemed bereft of speech for a moment. It was Miss Groom who cried in a shocked voice, 'Mary Bray! Sit down this minute.'

'I will not sit down. And I am not Mary Bray. Mr Loveridge gave me that name. He thought it more appropriate for an apprentice and my real name too difficult to spell. I am Miranda Yasmin Henrietta Brehault. My late father was a baronet, Sir Anthony Brehault, of Guernsey descent. My mother's grandmother was the daughter of an Indian prince.' I swept a bold stare round the suddenly silent assembly. Even the hovering maids were struck still as statues. Every expression was registered, from disbelief on Ida Loveridge's face to something very akin to amusement on her step-mother's countenance. It was to Mrs Loveridge that I spoke now. 'Ma'am, we are not as well treated at Crossbank Mill as Mr Loveridge would have you believe. We labour from six in the morning until eight at night – later if there is a deal of work – and are badly fed. We are beaten awake if we fall asleep at our frames. When we fall sick we must get ourselves better as best we might, for a doctor attends us rarely. And, ma'am, there is a little girl, Maggie Armitage, who even now is desperately ill and needs help . . .'

I broke off, the words choking in my throat as I stared across the terrace.

'Maggie?' I whispered. 'Maggie?'

She stood on the terrace, just by the glass doors that led to the parlour. She looked at me and smiled. Then it was not Maggie any more, but Mr Loveridge standing glowering at me.

'What is this?' he said in a forbidding voice.

In an instant the spell was broken. The maids began to bustle about their duties. Alice gave a little whimper and shrank back from me as though fearing some infection. Ida Loveridge spun round and cried, 'Oh, Papa, I have been shamefully insulted! And these brats have stolen food!' And, try as I might to cling to it, the rage that had sustained my brief, bright flare of courage shivered to dull embers as sanity rushed in and I was Mary Bray again, quaking at the dreadful consequences of a headstrong and useless outburst.

But Mr Loveridge was no longer looking my way. He was regarding with surprise the tall man who rose to his feet and bowed stiffly. And Mrs Loveridge was on her feet too and going swiftly to her husband to take his arm and lead him to meet her cousin.

I seized my moment. I was out of my chair and running – down the terrace steps, across the garden and over the low wall – as though I had the devil at my heels. My feet seemed scarcely to touch the rough tussocky grass as I fled down the hill, uncaring of anything save that I must get back to the mill. To Biddie.

She was huddled on the steps of the apprentice house, her shoulders hunched. She turned a white, tear-streaked face to me. And I knew. I had known up there at Crossbank Grange.

'Her's gone,' she said, in a frozen little voice. 'Not half an hour since. Ma Hatcher's layin' her out.'

I could not cry.

'She's better off,' I said.

'Aye.'

I looked round slowly. All about us the limits of our prison. The apprentice house, the forbidding bulk of the mill, the cobbled yard, the gates, open still, but at sunset to clang shut and fasten us in. I thought of the aching, aching days of unremitting labour. I thought of Mr Hatcher and his seeking, lustful hands.

'I'm not staying, Biddie,' I said slowly. 'I can't bear another night here. And it has to be now. This minute.'

'You're running away?' The enormity of it almost took her breath. 'But you know what happens if they catch you . . .'

'Makes no odds. I'm taking my chance. Before they come down from the house.'

'You're not goin' without me.' She was on her feet. 'I 'ates this place. You're me only friend . . . but where will we go?'

'Home,' I said, and smiled. 'Home to Moondance.'

Chapter Two

Biddie gave a stifled yelp. 'Got cramp in me toe.' She eased herself into a more comfortable position and the laurel bush that sheltered us rustled alarmingly.

'Careful,' I hissed.

'There's nobody about now. 'Sides it's beginning to get dark.'

'Not dark enough. We can't afford to take risks.'

Biddie shivered. 'I hate bein' so close to the 'ouse.'

'I told you, it's our best chance,' I whispered urgently. 'It's the last place they'll expect us to be. Hush up your complaining. It'll be properly dark soon.'

We were huddled amid a windbreak of well-grown leafy shrubs which guarded a stone bench in the gardens at the rear of Crossbank Grange. There were several of these pleasant nooks set about the formal flowerbeds, where a person might rest protected from the breeze and enjoy a fine view down the valley or a particularly splendid grouping of flowers. Almost unconsciously the plan of the garden had imprinted itself in my mind as I glanced at it from the terrace and I had remembered the benches and the sheltering shrubs the instant I had decided to run. It was a calculated decision. I knew that however quiet the meandering valley road appeared, however empty and tempting the expanses of bare hillside seemed, they were routes to be avoided by daylight. Even if we were lucky and evaded those sent out to search for us, two young girls, strangers, passing through any village hereabouts would be instantly remarked upon. Mr Loveridge's net spread wide and he was generous to those who captured runaways.

The few apprentices I had known bold enough to try to leave Crossbank had been hauled back within days by some observant cottager eager for a reward and uncaring – or unaware – of the brutal punishment that would be meted out to the miscreant. And even in the apparently empty hills there was the risk of encountering a shepherd or a farmhand, or being espied from one of the scattered dwellings. There was the extra hazard, too, of becoming hopelessly lost in the dense mists or storms of rain that so often swept down from the wild and craggy heights.

No, we had to be cunning. It was our only chance. When we moved it must be at night, following the road and making what detours we must to avoid villages and farms. Daylight was our enemy. By day we must find a sheltered place to rest. I had only the haziest idea of the geography of the district, but the road, I knew, led to a place called Bakewell – I had passed through it all those years ago on my journey to the mill – and from there I hoped we should find a route to take us clear out of the county.

I would not allow myself to contemplate failure. But doubt and fear hung close, surging beneath my confident words to Biddie, waiting to take advantage of a moment's inattention in order to slide into my mind and sap my will and my strength. We had already had one close call. I could not expect we should be so fortunate a second time. I shuddered to think how close we had come to discovery.

Luck had been with us as we raced up the hillside, slid over the garden wall and dived for the nearest clump of shrubs. No one hailed us or set off in pursuit. But we had scarcely burrowed between the twiggy stems and settled ourselves uncomfortably squashed together in a damp hollow between two laurel bushes before we heard the crunch of feet on gravel, the rumble of male voices. His voice. Kit Warrener's. And, God help us, Mr Loveridge's!

We froze, Biddie's ashen face reflecting my own shock and fear. All of a sudden our shelter seemed hopelessly inadequate. There was too much light filtering in. The bushes looked solid enough from a distance but anyone coming too close might easily spy us through the natural gaps among the leaves.

Too late to think of that now. We were trapped. Might any moment be discovered . . .

Words became distinct and two sets of feet came into view and halted. It was all I could see of the men from where I crouched. I dared not even move my eyes, leave alone my head, to seek a better view of them, and the thump of my heartbeat rang so loud in my ears that it seemed they must surely hear it.

'It is not that I wish to appear inhospitable,' Mr Loveridge was saying in a cold, formal voice, 'but in the circumstances it would scarcely be appropriate.'

'I had no reason to believe, sir, that you would welcome me to stay as a guest under your roof. Indeed, had not my cousin insisted that I dine here, I should not have lingered once I had paid my respects. I will take my leave when dinner is over.'

'And you will not allow yourself to be persuaded otherwise by my wife?'

'You have my assurance on that, sir.' Kit Warrener gave a dry laugh. 'Caro may command my affection but not my will and I see no merit in embarrassing you further with my presence.'

Mr Loveridge cleared his throat and said stiffly, 'My wife has a generous and impulsive nature. Wholly delightful, it is true, and one would not wish it otherwise, but her age and sex naturally preclude her from a proper comprehension of the world beyond her own domestic circle. It is my duty as a husband to guide her in every aspect of her life and to protect her feminine sensibilities from unhelpful influences. I am grateful for your understanding in this delicate matter.'

Kit Warrener did not answer for a moment. The scuffed and dusty riding boots turned sharply and paced towards the stone bench that lay directly in front of our hiding place. The boots stopped, pointing straight at us. Biddie's nails dug into my arm. She buried her face in my shoulder as though by hiding her own eyes she might remain invisible.

Somewhere above my head a sharp intake of breath. He had seen us! All was lost! I should have listened to Biddie and not stubbornly insisted that we should be safer up here than anywhere else. Any second he would call out to Mr Loveridge and we should be dragged out of hiding . . .

I could not help myself then. I had to know for certain if he had seen us. I slowly raised my head and looked up.

My first instinct was to run. If we were quick we could make the wall and be over it before the men could stop us. But even as that thought flashed through my mind it fell away. Kit Warrener looked straight down at me through the gap in the lacing of leaves and branches. His eyes widened in surprise but there was no hostility, no condemnation in his expression. On the contrary his mouth twisted into a fleeting smile. Then, to my astonishment and relief, he winked before he turned away lazily and said to Mr Loveridge, 'This deeper matter you speak of being, of course, Caro's prospects as beneficiary under my father's will which would suffer if she disobeyed his wishes. She is to have no truck with me if she wishes to inherit his fortune. Is that not the case?'

'That was not my meaning,' Mr Loveridge said, rather too quickly, a certain falsity in his aggrieved tone. 'My prime concern is my wife's happiness and peace of mind, to which I believe your presence makes little contribution. And there is also the matter of the trust and friendship that has grown between your father and myself which is far more valuable to me than mere . . . mere pecuniary interests. How could I possibly face him if I became guilty of harbouring under my roof one who has proved himself so ungrateful and deceitful to a loving parent?'

'I stand corrected,' Kit Warrener answered, sounding more cynically amused than abashed. 'As to my deceit and ingratitude, what defence could I possibly offer in the face of condemnation by such an upright and worthy person as my father? Why, his business acumen, not to mention his benevolence and tolerance, is . . . legendary. From my brief acquaintance with your good self, sir, and the few of your apprentices I had the pleasure of observing this afternoon, I would suggest you have much in common. I can quite see that you would hit it off together.' That short, dry laugh again. 'Far be it from me to cast any blight on such a priceless friendship. No, sir, you may rest easy in the knowledge that I shall be gone before dark and will not trouble your household again. But now I should be glad to continue our walk around the garden. I have spent a deucedly long time in the saddle these last few days and it will be a pleasure to stretch my legs.'

The crunch of boots on gravel died away. Only then did Biddie raise her head.

'That were close,' she gasped. 'I thought he'd 'ave seen us.'

'He did. But he didn't betray us and I think we can trust him.' To calm Biddie's fears I spoke with a certainty I did not quite feel, yet I hugged the memory of Kit Warrener's smile, his conspiratorial wink, to my heart and, strangely, that memory seemed the best defence against the lurking spectres of doubt and fear.

As dusk deepened towards nightfall, a chilly wind sprang up and the scraps of sky visible through the greenery turned ominously heavy with cloud.

Biddie and I were hardy souls – those who survived at Crossbank Mill had to be – and used to extremes of heat and cold. We worked all day in the oily heat of the spinning floor that could be overpoweringly close in the summer. In winter we returned to the near-freezing chill of the apprentice house where a pot-stove on the lower floor was the only heating granted to us. But being rarely out-of-doors we were not used to taking account of the weather, and now I grew increasingly worried at the prospect of a storm hampering the first and most hazardous stages of our escape. Even my new boots, the gown which covered me decently from neck to ankles and the cap that hid my hair, would soon be soaked through. Biddie was even more vulnerable. Her ragged, outgrown dress and the broken shoes through which her dirty toes poked offered scarcely any protection.

But while I fretted over the practical matters of how and where we might find some means of protecting ourselves from the elements, Biddie's fears took a very different turn – and one that at this moment, with night settling in dense purple-black shadows and the bushes clashing uneasily in the wind, I did not in the slightest appreciate.

I was aware that she had grown increasingly tense and restless but vaguely thought it was the cramp disturbing her. I jumped when she suddenly pressed up against me and quavered, 'Mary, did you 'ear that?'

'What? What've you heard?'

'Noises. A . . . funny sort of scratchin' . . . there!' Her nails were at my arm again. 'Oh, 'tis a boggart! I knowed it!' she burst out. 'It's on the hill, waitin' for us . . . Perhaps it's the one Alice told us of. The one wi' the big fangs as walks the dale on moonless nights looking for children to carry off to eat in its cave.'

'Don't, Biddie!' Her panic set my own nerves jangling. 'Don't talk of such things. It's only a daft story. Alice made it up.'

''Er didn't! Mrs Hatcher said. She'd 'eard tell as a little 'un from the village disappeared one night an' all they found of 'im was chewed bones! And they knowed what 'appened to him because the lad's ghostie was seen moanin' and skrikin' and pointin' to t' boggart's lair!' She gave a gasp of terror and both hands latched on to my arm. 'Th-there it is again!'

I caught it now. An animal, I thought desperately. It must be. Some animal hunting stealthily among the loose stones of the wall. I had longed for concealing night to arrive but of a sudden the night was no longer our friend but a sinister stranger with flesh-creeping monsters dangling at its coat-tails, and I found myself wishing most heartily that I had never been one of the scared but avid audience when Alice was in the mood to entertain us with her bloodthirsty tales of phantoms and horrible murders. It was one thing to listen and giggle nervously at such stories safely indoors and in the comforting presence of the other apprentices. Quite another to remember them out here, in the bleak country night, when we were alone amidst whatever sinister forces the darkness concealed.

A thump as of something heavy falling to the earth.

'It's comin' for us! The boggart!' Biddie's voice was hoarse with terror. 'That was its footfall!'

'No! Hush up, Biddie!' But my voice was low with fear because there was another thump, followed by a weird low muttering.

Then, quite distinctly, a man's voice said, crossly, 'Damn you, Miranda Brehault. If you are still hiding in the bushes I shall hold you personally responsible for causing me to rip my breeches on this wall,' and a great wash of relief sent the fear spinning away.

'It's no boggart, Biddie.' I choked on a hysterical laugh. 'It's a gentleman – Mrs Loveridge's cousin – and I think he might be a friend.'

The branches above us were roughly pulled aside.

'Not gone then?' Kit Warrener was a tall black silhouette against a sky that still held a trace of evening light behind the streaming clouds. He gave an impatient grunt. 'You can come out. It is safe enough now.'

We eased ourselves, stiff and scratched, out of the bushes and without ceremony were thrust to the wall and, hampered by the chill of limbs that had been immobile for too long, roughly hoisted over it.

'With my cousin's compliments,' he said, pushing a soft bundle at me when we had stumbled to the rough grass. 'A few gew-gaws. If you are to travel with me you must look the part of respectable maidservants.'

'M-Mrs Loveridge sent this?' I groped at the bundle, clumsy with cold and shock. Half the contents fell to the grass. His words baffled me. 'Travel? Travel . . . with you?'

'Yes, yes,' he growled, swiftly retrieving what had fallen. 'Or do you have some better plan in mind? No? Well, I have no intention of standing here all night discussing the matter, so if you would both be so kind as to dress yourselves . . . Here, there's a bonnet apiece and a shawl – you take that, Miranda – and you, what's your name? Biddie? You had better conceal yourself under the cloak. It is the best my cousin could do in the time available – and deuced tricky it was to smuggle 'em out of the house without the servants' knowledge. It was only by dint of a convenient upstairs window my cousin was able to throw the bundle to the side path so that I could pick it up on my way out. Now make haste, the hunt is called off for the night but it is best we get well away as quickly as possible.'

In a daze I pulled the straw bonnet over my cap and drew the warm soft shawl around my shoulders. The moment I touched it, I remembered my mother. Remembered being curled on her lap with my head on her breast, my cheek pressed to the deep softness of her precious Kashmir shawl, remembered the way the vibrant colours shed a faint luminous reflection on the creamy-olive skin of her neck; how it smelt of the spicy oils she used on her silky black hair and how she sang to me, her voice rising and falling in cadences that were strange and in a tongue that I could not understand save that that it meant love and comfort. Though Caroline Loveridge's shawl smelt of a different, rose-petal fragrance and in the dark I could not know its colours, to touch it brought reassurance. It was an omen of good fortune, surely, this Kashmir shawl that felt so like my mother's?

'Come.' There was no time for dreaming. Kit Warrener had a grip on both of us, propelling us over the rough tussocks to where he had left his horse. 'I would hazard the beast's ancestry is pure carthorse,' he said, hauling me up before him on the saddle and then Biddie behind him on to the nag's rump. 'I cursed the brute mightily on the way here for its inability to achieve more than a slow plod, but I daresay it is better designed than a lesser mount to carry an extra brace of passengers, though not in any comfort, I will guarantee you that.' Then he added in a growling voice, 'And let me make it clear that if either of you utter a word until we are off this hillside and I give you permission to speak, I will take the greatest satisfaction in wringing your grubby little necks and flinging you into the river to feed the fishes. Understand? Not a word. I have problems enough already without being caught in the act of assisting a pair of runaways.'

So we passed the first miles of the journey in total – and terrified – silence. Terrified not so much at Kit Warrener's lurid threat but at the real possibility of discovery, for a few glow-worm lanterns bobbed along the road between the mill and the village to remind us that determined searchers were still about. And though we kept high on the hillside following sheep tracks until we were well clear of the village, every stone dislodged by the horse's hooves, every creak of leather, seemed likely to betray our presence. Even after we descended to the road and could press on faster there was little conversation. What was there to say beyond a few whispered words of thanks? And when he rebuffed these with a curt, 'We are not properly safe yet,' I made no further attempts to speak and he confined himself to encouraging remarks to the horse. At one point, when we came to a crossroads, he broke his silence to say brusquely, 'We have some way to go yet.' But I did not care how long the journey would take, nor that a thin, penetrating drizzle had set in. All that mattered to me was that every dark and desolate mile took us further from Crossbank Mill.

We were on a broader highway now but my fears of meeting travellers who might note the ungainly horse with its three passengers were unfounded. The only alarm we had was when a coach roared past us, spewing mud from pounding hooves and churning wheels. The dim yellow flare of lamps was here and gone in an instant and as we had prudently drawn well into the hedge when we heard the horn trumpeting its approach, I did not think that even the most sharp-eyed of the outside passengers could have seen much of us.

Sometime later the pace of the horse quickened. Then it launched into a trot, to set Biddie squealing as she bounced on its rump while I clutched frantically at its mane and Kit Warrener muttered imprecations as he tried to rein the beast in. 'It senses its stable, damn its hide!' he cried and continued to wrestle with the horse until we reached a black huddle of buildings, leaking slivers of light around ill-fitting window shutters. The horse turned by a creaking sign that pronounced the place to be The Plough, and into a stable yard where, stiff and sore, we alighted – or rather were yanked down from the horse's back and ordered curtly to wait in the shadows cast from the solitary lantern. He disappeared into a small side door. The wizened old man, head and shoulders shrouded in a sack, who had hobbled out to claim the horse, was thankfully more concerned with getting himself and the nag back to the shelter of the stable than in taking much note of us.

'Where's this place?' Biddie whispered. 'Are we far off from t'mill?'

'Not far enough,' I said grimly. 'I'll not rest easy until we've the length of the country between us and Crossbank.'

'P'raps he's gone to fetch us supper,' Biddie said hopefully. 'Seems a long time since we 'ad dinner and me belly's fair stickin' to me backbone.'

'More like he's seein' to getting a fresh horse. I hope he is.'

'Gawd 'elp us,' Biddie groaned. 'Me legs is rubbed raw already. Not to mention the rain comin' down in pokers.'

'We can't afford to hang about a public place like this for too long. Might be coaches stopping . . . 'Sides, I didn't say runnin' away was goin' to be easy, did I?'

'Eh, Mary love, I'd sooner be 'ere wi' you and the weather than facin' old Hatcher any day,' Biddie said hastily, adding as though to bolster her own spirits as well as mine, 'Mind, this is a grand warm cloak. Not a bit o' wet coming through. And Mr Warrener talks like proper gentry. Mebbe he's rich, like master. P'raps we'll be drivin' off in a carriage and pair.' There was a wistful note in her voice. 'I'd fancy that.'

'You've been listening to too many of Alice's fairy tales,' I said. 'Just be glad we got to ride this far. We might have to walk the rest of the way. And I'm not Mary now, I told you. I don't want ever to be called that again.'

I felt a pang at putting her down, but neither of us could afford to start daydreaming about what we could not have. It would only make the reality of our position all the more uncomfortable – and highly uncomfortable it was at this minute, too. I pulled the shawl tighter about my shoulders, and tried not to envy Biddie her possession of the cape. A Kashmir shawl, soft and agreeable as it was when dry, was little protection against the downpour which had now set in. Though we huddled under the eaves of the building, the wind drove the rain relentlessly at us. I was becoming soaked through. I could feel water from my sodden skirts seeping down my legs and into my boots and the deep brim of my straw bonnet began to sag limply down over my nose.

By the time Kit Warrener reappeared I was hard-pressed to stop my teeth from chattering from a mixture of cold and anxiety at the long delay, and the chill seemed to have settled like a weight under my ribs. We slithered across wet cobbles to the door when he called to us in an urgent whisper. His hand reached out and grabbed my shoulder, tugging me into a narrow passage lit by a smoky taper, Biddie stumbling at my heels.

'Up the stairs with you,' he said, jerking his thumb at a flight of rickety steps disappearing into the gloom of an upper floor. 'Mrs Turpin will show you where you will sleep.'

'Sleep?' I looked at him blankly. 'But how can we stay here? An inn? We'll be seen . . .'

'From my brief acquaintance last night with the landlady of this establishment,' he said brusquely, 'I would suggest that any contact with the forces of law and order would be the least of her ambitions. Also she owes me a favour. I was persuaded to bring a deal of cumbersome gifts from her brother when he knew I was bound this way. And, if that is not enough for you, I tell you frankly that I have no mind to spend a sleepless night on the road in miserable weather like this, though you are of course at liberty to do so.'

'But . . . but if we stay, what then?'

'You travel south with me in the coming days, to friends who may be able to find you kindlier employment in Dawlish.'

'But that is . . .'

'Devonshire, yes. Would you not wish to return there? My cousin seemed to think it appropriate.' He shrugged, frowning. 'However, if you have some cleverer plan in mind do not think I shall be discommoded if you choose to make off by yourselves. Believe me, had it not been for my cousin's insistence that I should escort you – and that she provided the financial support for the journey as I am sadly lacking in that particular commodity – I should have no hesitation in bidding you adieu. I much prefer to travel solitary. But if nothing else, I am a man of my word. I said I would do my best for you and I shall. Is that sufficient answer for you, Miss Brehault?'

I stared at him, fighting the weakening thought of being dry and sheltered on this wild, wet night, of letting someone else take the responsibility for our journey. And all the way to Devon! That was far more than I had ever expected. But could we trust him? His expression was not encouraging. His face was drawn and pinched, his eyes mere slivers of a chilly green-grey in their deep-set, shadowed sockets. His words were spoken carelessly, as though his mind was elsewhere, occupied with thoughts that were far more important – and deeply unpleasant. The young man who had winked at me and smiled and had appeared a co-conspirator, seemed to have entirely disappeared and been replaced by someone harder, far less appealing.

No, best not be beholden to someone with an unpalatable commission forced upon him. And thoughtful and generous as Mrs Loveridge had been, how could I rest easy here knowing that we were still dangerously too close to Crossbank? I steeled myself. 'You've helped us, sir, and me and Biddie's grateful, but we won't trouble you further. I was planning we'd travel by night. You've given us a good start and I'd rather we pressed on to Bakewell.'

'Bakewell?' His bark of laughter was without humour. 'That is some miles back. You are close to Buxton now.'

'Oh,' I said, dismayed. Buxton was just a name to me. I had no notion of its geography. 'Is that a big place, sir?'

He shrugged. 'I believe so. But tomorrow . . .'

He did not finish what he had to say. And I have often wondered since what would have happened had I been able put my plan into action, overriding Biddie's protests and urging her out again into the rainswept darkness to take our chance in a friendless world. We should have been gone to a very different future, to be sure. But it was not to be my destiny to find out, because two things happened then. With a swish of heavy skirts, the shushing of soft slippers on the stairs and a cry of, 'Where are these waifs, Mr Warrener? Why do you keep them standing in this draughty passage?' the landlady of The Plough bore down upon us. And, as she swept towards us, displaying an alarming expanse of powdered white bosom that spilled from the dangerously low bodice of a crimson velvet gown, my chilled and exhausted body chose that precise moment to overcome my determination to leave.

My stomach clenched, sending waves of sickly weakness through my legs. I fought down the spasm, took a deep breath and immediately regretted it for the unfamiliar smell of the inn, a compound of tallow grease, spent tobacco and ale dregs, caught queasily in my throat.

'You did well to bring them to me, sir,' Mrs Turpin was saying. 'I'll soon have them warm and dry. Such starveling creatures! Why, I've seen broomsticks with more flesh on them. They're from Crossbank, you say?' Her voice lowered to a stern whisper. 'Charles Loveridge is free enough with his money where it shows him up well in the public eye. A pity he never thought to spend more on those who labour to provide him with a fortune! But he's not the only one that's blind to what's under their nose, nor the worst of the mill masters, sad to say. If I told you some of the tricks of the Needhams over to Litton . . . well, best not to dwell on it.' She swept a plump white arm about us. 'But these pair shall eat and sleep royally tonight, I promise you.'

I opened my mouth to protest and shut it quickly as another

spasm wrenched through me. I prayed that Mrs Turpin would not mention food again. I did not wish to think of eating. I did not wish to remember the rich pastries I had guzzled this afternoon. I wanted to fight down this sick dizziness and walk out of the inn, not be tempted by the prospect of being able to lie down, warm and secure. But the nervous energy that had sustained me through this strange, eventful day was deserting me. I felt as though bones and muscles were sagging with relief at the thought of rest and my mind did not have the energy to direct them otherwise.

'I shall have supper sent up to you directly, Mr Warrener, and I should be obliged if you would later favour the company with a tune or two,' Mrs Turpin said, in a more cheerful tone. ''Tis an age since we'd such fine entertainment as you gave us last evening. And don't fret yourself over these young ones. They'll sleep safe close by me tonight.'

I gave up all pretence of resistance as nausea swept through me again. I prayed that I should reach where I should sleep before my legs gave way. I needed all my strength to drag each leaden foot from tread to shallow tread of the stairs and then along a dim passage that narrowed and turned corners in a highly erratic fashion. Several times I stumbled and without Mrs Turpin's stout arm propelling me forward, I should have fallen. When she eventually opened a door and we went inside I felt so dizzy that I staggered from the assault of heat and light that met us. Flames roared upwards in the grate, an extravagance of candle flames twisted and flared in the draught from the opened door, soft rugs deadened our footsteps and it seemed that the chamber – Mrs Turpin's own bedchamber I learned later – with its vast crimson-curtained bed was full of beautiful, angelic beings with shining hair and flowing silk gowns.

These beings – three young women, I gradually realised, though my vision was strangely blurred and their voices seemed to be loud one moment and fade the next – pushed us to the fire. The object standing there I recognised, dully, as a hip bath full of gently steaming water. Beyond it, a long mirror reflected two weird skinny creatures. Could that hollow-eyed, whey-faced bag of bones really be me? I giggled but the sound was so remote that I scarcely recognised it. How comical we both looked. Biddie, her over-large bonnet askew, her small person lost under the smothering folds of a vast brown cloak that spread behind her like a train. Me, bonnet drooping over my nose, stringy tails of black hair dangling forlornly at my neck, the coarse cotton of my sodden new dress clinging like crumpled blue paper to my legs. He had said, Kit Warrener, that we were to pass ourselves off as maidservants. Small hope of that! We looked better fitted to stand in a field and scare the crows. I wanted to share the joke with Biddie but it was too much effort to catch her eye. And the smothering heat in the room made it difficult to catch my breath enough to form words.

Mrs Turpin caught me as I swayed. 'This one is passably clean,' she said sharply. 'Get her dry and into bed straight off, Dinah. She's half dead on her feet. Maud, you and Violet had better see to the smaller one. Into the bath with her, however she protests. Get rid of the stink of the mill before you give her supper.'

Then gentle hands were stripping me of wet clothes, drying me with soft linen, easing me into a nightgown – and trying to separate me from the Kashmir shawl to which I obstinately clung, protesting, as I was half carried through a doorway into an adjoining smaller bedchamber. Once there, the nausea came back in a blinding wave that could no longer be denied. I was profusely sick into the chamberpot. Once rid of the unaccustomed richness of the food I had eaten at Crossbank Grange my stomach felt easier. And, curiously, my mind also. As though the violence of the attack had been a cleansing, a physical snapping of the chains that bound me to the mill and my mind was left clear to appreciate that I had truly fallen among friends.

I wrapped my icy hands round the mug of hot liquid – herb tea laced with brandy – that was pressed upon me, almost choking on the first sip then feeling its soothing fire bring blessed relief. Then bed drew me down, enfolded me in its feathery depths. I scarcely felt the covers being drawn over my shoulders. My fingers dug into the damp softness of the shawl and its colours seemed to flow into my head, melting, spinning . . .

I half woke once, shaken with sobs. I had dreamed of Maggie and I grieved for the waste of her young life. But there had been music in my dream too. Music that wove soothing harmonies around my grief and lulled away distress . . . A flute, I thought. Trickling, haunting notes. Moonlight shimmering on water . . . I slipped back to the blessed oblivion of dreamless sleep and did not wake again until morning.

We were three days and nights at The Plough. Three days when the wind tore at the stout walls of the inn and hurled rain against the small-paned window of the bedchamber where Biddie and I lived and slept and thought ourselves in paradise. Mrs Turpin had apologised that we should be so restricted, though heaven knows we should have been content in a bare garret. 'Best to be on the safe side. One never knows with prying eyes and clacking tongues. I regret my duties keep me busy but my girls will keep you amused. And don't worry that Mr Warrener will carry you off before you are properly rested. He is persuaded to stay until the weather improves.'

By daylight Mrs Turpin seemed larger, older, more intimidating, than she had the evening before. Crimson velvet was replaced with plain black bombazine, frizzed grey hair was hidden under a large widow's cap and the expression in her eyes seemed cold when she gazed at us. But she was clearly distracted by more pressing matters than two waifs the storm had washed up on her doorstep and was happy to leave us to be cared for and amused by the three young women she called 'my girls'.

They drifted one by one into our bedchamber late each morning, crumpled wrappers carelessly tied over nightgowns, hair in curling rags, draping themselves with boneless grace over the bed, the window seat, a chair. They brought cards and fashion papers, sewing and gossip, and set themselves to fuss over and entertain us. The first day I had woken languid and queasy still after my bout of biliousness and was ordered to stay in bed. There, in drowsy contentment – and half believing that I should wake any moment to find that I had been caught up in a dream – I watched Biddie being groomed and petted and fed titbits as though she were a kitten or puppy they were intent on spoiling. Biddie, bewildered and apprehensive at first, stood quiescent as one or other of the girls scraped her hair to root out the lice, applied scented lotions that they assured her would despatch any of the troublesome creatures that were left, and teased her gingery mop into fat curls with hot irons. By the time they persuaded her into an old print dress of Maud's, snipping and stitching round her to make it fit, she was giggling with the wonder of it all. 'We shall do the same for you tomorrow, Miranda, when you're feeling better,' the girls cried. 'Ma insists we make you look decent.'

'She's very kind. You all are,' I said.

They were very different in looks, these three, and not one of them favoured their mama. In my innocence I remarked idly that for sisters they were not very alike and caught the glance that Maud and Dinah exchanged over Biddie's head.

'Not sisters, duck,' the small dark one called Maud said carefully. 'Ma – Mrs Turpin's – our . . . well, let's say she's our foster mother.'

'We were all orphans, see, like you,' said Dinah. 'And in a very poor way when she took us in.'

'There've been others, too,' said Maud, 'that Ma brought in starving from the streets, though they've . . . well, they've – er – left home now.'

'Married,' put in Dinah.

'That's it, married,' agreed Maud. She sighed dramatically. 'Lord knows where I should be now if Ma hadn't rescued me from destitution.'

Violet, after her performance with the curling tongs (she was, they said, the most skilled at dressing hair), had retreated to the window seat with sewing of her own. She looked up as though challenged. 'Where would you be? Pox-ridden, most likely, and glad to lift your skirts for tuppence in some alley behind a potbank,' she said in a cool voice.

'Hush up, Vi! No need to be coarse,' said Maud, flushing. 'You know Ma don't like us to talk so.'

'It's only the truth, Maud Povey. You were whoring on the Potteries streets at thirteen. We all were, give or take a year or two. Had Mrs Turpin not picked us out for better things when she did we'd have been there yet. And sorry sights we should have been by now.' She smiled. She was the prettiest of the three, small and blonde and vivacious, but her prettiness was hard-edged and there was cynicism in that glimpse of sharp, white teeth. 'And don't tell me that this pair's so innocent as not to understand what I'm saying. We've all heard tales of what goes on in 'prentice houses. Stands to reason. Lads and lasses thrown together all hours of the day. It's only nature.' She jabbed her needle into the heavy lace she was stitching to the bodice of a blue silk gown. 'Men are no different whatever their station in life. Pauper or prince, they're all the same when what lies under their breeches will have its way. I daresay both of you have seen Master Pillicock rampant a-many times, haven't you now?'

'No, miss, you're wrong,' I burst out. We were not innocent, Biddie and I. How could we be, living in a place like Crossbank? Innocence was one of the first casualties of existence there. What we did not already know when we arrived, we soon learned from salacious gossip among the girls or bawdy exchanges between the boys. But the injustice of Violet's words fell like acid on raw skin. 'It wasn't many 'prentices that got up to tricks like that at Crossbank, or leastways when they did both parties were willing – and it was out of affection for each other. The Hatchers was always watching and prying whenever we had a few minutes to ourselves – and that was rare enough with the hours we worked. They'd thrash anyone who stepped out of line. No, it was him – our overseer – that had the minding of us. He was the one who picked out girls he fancied and forced them to go with him. Tears and pleas didn't make no odds to him.' I shuddered, remembering the lustful threat in his eyes, the feeling of helplessness under that slimy gaze. 'It . . . it could have been me next.'

'Then you're well out of it.' Maud's voice was full of sympathy. 'Believe me, lovey, we understand. We all know what it is to be alone and in the power of others – and what it can lead to.' She broke off then said angrily, 'How could you, Vi? Can't you see how you've upset the poor wench?'

'I'm not upset,' I said slowly. And it was true. The emotions I felt were far stronger than that, far darker . . . far more strengthening. So long suppressed, their release seemed to rise to my head like a stream of invigorating air bubbles. I looked Violet in the eye. 'I've heard worse, many a time.'

Violet smiled again, shrugged. 'There you are then. I was only going to tell you how *grateful* we all are to our *benefactor*, Mrs Evangeline Turpin, who rescued us from the streets.' If her eyes had not been so hard and mocking I might have believed she was sincere. 'You can see what a comfortable life we lead here. She's given us nice clothes and taught us fancy manners and lets us mix with the fine company she entertains. Such a generous lady.'

'Well, she is,' said Maud. 'So there's no need for you to be sarky.'

'Ah, but that don't disguise the fact that we still sell what we did on the streets of Burslem and Longton, only it's to the carriage trade in a feather bed. Gentlemen out of Buxton, come to take the waters, looking for a livelier time than their dull wives can give them.' Violet's hard eyes glinted. 'I only mean to give Miranda and Biddie a word of warning. They've been locked away for so long, they're like fledgling chicks unaware that there are cats and hawks waiting to pounce. Remember this. Nothing comes for free. You don't get owt for nowt. Oh, yes, Ma Turpin took us in and looks after us well. But it's to her advantage that we stay . . . Do you take my meaning, Miranda? True kindness and generosity are noble qualities, but there's just as many who make a pretence of them to disguise their own purposes.'

An image pressing into my mind. An image I had done my best to banish these last years. Now I released it, let it fill my head. That looming, black-clothed figure stepping from the carriage, walking into the house, bending over me. The smiling, kindly, reassuring face – sallow against the mane of thick black hair. *You must not be afraid, my dear. Of course it is sad that you must leave your home, but Moondance belongs to me now and I have made arrangements for you to be properly cared for in a new place . . .*

'I understand, miss,' I said slowly. 'But there was no need for you to tell me. I've known it for a long time.'

Known it, hoarded it against this day when it was possible to let free all the memories I had suppressed out of despair and helplessness. Now I was no longer despairing. Now there was hope, and my vague desire to return to Devon, to Moondance, where I had been born, sharpened, hardened. Now I knew quite clearly what I wanted. I wanted to oust the interloper, Theophilus Crowe, the man who had claimed Moondance. The man who had destroyed my childhood by sending me into slavery. And there and then, as the women chattered round me, I vowed that even if I were an old, old woman before I had the means or the opportunity, one day I would walk into Moondance to claim the inheritance that was rightfully mine.

We saw nothing of Kit Warrener during those three days at the The Plough. Mrs Turpin on one of her brief visits assured us of his concern for our welfare. 'He was greatly upset to hear about your indisposition, Miranda, and is anxious that you recover properly before you continue your journey.'

Violet gave a scornful laugh when she had gone. 'She turns everything to her own advantage. Your bout of sickness gives her a good excuse to keep him here. He's as edgy as a horse in a gale and, rain or no, he'd have been off before this if she hadn't hinted that you were so poorly he'd be like to find you dead before journey's end.'

'Ouch,' I said, wincing, as the comb was dragged relentlessly through the knots in the hair I had left, Violet having already ruthlessly attacked it with the scissors. 'But why? Why should she want to keep him here?'

'Hold still,' Violet said, 'or I'll cut off the lot and save myself the time and trouble of making you look halfway respectable. He's useful as an entertainment – a diversion – to the company, that's why.'

'He plays the flute like an angel,' Maud said, with a wistful smile. 'I was quite carried off by it. He's been somewhere foreign, studying music, Ma told me, and only recently returned.'

'I prefer the squeeze box myself,' said Dinah with a sniff, looking up from the cards she was dealing to Biddie. 'Something jolly that you can dance to. Not that mournful stuff.'

'Sour grapes!' Violet snapped the scissors around my ears. I managed not to wince. 'Just because he wouldn't take any notice of you. I saw the way you were ogling him.'

'I heard the music, too,' I said quickly, before Dinah, looking mutinous, could draw out the argument. 'When I was feeling poorly. It was . . . I don't know, sad.' Comforting, too. Weaving restful, haunting patterns of sound, though I did not say that for fear of sounding foolish.

'You couldn't have heard him playing.' Violet, annoyingly, had a tart answer for everything. 'You're at the opposite end of the house. The oldest bit with the thickest walls. The pantries and scullery are below and you don't hear any noise from there, do you? Ma likes quiet in her own quarters. She put you up here because no sound was likely to carry either way.'

'But I did!' I protested.

'Have you heard it since? Or any other sort of commotion? There was plenty of drunken singing last night.'

'No,' I said grudgingly.

'There you are then.'

'I expect you were a little fevered, lovey,' said Maud.

Perhaps. I still preferred to believe that they were wrong and some trick of the storm outside had carried the sound to me. It was too disquieting to think that it had been anything other. Like my name spoken in an empty garden. Like the glimpse of a dying child, smiling at me across a sunlit terrace.

'Mr Warrener knows Mrs Turpin's brother,' I said quickly, to divert myself from uneasy reflections. 'He told me he'd brought presents.'

'Ah, yes, her good brother, Aaron Luscombe. Surprising the number of acquaintances of his that just happen to be travelling to Derby or Buxton or Manchester and are pressed into delivering bundles and boxes to The Plough.' Violet swished aniseed-scented oil from a flask on to her palms and began to rub it into my hair with hard, quick strokes. 'Why, sometimes it is as much as once a month. Devonshire men must be restless souls, indeed.'

'Hush, Vi,' Maud said, lowering her voice with an uneasy glance at us. 'You're speaking out of turn. You know Ma don't like us to blab about her business.'

Violet sighed. 'Sometimes I wonder why I try to make pleasant conversation when I'm always being put down.'

'Because you don't mean to be nice, Violet Briggs! You only say things to vex folk and stir up bad feeling!'

'Me? Fiddlesticks! I only speak as I find.'

I heard them squabbling on but my mind had latched on to a name that opened the door to a raft of memories. Memories that I no longer wished to suppress. They belonged to Miranda, not Mary, and they glinted through the dross of recent years like flecks of true gold that Papa had once told me might be found among the peat-stained gravel of the streams that scoured down from the heights of the moor. I was a prospector now, scrabbling for every scrap, intent on hoarding each precious fragment. And when I had enough pieces I would build a shiny, unbreachable tower into which I would thrust Mary Bray and everything she had suffered and forget her for ever and ever . . .

'Luscombe,' I burst out. 'That's a proper Devon name.

There was a family of them in the village where I used to live. The man who mended boots, he was a Luscombe, and the carrier and the blacksmith . . .' The hot, clanging cavern of the smithy . . . A slick of sweat on the blacksmith's brawny arm as it rose and fell and my hand very small and trembling in Papa's. Laughter in his voice. *No need to be upset, sweetheart. Of course the nails don't hurt the horse's hoof. I would not allow anyone to harm Rajah any more than I would let them harm you . . . Rajah knows that. See how bravely he stands*. What age was I then? Three, four? Already I knew that bravery – be it in a hound, a horse or a person – was a quality that pleased Papa, and that tears, however justified by grief or pain, were a sign of weakness, a betrayal of the strong, proud Brehault blood that ran in my veins.

'Don't think I heard her mention a blacksmith in her family,' Maud said, shaking her head. 'They live by the sea. Fishing folk.'

'Luscombe . . . it's a common enough name,' I said absently, faces looming and fading in my mind. 'Like Hawkins and Davey – they were farmers – and Tozer – Meg was a Tozer, and Jed – that was her grandson. He was an orphan. Meg looked after me when I was little and Jed, too, after his ma died. We used to play together . . .' I broke off. The habit of secrecy was still too strong. The memories too fragile and disjointed – too precious – to share with these near-strangers. But my mind would not be still. While Maud rattled on about Mrs Turpin, half-forgotten images of my bold handsome papa came swirling to the surface.

Had he not been the personification of the valour and endurance for which the Brehaults were renowned? Guernsey men who had made and lost fortunes in all manner of adventurous enterprises on land or sea. How else, if not with great courage, would he have survived travelling alone the length and breadth of India, a place of unimaginable heat, of tiger-infested jungles and scorching, waterless plains? How else could he have snatched Mama, his adored Yasmin, from under the nose of her authoritarian Scots ship-owning father and her half-English, half-Indian mother, who had already planned her marriage into a family of equal prestige and wanted no truck with a footloose Englishman of no great fortune? Which elopement had involved him in a hazardous escape in a small boat down a crocodile-infested river with armed men in pursuit.

Maud's voice was a faint counterpoint against the growing rush of memories. Once released there was no stopping them. Like water filtering through a breach in a river bank, the trickle widened to a flood, the torrent fetching up a sediment of impressions that, however painful and poignant for the moment, would resettle, I knew, to provide a rich and necessary nourishment for the resurgence of my true self.

I remembered listening agog to Papa's tales. Snarling man-eating beasts with gory fangs, bloodthirsty bandits, the extremes of heat and cold, rain and snow, huge poisonous insects, storms at sea with waves as high as mountains – Papa not only accepted such hazards as the price of satisfying his wanderlust, but relished pitting himself against them. I had longed to be like him. Longed to show him that there was no need to be disappointed because I was not the yearned-for son. In my imagination I faced bloodcurdling danger with ease. But reality proved my courage to be a puny thing.

However I tried to slow my steps I could never do other, on dark winter evenings, than scuttle – eyes averted – past the cold, shadowy corner in the hall where a maid had once been frightened by the ghostly, beckoning figure of an old crone. I schooled myself more than once to pick up one of the black beetles that by night haunted the kitchen and scullery and which darted across the flagstones with a peculiarly horrid rustling sound, like blown dead leaves. But the moment my fingers touched the flat, loathsome body my nerve deserted me and I fled as speedily as the nasty creatures from candlelight. I eagerly accepted Jed's challenge to climb to the topmost branch of the ancient, spreading Cedar of Lebanon tree but once there a glance between my feet at the ground a dizzying distance below smartly removed the sense of elation. It took two gardeners to fetch me down and my humiliation was not eased by Papa's amused dismissal of the episode. I wanted to see pride in his eyes, not laughter. I wanted to hear him say, 'Brave girl! Such a feat for you to have climbed so high!' Not, 'Silly little goose! Look how dirty and scratched you are. But perhaps this has been a timely lesson. Small girls should be content with their dolls and their story books, and not allow themselves to be led into mischief.'

It was all the fault of being born a girl! Climbing up and down trees would have been easy for a boy who would surely have inherited the finest characteristics of the Brehaults. But Papa had already had his hopes dashed twice by Mama's miscarrying. He had both times been extra tender towards her and remained cheerful in her presence. Away from her he looked sad and Meg said that he was greatly disappointed. ''Tes natural for a gentleman to want a son. But there 'tes. The Lord gives and the Lord takes away. No sense in frettin' when they'm both young enough to have a dozen healthy babes yet.'

A dozen! I was in two minds about that. Of course, it would be fun to have so many extra playmates – but it would mean sharing all Mama's cuddles and kisses. And perhaps if I had a brother – brothers – Papa would have even less time to spare for me. I cherished the occasions when he was in the mood to whisk me off for a walk about the grounds, entertaining me as we strolled with stories of his adventures, or those of his swash-buckling Brehault ancestors. A little, too, of our quieter, more shadowy, Northfield forebears, who had built this house and created the lake and planted the gardens in a sheltered fold of south-facing land below the moor in the days when Queen Elizabeth reigned. There would be no time for any of that once Papa had sons whose company he would naturally prefer.

'Ma Turpin was in service, see, till she met her husband who was the coachman, and they bought this place near to where he was born. But he died soon after, leaving her to manage alone. Sad that she never had any children of her own to comfort her.' Maud's voice impinged for a moment.

Then it was Mama saying softly, delightedly, in her voice with its charming, lilting intonation that was so different from any other I knew, 'You are to have a very special birthday present this year, Miranda. A new brother or sister. We must pray that this time all goes well.'

I wanted to be wholeheartedly glad but as her time drew near I became more and more troubled. I knew it was wrong to be selfish about losing my parents' undivided love and attention but that was only part of it. There was something else – a terrible, frightening wash of foreboding – that seemed to grip me at times. A fear far more deep-seated and powerful than mere selfishness. At six years old I could not understand or express the nature of it, only that sometimes, unexpectedly, I would look at Mama lying swollen and exhausted on the sofa and have the sensation that I could not quite see her clearly. As though a grey mist hung between us, making her seem insubstantial and remote. At the same time, on some profound and instinctive level, I would feel achingly unhappy and bereft. Having no understanding of these disagreeable and frightening sensations, I was inclined to vent my feelings by bouts of fierce possessiveness, throwing my arms about her neck and smothering her in kisses, or clinging to her side and stubbornly refusing to obey Aunt Hettie's instructions to return this minute to the sampler I was embroidering under her instruction, or to writing in my copybook. Aunt Hettie's nostrils were inclined to flare at such hoydenish behaviour and she would make scornful remarks about sparing the rod, but Mama would not allow her to pull me off. She would stroke my hair, and whisper soothing nothings in my ear until I was calm and myself again. Nothings? Perhaps not so unimportant, after all.

Long after she and her stillborn twin sons had been laid to rest in the family plot in the village churchyard, I remembered the infinite sadness in her voice. 'You will understand and accept in time. We are given gifts that we do not always wish for. Remember, afterwards, that I love you and that my love will be with you always.'

The words had no meaning, then. But later Meg, who was not above busying herself outside a door when something interesting was going on on the other side of it, told me that Mama had informed Aunt Hettie plainly that she would not survive the birth. 'Seems your poor ma was warned,' she said in a dramatic whisper. 'In a dream or some such. Well, 'twas like a red rag to a bull, for Miss Brehault don't hold with anything 'er considers ungodly. Fortune tellin' and the like. 'Er argufied with your ma, but it did no good. Your ma wasn't having any. Proper surprised me that did for 'er was such a quiet, biddable soul, in the usual way o' things, and properly caring of Miss B's views, but 'er wasn't to be set down this time. "It'll happen. I knows it," 'er says. "I've the gift, Hettie. I sees things. Sometimes good. Sometimes bad. Nothing I can do about it. And now, I'm tellin' you, within the week my poor Anthony will not have a wife or a son . . . But it's Miranda I fear for. My dear child. There is such a shadow over her . . ."' Meg had broken off, gathered me to her bosom. 'Well, that was it, really. Made your auntie promise to take good care of you after she was gone.'

I understood, then, even as I wept into Meg's white apron, that somehow I had sensed what Mama already knew. And though there was comfort in having that strange, indefinable link with my mother, there was loneliness, too, because it must not be spoken of. Aunt Hettie would have no truck with what she termed superstitious nonsense. Even dear Meg, who would never have washed a blanket in May or harmed a robin for fear of ill-luck, and believed firmly in hobgoblins and piskies and ghosties, might have regarded me with different, more wary eyes.

In the weeks after Mama's death I coped as well as I could with the desolation and misery of loss. It might have been easier if I could have shared something of what I felt with Papa, but grief made a stranger of him, cut him off from me and Aunt Hettie. He had seemed to age twenty years in those weeks, becoming so thin and haggard that I was terrified he too would take a fever and die. I did not know how to comfort him and Aunt Hettie said he must be left to mourn in his own way and that time was the best healer. So Papa locked himself in his study, or rode out on Rajah for hours at a time, and ate his meals alone and hardly spoke a word to anyone. I suppose it was during those solitary hours that the inherent restlessness in his character, curbed since his marriage, rose up to fill the void left by the loss of his adored Yasmin. When he did at last join us for supper, it was merely to explain his plans. He would travel east again, embark on a journey of exploration. He had heard, he said, of great treasures to be found in the East Indies. A myriad islands, as yet uncharted, where palaces and temples were fashioned of gold and precious stones and where a bold man might seek his fortune . . . He looked at Aunt Hettie, at me, as he spoke, but I think he did not truly notice either of us. His vision was already set on far horizons.

In less than a month he was gone. We did not set eyes on him again. Aunt Hettie kept Rajah as long as she could, always hoping for news of her brother's return with the promised fortune. But by the time the last of Papa's infrequent letters had grown dusty, she had been forced to sell Rajah, along with the remaining silver and the last of Mama's gold bracelets. And still it had not been enough. One by one the servants were dismissed, the gardens rioted to a barely contained wilderness, and the house, never more than comfortably shabby, now fell prey to the elements. Broken roof slates littered the ground after every gale. Rain and melted snow dripped and seeped into the upper rooms. Ornate plaster ceilings sprouted black mould, damp patches spread down walls, timber rotted and crumbled. Aunt Hettie, who had devoted her life first to her parents until they died, then to her adored young brother and always to the house that she loved, did her best but it was not enough. And though her proud and severe nature – her loyalty – would not allow her to admit it, her faith in Papa began to falter. The struggle against undermining doubt, against accumulating debt, against the corruption of decay and neglect she saw all about her, contributed to her final defeat as much as the congestion of the lungs that carried her off. At least she was spared the final blow, the letter to inform us that Papa was dead, killed months before by bandits in a jungle skirmish. The letter delivered by the hand of the man who banished me to slavery at Crossbank and who subsequently became the new owner of Moondance: Theophilus Crowe.

'So that's how The Plough comes to be so popular with bored gentlemen out of Buxton,' Violet was saying in her sharp, clear voice. 'Fine brandy at excellent prices, a gaming table or two, and a few pretty doxies on hand to wait on them in public and entertain them privately when they're bored with cards or dice.' She scraped the comb through my oily locks for the last time. 'There, that's the best I can do with it. No use even thinking of trying to curl hair so defiantly straight.' Violet whisked round the chair to face me and regarded me with a frown. 'Curls wouldn't suit you, anyroad. Mind, it's hard at present to say what would. I can only hope that a bit of rest and fattening up will work an improvement on your looks, for they're sadly in need of it.'

'I'm not a prize pig, miss,' I said, still half lost in my thoughts so that the words were on my lips before my mind had time to recall them. 'And I don't care to be treated as such by someone who's no better than she should be!'

I instantly felt my face burn with shame, with embarrassment, and with an instinctive recoil of fear – borne of recent years – against the punishment such dreadful impertinence was bound to produce. 'I . . . I'm sorry, miss,' I stammered. 'I shouldn't have said—'

Violet, who I'd fully expected to fly into a temper, surprised me by cutting short my apologies with a shout of laughter.

'Well, well, one little mouse still has a spark of spirit left,' she chuckled. 'I should box your ears for your cheek, save that I know it wouldn't do any good. If you can still be lippy after five years of Crossbank, then a clout or two from me won't mend matters. Besides, who am I to dowse such a spark when it might serve you well in the future? Now, tell me, have you got any other advantages? Can you number and read?'

'Mar . . . Miranda was the best scholar at Crossbank,' Biddie put in proudly. ''Er can read a treat.'

'Better and better,' said Violet. 'You can make yourself useful.' She handed me a book she produced from her sewing basket. 'You can entertain us all by reading aloud while I finish this sleeve. From the beginning, if you please.'

I took it and turned the pages with careful fingers. I felt a thrill of pleasure. The only books Miss Groom ever brought with her to our Sunday lessons were a well-thumbed Bible and a great tome of sermons from which we might be privileged to read a paragraph or two. This book was almost new. I inhaled the smell of its smooth leather binding, the crisp, clean paper. A heady fragrance, redolent of the world I was about to re-enter. A world where people had time and freedom to indulge themselves in the ordinary – to me extraordinary – pleasure of taking up a book and wiling away an unplanned hour.

Maud rolled her eyes when she saw the book. 'Aha, your admirer been trotting off on errands for you again? He's fair besotted. He'll be offering to set you up in a place of your own next.'

'He already has, if you must know,' Violet said offhandedly. She regarded Maud with her hard blue stare. 'But if you think I'll put myself at his exclusive disposal – or any young man's – for the price of a few trinkets and a supply of novels from the circulating library in Buxton, then you're much mistaken. I've got different plans.'

'Plans? What sort of plans?'

But Violet lowered her lashes and picked up her sewing as though she had not heard the question. 'Please begin, Miranda,' she ordered.

'*The Lake of Killarney*,' I read, hesitantly, my voice sounding strange in the attentive silence, 'Chapter One . . .' And plunging into the adventures of one Rose de Blaguère, a foundling, became so caught up in the story that the intrusion of the clock in Mrs Turpin's bedchamber striking the hour when the girls must go and change for their evening duties came as a shock.

'I find the story very simple,' Violet said in a bored voice as she packed away her sewing. 'I daresay it's like many another and the foundling proves to be the daughter of a duke and all ends happily. I reckon I'll send it back and ask for something more original.'

There was a chorus of dismay.

'You always do this, Vi,' Dinah wailed. 'Read us a bit and get us all worked up and then don't tell us the rest. All we ever gets is half a tale.'

Maud, who had been hanging on to every melodramatic word, scowled. 'Like I told you, she does it a-purpose to vex us.'

Violet pretended surprise. 'Certainly not. In fact I may glance through it just to make sure I'm right and I'll explain the ending to you, though it's more than you deserve. After all, I offered to teach you to read. I've always been thankful my grandma taught me before she died. Once you can read you can educate yourself, like I've done. I've told you that many times but you won't take advantage.'

'I'm not a scholar like you. I don't have the brain for book-learning,' Maud wailed.

'You don't have the willpower or the determination, you mean,' Violet said. 'But then, you're not prepared to look further than the end of your nose. You're forgetting that time don't stand still. We'll none of us stay twenty. We won't always have the looks and figure to bring a lusty gleam to a man's eye. Have you thought what'll happen in another few years, eh? By then Ma Turpin will already have been on one of her jaunts to Derby or Sheffield or Stoke-upon-Trent in search of younger girls to train up. There'll be no place here for us then. Remember Hannah and Edith who were here when we first come? I'd like to know what happened to them once we became popular and they fell out of favour. One day they were here, the next they were gone – and if Mrs Turpin found them good honest work, as she told us, it was strange how her memory failed when I asked for Hannah's address in order to write to her. If you ask me, she sent 'em back to where she'd found 'em and left 'em to get on as best they could. And what happened to them, could happen to us.'

'You're only guessing,' Dinah protested. 'Making it up to suit yourself.'

'And forgetting Annie, who got wed,' Maud said triumphantly. 'Not to mention Sal. Look what happened to her. Set up in her own place in Manchester by a fine, rich gentleman—'

'Hah! Rich he might have been, but a more disgusting old rake I never did see. A withered bag of bones with a mouthful of rotting teeth and a nasty lust for young flesh. To be within a yard of him made my flesh crawl. Sal's too, I reckon, if I'm any judge. She put on a good, boastful show, but I saw the bruises she tried to hide when she'd been with him. And the way she watched him when he was pawing her. Sort of sick and frightened. As for Annie, she was a fool. Must have been, or she'd not have given her favours for free to the miller's lad in order to trap a simple bumpkin into marriage. Well, she's paid a high price for a wedding ring and respectability.' Violet lifted her elegant, muslin-clad shoulders in a shrug, her tone scornful. 'But if that's what you want – to live in a hovel with a parcel of screaming brats at your skirts and poverty reducing you to a careworn hag by the time you're thirty – so be it. But it's not for me. Not if I can help it.'

She had sauntered to the door as she spoke, casting her words airily over her shoulder. With her hand on the latch she turned and looked first at Biddie, then at me, and the hardness in her eyes seemed for an instant to be less pronounced; 'Nor for anyone else with an ounce of pluck and the intention to better themselves. It's always possible to improve your lot, even when you're poor and female. But bear in mind that what seems to be the easy way might turn out a sight harder and more unpleasant than you imagined, as Sal and Annie found to their cost. As any of Ma Turpin's girls might do lest they look out for themselves.' She slowed, stopped, her glance still on us. Then her eyes widened, as though a sudden thought had taken her. 'The bitch,' she breathed. 'I wonder . . .' Then, her expression changing to one of malicious amusement, she said mysteriously, 'An eye to a little extra profit, eh? Bitch. We'll see about *that*!'

When she had gone Maud put her arms around our shoulders. 'Take no notice,' she said comfortably. 'Vi's always got some bee in her bonnet. She was born sour and bossy. Anybody would think she was hard done by when we none of us wants for anything. You can see that for yourselves, can't you?'

Was there the faintest plea for understanding in her soft brown eyes?

I merely smiled and nodded, wanting to please Maud who had been kind. Unable, quite, to dismiss the ugly pictures raised by Violet's words. Biddie had no such reservations.

'I think it's lovely here,' she breathed. She reverently touched the satiny frill on Maud's wrapper. 'I never seen such pretty things in all my life before. Nor ever ate so well, neither.' She patted her stomach and grinned. 'Fit to bustin', I am. It feels grand.'

Dinah and Maud departed giggling, returning later to parade their finery. They preened before us, pouting, smiling, snapping open embroidered fans to peep above them with their shining, teasing eyes. Pink silk, lemon silk, heavily flounced, floated and clung round pampered white flesh. Ornaments sparkled among the glossy curls, on wrists, in the cleft between swelling breasts. They were like a pair of pretty, scented butterflies. Butterflies that were well aware of their attraction. Revelled in it. Made it impossible – in their self-assurance and conceit – to believe they had once been poor urchins like Biddie and me. Or to envisage them as the used and broken chattels of Violet's warnings. Yet the unpleasant images would not be shaken off. They remained lodged in my mind for the rest of the evening, like a bothersome piece of grit in a shoe.

That night – drifting to sleep – I caught the scurry of light feet along the passage beyond our room. A woman's voice and a man's deep tones mingling in laughter, whispered words, the distant click of a door closing.

One of Evangeline Turpin's girls about her work.

Violet was wrong, I thought drowsily. The walls are not so thick that they block all sound, though I had not heard music tonight. Perhaps Kit Warrener had rebelled against playing for his supper . . . If Violet could be wrong about one thing, then she might be wrong about the rest. Maybe Maud was right and Violet's cynical turn of mind blinkered her from seeing good in anything. True, the girls paid for the idle luxury of their days in ways that would cause respectable people to throw up their hands in horror. But those same respectable people wore on their backs the products of Crossbank and many another hell-hole like it, with never a thought for how the fine cotton was made and the wretched conditions the apprentices had to endure . . . I had seen so much that was cruel and degrading at Crossbank that I could not be shocked by the way of life of Ma Turpin's girls. They had, after all, been earning their living on the streets by the same means before they came under her protection. Violet had said so herself.

I snuggled further down under the soft sheets. It was none of my business, anyway. Before I let the blissful feather bed work its restful magic, I had already decided I would not allow myself to be unsettled by Violet's carping. I would be like Biddie and accept with gratitude all the comforts Mrs Turpin showered upon us. After all, we should be gone from here soon enough and there was no knowing what privations we might have to suffer in the future. We should make the most of our stay. We might not enjoy a time of such cosseting and luxury ever again.

But our spell of sybaritic living ended as abruptly as it had begun. Kit Warrener's patience, it seemed, had run out. Violet shook us awake before it was properly light on the fourth morning and informed us that we were to leave immediately.

'Be quick, and quiet about it,' she said, snatching the bedclothes from us. 'And no use pulling long faces. He's made up his mind and he'll not take it kindly if you keep the carriage waiting.'

While we washed and dressed she made bundles of the spare undergarments we had been given before hustling us out through Mrs Turpin's bedroom. I had expected to see the lady herself, propped up in bed drinking chocolate and surrounded by ledgers and papers as she usually was until late in the morning, but the room was empty. Downstairs, the low front door stood open to reveal a bony, sway-backed horse standing in the shafts of a farm wagon. The driver – merely a huddled heap of sacks topped with a shapeless, filth-encrusted hat – leaned down in conversation with Kit Warrener. A strong smell of pig muck wafted towards us.

'Perhaps not quite the sort of carriage you expected, but the best we could do at the last minute,' Violet said with sly amusement. 'With luck it will get you to Buxton before the horse drops dead from old age.'

'But – but where's Mrs Turpin?' I said. 'We ought to thank her . . . say goodbye . . .'

'She's busy,' Violet said. 'Trouble in the kitchen.' Her eyes glinted. 'Cook's having hysterics. Some villain got in overnight and turned the pantry upside down. Make haste now. You need to be off before she gathers her wits. Mr Warrener's fair dancing with impatience.'

'Gathers her wits?' I said, puzzled.

'Go!' Violet snapped. 'Keep your questions for later.' She pushed us roughly over the step, but we were immediately brought up short by the sound of Mrs Turpin's voice. A very angry Mrs Turpin.

We turned to see her pounding up the dark inner passage, chins a-wobbling, clutching her striped dressing robe to her vast, uncontained bosom, her hair in a thin grey plait hanging like a rat's tail below her nightcap. 'What's the meaning of this?' she demanded, brushing Violet to one side with one sweep of her arm. She caught at our shoulders, drawing us back into the hallway. 'Whatever is the hurry? Would you leave without saying goodbye? And why was I not told?'

'Dunno, missus,' Biddie stammered. 'We was got up early—'

'At Mr Warrener's insistence,' Violet put in smoothly. 'I couldn't dissuade him, Ma. He was determined to go at first light.'

Mrs Turpin clicked her tongue. 'Such ill manners. To leave so . . . so precipitately, without a word of thanks. And there was I, taking him for a gentleman. Well, it smacks to me of deceit and ingratitude, indeed it does, when I think of the comforts I have showered on him – on you all.' She made a visible effort to soften her tone, to smile, but the anger – laced with an odd kind of anxiety – still simmered below the surface. 'There, there, my dears. I don't mean to be cross with you. It's not your fault. No need for you to be worried.'

'I'm sorry, ma'am,' I said, awkwardly. 'Perhaps he – Mr Warrener – didn't think. I know me and Biddie's very grateful for what you've done. We've not known such kindness for a long time.'

It was from the heart and Mrs Turpin smiled. She put her hand to my cheek. Her fingers moved, plump and warm, against my morning-chilled skin. 'Oh, my dear child, I am moved. I truly am. Though I assure you, I wasn't looking for compliments. Dearie me, no. 'Tis enough reward for me to see such improvement in three days.' Her small dark eyes scrutinised me from the top of my neat straw bonnet to the hem of my cut-down dark print dress, one of Maud's cast offs. With Violet pressing us to hurry, I had not been allowed more than a glimpse of my newly turned-out self in the bedchamber mirror but I knew that the skilful arts employed by Dinah, Maud and Violet had worked wonders. She inspected Biddie in the same careful manner, then nodded, well satisfied. 'Though I say it myself, your stay at The Plough has served you well. Yes, indeed. Quite a transformation. Most satisfying.' Her glance had lingered on Biddie. 'I thought there might be hopes of a pretty child under the grime and I see that given a year or two you will grow very fetching, my dear. Even now, you have qualities that will soon have you setting hearts a-flutter.'

Surprised, I looked at my friend. Biddie, with her gingery curls escaping from under her bonnet to frame her cheeks . . . Biddie, clean and neatly dressed and smiling with pleasure and gratitude, so that her green eyes sparkled and her face filled with an animation that momentarily plumped out the sharpness of her starveling bones. Mrs Turpin was right. It was possible to see the young woman – the attractive woman – she would become.

Mrs Turpin heaved a sigh. 'It would have been a great joy for me to have been allowed to care for you a while longer, to see you both properly well and bonny. But if you feel duty bound to go with Mr Warrener, then go you must . . . I daresay you will soon forget Evangeline Turpin who took you in out of the storm and provided everything within her power to make you comfortable.'

'But we won't forget,' Biddie cried, reaching out a timid hand to touch Mrs Turpin's sleeve. 'Will we, Miranda? An' we're really sorry we got to go. It's been lovely 'ere.'

'Has it, dear?' Mrs Turpin said. 'Well, I try my best to make a pleasant home for all who live under my roof. And it always pleases me to help young people in any way I can.' Her large hand closed over Biddie's. 'Remember this. You will always find my door open, poor motherless lambs that you are, should you ever find yourself in need of a friendly word of advice.' A pause, then, lightly, a casual afterthought but again with that curious hint of anxiety, as though she was eager to settle some matter of importance: 'Of course, if you were so minded, we could work out a plan so that you need not leave at all. If you really want to make The Plough your home . . . well, perhaps it would be as well to leave the district until the hue and cry dies down.' She paused, frowning, then brightened. 'I have it! I have good friends in Sheffield. I will arrange this very morning for them to take you in until it is safe to return here, to me and these dear girls whom you may now count among your friends. I'd willingly have a word with Mr Warrener on your behalf.'

Such cosy warmth and friendliness in her voice, such a tempting possibility.

I felt its seductive pull. We had seemed so safe here. After the cosseted seclusion of the past three days, the prospect of stepping out into the remorseless daylight to make a journey in an open waggon, with heaven knows what to face in Buxton and beyond, was intimidating. Biddie's thoughts must have been much the same. She turned to me, her eyes wide and bright. 'Oh, Miranda,' she breathed. 'Just think 'ow that'd be.'

Think of it. How easy a solution . . . Involuntarily I glanced at Violet. The cynical twist of her smile was like a dash of cold water that swilled away all that was cosy and comfortable about Mrs Turpin's words. I looked at Mrs Turpin again. Looked this time with unclouded eyes and did not like what I saw behind her easy smile and coaxing voice. Whatever it was Mrs Turpin wanted of us – whatever it was that made her anxious to keep us at The Plough – was to her advantage, but not to ours.

'No need to make up your mind right away,' she was saying easily. 'I think we should take breakfast while you think about it. Even with the kitchen in disarray, I cannot allow that ungrateful young man to carry you off without allowing you to take a bite to eat . . . I think a few rashers and some boiled eggs might be managed, and while you eat you may consider the advantages in remaining with loving friends instead of hurrying off to somewhere strange where you will not know a soul. Come this way, my dears. You shall take breakfast in my own little private parlour—'

'Tempting, but I think not, Mrs Turpin.' Kit Warrener's voice cut across her wheedling words like a cold knife slicing into warm butter. He had come silent-footed into the hallway. 'There is no need to put yourself out any further on our behalf.

We shall buy what food we need in Buxton. Come, Miranda, Biddie. It is time we were off.'

Mrs Turpin's smile did not falter. She was fully herself again. She had regained her air of formidable, matronly composure. She sounded very sure of herself as she said, smoothly, 'Of course, sir. Far be it from me to delay you. Pray don't forget to convey my thanks and best wishes to my brother Captain Luscombe, when you are returned. As to these dear girls –' she shook her head at him almost playfully '– I think you may well be relieved to find that they are considering alternative arrangements.'

'Is that so?' He sounded unsurprised. 'And does a certain Samuel Foster of Sheffield come into these arrangements? I believe he is an occasional visitor at this establishment.'

Mrs Turpin raised her eyebrows. 'Foster?' she queried, shaking her head. 'I cannot recall that name in particular, but then I can hardly be expected to remember all the gentlemen who frequent The Plough.'

'Then allow me to jog your memory.' Kit Warrener stepped closer.

She was such a large woman that he, though a good head taller, looked slight by comparison. Even so, it was Mrs Turpin who drew back and said warily, 'Really, sir, I cannot think what you . . .'

'Samuel Foster,' he said as though she had not spoken, 'is the man you sent word to yesterday regarding a . . . well, shall we say a delivery you intended to make? Is that plain enough for you? Or should you like me to tell you how I came to overhear your instructions to the carter who carries your messages? And my subsequent greasing of a few palms that turned up some interesting facts about one of the more sordid aspects of your trade . . . Well?'

Mrs Turpin's mouth fell open then instantly closed, her teeth snapping together with a sharp click. She reached out and clutched at Biddie, as though to drag her away. Kit Warrener was quicker. He grabbed Biddie's arm and yanked her backwards. At the same time Violet stepped forward briskly, crying, 'This is for you, Miranda. I nearly forgot. A little farewell present.' And she pushed a package into my hands, threw her arm about me and managed to set herself between me and Mrs Turpin.

'Violet! What are you about? Make yourself useful and take Miranda into my parlour.' Mrs Turpin was blustering now, her hands groping uselessly at thin air. 'Biddie, come here this instant! Sir . . . Mr Warrener . . . you have quite the wrong idea. Give me a chance to explain . . . I shall order breakfast and we can talk . . .'

But Kit Warrener was already outside and hefting a protesting Biddie none-too-gently into the waggon. Violet, who seemed not to have heard Mrs Turpin's order, swooped a kiss on my cheek and pushed me once more over the step. 'Travel safely,' she said. 'And if a whore's blessing counts for anything, then you have it.'.

I followed Biddie into the waggon. Kit Warrener tossed our bundles after us and ordered the waggoner to drive on as he threw himself down beside his own shabby leather bag. I half expected Mrs Turpin to come after us, calling and cajoling, but only Violet remained at the door to watch us jolt away, her face full of some private, malicious amusement. Then she went inside and the door closed after her.

'I'd rather have stayed,' Biddie wailed. 'Missus wanted us to. It was lovely there.'

'I daresay.' Under the rim of his worn beaver hat, Kit Warrener's thin, bony face was pale, his narrow eyes underlined with shadow as though he had slept little. 'But it would not have been to your advantage, I assure you. Be glad you are safely away and let me hear no more whining.'

The habit of submission to authority, of obedience to the rule of fist and boot, was still too harshly imprinted, too close, for Biddie to make any further protest. Still looking sulky, she contented herself with kneeling up on the passably clean straw that had been spread over the odorous remains of the previous cargo and watching until the bend in the road cut off the last glimpse of The Plough. But my curiosity was roused and I could not hold it back.

'Why *safely* away, sir?' I burst out. 'What was the danger?'

'Nothing you need worry about now,' he said curtly. 'You are out of that woman's hands. Let that be enough.'

His reluctance intrigued me all the more. There was some mystery here that I needed to understand.

'She only promised to find us a place with kind friends in Sheffield, sir,' I persisted. 'That Mr Foster you spoke of, who's he, sir? Was he the one we were to go to?'

He did not answer straight away and I thought at first the colour that came into his face was a symptom of his anger at being questioned. But his glance wavered from mine, fixed itself at some point beyond me. I suddenly realised that he was for some reason deeply embarassed. 'Samuel Foster is by repute a man involved in a sordid trade,' he began. 'Mrs Turpin – er – assists him from time to time . . . with suitable acquisitions.' He cleared his throat. 'Young girls, orphans . . . *untouched* young girls . . . There are some men, you see, who pay well to be . . . well, to be the first to . . . to . . .' He broke off, said crossly, 'Dammit, I see no need to spell it out! Just be grateful I was warned in time to foil that wretched woman's plans.'

For all that he must be at least one-and-twenty his embarrassment momentarily gave him the air of someone much younger, an effect heightened, I realised, by the length of gangling wrist protruding from his sleeve, and the way that outgrown coat strained across his shoulders and chest. Even as I shivered with the sickening understanding of what he was saying, there was some part of me that seemed to be more interested in these trivial observations than in our lucky escape from Mrs Turpin and her trade in virgins. A sharp inner sense that noted the fine down of black hair on that exposed length of wrist and the broad hand with the strong, supple musician's fingers; that found significance in – that was strangely moved to sympathy by – the glimpse of a threadbare cuff lying against pale skin, of the hole visible in the sole of one boot and a clumsy darn half-concealed by the carefully folded and tied cravat.

'Was it Miss Violet who warned you?' I asked, drawing my thoughts sharply from these distractions.

He nodded, said gruffly, 'She believes Mrs Turpin meant to hand you over secretly to this man Foster. Then she would spin me some cock-and-bull yarn about you running off. I thought it best to take Miss Violet's word even if she is only a . . . a . . .'

'A doxy,' I said, wanting to put him at his ease. 'There was plenty of rough talk at Crossbank, sir, we all knew of such things. Will she get into trouble, Miss Violet, for helping us?'

'I think that young lady is well able to take care of herself,' he said, his embarrassment fading to be replaced by grim amusement. 'She seems to enjoy playing her own devious games. It was she who told me that you were not at death's door, as Mrs Turpin insisted you were. The damned woman told me it would be fatal to move you.' He paused then added stiffly, 'I cannot say that I was – or am – pleased to have the responsibility of escorting you to Devon thrust upon me. But I would not have knowingly led you into danger, or let you remain a moment longer than necessary at the inn, had I been aware of Mrs Turpin's evil intentions. Will you believe that?'

His narrow, deep-set eyes were steady on mine. I held his glance and as I did so, I felt the first tentative stirrings of trust, of hope.

'Yes, sir,' I said quietly.

He nodded brusquely, then deliberately turned his head to stare in silence at the passing scenery, his stony profile prohibiting all further attempts at questions or conversation.

After a moment I remembered the package Violet had pushed into my hands. I pulled the Kashmir shawl more tightly round my neck against the thin wind and broke the seal on the wrapping paper. Inside, to my astonishment, was the book, *The Lake of Killarney*, and a note from Violet in a careful hand.

I shall say I have mislaid this. It can be well afforded by he who brought it for me and will give you, I trust, some pleasure. May Fortune be your Friend, as I have tried to be.

V.B.

The page that bore the impress of the library had been carefully cut out. Above the title on the frontispiece Violet had written: *Miranda, her book, the fourteenth day of September, 1812.*

I could not remember the last time I shed tears. Within Crossbank's grim walls I had quickly learned to suppress weaknesses of that sort. But now I was glad that Kit Warrener chose to set his attention on the landscape and that Biddie hung over the tail of the cart, her face wistful and her mind clearly on the delights of The Plough from which she had been so rudely snatched.

Eventually I managed to swallow the great lump that had risen into my throat and blinked hard until the wetness in my eyes had subsided. Violet could not have known. I had almost forgotten it myself until I saw the date she had written.

Today was my birthday. Today I was fifteen years old.

Today, I had been given a gift. That seemed something of an omen.

And even though the malodorous waggon, the sway-backed old nag and the louring clouds might not seem to cast an auspicious lustre on the beginning of our journey to freedom, I could not help but feel my spirits lift.

Chapter Three

We were four days and nights in reaching Exeter. We were tired and travel-stained, but when we clambered down from the coach outside the London inn I could have knelt and kissed the greasy cobbles or hugged one of the dirty little ragamuffins who always haunted any hostelry in the hopes of earning a copper from carrying bags or sweeping away horse-muck or running errands. I was safely back in Devon with no more, Kit reckoned, than fifteen to twenty miles to go to journey's end. Well before nightfall Biddie and I should be with Mrs Loveridge's friends in Dawlish. There seemed little now that could go wrong.

I was sadly mistaken on both counts, but I was not to know that as I stared about me, drinking in the sight of the mild September sunlight washing over rosy Devon stone and sturdy red brick.

How warm it all seemed, how welcoming, after the stony grey villages of the north. Even the faces of the passers-by and the travellers moving in and out of the inn seemed more alive, more inclined to smile, as though the sunshine and the balmy air had a benign effect upon them. It certainly had that effect on me. I lifted my face to the sun, no longer feeling the need to shade my face from the gaze of other people. The sensation of believing the word 'runaway' to be branded across my forehead for all to see had quite gone. Our respectable dress and the company of Kit Warrener had ensured an unremarked passage, though at first we had been very cautious. We had not lingered in Buxton where our names and descriptions were bound to have been cried, but had left on the first available coach which fortunately was travelling south to a small town called Leek, in Staffordshire, from where we were able to travel to Newcastle-under-Lyme on the busy London Road.

With every passing mile after that my confidence rose, and it did not matter in the slightest that we were constrained to using cheaper and slower forms of transport than the fast coaches that would have had us in Exeter in half the time. Mrs Loveridge had pressed all her available pin money on her cousin – to have done more would have drawn Mr Loveridge's attention – but it had to be stretched very thin.

'I've very little of my own,' Kit warned us. 'So do not expect to be dining on larks' tongues and roast swan.'

'I don't care if we have to walk the whole way,' I said stoutly. 'As for fine dining, I'd prefer to see swans and larks alive and beautiful, not slaughtered for the pot.'

He grinned. 'I reckon bread and cheese and Adam's ale can taste just as good when you're hungry and thirsty.'

So bread and cheese it had been most of the time, with the only variations a plate of roast pig's cheek with onions shared between us at the New Inn at Hereford and a beef pie each from a pie seller who was selling off his wares cheap late at night in Bristol. Our hunger was well sharpened by being in the fresh air, outside seats being all we could afford. This was no hardship for the weather had settled back to being dry and warm.

Though Biddie swathed her cloak up round her face and refused to take any pleasure in what she called 'empty places', only perking up when the conveyance clattered to a halt in whatever the town or city of our destination, I wanted to stretch all my senses. To feel the wind in my face, to breathe in the tang of horsflesh and dust, of turned earth from a newly ploughed field, the stench of a farm midden, the sudden sweet waft of late roses blooming in some cottager's garden. As my body relished the plain honest food, so my starved, bruised spirit feasted greedily on these ordinary things. There was such joy in the sight of yellow harvest fields where women and children gleaning in the stubble turned to wave to us, on the pattern of stars piercing the velvety night sky, or the sudden contrast as we swept from open countryside into the vibrant clamour of the towns. Every sight, every scent, every noise – every discomfort – reminded me that I was truly alive and free, and continued the restorative process of healing that had begun the moment I had turned my back on Crossbank.

The tentative seedling of trust in Kit Warrener had sprouted a little more each day of the journey. Though we were stiff with each other at first, from a wariness of his temper on my side and a residue of truculence at being encumbered on his, it was scarcely possible to remain on formal terms when we were together for twenty-four hours of the day. I was at first suspicious of his declaration of poverty, half expecting that he would seek out extra privileges for himself in the way of a better class of seating or a more substantial diet. My suspicions were quickly allayed. He said we would share everything and we did. Whether it was precarious outside seats on lumbering country conveyances, a ha'penny cup of milk – or even a few blissful hours of abandoned sleep one warm afternoon under the sun-drenched hedge of a stubble field on the fringes of Gloucester when there was ample time for him to have bespoken a feather mattress at the nearby inn. The farmer we had fallen into conversation with while buying bread at Tewkesbury market had brought us this far along a winding byway, being glad, he said, of the company on his now-empty waggon and stoutly refusing any payment. We decided to eat our midday bread and cheese in the field before walking into the city to find the Bristol coach. The heat and peace had lulled us all to a comfortable torpor.

'We might as well rest for a few minutes,' Kit had said, stretching his long legs and sinking back against the grassy bank. 'I believe I might take a nap . . .'

That was the last I remembered until the sound of the flute wove its gentle insistent way into my dreams and I woke to find Kit had moved to sit a little way off under a spreading ash tree. He had taken off his coat and carelessly rolled up his shirt sleeves, and with his eyes half closed, the dappled, greeny shade rippling over the pale skin of his forearms, his bony profile remote in its concentration on the music, he looked like some pagan deity strayed from the distant woodland.

There was nothing mystical or fey about the music, though. The tunes were clearly recognisable. I sat up, captivated, hugging my knees as the notes cascaded like birdsong to link snatches of country airs. I picked out 'Blow away the Morning Dew' and 'Dame, Get up and Bake your Pies' and 'Lavender Blue' amid others that I did not know. Then after a rippling crescendo of sound he broke off, turning quickly as though suddenly remembering he was not alone. He beckoned me over, looking crestfallen.

'I did not mean to wake you.'

'I'm glad you did. It was lovely music.'

His grin was rueful. 'Which proves you are no musician. Though I love these old airs, there were far too many wrong notes and I would be the first to admit that such talent as I have does not lie with the flute. But I am temporarily parted from the violin which is my first love, so must make do.' He patted the grass. 'Come, sit beside me. I am willing to play an encore for such an appreciative audience. What will it be? Do you know any songs? "Greensleeves", perhaps, or "Raggle Taggle Gypsies"?'

He piped the first phrases of each and before I could answer swept into a lively rendition of a tune I did not know. Then he stopped playing and burst into song, in a robust baritone:

> 'Now welcome, Summer, with thy sunne soft
> Now welcome, Summer, with thy sunne soft,
> That hast this winter's weathers overshake
> And driven away the longe nightes black'.

And pausing only to cry, 'Catch the tune, Miranda. Sing out! It is easy,' played it several times more, encouraging my hesitant efforts to follow the tune.

'Well done,' he said at last, laughing. 'An appropriate song,

I thought, for such an afternoon. This seems a day snatched from summer, does it not?'

'Indeed, sir,' I said.

There was about him an air of total ease, as though some effect of the music had for the moment cast off the dark broodings that so often shadowed his face and made him withdraw into silence. He looked at me curiously.

'You sing true. Did you ever have singing lessons or learn to play an instrument? In your old life, that is.'

I shook my head. 'Aunt Hettie had a harp she'd learned to play when she was a girl, but the strings were all broken and loose. She was always promising to get it mended and teach me, but she never did. Mama and I used to sing together when I was very little and Aunt Hettie wasn't about. She didn't like Mama's songs. They were foreign, you see. Strange.'

'And this Aunt Hettie . . . and your mama? What happened to them?'

'Dead,' I said. 'Papa too. The house sold off.'

'What about other relatives?'

'No one. Papa and Aunt Hettie were the last of the Brehaults.' I shrugged. 'I might have aunts and cousins in India but Mama cut herself off from them when she eloped with Papa.'

'I wondered, you see, if there was anyone who might usefully be contacted on your behalf?'

'That's kind of you, sir,' I said, taken by surprise.

He grinned, half-embarrassed. 'We waifs and strays must look out for each other. And to be honest, I am trying to make up a little for my earlier churlishness.' He delved into his travelling bag and drew out a soft rag which he folded carefully around the flute. 'I should have had more sympathy. I know what it is to be out in the world, alone and penniless. And your case is so much more understandable – more deserving of support – than mine. Indeed, there are those who would condemn me for a fool – and worse – for defying my father's sensible rules, leave alone that I should cut myself off entirely from him.'

'What rules were those, sir?' I asked, prompted by the easiness of the moment His answer was so long in coming that I feared I had offended him by my question. But his voice was light when he answered, impersonal almost, as though all that had happened had quite lost any significance for him. It was only the way his hands slowed over the small task of settling the wrapped flute into his bag that betrayed him, as though the intensity of memory caught him unawares.

'Oh, the rules of a man who believes his son to be a wastrel. When I grew too big to be thrashed out of my foolish ideas of becoming a musician, I was forbidden to practise in the house or out of it.'

'Wasn't he proud that you played well?'

He laughed. 'Proud? No, indeed. He saw it as an unhealthy obsession. He was unable to understand that I could no more part myself from music than cut off my arms and legs. While my mother was alive she protected and encouraged me as best she could, even though she was delicate and often ill. I was twelve when she died. After that there was to be no more "spoiling", as my father termed my violin lessons. Just to be sure, he sold the violin Mama had bought for me . . . Still, it is old history and of no consequence to anyone save myself.'

This was the first time we had held a conversation of any length, or touched upon personal matters. Watching the play of light and shade over his face, I felt the echo of that first strange, knowing moment when I had watched him riding the valley road and heard his voice speaking my name. The feeling fled almost as soon as I recognised it. All that was left was the faint but clear compulsion to know more about him, to probe further.

'It must have been a hard, sad time for you, sir,' I said.

He shrugged. 'Not nearly so hard as you had, Miranda.'

'But . . . but you did keep up with your music. You defied your father . . . That was . . . brave.'

'Brave? I think not. Bravado I had in plenty, certainly. And a generous helping of my father's own pigheadedness. I learned to be devious and to lie fluently, but half the time I was quaking in my shoes lest I be discovered in my deceptions.' He laughed. 'I would hardly call that heroic behaviour.'

He told me a little more. Bare facts, his flippancy a bright and steely shield. But it was not difficult for me to flesh out these bare bones and imagine the unhappy years he must have suffered. A clever, sensitive boy, grieving for the loss of his mother, desperate to continue with his music despite the cold animosity of his father and the servants paid to spy on him. He was not entirely friendless, though. The German music master at the school he attended, unable to bear seeing talent go to waste, gave hours of his time entirely without payment; a sympathetic housemaid had helped him in small ways wherever she was able; and, in due course, when Kit was fifteen and had been taken, protesting, from school and put to work in his father's counting house, there was the friendship of his cousin Caroline.

'Though I loathed the counting house, my old music master was still my ally. I visited him to practise on his violin – a magnificent Cremona – whenever I could sneak away for an hour. Also I was composing more and more, working until the small hours shaping the melodies and harmonies that constantly flowed through my head into some sort of order.' He laughed. 'And sleepy and sulky it made me in consequence. I had many a clip round the ear from the bad-tempered chief clerk for dozing over my ledgers. But I did not care so long as I had my music, and it became easier after Caro – that is, my cousin, Mrs Loveridge – moved in with us. She thought it a great game to devise ploys to deceive my father.'

I could imagine that sharp intelligence at work, scheming, manipulating, as perhaps even now she did at Crossbank . . .

'She had no love of him, d'you see? A few weeks after her mama died – she was sister to my own mother, who succumbed to the same weakness of the lungs – her papa, too, was tragically taken from her when his horse bolted and threw him under the wheels of a carriage. We were her only relatives and my father, whose idea of moral duty had no acquaintance with compassion, immediately removed her from Furze House, the school at Dawlish where she was exceedingly happy, and brought her to London. You will meet Miss Swann and Mrs Greenwood, the owners of the school, before long. Their establishment is our destination and you may be assured they will do their utmost to help you. I believe they were as heartbroken as Caro when she left, but my father did not believe in wasting money on educating girls, or in employing a housekeeper when there was a grown niece of nearly fourteen who could be trained up to take that role.'

For the first time his eyes were shadowed by his dark lashes, his voice laced with sadness. 'My poor Caro. So bewildered and unhappy. Mourning for her parents, hating the noise and dirt of Cheapside, hating her confinement in that gloomy house. And now I return to find her in worse case. Forced to submit to the demands of a husband she does not even like and could never love.'

There had been little submissive about Caroline Loveridge so far as I had seen. She had seemed to have the management of her husband well in hand. But I could not break the brooding silence that had fallen with so impolite a comment.

He gave a short, bitter laugh, then said softly, 'Had I but known . . . ah, such a tormenting thought. But I did not, because I chose to go my own way, all the time deluding myself . . . hoping . . . that she would still be there, and all unchanged, awaiting the prodigal's return . . .' He broke off with a guarded glance at me, as though suddenly realising he was speaking aloud thoughts which were too private to be shared. With a visible effort he returned to his story, glossing the hard facts with a lightness intended to disguise the pain of them. 'Where was I? Ah, yes. Papa found us out, as he was bound to do, I suppose. His revenge was to order all my belongings searched while I was out and a bonfire made of every piece of paper he found, every personal item. All went. Books, music, including all the pieces I had composed and kept hidden in what I had thought a secret place under a loose floorboard . . . letters Mama had written to me and a likeness she had had painted before she died as a remembrance . . . everything he considered distracted me from the path of duty. Everything dear to me. All gone to ashes by the time I returned.'

'How dreadful,' I murmured.

'Perhaps it was for the best. I had tried, until then, to love him as a son should love his father, to placate him in the hopes, perhaps, that we could some day reach an understanding. That was the moment I knew it was impossible. Deprived of music, my spirit would have shrivelled and died. I could never be the son he wanted. He could never be the father I needed. So I ran away that night. And, thanks to the help of my music master, I was able to set out for Vienna where he had friends. His parting gift to me was the violin upon which I had so often practised, a magnificent Cremona, his most treasured possession which, alas, he could no longer play due to his fingers becoming crippled with rheumatism.' He shook his head sadly. 'More than anything I wished to repay Herr Schmidt for his gift and his many kindnesses. Soon after I left he moved to Bath on account of his declining health, though he kept in touch with my progress. His wife wrote to tell me of his death in January. I shall never play for him now.'

A cloud drifted across the sun and the breeze suddenly had an edge to it. Kit cocked an eye at the sky. 'I reckon we had best be making a move, else we'll not be in Gloucester before dark.' He got to his feet and snatched up his coat, saying cheerfully, 'Does it trouble you to travel with a prodigal son for whom no fatted calf will ever be slain and roasted?'

'Not much, sir,' I said, standing up and smoothing down my crumpled skirt. 'Leastways, I think you've done the best you could for us so far. I hope you'll keep on doing so.' The words sounded grudging but though I had been touched by his story, I was still too wary to trust him completely.

'I will do my best,' he said gravely.

He dusted his coat with his hand to clean it of the strands of dead grass and seeds it had acquired as it lay on the ground. Then he shook it vigorously so that the tails flew up and out.

There was a tearing sound and a small, heavy missile flew towards me and dropped with a thud at my feet. I bent and picked it up. It was an old and greasy doeskin purse, heavy in my hand. I could feel the shifting shape of coins under my fingers.

'I am a better musician than tailor,' Kit said lightly, as he reached for it and stuffed it back into its hiding place. 'I had thought I had sewn this little hoard safely in my inner pocket. And as you are perfectly aware of what I have here, for I can see it written all over your face, I will tell you that it is not mine. If it were we none of us would travel so frugally, believe me.' He hesitated, his narrow eyes intent upon me, as though judging how much to say. 'It is the payment for goods I delivered to The Plough.'

'To Mrs Turpin? From her brother, Captain Luscombe?' I remembered scraps of Violet's conversation that had scarcely registered at the time. It triggered an older memory. 'Miss Violet said something about regular callers from Devon . . . and the best French brandy selling cheap at the inn. Was that what you delivered, sir? Or was it tobacco, perhaps?'

He paused then said quietly, 'Both.'

'So Captain Luscombe's by way of being a freetrader? And you one of his runners?'

'This was my first trip. And my last,' he added quickly. 'I have no wish to tangle myself more than necessary with Captain Luscombe and his ilk. It was mutually convenient this once. I wished to travel north but did not have the means. He had goods to be delivered and offered to pay my way. You do not seem surprised.'

I shook my head. 'I've known about such things since I was little. Papa bought smuggled goods. Plenty of folk did. It used to be a packman come to Moondance. He'd turn up late at night and be given leave to sleep overnight in the cellars. There was always a new keg of brandy or gin in the cellar after he'd gone.' I smiled at the recollection of sitting wide-eyed and breathless, listening to Jed's melodramatic tales. 'My friend Jed was full of stories about how the goods were brought in and where they were hidden and what was done by the brave, daring smugglers to outwit the excisemen. We both thought it vastly thrilling.'

'Keep your romantic view if you wish,' Kit said dryly. 'What little I have seen of the trade inclines me to a more sober opinion. It is a hard and rough business. Those who deal in it must needs be cunning and ruthless to survive – and Captain Luscombe has survived a-many years and grown rich in consequence. He is a man made dangerous by his knowledge of other men's weaknesses which he has used to his own advantage. He knows which palms to grease and who to bend to his will by blackmail or violence. He has woven a fine protective tangle about himself. I was an innocent fly who stepped too close to his spidery web and am now temporarily caught up in it.'

'Then why . . . ?'

'Why did I agree to involve myself?' He pulled on his coat and fastened the buttons. 'Oh, I thought I had reasons enough. Let us say it was a moment of weakness.' His tone was momentarily curt. Whatever the true reason he was not about to share it with me. 'The opportunity seemed heaven-sent. It was later, when two of his cronies parted me from my violin, that I understood the captain was not the jolly, good-natured buffoon I had thought him on first acquaintance.'

'He stole it?'

'I was walking back to Furze House from a friend's cottage. He had been confined indoors after an accident. I had thought to cheer his spirits by playing for him. I was waylaid as I returned to Furze House and my violin confiscated. As surety of my good behaviour, they said, in case I had ideas of tricking the captain.'

'Do you trust him to give it back?'

'I have no other option. He knew I could not challenge him. There was too much at risk.' Again that tightness in his voice, that sense of a shutter abruptly closing on something he did not wish to disclose. He picked up his bag and we began to walk back to where Biddie, still wrapped in her cloak, was sleeping soundly. His voice was level, dispassionate, giving nothing away, as he said, 'I had the misfortune to cross his path when he was short of men and there was a cargo to be shifted quickly, otherwise I should not have been recruited. The press gangs had been active in the district. Several of his men had been rounded up by a gang operating out of Teignmouth. Others had suffered injury during a chase by revenue officers off Guernsey.' He halted just short of where Biddie lay and caught my arm. 'Keep what I have said between ourselves,' he said softly. 'In particular, I should not like you to mention it to Miss Swann or Mrs Greenwood. I would not wish them to be distressed. They have been more than generous in offering me the hospitality of their home as long as I remain in Dawlish. It is best you forget what I must secretly carry. Now, rouse your friend and we will be on our way.'

Until we reached Exeter I truly did not give much thought to the money Kit Warrener carried, being more interested in piecing together the story of his runaway years which he had spent in Vienna – a city, he said, that ate, lived and breathed music despite its occupation by Napoleon's armies. The recommendation from his old music master had opened doors for him, enabling him to set up as a teacher of English, so establishing the means to pay for his own music lessons until, he said, he had felt the pull of his own country and his own people.

We had a long wait before we could board the coach for Dawlish. Kit counted out his remaining coins. 'We can afford the coach fare and a good breakfast,' he declared, ushering us into the inn where we ate heartily of beefsteak pie and scrambled eggs and steaming bowls of coffee.

We came out into the warm sunshine well satisfied and looking for a diversion to while away an hour. I had only been to Exeter once before, when I was very small, with Mama and Papa. My memories of the place itself were hazy, though I did remember a particularly fine toffee apple Papa had bought for me from a tiny shop set close against a massive stone arch which Kit said was probably one of the gateways leading into the city through the old walls. He, too, had visited Exeter several times as a boy when his delicate mother came to visit her sister during the summer. 'But we never stayed for long. The household would decamp to lodgings by the sea, ozone and sea breezes having been recommended as beneficial by my aunt's doctor. That is how I first made my acquaintance with Dawlish and the kind of people there. But come, we have time to take a stroll and look at the sights.'

We threaded our way down alleyways of ancient houses whose upper storeys loomed over us to block out the light, and out into the High Street where crowds thronged round the market stalls that had been set up in front of the shops.

'We shall come back to the market and buy apples for our journey,' Kit cried, diving into the press of people haggling and hunting bargains round the stalls. 'But you cannot leave Exeter without viewing its greatest glory. This way!' Then weaving round panniered donkeys, gentlemen on horseback, small ragged boys with large brooms at the ready to sweep litter and horse droppings from the path of the fashionable ladies and gentlemen, and sweating chairmen crying passage for their conveyances, we went down another alley and found ourselves in the quiet open space before the cathedral.

'It's just another old church,' Biddie muttered rebelliously in my ear. 'We passed plenty o' them on the way. I'd sooner go back where there's summat goin' on.'

But Kit was already striding ahead, to pause before the west front, head thrown back, staring at the great carved façade.

'Just as I remember it,' he said. 'As a small boy, if I half closed my eyes, I fancied the rows of saints in their niches appeared like notes on a sheet of music. I quite believed it was some mysterious anthem carved in stone by the medieval masons only I did not have the means to interpret it. It was only God, I thought, who was allowed to hear the melody. Perhaps, in a childish way, I was right.' He swung round, his face, the whole taut length of his lean body, expressing the intensity of feeling I had glimpsed when he had been sitting in the dappled shade of the ash tree like a pagan deity, absorbed in his playing. 'The music is here, waiting for me.' He flung his arms wide as though to encompass the stretch of grass, the buildings circling Cathedral Yard, the calm blue of the September sky and all the clutter and noise of the city, spreading and spilling beyond its ancient walls into the rich Devon countryside. 'This is why I had to return. I do not want to compose mockeries of the Italian style. I cannot think or feel as an Italian – or as an Austrian or a German or a Frenchman. Though I am grateful for all that I learned in Vienna, the fact remains that I am English. This . . . this *Englishness* is exactly what I wish to capture. All the energy and charm and ribaldry that is expressed in folksong and myth . . . the diversities of the countryside and the people who inhabit it . . . the vigour of the cities, the moods of the sea. Ah, if I could transcribe but half of what I feel in my blood and my bones into music, I should be a happy man.'

'He's skewpated, him,' Biddie whispered, scowling. 'I don't know the 'alf of what he's on about.'

'There speaks an honest woman.' Kit's hearing was sharper than she realised but he was laughing as he spoke. Biddie flushed and, out of an instinct borne of many a hard-earned lesson in self-protection, shrank back into my shadow.

'No need to hide behind Miranda, Biddie,' he said gently. 'I am not in the least put out for I have had far harsher judgements made on my ambitions. The most recent being in Vienna where a distinguished composer with whom I had taken some tuition in counterpoint was particularly scathing about a string quartet I had written especially to impress him. I can freely admit that Salieri's criticism did cut me at the time, but in a way he did me a favour. It brought matters to a head, you see. I had become restless. I felt that I had absorbed all that I was able to in Vienna. It was time to move on. I wanted to come home. And where better to start than Devonshire, where I had been happiest as a child? And which held many warm memories that had sustained me through comfortless times. I had planned to go to London quite soon. Perhaps

I shall yet though all the ties of . . . of affection are broken now. My old music master dead . . . Caro gone . . . well, there is no one else that I care about there.' He shrugged, straightened his shoulders, grinned. 'And you are quite right, Biddie, I should not have dragged you into Cathedral Yard for my own selfish pleasure. We shall find entertainment enough in the High Street while we search out apples.'

So we returned to the thronging market, and while we paused to watch a juggler tossing knives from hand to hand and to listen to the patter of a man selling some cure-all, I found myself daydreaming, as though all the sights and noises produced some echo of that other, barely remembered, visit with Mama and Papa. The thought that we might have strolled here, seen similar sights – perhaps even on such a day as this one for I seemed to recall sunshine and warmth – contrived to bring them very close. As if I might suddenly turn and catch a glimpse of them sauntering behind me, Papa's hand over Mama's lacy-gloved one as it rested on his dark sleeve, both of them regarding me with warm, loving smiles.

Absorbed in my own thoughts, I gave no heed to the people who pressed about us until the moment when we came to the stall where we were to buy the apples.

Where Kit discovered that all his money had been stolen.

'Hell and damnation!' The words came out in a breath as he searched through his outer pockets. His hands came out empty. 'Our travelling money's gone . . . not even a farthing left,' he gasped. Then, panic-stricken, he delved into the inner secret pocket. All that clung to his fingers after a moment of frantic searching was a tell-tale scrap of loose thread. His face, paling to an ashen white, told me all I needed to know.

The kindly old woman on the stall gave us an apple each out of sympathy. ''Tes a wicked world that spawns such varmints. Pickpockets? Scum!' She removed the clay pipe from between her toothless gums and spat on to the cobbles. 'Nary a chance o' catchin' one o' they, even if 'ee calls out the watch. They'm well 'idden by now. Back in their rat holes.'

Kit and I stared at each other aghast. The loss of the travelling money was unpleasant and inconvenient but we were so close to our final destination that it was scarcely important. The loss of Captain Luscombe's money was a very different matter.

'Christ, how will I tell him?' Kit burst out.

'You're not to blame, sir,' I whispered.

'I knew it! I knew I should never have mixed myself up with any of it . . . And as for you pair, I wish to God I had never clapped eyes on you!' His narrow grey-green eyes were hostile with uncontainable anger and despair. 'But for you I should have been back long since. This need never have happened.'

'What'll we do now?' Biddie quavered.

'We walk! We walk to Dawlish. What else is there to do? And, by God, if I have a squeak of complaint out of either of you, I swear I will strangle you with my own hands.' Then, running his hand over his face, his shoulders sagging, he said in a flat, tired voice, 'I am sorry. I should not lash out at you. It is not your fault. I am the one responsible. I am the one to blame. Come, it is not yet noon. We should still make Dawlish by nightfall.'

It was a wearying journey. In happier circumstances the way would not have seemed so long. We would have talked together and enjoyed the green and gold countryside as we passed through it. But Kit was in no mood for conversation and his stony expression forestalled any attempt on our part. So Biddie and I spoke quietly together, though due to the rapid pace he set, before long she was flagging and complaining of sore feet and aching legs.

My own case was no better. The young ladies at the inn had generously found a pair of boots each for us. The ones I wore were very tight, Biddie's overlarge. Up until now we had done little serious walking and we found the sun-baked, dusty surfaces of the roads unforgiving to feet that were more accustomed to broken down shoes or no shoes at all.

After the umpteenth time Kit had waited for us to catch up then impatiently ordered us to hurry, I could not hold back.

'Sir, we are trying our best,' I cried. 'It's not easy to walk quickly for any distance in badly fitting boots. If you'd be a bit patient and walk slower, we'd manage better.'

'If I am impatient it is because we have some rough heathland to cross before we reach the coast. It will be more difficult to find our way once it goes dark.' Then, looking somewhat contrite, he said gruffly, 'Give me your bundles. I can easily hold them in my free hand.'

He swept them up before I could protest and strode out once more. But after that he stopped whenever there was a brook where we could quench our thirst and rest for a few moments, for the road was not only hard underfoot but increasingly hilly. And presently, with gathering dusk softening and purpling the distances, we left the road altogether and followed a rough track that climbed among scratchy furze bushes, bracken and purple heather.

'We need to be to the west of the town, towards Holcombe,' Kit said. 'I used to come up on this heathland as a boy with a friend when he came to empty his rabbit snares. If I can find the right path it will lead us almost to the door of the school.'

Finding the right path was easier said than done. There were a myriad little tracks meandering through the scrub, and several times, as it grew increasingly dark, Kit cursed roundly as a seemingly established track fizzled to nothing and we had to retrace our steps. But the breeze in our faces brought the salty tang of the sea and presently we could see the glimmer of lights in the town below and, slithering and sliding on a steep descent which was the last refinement of torture on blistered feet, we came to a stile which took us into a high-banked lane. We stumbled over the deep, hard ruts, the only habitation we passed the black huddle of a small cottage with the merest sliver of yellow candlelight leaking round the tight-closed shutters of its single window. Eventually we came out on to a wider road.

'At last,' Kit breathed. 'Almost there.'

The plain stone house lay back from the road behind a low

hedge. The blinds had not yet been drawn nor the shutters closed. Light spilled from the tall windows on either side of the porch where a discreet sign announced that this was Furze House School for Young Ladies, Tuition in All Useful Academic and Genteel Accomplishments. Through one of the front windows a diminutive young maid could be seen clearing the remains of a meal from a long dining table. Through the other I caught no more than a glimpse of movement, a girl in a blue gown, arm outstretched, passing a cup and saucer to someone out of sight.

Kit rang the bell and after a moment the door opened a crack and the maid put one eye to it. ''Oo's that?' she demanded in a loud, suspicious voice. 'What do 'ee want this time o' night?'

'No, no, Flossie, that is not the way,' hissed another voice from within. 'I have told you before. Enquire the caller's name and business in a civil manner then ask them, politely, please, to wait while you see if your mistress is at home.'

The eye disappeared as the maid turned her head to speak over her shoulder. 'But you an' the other missus is both in,' she said indignantly. 'An' 'tes fearful dark. Might be any hobbledehoy out there . . .'

'Flossie, do as I have told you.' The voice was threaded with exasperation.

The eye reappeared in the opening.

'I bin bid to ask your name and business,' she said in a threatening tone.

'Mr Christian Warrener and friends. We are expected.'

'Not by me you en't,' said the maid. 'But I'll tell 'en . . . 'Ere, get your foot out o' the door . . .'

'Miss Swann, is that you?' Kit said loudly, his boot wedged in the doorway. 'This small dragon of a doorkeeper seems disposed not to admit us.'

'Kit? At last! Open the door at once, Flossie! Really, child, I know you mean well, but you will have to learn to listen and obey my instructions if you truly wish to better yourself.'

The door swung wide to reveal the still fiercely frowning

maid and behind her a tall angular woman who strode forward and held out her hand to Kit.

'Dear boy, come in. Come in. You have been expected these last two days. We were beginning to worry that some misfortune had overtaken you. And these are the two girls Caroline wrote to me of. Let me look at you.'

Biddie and I bobbed our curtseys and I looked up warily. Our recent experience with Mrs Turpin had done nothing to relieve my in-built distrust of strangers and Miss Swann's appraisal was not calculated to give instant reassurance of having fallen among friends.

The little maid banged the door closed behind us with a thump that set my stomach lurching nervously.

'Quietly, Flossie, quietly,' said Miss Swann in a stern voice. 'And do not stand there gawking. Finish your duties in the dining chamber then kindly advise Mrs Hawkins that there are three guests for a late supper.'

Everything about Miss Swann was sharp and severe. The mellow candlelight did nothing to soften the long, square-jawed face with its over-large features, the iron-grey hair scraped back from a bony forehead under a cap starched to stiff white points, a high-necked, unadorned grey gown.

She did not launch into fulsome words of welcome. Yet as she scrutinised us in silence I felt unaccountably heartened. Perhaps it was some quality I glimpsed in her eyes, a deep speedwell blue I saw now, the only handsome feature in the plain face. Perhaps it was the very fact that she did not smile, for I knew from bitter experience that easy smiles, like easy words, could mask the blackest of motives.

Whatever it was, the panic that had flared up as the door banged shut fell away and I knew, beyond doubt, that we were not trapped inside but that the closing of that door had done nothing more than shut out the darkness of the night.

I awoke to the greyness of dawn. For a moment I could not think where I was. My heavy eyes opened to a room I did not recognise. An uneven sloping ceiling and white walls set at odd angles, the dark shapes of a washstand, a press, a half-tester overhead draped with some sort of sprigged material. I turned my head to see the same sprigged cotton at the open window. And heard a noise. A strange, continuous background hissing.

I remembered. We were in Dawlish, at Furze House.

Biddie did not move as I slipped out of bed, wincing as my heels with their broken blisters touched the floor. I hobbled to the window, every overstretched muscle in my legs burning painfully, but when I drew back the curtains and raised the sash I forgot the pain as the chill, salt tang of the air filled my lungs and I realised that the sound I heard was that of the sea.

In time I should come to know intimately the view that spread before me and to become familiar with it in all its seasonal changes. But that September morning it was fresh and new. An undiscovered country.

The sun was not yet up, though the clear sky was already light and a few frail filaments of cloud, low on the horizon, were beginning to turn pink. The land still clung to the monochrome greys and inky blues of night, the details of fields and hedgerows and woods becoming increasingly discernible.

I knew we were on the attic floor and now I saw we were at the back of the house overlooking a large walled garden. Directly below were beds of flowers set about with benches and further on a strip of orchard, a pond that lay flat and dull as a pewter plate in the still dawn air, and a substantial vegetable patch. Presumably the cluster of cob-and-thatch outbuildings at the far end of the vegetable patch marked the boundary of the property. There was a wicket gate set into the high wall to one side of the outbuildings, though I could not make out what lay beyond. Perhaps it opened to a lane that led to the cliffs and the shore. I felt a tingle of excitement. I had never in my life been so close to the sea. And there it was, beyond the strip of fields and the dark hump of the wooded cliff edge, a vast length of crinkled crêpe.

Far out, a ship the size of a child's toy inched slowly

westward. Closer in, a few fishing vessels seemed almost motionless, with scarcely a ruffle of breeze to fill their sails. Dawlish boats, I supposed. I knew the town lay somewhere to the east, though I could not see it from this angle, hidden as it was in the fold of the combe. Or maybe the boats were from beyond there . . . Dawlish Warren, Starcross or Exmouth with its harbour tucked safely inside the shifting sands that marked the river's plunge into the sea. A few miles the other way, to the west, Kit had told us, the sandbanks at the mouth of the River Teign were equally treacherous and could move from one tide to the next, laying a silent, deadly snare for the unwary vessel running in to Shaldon or Teignmouth. Just names to me as yet, carelessly tossed to us by Kit as we walked yesterday. How I longed to discover them as real, solid places.

It seemed as I watched that for all the lack of wind the fishing smacks were making their way steadily on some course that was bringing them closer to land. Fetching the catch in, I supposed, or seeking shelter before the change in the weather Miss Swann had spoken of last evening.

'I was concerned that you would not arrive before the storm,' she had said. 'We are in for a lively blow and a deal of rain, I am afraid.'

It was hard to believe on such a clear morning with the wind no more than the touch of a feather on my cheek. On the other hand, if my first impressions of Miss Swann were correct, she was not a woman who would make such a statement out of a mere wish to make polite conversation. Unlike Mrs Greenwood whose tongue never seemed to rest.

I smiled now to think of the contrast between the two ladies. I had fully expected Mrs Greenwood to be another in the same sober mould as Miss Swann. Instead I found myself making my bob to a vision in canary yellow muslin, the faded prettiness of her small, pointed face quite swamped by a high frilled cap tied with a yellow ribbon into an excessive bow under her chin, and a number of brown ringlets, of a rather harsh hue, hanging low over her eyebrows.

'My dear girls,' she cried in a breathy little voice, 'Mrs

Loveridge's most eloquent communication as to your circumstances has touched our hearts, has it not, Tryphena? Of course, we cannot condone the fact – no genteel person possibly could – that by assisting you, and continuing to assist you, our dear Caroline – Mrs Loveridge – has defied the natural laws of affection and obedience that bind a wife to her husband.' Small white hands in lacy mittens fluttered to her bosom as though to still the distress she felt. 'But Miss Swann and I have searched our hearts and find that in all conscience we can do no more than offer you the shelter of our home where so many lonely and abandoned children – albeit by virtue of their parents' absence in the colonies, et cetera, rather than any unfortunate escapade – have been harboured.'

As I listened to the flow of words, I found myself thinking of the ancient singing bird of uncertain temper that my Aunt Hettie had kept in a wicker cage in her bedchamber. It had quite lost its ability to sing but kept up a ceaseless twitter, maddening to anyone who did not have my aunt's fondness for it. That same little bird could also deliver a painful peck to anyone gulled by its innocent appearance into coming too close, scarcely pausing in its chirping to do so. Mrs Greenwood seemed somehow gifted with the same ability.

I tried to tell myself that she meant well and that she did not intend to provoke, but through the repeated phrases of welcome and assurances that not a word that we were runaways should pass her lips, I caught all too clearly the sharp little reminders that she did not entirely approve of our situation or of Mrs Loveridge's involvement in it. Her words reinforced my deepest doubts. The precariousness of our situation, the guilt that other people should be involved, our dependence, seemed to take on a stronger, bleaker emphasis in my mind. By the time Miss Swann ushered her away I had twisted my fingers together so hard it was painful to unknot them.

'The girls will be getting into mischief if you leave them too long, my dear,' Miss Swann said, firmly guiding her to the door. 'And remember what we had decided to tell them. After all, it is no more than the truth. The newcomers are orphans, with a benefactor who wishes them to be educated.' She closed the door quietly and turned back to us. 'Pray be seated and help yourselves to whatever you wish. There is only a little of Mrs Hawkins's rabbit pie left – the girls are very fond of it – but there is plenty of cold mutton and a good dish of beetroots.'

'Miss . . . begging your pardon, miss.' I could not move. Despite hunger, despite the wash of guilt Mrs Greenwood's words had aroused, I was riveted by the implications of what Miss Swann had just said. 'Are we really to be educated?'

'Indeed,' Miss Swann confirmed. 'We always have a few girls boarding with us. You will be safe here. As Mrs Loveridge knows, there is no reason for anyone to comment upon the arrival of two new pupils.'

'But what'll we tell folk . . . these other girls? They're bound to ask.'

'I see no reason to hide the fact that you worked in a cotton mill, from which labour you had the good fortune to be rescued by an anonymous benefactor. That is all they need to know and has the virtue, as I have said, of being the truth. You may draw a veil of discretion over the rest.' She regarded me steadily. 'There is something else that troubles you?' she asked, as though she could look straight into my thoughts and see the muddle of suspicion, disbelief and distrust that churned there.

'What about our keep, miss?' It was all I could bring out. How could I say anything of my fear of being betrayed yet again? How could I demand a promise that we were truly safe when I knew a promise to be something as ephemeral as a mayfly that lives but a day before falling to corruption? 'Will you find us work?'

'Mrs Loveridge will pay for your upkeep as and when she is able. She tells me her husband is generous to a fault.'

Biddie gave a disbelieving snort. 'Generous? Him?'

'*He's* always lived fatly. And his spoilt daughter,' I added bitterly. 'Pity he couldn't have spared some of his riches for those who help make them.'

Miss Swann's calm gaze did not falter. 'Mrs Loveridge hopes she may in time be able to wield some influence upon her husband in improving conditions for the apprentices. In the meantime she feels that by helping you she is in some small way making reparation for your treatment at Crossbank. She particularly wished you to know that her reward will lie in knowing that you will take every advantage of your time here. As for work, do not think for a moment that we tolerate idle hands in this establishment.' Was there a suspicion of understanding in the speedwell blue eyes as she added, in that same stern voice, 'All you need to do for the moment is accept that you are among friends. Now, eat your supper and off to bed with you. There will be time enough for questions tomorrow.'

Among friends. Could that be true, at last? I leaned from the window, breathing deeply of the salt breeze. Its clean sharpness seemed to fire my blood with energy and brought a lift of the spirits that was almost dizzying in its intensity. On such a morning anything seemed possible.

Even happiness.

I pulled the window down and went back to bed to snatch a little more rest before we should be called to breakfast.

Miss Swann was right about the weather. By eight o'clock, when Biddie and I nervously presented ourselves in the dining chamber, clouds were already beginning to thicken and stream across the sky, driven by a freshening wind.

'I hope Kit does not dawdle too long in town,' Miss Swann said, 'or he will be in for a soaking. Now take your seats if you please. It is Bertha's turn this morning to say grace.'

Grace before meals was something new to Biddie and only a distant memory to me. At Crossbank the Hatchers had been concerned solely with getting us through our scanty meals as quickly as possible. Dutifully we copied the others by closing our eyes while the youngest of the three fair-haired, stolid-faced sisters opposite chanted in one long breath, 'For-what-we-are-about-to-receive-may-the-Lord-make-us-truly-thankful-Amen,' and my thoughts darted away to Kit. I breathed a silent prayer that all would go well for him, for I guessed he had already gone in search of Captain Luscombe.

Last evening Kit had been very quiet over supper, responding politely only when Miss Swann addressed him directly, his face pale and drawn. He excused himself the minute it was over, pleading fatigue, but it was more than that, as I well knew. I could not help feeling for his distress. Not only had he to confess the loss of the money to Captain Luscombe, but somehow he had to retrieve the precious Cremona which had been taken as surety for his good behaviour. From what he had told me of Captain Luscombe, I did not hold out much hope that he would find a sympathetic hearing on either count.

As soon as grace was said, Flossie scuttled round the table thumping down before us bowls of steaming porridge. We were to help ourselves from the jug of yellow cream and bowl of honey that were politely passed from hand to hand as accompaniments. As though this bounty were not enough to start the day, the table also bore a large platter of fried eggs and mushrooms kept hot on a stand set over a tiny lamp, a slab of butter, a crusty loaf cut into crumbly wedges, a bowl of pears and apples and several small dishes containing jam of various sorts. Biddie was round-eyed, as I daresay I was myself. The food at The Plough had seemed wonderful after the near-starvation diet of Crossbank, but in comparison to what lay before us it had been rough, plain fare indeed. Even the Loveridges could scarcely breakfast better than this! For Biddie's sake I was glad. At least the good food would help her to accept the prospect of having to learn to read and write.

'What do I want wi' schoolin?' she had wailed as we wearily prepared for bed last evening. 'I'm no scholar. I 'aven't the head for book-learnin'.'

'You don't know until you've tried properly,' I said, gingerly plunging my dirty, bloodstained feet into the bowl of warm water pungent with some herbal mixture Miss Swann had said would be soothing. 'Ow, it stings . . . no, it's going off. Mmm, it feels really nice . . .'

'Never mind your feet!' Biddie said mutinously. 'Why do I 'ave to try?'

'Because it's a way of getting on.'

'Plenty o' folk manage wi'out.'

'Yes, folks that slave their lives away in mills like Crossbank and nasty places like it.'

'Bein' able to read and write don't mean you'd be any better off. Or any 'appier. Look at that Miss Groom, miserable an' sour as a vinegar-fart.'

I turned on her fiercely. 'So what else do we do if we don't stop here and make the best of it?'

She shrugged helplessly and my irritation died as quickly as it had arisen. My heart went out to her. My friend Biddie. My only good friend through the long years at Crossbank, standing there in her shift, exhaustion from the journey written in the droop of her body, the legacy of years of undernourishment revealed in her skinny limbs, the grey-white pallor of her skin. How could I be cross with her? I had no right to take for granted her appreciation of something that seemed so important to me. The only life she had ever known before Crossbank was the stark struggle to exist in a foetid slum until her widowed mother died and she was put into the Clerkenwell workhouse. How could she have any comprehension that a decent sort of life existed in which there might be a place for us? She was frightened, bewildered, apprehensive. About everything, not just the prospect of schooling. I was in little different case myself, save that I burned to escape the grievous state we had been reduced to and understood the need to haul ourselves out of poverty and dependency by any means open to us. So much had happened in so short a time it was hard to take in. But we still had each other. Whatever was to come, the bonds of friendship must hold firm, to hearten and support us.

'Don't fret about it,' I said gently. 'I'll help you all I can.

All that matters is that we're safe for now and we've got a good bed to sleep in.' I was suddenly overtaken by giggles. 'But watch what you say from now on, Bridget Riley. Call anybody in this house a vinegar-fart and you'll have 'em all fainting dead away from shock!'

'Bleedin' clever-arse,' said Biddie, starting to grin.

'Piss-drawers,' I said sweetly.

We eventually tumbled into bed, still capping each other's earthy phrases and weak with the laughter that so often comes to bring release from cold and difficult reality.

At breakfast I found that we were not the only ones to whom coarse and colourful epithets were the common currency of everyday life.

While Flossie removed the empty porridge dishes, Mrs Greenwood poured fragrant dark coffee into two fine china cups for herself and Miss Swann, explaining that new milk or fresh-drawn spring water was the most wholesome beverage for young girls and we were to drink as much of each as we wished.

'Such a regimen when I was young contributed to the fineness of my complexion.' She patted her powdery cheek like a girl of eighteen with a skin of silk. But daylight was less kind to her than candlelight. It revealed the net of fine wrinkles round her eyes, the soft sag of the crumpled flesh below the pointed chin. I had thought that she was much younger than Miss Swann, but now I saw that they were of a similar age. Neither would see fifty again and in the sharp morning light Miss Swann's sober attire seemed far more becoming than Mrs Greenwood's youthful muslin. The grey gown bestowed dignity on her angular figure, the plain cap and severely drawn-back hair gave a certain stern distinction to her strong features whereas Mrs Greenwood's frilly pink gown and excess of bows overwhelmed her prettiness, giving her the look of an overblown rose ready to lose its petals to the next gust of wind. 'I begged dear Kit to take refreshment before he left.' She went on to enlighten me as to his excuse for leaving before breakfast. 'He was intent on making off early, eager to see for himself how his poor friend Billy fared. I begged him at least to partake of a little bread and butter, but he was impatient to be gone.'

'Billy Rossiter? He'm still crippled, but mending,' put in Flossie helpfully, setting down a large rack of toast. 'I'd've told 'en that if he'd have asked. 'Eard it from Mrs King when 'er fetched back the bagwash yesterday. Now, will 'ee be wantin' more of anything? Seems to me you've plenty to go at 'ere – proper belly-buster, I'd say, if you gets through that lot.'

'Flossie!' Miss Swann managed, before swiftly putting her napkin to her lips, seemingly attacked by a sudden choking fit which took a few moments to control. Her voice still sounded a little uncertain when she was able to speak again and she held the napkin ready to stifle another attack. 'I beg you to resist the temptation to interrupt private conversations.'

'But, miss, I knowed about Billy—'

'I daresay, but it is not your place to say so when you are waiting at table. A good servant is discreet, goes about her duties quietly and closes her ears to anything but instructions given directly to her.'

'But I can't 'elp hearin' what 'ee all says, miss,' Flossie protested. 'Stands to reason when I'm standin' next to 'ee.'

'Then you will have to learn to forget what you hear as soon as you hear it. As to your other . . . er . . . comment.' The napkin was employed again. 'You must refrain from making any remark on the quantity or quality of the meal. It is most impolite. Now you may return to the kitchen until I ring for you.'

Flossie went off, looking crestfallen. Biddie kicked my foot under the table and I dared not look at her in case I dissolved into giggles. Miss Swann dabbed at her eyes and said faintly, 'That child – oh, dear, such an eloquent turn of phrase.'

Mrs Greenwood, who had not fainted away as I had predicted but was clearly and profoundly unamused, said with a little shudder: 'I do truly believe you to have made a misjudgement in employing Flossie Parker, Tryphena. I should have expected by now to have seen some slight evidence of improvement.'

'Give her time, Harriet. She has been here scarcely a week.'

'I fear I cannot find it in me to believe she will alter a great deal given a week, a month or even a year. She is a Parker! What good ever came out of that shiftless brood? I cannot think, dear, what possessed you to take her on.'

'I admired her spirit,' Miss Swann said simply.

Mrs Greenwood sighed. 'Your heart is too tender. You allowed sentiment to override reason. A girl who has spent all of her thirteen years in a hovel on the banks of the Teign and has been subject to the most deleterious influences is scarcely suitable material to introduce to a genteel household.' Was it deliberate that her darting gaze rested momentarily on Biddie and me? That I felt the needle-prick of her distaste and saw that she ranked us no higher and no more worthy to be here than the maidservant? 'Why, the womenfolk in that family are slatterns every one, and scarcely a month goes past, it seems to me, without we hear of one or other of her brothers up before the magistrate or sentenced to a spell in the house of correction.'

'It takes a brave heart to transcend such a background,' said Miss Swann.

'There were any number of decent Dawlish girls from respectable homes with God-fearing parents who would have jumped at the chance of taking up employment at Furze House.'

'But how much more worthy of a helping hand is a girl who has remained decent when her home is not at all respectable and her father has no regard whatsoever for the Almighty.'

Mrs Greenwood helped herself to a piece of toast and spread butter upon it somewhat impatiently. 'To have come harassing us as she did! Sitting on the doorstep the minute she heard our dear Rose was to marry and move to Dorset. And refusing to budge until you agreed to take her on. I believe she would have been there yet had you not submitted to her importuning. I would have sent her packing, I would indeed.'

'She deserves encouragement,' Miss Swann said firmly. 'I think she will do well once she has settled.' Then she moved swiftly to the timetable for today's lessons. If she had hoped to have found a more amenable topic she was soon disillusioned. Mrs Greenwood, still piqued, immediately disagreed that geography and singing lessons should occupy the morning.

'With the weather closing in we may well need to light candles by midday,' she said sharply. 'The still life I have prepared for sketching most certainly needs benefit of natural light or the effect will be lost. The girls have learned the words to the new ballad so they would be well able to sing were it pitch dark. And you may easily expound upon the globes by candlelight, Tryphena. I feel that I must in this instance prevail upon you to see the good sense of allowing the sketching class to take precedence.'

Miss Swann hesitated, as though prepared to argue. Then she nodded. 'Of course, my dear. You are quite right. I had not given the matter enough thought.' And seemed not a trifle put out that her diversionary tactics had not worked. On the contrary, she cast an affectionate and tolerant glance at Mrs Greenwood whose air of triumph, and subsequent good humour prevailed throughout the rest of the meal. Miss Swann, I thought, had the measure of her less subtle friend, allowing her victory in a minor skirmish in order to distract her from a defeat of greater significance. I wondered if by such means Miss Swann had persuaded Mrs Greenwood to submit to Mrs Loveridge's request to house a pair of runaways, and tucked away the comforting thought that if that were so we had the kindlier and cleverer of the two ladies on our side.

Perhaps such arguments were quite common. Certainly the three fair-haired girls sitting opposite seemed indifferent to the gentle wrangling of the ladies and after a few curious glances at Biddie and me, returned to whispering among themselves and chewing their way stolidly through the meal. They were the MacBride sisters of ten, twelve and fourteen, Miss Swann had said when we were introduced, who had been at Furze House for two years and whose parents were even now on the high seas on their way back from the East Indies, their papa having been ordered home on account of his health.

'Pissed in the same pot, them three,' Biddie giggled when breakfast was finished. We had hung back uncertainly as the others went out into the hall where a babble of voices announced the arrival of the day girls. 'Like as peas in a pod.'

'But none too bright, I think,' I whispered back. 'That's a blessing. They'll believe anything they're told about us. Besides they're too full of their own plans to have room in their heads for anything else.'

'By Christmas they reckon they'll be back in Scotland wi' their ma and pa.' She gave an envious sigh. 'The big one, Catriona, says they'll be livin' in a grand big 'ouse wi' twenty servants and new gowns for every day o' the week.' She picked at a stain on her skirt. Despite shaking and sponging them this morning, the dresses we had travelled in – our only ones – looked decidedly crumpled compared to the fresh-laundered muslin gowns the sisters were wearing. 'D'you suppose we'll be gettin' anything new?' she added hopefully.

We did, though perhaps not what she had in mind. Miss Swann returned to the dining chamber almost immediately and gave us each an enveloping apron. 'We provide these for all our pupils to protect their clothes while they work,' she said. 'And to prevent the somewhat foolish competition between the better-off mamas in the matter of dress. Whether a girl arrives clad in fancy silk or everyday cotton, it makes no odds if all is concealed under breadths of sturdy unbleached linen.'

When we had fastened on the aprons, which enveloped us back and front in the manner of a sleeveless wrapper, Miss Swann made us hold out our hands to see they were clean, tweaked one of Biddie's curls into place and nodded approvingly. 'You look well enough for now. Do not look so nervous. You will soon settle in. Follow me.'

The schoolroom was on the first floor, a long room stretching from front to back of the house. It seemed that a hundred pairs of eyes turned to inspect us when we went in, a hundred voices stilled their chatter, though I later counted only twenty-two girls. Mrs Greenwood clapped her hands to draw their attention back to the business of setting up of drawing boards and sketching blocks around a small table upon which a selection of fruit, a stuffed cock pheasant and sprigs of autumnal foliage had been arranged.

The hum of voices broke out once more as we followed Miss Swann to the far corner of the room. We seated ourselves at one of the tables which had been pushed back against the wall out of the way of the would-be artists.

'We shall stay quietly here during the drawing lesson,' Miss Swann said. 'And we shall talk a little and read a little and be thoroughly comfortable together.'

I looked at the books spread in an orderly row before us. At one end a large, well-thumbed A-B-C, at the other a small pristine volume proclaiming itself to be the *Poems of William Cowper*.

Miss Swann produced a pair of eyeglasses and fixed them on her nose. 'I know nothing yet of your ability, your aptitude or the extent of any education you have had. When I do, I shall know how best to help you.'

I had already reached for the books in my greediness to investigate them, momentarily forgetting that I should wait to be asked. I brought myself up short with the poetry book in my hands and already open, glancing shamefaced and apologetic at Miss Swann, fully expecting a reprimand. But Miss Swann's speedwell blue eyes held only encouragement.

'You read, Miranda? Good. Would you care to speak a few lines to us?'

'Yes, Miss Swann,' I said softly. Then cleared my throat and eagerly began.

By midday the wind was flinging gouts of rain against the windows. When the day girls left for home at half-past two o'clock it was a downpour. They scuttled off down the long hill into the town huddled together under bobbing black umbrellas that threatened any moment to fly inside out.

Kit still had not returned.

I felt guilty that during the whole busy school day I had not given him a thought. There had been so much to absorb, so much to occupy my mind: from trying to remember the names of the girls – mostly the daughters of local farmers or of tradesmen in the town – to learning the principal trade routes of the world which Miss Swann pointed out on the large globe on its ornamental stand.

Now that I did remember Kit, the memory of his pale, drawn face seemed to lodge accusingly in my mind, giving me troublesome, unwanted reminders of his absence through the continuing orderly routine of the Furze House day. I tried in vain to brush away the thought of him. I could do nothing to help him. His involvement with the likes of Captain Luscombe was of his own choosing and no concern of mine. But the uneasy knowledge haunted me that, travelling alone, he would have had a swifter, more comfortable journey back to Devon and the fateful delay in Exeter might never have occurred.

I had thought the milk and bread and butter that had been brought to the schoolroom at noon must see us through until suppertime, but promptly at a quarter to three we were sitting down to dinner, yet another substantial meal, this time of parsnip soup, crimped skate, buttered green beans, apple tart and the thick yellow clotted cream that was a taste straight out of childhood.

'Usually after dinner we take exercise out of doors,' Miss Swann explained, 'but as that is out of the question today we shall occupy ourselves in the house. Catriona, dear, you may help your sisters to turn out the contents of the press in your room. The change in the weather is a timely reminder that you should fetch out your warmer clothes to see what you have outgrown and what might be refurbished for the coming season.'

'There is the silver to be cleaned, Tryphena,' Mrs Greenwood put in quickly. 'It is a task Bridget and Miranda might be usefully instructed in. I will be happy to supervise them, for I know you will be wishing to attend to the weekly accounts.'

If Mrs Greenwood had hoped that we would be be discomfited by being relegated to this household task she was wrong. Set against the drudgery of cleaning and oiling our drawing frames, with kicks and blows to speed us on, the polishing of cutlery and candlesticks while sitting on comfortable chairs at the well-shrouded dining table was as nothing. Even though she found fault with every piece and made us go over them again and again until some speck of tarnish, visible only to herself in the deepest recess of the ornamentation, was removed, we were not at all distressed. Indeed, Biddie threw herself into the work with extra vigour. This was something she could understand and excel at. Much more satisfying than copying letters on to a slate. She beamed when Mrs Greenwood grudgingly admitted that we had done well which, I suppose, was more thanks than we had ever received at Crossbank.

The storm worsened as the afternoon went on and the buffeting of the wind grew to an alarming intensity. Flossie drew the parlour blinds which rattled in the draughts. Even the heavy green brocade curtains which were pulled across the blinds continued to sway and shudder until Miss Swann shrouded herself in a vast black cape and hood and went to help Flossie close and fasten the outside shutters. She returned, breathless, to the now-snug candlelit parlour to dry the hem of her skirt before the snapping fire where Biddie and I sat unpicking the hems of sheets that were to be turned sides to middle, the others employing themselves with the household mending.

The clanging of the bell made us all start. Miss Swann hurried into the hall, for once overlooking Flossie's cry of, 'Watch where 'ee puts your muddy boots, sir! I sweated cobs over they floorboards this mornin'.'

'Dear boy, you are drenched,' boomed Miss Swann. 'Upstairs

to your room at once and change into dry clothes or you will catch your death!'

I heard with relief the rumble of Kit's deep tones. When he eventually came down to the parlour the only sign that he had been out in the rain was the damp hair drying into dark curls about his ears and collar and the colour whipped into his face. He looked a deal more relaxed than he had last evening.

'I had hardly left Teignmouth before my hat blew away,' he said cheerfully. 'It is probably half way to Haldon Moor by now.'

'Teignmouth?' said Mrs Greenwood. 'But I thought you were only going into Dawlish to visit your friend.'

'My deepest apologies for not returning for dinner, as I'd hoped to do,' he said, taking her hand and bowing low over it. 'But Billy asked me to go on an errand for him and I could scarcely refuse. Even though I would rather have been back here in the company of so many charming ladies.'

Mrs Greenwood gave a pleased, girlish laugh as he placed a kiss on her hand. 'You may have learned elegant manners in Vienna,' she said in mock-scolding tones, 'but I insist you draw up a chair by me and give me the fullest explanation of your activities before I decide if I shall forgive you or not.'

He did as he was bidden, launching into a tale of having to take some small woodcarvings to Billy's brother in order that he might try to sell them for him when next he went to Newton Abbot market. Perhaps it was true so far as it went. His concern for his friend was certainly genuine. 'Billy is reduced to whittling figures from driftwood in order to make a copper or two.' Kit shook his head, his face sombre. 'He talks all the time of returning to sea, but I think it will be a long time before he is fit. The gash was a severe one and I fear it has severed more than mere flesh. It happened when they were dropping anchor in a northerly blow off Alderney and a loose coil of rope whipped round his leg. But for the rest of the crew he might well have lost his foot or been dragged overboard and drowned. As it was they managed to free him, but he was sadly injured and even now can barely hobble. But with a wife and child to support – and there will be another baby within the month – he must work or they will all starve.'

'I did hear – I believe it was one of the girls told me – that Captain Luscombe had got up a subscription to help the family. It was upon one of his boats the accident occurred, was it not?'

The name dropped into the room like a stone. At least so it appeared to me. Kit's expression did not betray him, but his glance caught and held mine for a fraction of a second before his lashes dropped to mask his narrow green-grey eyes and he said shortly, 'That was all spent long ago. There will be no more from that quarter.'

'Our hens are laying well at present,' Miss Swann said. 'You must take Billy a dozen when you next visit, and a basket of apples, and I will see what else we can spare.'

'Thank you. He will be very grateful. As he has been for the other comforts you have sent down over the last weeks.'

'Oh, that was nothing. Mere bits and bobs we happened to have by when Mrs King, our washerwoman, called. She is married to a cousin of Billy's wife and kept us up with his progress. Such a misfortune.' Miss Swann sighed. 'I have always liked Billy. An imp of mischief at times as a boy, I know, but always so cheerful and polite one could forgive him anything. I can see him now, struggling up the hill to deliver our fish and the basket nearly as big as he was. But it never seemed to daunt him.'

Mrs Greenwood, having spied Biddie digging too deeply at the stitches with the point of the scissors, cried sharply, 'Not like that, you will drive a hole through the sheet! Take more care!' When the conversation resumed Miss Swann wished to learn more about Mrs Loveridge's new house and garden and Miss Swann demanded to know if Caroline had been wearing one of the white muslin spencers which she had heard were all the fashion among ladies in society.

I had to wait until we were called for eight o'clock supper

before I managed to speak to Kit privately. I dawdled behind the others to whisper urgently, 'Your violin?'

'I am to work for the rogue. For nothing,' he hissed back. 'When he reckons I have paid off my debts he will return it to me. Hah! The truth is, he will use me to his advantage for as long as he wishes. And enjoy watching me jump each time he pulls the strings. I could read that in his face once he had given over his blustering.'

'What kind of work?' I whispered.

He shrugged. 'Whatever it is, I shall be made to pay back my debt with interest. Captain Luscombe is a man well practised in the fine art of bending men to his will and turning every situation to his own profit.'

After supper we were allowed to enjoy some recreation of our own choosing before we went to bed. The two younger MacBride girls played spillikins with Biddie. Miss Swann and Mrs Greenwood brought out their embroidery. Catriona MacBride began sorting shells to fashion into a picture and I fetched down the book Violet had given me.

'Will you not give us a tune, Kit dear?' Mrs Greenwood asked. 'We have only had the privilege of hearing you play your violin the once, when you first arrived. Quite, quite delightful. Perhaps that little scherzo . . . what was it?'

'The Mozart,' Catriona burst in, then flushed and stammered, 'I . . . I remember it because it was so pretty.'

'How clever of you,' Kit said easily.

'I . . . I am musical myself. I . . . that is, we all three have lessons upon the forte-piano.'

'Catriona is my best pupil,' Mrs Greenwood said proudly. 'I am sure she would be delighted to provide an accompaniment.'

'I regret I must refuse,' Kit said, his tone innocently rueful. 'I am rather tired – and somewhat out of practice. The violin requires my fullest concentration. However, I will fetch down my workaday flute, if you like, Miss MacBride, and we will try a duet or two.'

Kit smiled at her. He should smile more often, I thought

idly, glancing up from my book. In repose, his thin face and narrow eyes gave him an air of watchful reserve. He looked withdrawn, unapproachable. Perhaps it was merely that his mind was on his music, though I seemed to sense there was a dark edge to his introspection, something deep and secretive and devious. He had, after all, a history of lying and deception in order to gain his own ends, however justified. Even now the fluent excuse – the lie – slid from his tongue with the ease of long practice. Yet when he smiled, how it changed him. All that darkness lifted. His eyes glinted with good humour. The hard planes and angles of his face subtly shifted themselves to a far more agreeable alignment. He might even be thought handsome . . .

Catriona MacBride certainly thought so. If Biddie had been closer I would have nudged her to share the joke. Catriona leaned towards him, shells forgotten, positively mesmerised by that flash of white teeth. I felt embarrassed for her. How very silly she looked, blinking at him with her pale lashes, her prominent blue eyes awash with a particularly fatuous expression of admiration. And he no better for encouraging her with the kind of teasing repartee that I daresay was perfectly acceptable in the sophisticated drawing rooms of Vienna but only succeeded in making gauche Catriona blush and stammer the more. I did not think I cared much for Viennese manners – or for him when he so carelessly played upon the sensibilities of such a simple creature.

I went back to my book finding myself more irritated than amused. When they began their duets the music, however harmonious, only served to interrupt my enjoyment of Rose de Blaguère's adventures. I wished, tetchily, that they had gone off to attend to their music-making in another room. Each time I looked up, there was Catriona suddenly looking assured now she was seated at the forte-piano and perfectly able to counter Kit's suggestions as to what they should play with ideas of her own. And there was Kit, laughing and flattering and addressing her as 'Miss MacBride', as though she were not just a silly schoolgirl but a grown-up young lady . . .

It was the first of many times in the following days when I was to become irritated with Catriona MacBride. Later, much later, I was sorry that I was not kinder to her. The poor girl could not help her innocent feelings for Kit and puppy love can be as painfully consuming at the time as the more adult emotion. But I did not know, any more than she did, the manner in which her innocent passion would be so abruptly cut short. After the news was brought to us she was inconsolable and drooped about the house like a wilted daisy. But by then I was too racked with despair myself to have feelings to spare for her. For I could have – should have – done more to stop Kit going out on that October afternoon.

Would he have listened? Would he have understood? Would my warning at least have made him more cautious?

Perhaps. Perhaps not.

But I was too scared of ridicule to try. Instead, I played the coward's part and let him go blindly to meet his fate.

It is something I will regret until my dying day.

To my surprise Captain Luscombe relented and returned the violin to Kit within the week.

I was out in the linhay – the barn – when he came to tell me the news. I had been given the task of calling up the chickens and shutting them in for the night when I looked up, startled, to see Kit standing in the doorway.

Feeding the hens was a chore I had taken to right away and begged to be allowed to do each day. There was something very comfortable and droll about the speckly creatures. I loved their plump, motherly shapes and their contented clucking and crooning as they rushed from all directions to peck up the corn I scattered to lure them inside.

'Are you all in, my pretties?' I enquired, in the silly way one does. 'All safe and sound indoors before hungry Master Reynard comes out of his den? I wonder how many eggs you have for me tonight . . .'

'I hope you do not expect an answer,' said an amused voice. 'I believe chickens do not have the mastery of English.'

'Oh! Sir . . . creeping up like that! You made me jump.'

He was leaning over the half-door, grinning. I felt very foolish.

'My apologies. I merely wished to tell you the good news. Look.' He hoisted a violin case into view. 'My powers of persuasion must be better than I realised. The old rogue has relented.'

'Then perhaps he's not so hard-hearted as you like to make out,' I said, huffy from embarrassment at being caught in conversation with hens.

'More like he is rendered generous by a successful run last night,' he said. 'Fifty tubs of brandy brought in by way of Holcombe Cove. Not to mention a quantity of other packages. Tobacco and silk stockings, it was whispered.' He grimaced. 'Those cliffs are devilish steep, I can tell you – and become steeper as the night goes on and you must climb them again and again.'

'So that's where you were.' I threw the last handful of corn to the earth floor and dusted my hands. I was disinclined to be congenial. 'I hope the ladies don't find you out. Such a cock-and-bull tale you told before you left yesterday! What was it? Another errand to Teignmouth for Billy? And such a coincidence that Billy's brother had heard of someone wanting to engage a musician . . .'

'And the hour being late when I set off, I said I would lodge with Billy's brother overnight and seek out this prospective employer.' His eyes glinted with excitement. 'I did call upon Sam Rossiter. That is the truth. But I did not stay and I confess that all the sleep I had was but an hour or two under a hedge when the cargo was safely borne off to safe hiding. Neverthless, I was perfectly honest in stating that I was to seek more respectable employment today. In which quest I was successful.'

I walked slowly to the door, curiosity overcoming my crossness. 'You have work?'

'For Captain Luscombe himself. Or rather his wife.' His excitement erupted in a shout of laughter. 'A more disagreeable, sour and proud woman I never met, yet I could kiss the ground she walks upon. She engaged me to play at a grand function she is planning – and so gave me the means to twist Captain Luscombe's arm in the matter of returning my violin. For how could I be expected to dazzle the company with my playing and so add to Mrs Luscombe's standing if I were not allowed to practise? After all, he had ordered me to audition for the lady, thinking to put himself in her good favour.' Again a roar of laughter. 'If I had not seen it with my own eyes I should never have believed the tattle I had heard that the good Captain, so hard and powerful and devious in his business affairs, legal or illicit, is sadly henpecked in his own home.'

In a few swift words he painted a picture of Captain Luscombe's household. A wife with a distant connection to the Duke of Somerset who in middle age – and barely surviving in genteel poverty, it was said – had seized the chance to marry a younger man anxious to raise his status in society well above his lowly origins, and once the ring was on her finger, never allowed him to forget that she had married beneath her.

'Oh, she knows how to spend his money, even if she despises the means of making it. You should see the new house they have had built outside Teignmouth! It has a veritable hill of its own to stand upon – and offers not a glimpse of the Luscombe boatyard lest madam's eyes be tainted by the sight of honest men about their labour. It is stuffed with fine furniture and carpets, and deuced formal and uncomfortable it looks to my way of thinking. Even the servants tiptoe about as though they fear to disturb the very air. Or to catch her martinet's eye. As for the Captain, it was all, "Yes, my love. No, my love" – docile as a lamb in her presence and snarling imprecations and threats once we were alone again.'

I looked him in the eye. 'And do you really intend to play at this . . . this function?'

He grinned. 'Have I not said so, Miranda?'

'You say many things, sir, but you don't give me cause to believe all of them. You have your precious violin back. I'd not be surprised if you made off, safe out of Captain Luscombe's way.' I sounded more grudging than I'd intended.

He did not take offence but merely said, in a teasing voice, 'Dear me, Miranda, you do not mean to set yourself up as my conscience, do you? I fear you will have a thankless task if you do.'

'I don't care a jot about your conscience, sir,' I said tartly. 'But I shouldn't want . . .' I broke off. It was hard to put into words the many conflicting fears that lived with me every day. Fears that I scarcely dare voice, even to someone who would understand more than most.

'Want what?' His glance sharpened. He leaned across the door and caught my arm as I stepped back into the dimness of the barn. 'What is the matter? What is troubling you?'

His grip was like iron. I tried to prise his fingers away without success. 'Get off me,' I muttered, wriggling helplessly.

'The quicker you speak up,' he said with mock-sternness, 'the quicker I shall release you.'

'Why should I tell you?' My indrawn breath was a gulp. I felt my blood suddenly on fire as a bubbling rush of anger and indignation overtook the quivering, docile instinct that had made me shrink back from revealing what I was thinking. His imprisoning grip was too fierce a reminder of all that I had left behind in Derbyshire. It might be a teasing game to him, but to me it had too many unspeakable overtones. I would not submit! Not today. Not ever! 'Just because you're bigger and stronger, you think you can bully me! Well, I won't let you! I'm not a naughty child and you're not my master!'

It was just like that afternoon at Crossbank when, heedless of the consequences, I had stood up and raged against Ida Loveridge and all she represented. If anything my feelings now were even more intense, as though the days of freedom had already begun to affect the tight control I had kept for so long over deep resentment and pain.

'I'm a person!' I cried. 'With feelings! Not some . . . some creature you can treat as you please. Get your hands off me, and get about your business.'

I battered wildly at his arm with my free fist and tried to tug my own free. My feet scrabbled for purchase, my skirts flapping as I threw my whole weight against his grip. My boot caught a feathery body. At once there was chaos in the linhay as the hens took panic.

Desperation to escape this dancing, slipping, shouting monster rippled through the flock. Hens flew everywhere, squawking and flapping in their attempts to find the farthest, highest corners to hide.

'Damn you, Kit Warrener,' I yelled. 'Now look what you've done! I was nice an' peaceful till you came!' My careful attention to the remembered speech of childhood lapsed, in my anger, to a more recent vernacular. 'Bugger off, why don't you!'

But still he held me, keeping me at arm's length, laughing at first, then the laughter fading to puzzlement at the strength of my fury, and finally to shock and concern. I took little heed. I was past caring. The volcano of rage roared through me. A searing lava flow that could not be contained. Nor did I wish to hold it back. The powerful sense of violence and ferocity in it was strengthening. I lashed out with my foot. It slammed against the half-door that separated us.

'I wish it was your head or your balls,' I screeched. 'An' if it were I should laugh fit to bust.' My hair tumbled out of its tight-drawn knot in a cascade of hairpins. Uncaring I trampled the pins into the detritus underfoot. 'You're nowt but a coward,' I taunted. 'Only yeller bellies fights with lasses . . . and hides behind doors. What's the matter? Too skeered to step right in here with me? Skeered to let go of me arm lest I gets too close and claws your eyes out . . . ?'

I raged on. Mindless with fury, lunging now for the pitchfork that stood propped against the wall. Spitting with rage because it was tantalisingly out of reach . . .

'Miranda.'

His voice was so quiet as to be almost lost in the heat of my own ravings.

'Miranda,' he said again. Still quiet, but with a timbre of compassion so strange to my ears that my own voice faltered.

He spoke my name again. I choked on my words, though the raucous sound of my curses still seemed to ricochet from wall to wall after I had fallen silent. Or perhaps I still heard it only in my head like the dying echoes of a suddenly muffled clarion. We were very still for a heartbeat, two, no more. Then, his eyes never leaving my face, his grip eased on my arm.

I believe now that had he released me roughly or answered me back in kind, my anger would have erupted again, and God knows what the outcome would have been. I scarcely dare think of it, because for those few moments I had been out of my head, without principle or conscience. I could have gone for his eyes with my nails, as I'd threatened, or seized the pitchfork and run it through him, as I had once seen Mr Hatcher despatch a cornered rat. Perhaps I did not even truly see him, but thought Mr Hatcher himself stood there. Or Mr Loveridge. Those two loathsome people whom I hated most in all the world.

But Kit did not shout or threaten. Instead, as I stood there, he eased his fingers gently down my sleeve until his hand reached mine. There he gathered my still-rough, broken-nailed paw with infinite tenderness into his palm.

It was my undoing.

I had learned to cope with hard words and cruelty. Against tenderness I had no defences.

The trembling began somewhere near my toes. Blind rage crumpled to a pathetic shred of deflated vainglory that could do nothing more to hide the cowering emotions that now lay exposed. The trembling reached my legs, my arms, my heart . . . as all the strength that had fired my muscles evaporated to a sickly weakness.

My hand slipped from Kit's grasp as my knees gave way. I dropped like a stone to the cold earth among the chicken droppings and corn husks and buried my head in my hands. I began to cry.

No dainty, ladylike weeping, this. Far from it. These were the ugly, racking, retching sobs fetched up from a nightmare abyss of pain and hate. I heard nothing, saw nothing, thought nothing. Felt nothing but the tearing rawness in my throat and chest and the hot tears spilling through my fingers.

I do not know how long it was before I became aware that Kit was holding me. When I did, I could not feel shame or embarrassment or even concern that he was kneeling in the dirt to the detriment of his clothes. I wanted, instead, to lose myself in the pleasure of being comforted.

I leaned against him, as I had once as a small girl leaned against Meg or Mama, knowing they would soothe away whatever childish distress I had brought to them and put my little world to rights. It seemed perfectly natural that he should rock me in his arms and mop at my tears with a grubby handkerchief and gently apologise for upsetting me. Perfectly natural that as the racking sobs diminished, all the worries I had been so careful to hide should now spill out without thought or effort. Stammering, I confessed how the fear of being returned to Crossbank had never left me and every precious day spent at Furze House made the prospect of discovery as a runaway apprentice more terrible. How his frivolous talk of Captain Luscombe revived the dread that sooner or later the Captain would hear word of Biddie and me from his sister and his revenge would be swift and merciless, for had not Kit himself told me what a hard, cruel man he was? The kind of man, surely, who would have no compunction in turning a pair of runaways over to the magistrate . . . And mixed up with these logical fears were sillinesses that I knew I should be deeply ashamed of when I recovered my wits, but which at the time were revealed disjointedly with the rest. Like resentment at Mrs Greenwood's casual announcement that Catriona MacBride's cast-offs would be perfectly suitable for Biddie and me. Like Kit himself treating Catriona as grown-up. Calling her

Miss MacBride, while Biddie and I were given no such courtesy . . .

When it was all out Kit still did not release me. I lay cradled against his chest, hiccupping a last shuddering breath of release, of catharsis. I felt empty, drained of all strength. Yet I knew I must make an effort and move. The incongruity of our position, huddled together on the floor of the barn, was beginning, at last, to impinge on my consciousness.

As though the first hint of my embarrassment communicated itself to him, Kit said quietly, 'I think if you are recovered we might make ourselves more comfortable while we talk.'

With one brisk movement he was on his feet, pulling me up with him and drawing me towards a bale of clean straw.

I tugged my hands away and made a pretence of brushing down my skirts.

'Talk, sir?' I said in an uncertain voice. 'I think I've said enough for one day.' As I spoke I half turned from him, unable to meet his eyes for shame. 'Terrible things . . .'

'No!' he interrupted fiercely. 'Don't even think you were in the wrong. The bastards who brought you to this state are the ones who should be grovelling in apology. And I berate myself for an insensitive fool for not understanding how you must have been feeling . . . For Christ's sake, Miranda, look at me! Say you forgive me for my brashness.'

His face was pale and stern, his grey-green-eyes dark as granite and impassioned with remorse.

I shook my head. 'It . . . it wasn't your fault, sir . . . I think . . . I think perhaps it was meant somehow.' I groped for words to explain. 'It was as though something had been festering away inside me, like a . . . a sort of abscess . . . and all of a sudden it burst. Sooner or later it would have gone. Anyone – anything – could have set it off.'

He paused then said, dryly, 'I reckon that is the first time I have been likened to a poultice.'

I clapped my hand over my mouth. 'Suppose it had happened when I was with Miss Swann or Mrs Greenwood? If

I'd come out with all that rough Crossbank speech. They'd have been horrified . . .' I broke off, realising what he had said. 'A poultice? Oh, sir.' The giggle caught me unawares.

'That's better,' he said. 'Laughter becomes you rather more than tears.' He looked at me critically from under his straight dark brows. 'Though I have to say that even a smile cannot disguise your dishevelment, if you will forgive my frankness.'

'Lord help us, yes!' I cried, frantically beginning to scoop up hairpins. 'I must look a fright. What'll the ladies think!'

'I'll not dispute that red eyes and scarecrow hair, not to mention the adornment of lumps of chicken dung, might not be quite acceptable in the Furze House parlour.' He looked down ruefully at his once-cream breeches. 'To be sure, I am scarcely less disreputable. Apart from the evidence of sleeping in my clothes, I seem to have accumulated a certain amount of guano also. Shall we take a few minutes to restore ourselves to a state fit to be seen?'

With the aid of a handful of straw we cleaned the worst of the muck off our clothes. Then Kit fetched a bucket of water from the pump outside and I gratefully rinsed my hands and face and pinned up my hair – still too short from Miss Violet's cutting to be properly manageable – as best I could.

All the while he talked to me, repeating the reassurances that Violet had given me in the matter of Mrs Turpin's silence.

'She plays cunning games of her own, that one,' he said. 'And she has gentlemen of influence among her . . . well, let us call them her admirers. If there is a way to keep Mrs Turpin discreet she will find it. Violet Briggs has made it her business to know all there is to know about Mrs Turpin's activities at The Plough. She would not think twice about using such knowledge to her own advantage. And yours, Miranda.' He paused then said gravely, 'Or perhaps I should learn to say "Miss Brehault", if that will please you better?'

I felt my face grow hot. 'Please, sir. I did not intend . . .'

'Did you not? Then allow me to assure you I did not intend

any condescension by addressing you so.' He smiled. 'But perhaps we might begin again. In friendship, this time. Do you think that is possible, Miranda? Will you consider me your friend and address *me* less formally than you have done until now?'

'Sir, I . . .'

'My given name is Christian. Kit.'

'Well, then . . . yes, Kit,' I said shyly, though inside I felt not at all shy about it, for almost from the first he had been Kit in my thoughts.

Except for a heaviness about the eyes I was almost restored by the time we left the barn. And it was more than the drawing of a careful shield over inner turmoil. Something had changed. There was quietness deep within me that had not been there before. As though that violent outpouring had torn away the worst and deepest of the pain and fear, leaving behind a tiny core of calm. Whether it would last remained to be seen. But as long as it did, I knew I should be able to draw comfort from it.

And though I fully expected to feel awkward in Kit Warrener's company out of shame for my behaviour, I did not. Strangely, as we walked back up the flagged path to the house, I was quite saddened by the realisation that now he had recovered his violin there seemed little to keep him in Dawlish if he should choose to up and leave, save whatever sense of honour he had over the matter of his debt. But I had underestimated the force of his musical ambition.

'I hear that the cream of local society has been invited to the Luscombes' rout,' he said. The excitement was back in his voice. 'Just think, Miranda. Without patronage or connections, I might have waited months, years, for such an opportunity and it has fallen into my lap almost by default. I would be a fool to let such an opportunity slip. Who knows what it will lead to?' He lifted his left hand and stared at it ruefully. There was a deep scratch across the index finger and a bruise at the base of the thumb. 'I trapped my fingers when a tub slipped from the pony I was helping to load. I shall have to be careful next time. I cannot afford injuries that will affect my performance.'

'Tell the Captain that,' I suggested. 'He might let you off.'

He shrugged and said quickly, not meeting my eye, 'Oh, if I am called upon I shall take extra care, you may be sure of that.'

I raised my eyebrows. There was something in his voice that hit a false note. 'So *that's* the way of it,' I said, after a moment.

'What do you mean?' he said defensively.

'Last night's activities. I get the feeling that you won't be reluctant to go a-smuggling again. Don't tell me you've come round to my friend Jed's opinion that it's all a fine, brave adventure?'

Kit had the grace to look abashed. Then he laughed. 'I confess I did find it exciting. The darkness, the element of danger . . . the skill and speed of it all. I think I had half expected panic and confusion, but it went along in such an orderly fashion that I was somewhat astonished.' His footsteps slowed as we approached the pond. He stared down into the weedy water as though instead of scuttering pond-skaters and water-boatmen he saw the black outline of the lugger rocking in the moonless swell beyond the breaking waves, with the snail trail of men laden with a pair of tubs apiece, slithering through the sand and shingle and panting up the winding, perilous path to where the ponies waited on the clifftop. 'We were fortunate, of course, that we were not accosted. The whisper is that Captain Luscombe keeps certain revenue men in his pocket, the breed being badly paid and willing to keep to their beds on occasion for the price of a few pipes of tobacco and a glass or two of genever.'

'You might not be so lucky another time.'

'We should have plenty of warning even if there were a raid,' he said. 'Lookouts are posted all along the clifftops and we are well guarded by several burly fellows. There seems little likelihood of anyone sneaking up on us unawares and there are plenty of places to hide in if we were forced to run.'

A name from Jed's stories came into my mind. 'Batmen! That's what the smugglers' guards are called after the swingle-bats they carry. And they don't always confine themselves to those, either, as I recall. Pistol fights seemed to play a big part in Jed's tales—'

'I saw no sign of firearms,' Kit put in quickly.

'How can you be sure? It was pitch dark.'

'I cannot, of course, but . . .'

'And should you find that the batmen were armed with more than staves, and there could be bloodshed – deaths even – if there was a set to, would that put you off? There'd be hangings then, for sure, if anyone was caught.'

He shrugged. 'I have discovered that there are many local people involved in the trade one way or another,' he said. 'Respectable, decent persons from all classes of society who see the duty on tea and brandy and tobacco as an imposition on the common man's simple pleasures, and the avoidance of such taxes as a means of fighting injustice.'

'How very worthy.'

He scowled. 'Sarcasm, eh? You had best take care, Miss Brehault. A sharp tongue can make enemies of even the best of friends.'

'Not to mention pomposity, Mr Warrener.'

'Me? Pompous?' he cried in mock horror. 'Never!'

'Own up,' I said, laughing. 'It's nothing to do with fighting injustice that draws most people to the trade, but the prospect of cheap goods – like my papa – or the making of fine profits – like Captain Luscombe. And in your case, Mr Christian Warrener, I think that you're still a small boy at heart and it's the adventure and thrill of it all that draw you. Well, for your sake, I hope that the excisemen are kept sweet as long as you feel obliged to fight this injustice on behalf of the common man.'

But Kit was not called upon to take part in any more midnight runs in the two weeks before the Luscombes' rout.

Indeed there was little to disturb the household's quiet pattern of living. Kit even spent the hours of practice on his violin down in the linhay so that no one in the house would be disturbed.

Every orderly day that passed seemed to me to reinforce hope that we should be left in peace, though Biddie sometimes hankered for more lively company, wistfully remembering the gossipy chatter and easy-going life of the girls at The Plough.

'They were doxies . . . whores,' I protested as we dressed one morning. 'Paid to sleep with any man who had the asking price.'

'I know,' she sighed, 'but they was full o' fun and they had such pretty new things, not dull old castoffs.' She shot me a cheeky glance and grinned. 'D'you think it'd have been such a bad life if we'd been sold off as old men's darlin's like Ma Turpin had in mind?'

'I'm glad we didn't get the chance to find out.'

She wrinkled her nose. 'Keeping yourself pure's not much good if you've got to be miserable in consequence. I think I'd rather be wicked and have fun.'

I snatched a pillow from the bed and threw it at her. She dodged it, squealing with laughter. 'But if they keep feedin' me here, I'll be good. Honest!'

Even the regular Sunday visit to morning service at St Gregory's in Dawlish began to lose its terrors. On the first two Sundays I had been so frightened of public scrutiny that I had scarcely dared raise my head lest I meet the calculating eyes of someone who guessed our secret. With growing confidence came the understanding that the arrival of two new boarding pupils at Furze House was of little consequence in a town that was accustomed to the patronage of visiting gentry and nobility. There were far more interesting subjects than Biddie and me to fuel the gossip.

Once I began to look about me I was greatly taken with what I saw of Dawlish. It was a pretty little town, set in a deep, wide combe with a brook, the Dawlish Water, running between green banks along the flat valley bottom and pouring out on to the shingle and sand of the beach. The oldest cottages lay about a mile inland clustered round St Gregory's church and the mill and spreading in narrow streets along the lower slopes of the hills. But many modern villas had sprung up and the town now straggled all the way to the shore and up on to the cliffs to the east and west.

Mrs Greenwood said that it was truly astonishing how the town had grown in recent years on account of the mildness of its air, the health-giving qualities of its sea-bathing and the beauty of its setting. 'Why, the most particular and well bred of persons might now find suitable accommodation in new houses of an exceedingly comfortable and gracious style. And more are built by the month! I declare we shall not see East Cliff at all soon for the number of properties being built there.'

'Too rapid a change is not always advantageous,' Miss Swann reminded her gruffly. 'As Mr Manning found out after he drained the marshes and channelled the brook in order to create more land for building. It went quite against nature. Look at the dreadful flooding that ensued after the heavy snow on Haldon two years since. Houses swept away, bridges gone, even the poorhouse went, not to mention two of Mr Manning's fine horses. It can scarce be credited that no lives were lost.'

'But it is quite restored now, Tryphena, and we are assured that the new channelling with the pretty cataracts and plenty of grassy space on either side of the brook will prevent any possibility of a recurrence.'

'Time alone will tell, my dear. I am loth to trust the easy promises of businessmen who see nothing but profit in the rearrangement of an innocent little stream, and the removal of marshes and sandhills nature put there for the particular purpose of soaking up excess water. For myself I prefer Dawlish as it was when we were children and there was a certain wildness to the foreshore.'

'You are so . . . so backward in your thinking, Tryphena.'

'And you too anxious to embrace all that is new without a thought for the consequences.'

I was becoming used to the ladies' gentle squabbling.

'It is a hobby with them,' Kit assured me. 'Like découpage or embroidery. They have always been the same.'

I smiled. 'I'm glad to hear it. I wouldn't wish Miss Swann and Mrs Greenwood to have a horrible falling out and give up the school just as Biddie and I are getting used to being here.'

It was one of the rare moments when Kit and I could manage a few private words. Whenever he was not practising in the linhay or out visiting his friend Billy, he busied himself with some of the heavier chores in the garden for Miss Swann or helped Mrs Greenwood with the music lessons which gained a sudden popularity in consequence. Catriona MacBride was not the only silly young miss who harboured highly coloured sentiments about him.

The regimen at Furze House allowed for few idle moments for any of its residents. When school hours were over there were our rooms to keep dusted and tidy, the mysteries of mending and darning and other domestic tasks to be mastered.

'It is incumbent upon every young woman to understand the workings of a genteel household,' Mrs Greenwood observed. 'And how better to learn than through practical experience? Should she ever have her own establishment, then she must understand everything pertaining to the comfort of its residents and guests, from the provisioning of a kitchen and the drawing up of a menu to the best method of spring cleaning a room. Knowledge of such practical matters is vital if she is to gain the respect and loyalty of her servants.'

'Besides which,' said Miss Swann frankly, 'we would not wish to make Flossie's life more wearisome than needs be when we are able to lighten her burden.'

Even when Kit and I did get a chance to speak we were never alone for long.

Late one afternoon I was despatched with the two younger

MacBrides to gather the best of the windfall apples, Biddie being set to her favourite task of cleaning the silver and Catriona helping Mrs Greenwood to rearrange the music cupboard. The MacBride girls, having already lost interest, were involved in some game of their own under the wide branches of an old damson tree. Kit, who had spent the afternoon digging and raking the patch where Miss Swann intended to plant broad beans for overwintering, sauntered over when he was finished, whistling softly, his coat slung over his shoulder and his shirt sleeves still rolled up. For once, Catriona was not there to attach herself to his side and monopolise his attention.

'Let me help,' he said, scooping up an apple and tossing it into the basket I was filling.

'Watch out for wasps,' I cautioned. 'There are still a few about and if you get your hand stung, you'll not be fit to play tomorrow. Are you all ready for the big performance?'

He grinned, looking carefree, relaxed. 'As ready as ever I shall be.'

'You practise long hours,' I said.

'And yet it never seems enough. I hope the scrapes and screeches – and my curses when things are not going well – don't reach as far as the house?'

'We haven't heard a thing up here, so tonight will be a complete surprise.'

'Or a shock.'

I laughed. 'The ladies are proper thrilled that you're to give us our very own private concert tonight.'

'It will be in the way of a dress rehearsal,' he said, adding somewhat diffidently, 'and it will include a work never previously performed.'

'Something you composed?'

He made a deprecatory gesture. 'A mere nothing. Of very little consequence.'

The glint in his eye told a different story. I threw an apple at him. 'Don't tell fibs. You're proud as can be or you wouldn't have mentioned it.'

He retrieved the apple deftly, threw it high in the air and caught it again, laughing. 'You are too perceptive, Miranda Brehault.'

'Fiddlesticks. It was written all over you. You'd have to be blind not to see it.'

'I hope you will be as honest when you have heard the piece.' He looked me in the eye. 'I should appreciate your opinion.'

'Mine? Surely Mrs Greenwood or Catriona would be better judges?'

'Doubtless. But they are too . . . too frightened of giving offence to be truthful.'

'Too well mannered, you mean. And I am not.'

'I think that you and I have a better understanding.'

'Do we?' I shrugged non-committally but I knew it was true. There was an ease between us and had been since the day of my outburst in the barn when he had been so kind and comforting. But I had no inclination to wax soft and sentimental on account of it. Besides, I felt his compliment to be somewhat backhanded. There was little I found flattering in his assumption that I would speak out frankly if he thought me so coarsened by mill work that my nature could not possibly have the sensibility of a gently raised girl.

The momentary stab of triumph that he valued my opinion above Catriona MacBride's died the death and when at that instant I saw her hastening towards us from the house, as though my thinking of her had conjured up her physical presence, a most unladylike oath sprang into my mind. Which doubly peeved and depressed me because it confirmed what I already supposed: that I was indelibly marked by the years at Crossbank. As my skinny body bore the marks of deprivation, so did my mind and spirit. I feared those invisible scars would be much more difficult – if not impossible – to remove.

'Mr Warrener, there is a letter come for you,' she said breathlessly, the pale lashes a-flutter over adoring blue eyes. 'From Derbyshire. Mrs Greenwood sent me to fetch you in for she knew you would wish to have it straight away.'

My intention was to snatch up my basket and get on with the task of apple-gathering with my back firmly towards the pair of them. But I could not hold on to my prickliness when I saw Kit's expression. I knew who the letter was from.

Mrs Loveridge had written several times, enclosing a sealed note in letters to Mrs Greenwood or Miss Swann, with whom she had corresponded regularly in the years since she had left the school. It was no surprise to me that she was determined on flouting the instructions of her uncle and her husband, nor that she had set out her case cleverly and coaxed the ladies into understanding that those two loving and devoted sisters – Caroline's own mother and Kit's – would have most dearly wished for their children to keep in touch, whatever the forces that threatened to separate them.

'The poor child is quite beside herself with distress that having been reunited with her cousin – her one blood relative – she finds herself obliged to renounce him,' I had overheard Mrs Greenwood whisper indignantly. 'It is too bad.'

Miss Swann sighed. 'There is money involved, my dear. Caroline's inheritance. Cupidity is all too often the victor over compassion in such cases. But as you know from your own experience, the cleverest and kindest of women must subordinate herself to the wishes of her menfolk.'

'Indeed, indeed,' said Mrs Greenwood, her voice low and sad.

'There, there, dearest,' Miss Swann said comfortingly. 'We must be glad that those days are well behind us and remember how fortunate we are that we have had so many years when we have been beholden to no one but ourselves. Long may we continue do what our feminine instincts show us to be right.'

'And in this case?'

'I think you know my mind, Harriet,' said Miss Swann.

'And you mine, Tryphena,' said Mrs Greenwood.

For once, it seemed, the ladies were in complete accord and Mrs Loveridge had her way, though I noticed that these letters from the north only seemed to make Kit quiet and withdrawn. I wondered, now, what on earth his cousin had to say that even the expectation of reading this latest missive took all the animation from his face and brought a dark, bleak look to his eyes. I wished I could say something, do something, to comfort him.

'Thank you, Miss MacBride,' he said stiffly. 'I shall be along in a moment.'

Seeing that Catriona was inclined to dawdle in the hopes of walking back to the house with Kit, I said with an encouraging smile, 'There's not too many wasps about if you want to stay and help. And I don't think the big rat that was here just now will dare come back into the orchard while we're tramping about in the grass.'

She paled and shuddered. 'N-no . . . I . . . Mrs Greenwood is waiting for me,' she cried, clutching at her skirts and backing off.

'Rat?' Kit queried, watching her flee back to the house. 'What rat is this?'

'Something was certainly scuttling in the grass earlier,' I said airily. 'I thought it best to warn her. She'd have had hysterics if she'd glimpsed so much as a whisker of whatever it was. You know what a state she was in last week when she found a pathetic little mouse had taken shelter in her bonnet box. As for wasps . . .'

'Never mind wasps,' he said. 'You have a wicked streak in your character, Miranda Brehault. You meant to frighten her off. Why? What has she done to you?'

I grinned. 'Nothing. I gave in to temptation, that's all. And I know I shouldn't. But there it is. She's such a scaredy cat that it doesn't take much to set her squealing.'

'She's not likely to improve if you carry on teasing her,' he said sternly.

'But I find it excessively entertaining, Mr Warrener,' I said in such a passable imitation of Catriona's fulsome tones that his lips twitched as he fought to control a smile and the darkness in his eyes lightened a little.

'It is unworthy of you, Miranda,' he said. 'Just because she does not have your sharp wits or superior intelligence . . .'

'Do you mean to stand there lecturing me until the moon comes up or are you going to help me fill these baskets? You can rattle on while we work, if you're so minded. And I could do with a hand to carry the baskets to Mrs Hawkins before she fetches her rolling pin to us. She's wanting to start on making blackberry and apple jelly.'

It was the best I could do by way of distraction. I kept up the banter as we worked. It served its purpose, I believe. Kept his mind momentarily off the letter that awaited him. The letter that would, for whatever reason, sadden him.

And it was no effort, now, for me to put on a cheerful face. The prickliness I had felt earlier had quite dissolved with Catriona's hasty departure . . . and perhaps not a little with the knowledge that, attentive and polite as Kit might be to her, he thought her inferior in certain respects to a lass fresh out of Crossbank.

Kit need not have worried about criticism of his playing.

When the last note of the last piece faded into silence there was an outburst of genuine, spontaneous congratulation.

'Bravo! Bravo, dear boy,' cried Mrs Greenwood. 'A triumph. You will enchant them all tomorrow.'

'Oh, Mr Warrener, you play with such . . . such sentiment,' breathed Catriona.

'The Mozart piece . . . the scherzo. Magnificent!' said Miss Swann. 'Performed so beautifully. Most moving.'

'Excellent of course,' said Mrs Greenwood with a happy sigh, 'but as a musician myself, I appreciated the Beethoven as perhaps you cannot, my dear. The violin sonata was exquisite. The variations with which it ends – well, what can I say save that the irresistible theme was enhanced by the virtuosity of the playing? As for the *étude* – your own composition – it is a most innovative piece. I look forward to hearing you play it again for us sometime.'

'And I also,' Catriona said, blushing.

Kit bowed. His tall frame still seemed taut with the nervous energy that had fired the music. There was a dew of perspiration on his forehead where the black hair lay in a damp tangle above deep-set eyes that held a brilliance not entirely due to the flicker of candlelight. As his gaze swept slowly round the parlour, I felt that he still did not yet see any of us properly, as though his senses, his emotions, were still bound up in the harmonies he had created.

'You are very kind,' he murmured. 'I pray the audience tomorrow will be as generous.'

'They will be as delighted as we are!' Mrs Greenwood assured him, while Biddie muttered in my ear, 'He's right clever, I'll give him that. Though I'd sooner have 'ad a tune or two as we knew 'stead of all that scribbly stuff.'

I sat still and silent, the needle poised over the piece of old sheeting on which I was supposed to be practising hemming stitches. For the moment I could not find any words. They were lost somewhere in the dream landscape conjured up by the last piece of music, Kit's own composition. My mind reeled under the chill beauty of moonlight shimmering on black and silver ripples and the reflection of the house stirring in the water, as if it were some living creature caught in the slow currents.

More than a dream. I had felt the touch of the night breeze on my face; smelt the dank, rich odour of the earth; heard the heavy pad of badger paws on frosted grass and the yelping bark of a vixen echoing from the slope of the moor beyond the gates.

Moondance.

Kit's music had taken me there. The Moondance I knew and loved. Yet different. I had seen it through other eyes. I had been . . . someone else. Someone no older than me whose desolate, yearning spirit reached to me down the centuries. I *was* her. It was my voice begging the man riding beside me, my new husband, if we could stop a moment after the long wearisome journey, telling him that I was eager for a first glimpse of the fine house that he had created for me. But, in truth, delaying the moment I must enter, for my heart wept for the love I could not have, bound as I was by the fetters of duty and wealth to a more suitable union.

We dismounted, stepped out into the frosty night and walked to where the stand of leafless trees thrust twisting roots to the very edge of the lake, newly created from the imprisoned stream that had once run free and fast from the boggy heights of the moor. I shivered in the cold caress of the moon shadow despite my fur-lined overgown and the warmth of the heavy, possessive arm that lay about my shoulders. The granite of the house, unsoftened by the greens and golds of lichens and mosses that the passing years would bestow on it, gleamed pale and hard and unforgiving in the silver light. My gaze winced from it, was drawn to the water where its reflection stirred and shimmered as though the water, trapped as I was, strained to dash to its old wild, unfettered dance.

The name came to me and was spoken on an involuntary breath. My husband's answering shout of laughter splintered the icy night. *So be it! My house is named!* His lustful breath in my ear. His gloved hands impatient against the tender skin of my neck. *Come! Such a fine house must not lack an heir. We shall have merry games tonight in our bedchamber and set upon the business of breeding a quiverful of sturdy sons.*

'Miranda! Rouse yourself!' Mrs Greenwood's voice. 'Supper is on the table.'

She whisked past me with a flurry of violet frills. The others, save Kit, were already out of the room, their chatter floating back as they crossed the hall to the dining chamber.

'So, Miranda,' he said softly as, in confusion, I put down my sewing and jumped up. 'You stay silent. Does that mean you disliked my composition? Remember, I asked for your honest opinion.'

'Such sadness . . .' I broke off, gave myself a mental shake. Forced myself fully back to this room, this house, this day. 'Of course I'll be honest,' I said. 'I liked it very well.'

'But you thought it sad.'

The music or the despair of that long-ago bride? Both, I thought. Both.

'I confess,' he said, 'that I was in a melancholy mood when I was working on it. I was attempting to capture the feelings that those bleak Derbyshire hills aroused in me.'

I knew it was not merely the scenery that had affected him but the situation of Mrs Loveridge in her loveless marriage, their brief reunion and parting. Melancholy feelings that could be expressed in music far more profoundly than words. I felt a pang of envy. I wished I had been blessed with some talent that would allow me to express what I had just experienced. I knew I could not speak of it. Not to anyone. Even to me, now that I was recovered, it felt as though my imagination had lured me into a dangerous place where fevered nightmare slithered close to the perilous territory of madness.

I took refuge in action, marching briskly across the parlour, saying lightly, 'Then perhaps Mrs Turpin did you a favour after all. You might have grumbled at our enforced stay at The Plough, but at least it gave you chance to compose your piece of music. Even if you only had your flute to practise on.'

'What? Why do you say that?'

I looked up at him. 'Did you mean it to be a secret? If so, you shouldn't have been playing it so close to where Biddie and I slept. I heard it quite clearly one night, that very same tune. Magical I thought it was then – and even more so now I've heard it close up.'

He shook his head, looking at me strangely. 'But I did not compose the piece until I was back here, in Dawlish. Oh, I daresay the *idea* was beginning to shape itself in my head . . . but nothing else, for sure. It must have been something else – someone else – that you heard. There was an old man with a squeezebox who could knock out a fair ditty when he was sober.'

'No! It was . . .' I stopped, gave a shaky laugh. 'You're right. I'd been ill, hadn't I? I was nearly asleep. I can't possibly have been hearing anything properly . . . Now, will you come on or I'll be in trouble. Everyone else is seated.'

I made a good effort at tucking into supper, spoke and

smiled when necessary and generally made a good fist of appearing as normal as possible.

It was only in the long night hours that I could acknowledge the disquiet that teased away sleep and left me staring wide-eyed into the darkness, as my thoughts went back to that night at The Plough and the music that had lulled me to sleep.

The refreshment of deep sleep was something that continued to evade me in the nights that followed. It seemed that no sooner did I fall into a doze than I was awake again, fretted by an unaccountable restlessness and vague, unpleasant dreams. By day, in consequence, I felt thick-headed and heavy-limbed. Miss Swann remarked upon my drooping eyes and lack of concentration in the schoolroom and dosed me with peppermint and elderflower tea in case I was sickening for the head cold that was rampaging through the pupils of Furze House.

I obediently drank the tea but it made no difference. I still felt as if I had a sort of gloom, like fog, weighing me down.

'You're not 'zackly lively company,' Biddie grumbled one evening as we sat together on the parlour sofa, struggling with the inevitable hemming. 'What wi' Catriona's caterwauling and the young 'uns sent to bed to nurse their sniffles, we might as well be in the graveyard.'

'*My love is dead,*' Catriona quavered from the forte-piano, where she was accompanying herself in a selection of ballads, '*Gone to his death bed, All under the willow- tree . . .*'

'How many more times 'ave we got to sit through this one?' Biddie muttered. 'Hasn't she practised it enough?'

'She wants it to be perfect so she can show off to Mr Warrener,' I said sourly. 'After all, he set the poem to music for her. She's been boasting all week about it.'

'He buggered off to his room sharpish, I noticed, when 'er proposed to entertain us with her singin'.'

'Shush . . .' I hissed. 'The ladies'll hear you.'

'Not them!' She giggled. 'It's plain enough what they think of her warblin'.'

Mrs Greenwood's chin had sunk into the frills at her throat. She was snoring gently. Miss Swann, eye glasses perched on her nose, was lost to the world in her book.

'As for his lordship, 'im bein' musical, it must be torture to listen to 'er singing all out of tune. No wonder he 'opped it.'

'He's got work to do,' I said flatly. 'He's got to go to Exmouth tomorrow, don't forget. It's important he makes a good impression.'

The Luscombes' rout had proved fruitful for Kit. He had already been engaged to perform at a function to be held at Christmas at the new Public Rooms in Dawlish. And yesterday he had received a communication from a group of ladies and gentlemen who devoted themselves to charitable works in Exmouth. They were arranging a concert, they wrote, to be patronised by many eminent persons resident in the district, the proceeds of which would be donated towards coals and candles for the deserving poor in the coming winter. There would, of necessity, only be a small fee involved, but would Mr Warrener, of whom they had heard a most enthusiastic report, be prepared to give a short demonstration of his prowess to the committee? After which, if all was satisfactory, it might then be possible to come to some agreement.

'Would he not!' Kit had cried. 'Fee or no fee, I will play at their concert if I suit them. Who knows who might be in attendance? I might be summoned to Powderham Castle next, to entertain the Courtneys.'

I hoped he would be. It would divert him from his other, more perilous, activities. He had been out twice more of a night. Two more cargoes safely in at Dawlish Warren and the thrill of it growing stronger in him with each successful run. I feared his luck might not last. He brushed my protests aside.

'My stint will be over soon enough. I have put it to Captain Luscombe that I have nearly worked out what I owe. My appearance at the rout was part of the bargain and I swear I gave the finest performance of my life. It was worth ten guineas at least.' He grinned. 'One more outing with the owlers and after that I shall expect to be paid for my services.'

'And he agreed?'

'Grudgingly.'

'And you'll steer clear of the smuggling after that?

'Oh, I daresay I shall not be asked again,' he said, airily.

I hoped fervently that he was right.

> *"'Water witches, crowned with reytes,*
> *Bear me to your lethal tide."'*

Catriona's voice narrowly missed the high note she was aiming for then swooped down to the last soulful phrases:

> *'"I die; I come; my true love waits,*
> *Thus the damsel spake and died."'*

She plonked out a last chord and sighed. 'So very touching. I have often been brought to tears when I have read it. That was why I chose Mr Chatterton's "The Minstrel's Song" when Mr Warrener begged to be allowed to compose something for me. *Especially* for me. The tune he wrote matches the words exquisitely, does it not?'

'Not the way you sing it,' Biddie said under her breath, then loudly, giving me an evil wink, 'I'd have thought it bad luck to mention witches so close to All Hallows Eve. They'll all be out on their broomsticks tomorrow. Look well if they come a-riding in your window at midnight, screechin' and cursin', to cast a spell on you for speakin' of 'em so lightly.'

'Th-there's no such thing as witches!' Catriona said.

'That's not what I 'eard. There's one livin' scarcely a mile from here. Flossie said. Flossie knows everythin' about everybody round about.'

Catriona sniffed. 'I do not choose to converse with housemaids.'

'Then you won't want to know the witch's name so's you can speak kindly to 'er and p'raps stop her givin' you a face full o' scabs or turning you into a toad.'

'That's nonsense,' Catriona said, her voice quavering.

'Quite,' said Miss Swann, roused at last from her book. She peered at Biddie sternly over her eyeglasses. 'Shame on you for trying to frighten Catriona.'

'But, miss,' Biddie protested, trying to look innocent and failing, 'Flossie swears there's this strange old widow-woman as lives wi' cats and bats and such. Folks goes to her for love potions and charms . . .'

'I daresay she is referring to Widow Thomas, who is a perfectly innocent old lady. Because she chooses to live alone and is very knowledgeable about herbs and helps the sick – people or animals – silly tales have been invented by those with ignorant, idle minds.' Miss Swann closed her book with a snap. 'However, Bridget, you will shortly have the chance to see for yourself whether or not she is strange. In fact, by way of reparation for teasing Catriona, I shall insist you fetch whatever refreshment Mrs Thomas requires and make yourself agreeable to her when she calls. Which will likely be tomorrow or the day after as I have sent word that our stocks are low of the excellent honey we buy from her.'

Mrs Greenwood gave an enormous snore and woke herself up.

'Excellent performance, Catriona,' she cried loudly. 'I never tire of listening to you sing and play. Did you mention honey, Tryphena? Yes, I believe I might fancy a little on a slice of bread and butter before we retire . . .'

My attempts to sleep that night were made no easier by a fearful Biddie clinging limpet-like to my person. Her talk had been bold enough in the parlour but this careless chatter of witches inevitably reminded her, once our candle was snuffed, of the boggarts and monsters Alice Smith had told us of at Crossbank.

But by daylight her fears were banished by the brilliance of the day. Out in the garden the browns and ochres of the dying year were turned to the richest coppers and golds by a low sun that shone unmasked by cloud, from a sky of deep, untroubled blue. A day to rejoice in, for surely there could not be many more like this so late in the year?

I tried. I went to let out the hens before breakfast and made myself look for all the small delights that made each day of freedom an extra pleasure. The spider's web outlined with crystal drops of dew, the scarlet necklaces of black bryony berries glimmering among the fluffy grey curtains of old man's beard in the hedgerow beyond the gate, the satisfying warmth of a brown egg freshly gathered from its strawy nest . . . Nothing helped. Not today, because the heavy, sad feeling was worse. It lay on my spirit, my senses, a relentless weight. I seemed to reflect it physically as well. I found I was walking back to the house with hunched shoulders and downcast eyes.

The hall passage ran from front to back of the house, turning in a kind of dog-leg by the kitchen door which lay behind the dining chamber. The sound of voices came from the front hall and when I turned the corner I saw Kit taking his hat from Flossie, and Miss Swann, Mrs Greenwood and – inevitably – Catriona plying him with good wishes and advice for his journey.

'Try to leave Exmouth early,' Mrs Greenwood cried. 'I do feel that the river crossing is best accomplished by daylight. And pray do not linger in Starcross if it is dark. One hears so many tales of the rogues and smugglers and other low persons who frequent the alehouses near the ferry.'

'Really, Harriet, I am sure Kit is well able to take care of himself,' Miss Swann said stoutly. 'You forget he is a seasoned traveller.'

'And *you* forget that persons with evil intent may be found anywhere,' Mrs Greenwood retorted. 'My conscience would not allow me to do other than caution him.'

'Well, all I wish, dear boy, is that you return with good news of your audition,' said Miss Swann.

'And I,' said Catriona, blushing.

My steps slowed. At the foot of the stairs I stopped, my gaze riveted on Kit.

He stood head and shoulders above the women, his heavy, caped coat giving him the appearance of breadth as well as height. His clothes were well groomed and pressed despite their shabbiness, the stock at his throat crisply white and starched, his hair brushed neat and close and not yet disordered into its usual curly tangle. There was a glow of anticipation and excitement about him. A talented man with all the freshness and vigour and keenness of youth at his command. A young man looking forward enthusiastically towards a future that could hold marvels. Who would go from here towards that glowing prospect without a backward glance . . .

No! No!

I thought I screamed the word aloud, but nobody turned. Flossie opened the door, Kit went through it, clapping on his hat.

And on the porch hesitated and turned.

Had he heard? Had he caught the faintest echo of the voice that rang so loudly in my own head? His eyes met mine.

'Ah, Miss Brehault,' he called, smiling. 'Do you, too, come to wish me luck?'

I was impelled forward. As though, for a moment, the urgency of a message had overriden my will. All the power of those strange, sad feelings that had haunted me these last days was in the force that thrust me forward. They seemed to have coalesced into this driving, urgent need to prevent him from leaving.

I moved so quickly that I almost bowled over Mrs Greenwood.

'Kit!' I cried. 'Kit . . .'

'Such manners!' Mrs Greenwood's restraining hand closed tightly over my arm. 'I will not tolerate such hoydenish behaviour! Apologise at once.'

'Oh, I'm sorry,' I said desperately. 'It's just that I wanted . . . that is, I thought . . .'

My voice died away. I became aware of the curious, reproving faces around me. Of the incongruity of what I wished . . . what I needed . . . to say.

How could I speak and not be ridiculed? How could I tell him not to go?

I wanted to beg him, plead with him: 'I have had this terrible foreboding for days. Now I know why. I am terrified for you, Kit. If you leave here, you will run into the most dreadful danger. It will ruin everything you hope for, change your life irrevocably . . .'

Kit smiled, but there was a hint of impatience about him as he waited for me to speak. As I stared at him, I understood with cold certainty that even if I begged and hung on to his coat-tails he would not stay. Why should he heed something that sounded even to me only far-fetched nonsense?

Nonsense. They would all think that some madness had taken hold of me. Perhaps it had.

I opened my mouth. Instead of the beseeching cry there came a lame, halting whisper. 'I . . . I wish you well. Please . . . take care.'

'Thank you.' He grinned. 'I always do.'

A few short strides to the gate, and he was looking back to salute us before turning right to follow the road down to Dawlish. From there he would walk the few miles out past the Warren to Starcross where he would catch the ferry to the other side of river.

Starcross.

I shivered.

Miss Greenwood, still tutting reprovingly, released my arm and moved away with the others.

'Are you coming in, miss?' Flossie asked anxiously. 'Mrs Hawkins will be hollerin' for me . . .'

'In a minute,' I said. 'You get about your work, Flossie. I'll close the door.'

So I was the only one to watch him go. Gaps in the hedge gave me my final glimpses of a shoulder, his hat . . . then he was gone, swallowed by the bend in the road. I looked at the spot where I had last seen him and was transfixed by a trance of despair too deep for tears.

* * *

On the following afternoon Billy Rossiter's wife struggled up the hill to Furze House, her enveloping shawl hiding more than the swollen jut of her belly. Once in the parlour, she drew out Kit's violin case from under its fringes and thrust it at Miss Swann.

''Tes terrible, terrible, ma'am,' she cried. 'The press gang was on 'em afore they knew it. Took more'n twenty men as was refreshin' themselves in the alehouse down along the Starcross ferry and carried 'em off to Plymouth. Poor Mr Warrener was among 'em. The news just come and my Billy sent me straight off to tell 'ee.'

I felt strangely detached from the distress of the others. I was the one now who stayed cool and practical when Miss Swann seemed bereft of speech and Mrs Greenwood turned faint and sank into a chair. I found the smelling salts, asked Flossie to fetch glasses of cold water and told a snivelling Catriona to shape herself and see to the stricken ladies while I prised all the details I could out of Emma Rossiter.

They were precious few. The raid had been swift and sudden. Only one man had escaped by hiding in a pigsty at the back of the house. He had found Kit's violin stuffed behind a bench when he had crept back inside after the raiding party had left with their captives.

'He'm an honest man who knows my Billy. He thought it likely Mr Warrener had stowed the fiddle there less it got 'armed in the ruckus. Fetched it over as soon as he could. An' I brung it 'ere right off, for Mr Warrener's tried to do his best for Billy and me, miss, an' got naught for it but strife—' She stopped, cleared her throat, her gaze sliding uneasily to Miss Swann. 'Well, 'e's been a good friend,' she said awkwardly. 'Me and Billy's grateful.'

'Thank you, Emma.' Miss Swann had recovered her voice and her colour. 'I shall walk back with you and put in hard enquiries about having Mr Warrener released. It is a most dreadful mistake, I am sure. I will speak to the vicar. He will know best whom to approach.'

Emma shook her head.

'They'm well to Plymouth by now,' she said mournfully. 'Likely they'm put aboard ships and off to fight they Frenchies already, God 'elp the poor souls. Once they're to sea, mistake or no, there'll be no gettin' 'im back, whoever goes a-begging.'

She was right. Miss Swann's efforts were too little and far, far too late.

No word came from Kit. It was to be a long, long time before we knew that he had bribed one of his captors to carry a message to us. He might as well have kept the few coins that he had, for we never received it.

On that All Hallow's Eve of 1812 he vanished as surely as if he had been spirited away by the malicious entities that haunted Biddie's imagination.

Chapter Four

Kit's disappearance in such an abrupt and cruel manner cast a shadow over Furze House that took many months to lift. All that winter when we gathered in the parlour of an evening there were few occasions when his name was not mentioned with a sigh. Even when his name was not spoken aloud, it merely needed someone to note the fierceness of the wind as it rattled the shutters or to remark with a shudder that she pitied those who must be on the sea on such a wild night, for a poignant silence to fall in which Kit's image seemed to pervade the room.

Thomas Chatterton's doleful poem that Kit had set to music was a frequent accompaniment to our evening amusements, Catriona never failing surreptiously to wipe away a tear when she was finished. Thankfully by Christmas we were relieved of these nerve-grating renditions when Mr and Mrs MacBride arrived to bear their daughters off after the years of separation. Biddie and I were silent as we watched the kisses and tears of the family reunion and the bustle of their final departure in the hired carriage.

Afterwards, Biddie said wistfully, 'Must be nice to 'ave a ma and pa come to fetch you home.' I sighed agreement, then we hugged each other and said we must count our blessings because we were so lucky to be free when there were many still slaving at Crossbank and places like it. But nothing quite dispelled the empty feeling that haunted us for the rest of the day.

The house seemed very quiet after they had gone. But in the New Year three sets of boarders arrived in quick succession. Seven small girls in total, the eldest only ten, and including three forlorn sisters whose mama had recently died and whose distraught papa was at a loss as to how to cope with his daughters. In the business of comforting these homesick newcomers, the lingering pangs of self-pity soon dispersed.

It was clear that some rearrangement of the bedchambers would be necessary to accommodate all these new arrivals. Miss Swann had insisted that the room Kit had used be kept as he had left it lest he suddenly return. Now she admitted sadly that facts must be faced.

'If he is gone to sea in a ship-of-the-line, heaven knows where he might be or when he may be back. And so long as Bonaparte lives and the war with the French drags on, I fear there will be little chance of his release.'

'I pray night and morning that he sails in safe waters,' Mrs Greenwood quavered. 'I cannot bear to think of him engaged in battle with those dreadful Frenchmen. When one thinks of the tragedy of brave Lord Nelson, cut down in his moment of triumph . . . leave alone the countless others so cruelly mutilated or killed by shot and cannon . . .'

'Harriet, we must not succumb to morbid imaginings!' Miss Swann snapped upright, her tone severe. 'It will do Kit no good. Nor us. No, we must remain hopeful. And practical. Our priority is the care of those little ones now in our charge. We are pressed for space. Kit, I am sure, would not object to our clearing his room and storing his things to wait upon his return.'

So, one dark January morning, one of the two occasions in the year – the other being August – when the day girls were granted a month's holiday, Miss Swann called me to help in her self-imposed task.

Sleety rain slapped softly at the window of the narrow room on the half-landing above the adjoining bedchambers of Miss Swann and Mrs Greenwood. It was just as he had left it, even to the sheets of manuscript paper strewn across the table with the brass inkwell and pen beside them and the flute propped against the music books piled on the table by his bed. Miss Swann elected to attend to his clothes, probably deeming it unseemly for a young unmarried girl to delve among a man's undergarments and nightshirts. I was left to gather everything else and replace it in his travelling trunk.

It was an odd experience, this shuffling together of someone else's personal effects. As though we were tidying away Kit himself, stowing him neatly into a place of containment where we should no longer be troubled with reminders of him. Miss Swann said nothing as she worked, but I saw in her slow, careful movements and her downcast expression that her thoughts must not be a million miles from my own.

I traced with a hesitant finger the notations on the manuscript paper he must have been working on before he left. In singing lessons I was learning to interpret the symbols that represented the notes for a simple song, but these complicated patterns of rhythm and melody were beyond me. The music was inert and incomprehensible to my questing hand. Dead, until someone with the skill should bring it to joyous life. Joyous? Was that what it was? The notes certainly seemed to dash with cheerful vigour over the lines until they ended halfway down the page, the last crotchet scrawled in haste and the pen flung down ready to be taken up again the moment he returned.

He *would* return. One day. I must hold to that firmly, as Miss Swann insisted. And when he did all would be waiting for him because everything dear to him had been preserved by his friends, with loving care.

I added the sheet to the others in the trunk then wrapped the flute in its soft cloth and made to wedge the bundle next to the violin case. It was then I dislodged a much-worn German dictionary and saw the letters. They lay on the bottom of the trunk, unfolded, in a loose heap. I scarcely needed to read the signature on the foot of the topmost letter to know they were from Kit's cousin, Caroline Loveridge. The small spiky hand, an intense black, against the creamy paper, seemed to shout of her character. By the date, it must have been the last one he had received from her.

I did not mean to read it. Afterwards I was eaten up with remorse. How could I have intruded on a private correspondence? But the words and phrases seemed to spring out at me before I could turn my eyes away.

Oh, my dearest, dearest Kit . . . I vow each day that I will not write to you again, for the mere act of writing your name seems to fetch up the most exquisite pain in my heart. Yet how could I not, knowing you are so close after the long years when we were lost to each other? I cannot bear to deny myself this one frail connection, nor to hinder my imagination when it produces such tender pictures of the recipient of this letter as he reads the words I have penned with such deep emotion . . . Tho' I cannot have the joy of receiving an answer directly from you and have requested Miss Swann and Mrs Greenwood to forbear mentioning your name in their letters (lest the man I must call husband forbids me even the one small privilege he presently allows, of writing to these old, dear friends) I still have a strong sense – especially in Miss Swann's detailed and lively correspondence – of what you may be about . . . I know for certain you must be an eager participant in the musical entertainments you have of an evening and scarce a day passes when I do not glance at the clock at what I know to be that particular hour of recreation at Furze House and imagine myself there in the parlour. Such dreams are my only happiness, prisoner that I am in this miserable marriage. I cling to them, as I cling to the memory of the promises we renewed in that too brief time we snatched alone. The words you spoke then continue to warm my poor, unhappy spirit. I live for the day when I shall hear you say them to me again . . .

Miss Swann was advancing with an armful of folded clothes. Hastily I thrust the letters out of sight and stood up to fetch the last few books, Miss Swann looking up sharply as I let one drop to the floor. Guilt brought heat to my cheeks. It was not only shame that turned me clumsy but a kind of indignation on Kit's behalf. I knew I should not harbour such feelings towards the person who had directed our escape to Furze House but the memory of how her letters had always managed to cast Kit down into melancholy was strong. If all the letters had the same self-indulgent tone as this one it was no wonder poor Kit had been upset. But was that, perhaps, the intention? Did Caroline Loveridge hold Kit in part responsible for the situation in which she now found herself . . . grudging him the freedom she could never have and determining regularly to prod his conscience by means of these soulful and sentimental outpourings which he had no way of answering? If that were the case, I wondered what her true feelings were when she had learned of his abduction. Of course, to Miss Swann she had expressed her deep regret and sadness but did some other, less noble, sentiment stir in that sharp mind? A certain vengeful satisfaction, perhaps, that Kit's liberty had been as drastically curtailed as her own.

Miss Swann had chanced telling Caroline directly the misfortune that had overtaken her cousin. 'I cannot see that her husband could take objection to the relaying of these unhappy tidings. I have searched my conscience and I cannot see any other course open to me.' When Mrs Loveridge's answer came Miss Swann shook her head and sighed. 'She has taken it hard, poor child. The pity is she has no one save ourselves to whom she may pour out her grief.'

Mrs Greenwood patted her hand and said, softly, 'There, there, Tryphena. We have done our best for both of them. We can do no more. And at least her ogre of a husband has not forbidden her to communicate with us as we feared he might.'

So letters continued to be exchanged. Perhaps that was because Caroline Loveridge still had the management of the 'ogre' well in hand, for all that she painted an appealing picture of herself as a submissive, helpless victim. Miss Swann and Mrs Greenwood seemed quite unaware of this contradiction in her nature. Kit had been too. I seemed to be the only one who had glimpsed a different side to Caroline Loveridge. Had I been mistaken? My acquaintance with her had been brief. Yet something in me had responded instinctively to that clever, manipulative streak in her character. Something that stood back and remained cool in its assessment. Certainly I could not condemn her for seizing what control and profit she could from her situation. And I could do nothing but applaud the small improvements she was already achieving for the Crossbank apprentices, not least a slightly more generous and palatable diet and regular inspection and treatment of their injuries and ailments. To win even these little victories would have required all the cunning argument of which she was capable. There was no profit in what Mr Loveridge and the Hatchers regarded as 'coddling'. Profit was king and all at Crossbank were subject to his harsh rule. Anyone who set themselves to alleviate the lot of apprentices forced to suffer under the yoke of this implacable sovereign needed to be brave and clever and resolute. All of which qualities I was sure Caroline Loveridge possessed in abundance.

And yet . . .

I lay in bed on the night I had read her letter to Kit and wondered why I could not entirely like her, as the others did. But no answer came out of the lavender-scented darkness. Then, hunching over into the warmth of Biddie's back, I drowsily wondered what promises she had exacted from Kit while he had been at Crossbank Grange. I should not find out now. Nor, I thought guiltily, had I any right to know. Which thought led me on to wondering where Kit was and how he fared and, as so often had happened since he had gone, his was the last face I saw before sleep claimed me.

That winter I sank into the busy, orderly routine of Furze House as though into a comfortable armchair. It was a continual wonder to me that my appetite for learning was seen to be – by Miss Swann at least – highly commendable and something to encourage. She herself subscribed to the lending library and to the Exeter newspaper, taking pleasure in keeping herself informed of affairs and opinions in the wider world and relaying them for the benefit of her pupils. Miss Swann's lessons were a joy. She had the gift of great patience with the slowest girls while managing to fire the livelier ones with her own enthusiasm for knowledge. She encouraged questions, she opened our eyes to the enduring splendour of fine prose and poetry and to vistas past and present. With her we tramped with the Roman legions to the remote outposts of Britain, followed Hannibal across the Alps, travelled the silk routes to places with magical names . . . For someone who had never been further than thirty miles from Dawlish her ability to bring to life these distant places was extraordinary. As I came to know her better I realised that her stern and formal manner masked a profound dedication to her work as a teacher. She saw the improvement of our minds almost as a crusade, though all too often her efforts were unrewarded. Many of the girls – and their mamas – saw little advantage in learning more than was absolutely necessary of academic subjects when the drawing-room skills of artifice and amusement – as taught by Mrs Greenwood – would be far more useful in the necessary business of luring some young man into marriage.

By the spring it was perfectly clear that my abilities were not of the kind likely to endear me to Mrs Greenwood. However I tried, I could not make my embroidery stitches other than lumpy and uneven. Even the plain household sewing I was put to looked rough and coarse beside Biddie's increasingly neat work. As to drawing lessons, I grew to detest that stuffed pheasant. I am certain that it loathed me in return. Every time it was reverently removed from its glass case by Mrs Greenwood in order to enhance a still-life arrangement, I thought its eye grew more glassy and malevolent at the prospect that I should be encouraged to sketch its likeness.

'Really, Miranda, your efforts are quite pitiful,' Mrs Greenwood would say sharply, 'I find it impossible to understand how you have managed to turn a handsome bird into something resembling a feather duster. You clearly paid no attention to my talk on form and perspective. But then,' this with a deep sigh and eyes upraised as though expecting confirmation of her remarks to appear on the ceiling, 'your head must be so overloaded with facts and figures that there can be little room for serious study of the gentler arts more suitable to the feminine character. Embroidery, shellwork, découpage, the rudiments of playing the forte-piano . . . Whatever I do to assist you, you remain clumsy beyond belief.'

'Miranda is making excellent progress in her other work,' Miss Swann would reply mildly. 'It is not given to any of us to excel in all subjects.'

'Ah, yes, Tryphena, but it is the *importance* of these feminine arts that Miranda fails to understand. Do not forget it is Caroline's wish that Bridget and Miranda should eventually be found some occupation of a gentler nature than that to which they have been accustomed. The dear girl is quite adamant on that point, though I think she may not fully understand that one cannot make a silk purse out of a sow's ear.'

'Come, come, Harriet, that is unfair. Look at the improvement so far. Why, one would be hard put to remember the sad waifs that they were when they arrived.'

'*Physically*, my dear, of course, or it would reflect most badly on the management of our establishment. Bridget's looks have truly improved, though I have to say that Miranda shows an unfavourable tendency to grow lanky rather than plump.' This with an accusing glance in my direction as though I had grown taller on purpose to spite her. 'But as I was saying when you interrupted me, should either girl wish to advance herself in the matter of becoming a governess or companion to some invalid or elderly person, where she might find a home as well as making herself useful, then she must be prepared to cultivate the qualities necessary to these positions of trust. The womanly attributes of modesty and gracefulness, good manners, an ability to converse pleasantly when called upon to do so, skill in the gentler arts to which a woman's natural inclination and weaker constitution are suited . . . I am afraid I see little, yet, to encourage me that either Bridget or Miranda will attain these desirable attributes. Bridget clumps about the house like a hoyden and I have caught her more than once indulging in unseemly romps with the younger children or giggling in some corner with Flossie.'

Her flared nostrils and look of disdain managed to convey the impression that in striking up a friendship with the housemaid, Biddie had found her true level. 'As to Miranda, this adherence to inappropriate studies will surely lead to the sorry state of being branded a blue stocking if she is not checked. And what genteel household would wish to employ her then? None! Young persons and delicate invalids could not be trusted to the care of one who might have an untoward influence.'

Mrs Greenwood returned to this theme on many occasions. Miss Swann for her part would answer firmly, 'A thirst for knowledge should always be quenched.' Or, 'The world would be a poorer place if we were all cast in the same mould.' And serenely continue to ignore her friend's importunings. Which was a great relief to me. I could not have borne to have something so wonderful snatched away before I had scarcely begun.

The seasons changed. A moist and windy spring gave way to the soft, mild days of early-summer. Trees burgeoned with a new, leafy growth. Deep grassy banks bloomed with colour . . . creamy swathes of primroses, arcs of bluebells, pink and white campion, the sunny yellows of cowslips and dandelion . . . all thrusting with fresh life as birds nested and fledged their young in the dense tangle of thorn, elder and holly above. Everything about us was familiar to me now. Each hedge and field gate on the walk over Lea Mount and down into Dawlish, the rolling vistas of field and hedge and sea. I knew the names of the coves and headlands . . . the curious red sandstone outcrop named the Parson and Clerk, Horse Cove, Gentleman's Cove (where we were strictly forbidden to wander lest we chance upon some male person attired for bathing, or worse still in a state of nudity), Langstone Rock, the scrubby, sandy spit of land that was the Warren.

I seized any chance to be outdoors as the days lengthened, always quick to volunteer if there was an errand to run or joining Miss Swann in an hour's hoeing or weeding in the garden which she cultivated virtually single-handed save for the occasional days put in by a crusty old man from Hollacombe who had once been gardening boy at Furze House when Miss Swann's parents had been alive. I adored the rambles when all the school was taken out to wander the secret, winding little paths along the cliffs, gathering botanical specimens. Or when we walked along the beach at low water, examining the sea creatures darting about in the salty pools left by the tide and returning with a bounty of shells and pretty pebbles and pieces of driftwood that would later be used to adorn a trinket box or contrive into a picture.

After the years of confinement behind grim stone walls, this was freedom indeed. Even Biddie conceded that. Like Mrs Greenwood, outdoor exercise did not rate high on her list of pleasurable activities unless it was a stroll of a Sunday evening along the pleasant gravel walk set above Dawlish beach. There she could admire the latest fashions displayed by the leisured classes who promenaded like elegant, self-assured butterflies among the more soberly dressed – or downright ragged – lesser mortals. It was also a golden opportunity for her to exchange flirtatious glances behind Mrs Greenwood's back with the young bloods who also sauntered there.

'Did you see that tall gentleman in the green cutaway?' she would giggle later. 'He'd have spoke – spoken – if we'd been alone.' Or it would be the fine soldier. Or the handsome fishing lad lounging alongside the boat drawn up on the sand. 'And his friend,' she would never fail to add kindly. 'He looked straight at you. Proper admiring, he was.' Which was patently untrue, though I appreciated her attempts not to let me feel left out. I was glad that I attracted little attention. The mirror reassured me that the quietly dressed girl with the solemn hazel eyes and black hair scooped back into a severe knot was far too plain and ordinary for anyone to take much notice of – leave alone be worth a second glance. But fear of discovery still rose up to haunt me from time to time. I did not care to give it any encouragement by making myself anything other than self-effacing and commonplace.

So I was perfectly content to remain invisible beside Biddie, a mere backdrop against which her prettiness glowed with extra sparkle. I found it hard not to be dazzled myself, sometimes. The starveling child was transformed. No one looking at her could possibly take her now for a rag-tag runaway. Like any flower that has wilted in sunless, sour earth and then is transplanted into rich soil and tended with care, she had responded by a spectacular blossoming.

Early that June, though she did not know the exact day, Biddie turned sixteen and now it was possible to see what Mrs Turpin's professional eye had glimpsed in the grimy waif. She was, physically, suddenly a young woman, with round, high breasts and smooth limbs and a cascade of turbulent red hair that she spent far too much time curling and pinning in order to find some new, more fetching style. Her face was still pale though it was no longer the ashen grey of undernourishment and neglect but creamy-white, faintly flushed with healthy pink across the cheekbones and the full shapely mouth. But there was something else about her that drew – and held – masculine attention. Some quality in her walk that set the modest dark print gown which was her Sunday best swirling into the sensual movement of a far richer material. It was to do with the teasing dip of her lashes over her violet-blue eyes, the turn of her neck, so white and young and firm against the glossy tendrils of red hair that constantly escaped from under her plain straw bonnet.

Miss Swann often remarked it a pity that Caroline could not see for herself how much we were both improved. I thought it as well she could not. She was far too sharp, far too worldly. She would not miss the effect Biddie had on men. Neither age, nor class, nor state of health, made any difference. The wizened face of a decrepit old rake being wheeled along in a bath chair would turn towards her and brighten, as though he forgot the pain of the gout in his foot and the rheumatics that twisted his joints and was once again a virile, prospecting youth. The respectable, God-fearing tradesman would allow his glance to linger far longer than was properly polite, then quicken his pace, speaking irritably to the faded wife clinging to his arm as if questioning why she should continue to appear so *ordinary* when the makings of her new gown had cost him the best part of three guineas.

That look was always the same. Admiration, desire, lust . . . all combined in a sort of predatory hunger.

And well Biddie knew it, and revelled in this new-found power.

I smiled to myself. If Caroline could see her she would soon realise what I already knew: that any hope of turning Biddie into some kind of docile, biddable upper servant was rapidly declining with every month that passed. Biddie was becoming her own person. A person who was instinctively taking what she needed from the education Furze House offered and carelessly rejecting the rest. Who had already eased much of the coarse Crossbank dialect from her speech, refined her manners, had a steadily improving skill with a needle so that a practical cotton petticoat could be prettified with embroidered flowers, a plain dress tightened here, loosened there, to give it a more subtly elegant shape. Who had learned from Mrs Greenwood to play a genteel hand of whist, and watched the other girls in order to model herself on the one who struck the most graceful attitude whilst engaged in the chore of sketching a still life. She had even practised her drawing so that she had achieved a passable likeness of the wretched pheasant!

All because she had caught a glimpse of a better life. Her romanticised view of Mrs Turpin's girls, so lively and prettily dressed and carefree, was now reinforced by what she saw about her in Dawlish. There were poor people enough, to be sure, but she chose to ignore them. There were too many of the other sort to occupy her attention . . . and her dreams.

They came like migrating swallows and swifts on the soft warm winds. To spend a week, a month, a summer, in the mild and beneficial air of this charming resort. Gentry who had discovered that the coastline of southern Devon was markedly similar to the Mediterranean coast of France – now regrettably denied to them by the French war – and without having to undergo the many hazards of journeying on the Continent. Of course, the chilly waters of the Channel could be braved by the most hardy or the most desperate who felt they could only improve their health by total immersion in the sea, but there were perfectly adequate Public Baths where one might dip into agreeably warmed seawater without the danger of being buffeted by waves or inadvertently encountering some horrid sea-creature. Then there were the picturesque walks, the drives that might be taken to view the splendid houses of the nobility; the entertainments at the assembly rooms to which one might subscribe and much good company available for evenings of cards and dancing in the pleasant, newly built house one had rented. And all this might be found for a very modest expenditure. Why, a person might live a whole year in Devon for £400 compared, say, to Brighton or London where one would pay £600 at the very least for inferior lodgings and services.

Biddie's day-dreams took her into this rich, leisured circle. The reality was so close. She observed it every day. It was almost tangible; certainly, she persuaded herself, obtainable. The move from Crossbank to Furze House had been a far larger, far more difficult step than Furze House to the world of this fashionable company to which she would surely one day gain admittance? She must be ready for the opportunity when it came. Seize the chance. Make sure she was properly schooled in all the accomplishments necessary to be a proper lady who must pleasantly fill the idle hours of every idle day.

If the way in which this opportunity would present itself was vague and formless, other scenes presented themselves in a more precise manner. There would be an elegant drawing room into which a handsome young man would enter and halt in amazement, stricken instantly by Cupid's arrow as he clapped eyes on Biddie, seated gracefully, as she had practised, at her embroidery or at her drawing board. Or it would be at a ball and the same handsome gentleman would sweep her off her feet, refusing to allow her to dance with any other.

And after that? Happiness. Of course. For ever . . . was not that the way of dreams?

Ah, dreams. So sweet. And so dangerously deceptive.

But who was I to pour scorn on Biddie's imaginings, when my own would scarcely stand the scrutiny of cold logic?

And when August came and I had news, at last, of Theophilus Crowe it renewed my faith in my own particular dream and my determination to achieve it.

But before that there was other news too. From an unexpected source.

Billy Rossiter delivered the letter to me when I called at his house, the tiny thatched cottage huddled in a narrow alley not far from St Gregory's. Throughout the summer Miss Swann regularly sent to the Rossiters spare produce from the Furze House garden. I was often despatched with it, which was the greatest of pleasures to me. The Rossiters scarcely had two ha'pennies to call their own and their short married life had been dogged by misfortune, not least the constant worry over the baby which was a puny ailing little thing, but there was such a depth of happiness in the cramped little cottage that I could well understand why Kit had liked to spend so much time with his friend.

No one would have noticed Billy and his wife Emma in a crowd. Both undersized, wiry people of no distinction at all. Billy sandy-haired and freckle-faced. Emma mousy and shy. Yet between them was a tenderness and delight in each other that anyone would have been blind not to notice. And, as though the love they shared was too much to contain, it seemed to overflow and encompass every visitor. Even today when Billy looked washed out with fatigue, his face lit to a broad beam of welcome as I opened the front door and stepped down to the roughly flagged floor of the dark kitchen, and Emma, cutting up a loaf at the table, cried cheerfully, 'There, what did I tell 'ee, Billy! I knew in my bones we'd have the pleasure of company this afternoon. Now, young May, don't get under Miss Brehault's feet. Draw the stool out for 'er. That's a good girl. You'm just in time, maid. My Billy's just back from travellin' an' we'm about to 'ave a bite to eat.'

I sat on the opposite side of the hearth to Billy and drew May the toddler to my side where she proceeded to delve excitedly among the plump pods of peas and the two round cabbages in my basket in search of the special little treat she would find there. Something, usually, from the Furze House kitchen – a gingerbread man, perhaps, or a specially iced bun that fat, good-natured Mrs Hawkins had made – but today it was a doll that I had fashioned from a wooden peg. Remembering the ones Meg had made for me so long ago, I had inked in its features, pasted strands of yellow wool to its wooden pate for hair and covered up the rest of the peg with a scrap of old sheeting gathered into a kind of smock at the neck. There was certainly no criticism here of my cobbled stitching. May squealed with delight and rushed to show it to her father.

''Tis 'andsome,' he said admiringly.

I laughed. 'Scarcely that, but it is as far as my creative talents stretch, I'm afraid.'

''Twas kindly meant and it gives the little maid pleasure,' Billy said stoutly. 'That counts as 'andsome to me.'

'I wish I had your skill,' I said, picking up the piece of wood that lay on the shelf beside me. A half-carved rabbit was already emerging from the dry grey slab of driftwood. 'Even unfinished it's beautiful.'

'I could wish more folks thought so,' Emma said with a heartfelt sigh. 'Billy's brother sold not a one last time he was to market. Made a shillin' or two every time afore that, which we was powerful glad of and made me hopeful as we might build up a steady trade.'

'Don't matter now, my lover,' Billy said comfortably. 'Not

now I'm back on my two legs and good reg'lar work in prospect.'

'Reg'lar work? Humph.' Emma frowned at the gooseberry jam she was spreading generously on to bread. 'Reg'lar, mebbe. Good it's not. An' all this travellin' don't do that leg o' yourn a mite o' good.'

'Now, now,' Billy said. 'I'm managin'.' He winked at me. 'Listen to 'er. Away from 'ome for a week or so and I find her's turned into a proper nag.'

My answering smile felt strained. I understood Emma's anxiety. Billy's leg was unlikely to improve any further. His foot was twisted and useless and he was often in pain from an ulcer that had formed above his ankle. His sea-going days were over. Not, however, his involvement with smuggling, to his wife's distress.

I had learned of it on one of my errands to the cottage in the spring. I had found little May playing with her friends in the dust of the street outside and inside her mother cuddling the crying baby and weeping herself. She had begun at first to make apologies . . . she was tired because the baby had been fretful for nights on end and she was worried because Billy had just left, having been persuaded by Captain Luscombe to take on work he wasn't fit to do and it meant he'd be on the road for days at a time and he'd come back with his leg in a worse state than ever . . .

It was more than that, I could tell. But I quietly took the baby from her and jogged him against my shoulder until his fretful crying stopped. And presently when Emma had wiped her eyes on her apron and straightened her shoulders she said, 'That's what upsets me, to be sure.' Her eyes, filled with desperation, fixed on mine. 'For the rest . . . oh, 'tis hard when it worries away inside like a maggot and I can't speak of it to anyone. Billy won't 'ave me say a word, he'm that glad of earnin' again. As for they round here, they'm too beholden in one way or t'other to the Cap'n. In his pocket too many of 'em. But Master Kit, 'e told us you knew of . . . of what he was about . . . of a moonless night.'

'Ah,' I said. 'When you mentioned Captain Luscombe, I wondered. Billy's on . . . delivery business? Then I can see why you're worried. I would be in your shoes, though Kit seemed to think it was some sort of sport.'

'My Billy, too!' she put in fiercely. 'An' after all he suffered and goes on sufferin' on account o' that last trip to Alderney for the Cap'ns cargo o' brandy and tobacco . . . and not the first, by a long chalk. Men killed and maimed escapin' the Revenue men. Or caught and put to rot in prison. Or drowned in some chase at sea like my own pa when I was no bigger'n' my May. And who does the sufferin' then, eh? They poor wives and babes as must struggle to keep out o' the poorhouse while the likes o' the Cap'n stay well out o' trouble, goes on makin' his guineas, an' gives not a tinker's cuss for any of they.'

So it came out, all her long-held hatred and fear of the trade that had taken her father and reduced her mother to penury, and which now had her husband in its grip.

Other things, too, including why Kit had first become embroiled in the smuggling trade.

''Twas for us, Miss Miranda,' Emma admitted. 'When my Billy was so bad and me that desperate, I was fair out o' my mind wi' fear of losin' him. With no wage comin' in, everythin' we'd put by was gone an' I didn't know which way to turn. Master Kit – he did many a small kindness for us – was fetching in water from the brook one morning when the Cap'n called . . . 'im all smarmy like as usual. Come to 'elp us out, that was 'is tale, smilin' like 'e do, as though butter wouldn't melt. Folk bein' sorry when they 'eard of Billy's trouble had given 'im money, he says. He brung it for us, but there was no more'n two or three shillin's, for he'd kept most back for the rent we was owin' an' likely to go on doin'. To save us the worry of bein' in debt, he says, as though 'e ever give heed to anythin' but makin' money for hisself . . .'

'Captain Luscombe is your landlord?'

'Owns a good few o' the poorer sort of places in the town – and he'm keener on gatherin' his rents than spendin' on repairs, that's for sure. Howsomever, that was when Master Kit spoke up, sayin' a bit sarky-like that the good people who'd given money would be proper delighted to know of the Cap'n's thoughtfulness about the rent.' Emma smiled for the first time. 'Give the Cap'n a bit of a turn, 'earin' him speak. Taken Master Kit wi' a bucket in either 'and and 'is coat off, to be a common lad, not a gentleman. Set the Cap'n blustering I can tell 'ee. So after a bit more talkin', wi' the Cap'n all smiles and Master Kit all mannerly but proper cool, the upshot was Kit said straight out he'd heard the Cap'n was short of a man to take a delivery north an' 'e'd be willin' to do it, 'aving business up there himself. Wi' my Billy givin' him a good character the Cap'n no more than hummed and haahed a bit before 'e agreed. An' afterwards Master Kit said 'e didn't want none o' what the Cap'n would pay 'im for he'd intended goin' north anyway. He wanted us to 'ave it, to keep us goin'.' Her voice faltered. 'Only nothin' went right after that, as 'ee knows, Miss Miranda.'

I sighed. 'No, indeed. Poor Kit. The money stolen . . . ending in debt to Captain Luscombe . . .'

'Played right into his hands. As though the money was cursed.' She gave a wail of anguish. 'Oh, I've wished and wished they'd not met that day. Look where it's all ended, wi' poor Master Kit taken off heaven knows where.'

'We can hardly lay that at Captain Luscombe's door.'

'Can't we?' She rounded on me fiercely. 'I'd bet a pound to a penny they press men didn't fetch up where they did by accident. That's 'is way. He'm a devil to any that crosses him. 'Tis powerful strange how misfortune comes on those the Cap'n 'as a down on, though it's another matter to prove it.' Her face crumpled again and tears slid down her cheeks. 'I 'ad so hoped my Billy might get decent work but now he's in the Cap'n's pay again an' I don't know where it'll all end . . .'

The shock of learning that Kit's abduction might have been deliberately arranged had long since settled to a sadness that haunted me when my thoughts were idle or when I saw the stout, smiling Captain, high-nosed wife on his arm, bowing to left and right as he waddled to the pew he still maintained at St Gregory's though he now lived at Teignmouth. At first glance it was hard to believe that so affable a gentleman, who attended devoutly to the service and boomed out the Amens in ringing tones, could be the villain he was painted. But once I had been close enough to see him as he spoke to one of the ragged boys who hung about the churchyard gates in the hope of a copper for minding a horse. I could not hear what was said, but I had seen the boy shrink back as though he had been struck and, for a second or two, there was some alteration in Captain Luscombe's smile that shifted it from affability to something very cold and unpleasant indeed.

I remembered that now as I looked at Emma's worried face, and hoped to heaven that Billy would never give the Captain cause for complaint. But then, I reassured myself, good-natured Billy was the last person to incur anybody's wrath. I had never heard one bad word said of him.

'I almost was forgettin',' he said suddenly, dipping into his waistcoat pocket. 'I 'as a letter for 'ee, Miss Miranda. From a young lady o' your acquaintance. Sharp-tongued wench,' he said, grinning. 'Swore 'er'd cut me gizzard out wi' her embroidery scissors if I breathed a word to a soul that I was carrying it.'

I might have known. It was from Violet Briggs.

Violet's note did little more than briefly relate events at The Plough in the intervening months – Maud still there, Dinah gone off to Manchester to marry a coachman, Mrs Turpin fallen prey to an ague in the winter that had left her wheezy and breathless and increasingly reliant on Violet. The initial excitement of receiving the letter was soon tempered by an uprush of memories that I had sooner have left undisturbed, especially as the last lines exhorted me to destroy the letter and on no account to write back.

I should not like Long Noses to come upon what is not their

Business. The Bumpkin who fetches this gives me word of you to satisfy my Curiosity and of his Musical Friend, which is Tragical indeed . . .

I trusted Violet. I trusted Billy, though when I had first known he might be travelling to Derbyshire, I had been kept awake at night wondering how much Kit had told him of our circumstances. The gnawing possibility that out of ignorance – innocence – he might speak of us to someone alert to gain himself a reward for returning two runaway apprentices forced me brace myself to speak. But when I had begun, haltingly, to explain he had firmly cut me short.

'Don't 'ee fret, maid. Master Kit, 'e told me somethin' of the whys and wherefores. I'll not be talkin' out o' turn . . . 'specially to the likes o' Cap'n Luscombe's kin.' He had bestowed his good-natured beam on me. 'Every barrel 'as its rotten apples, to be sure. But there was good 'uns there, too, as I recollect. One in particler. Give 'ee good 'elp, Master Kit said. If 'ee has a message, I'll gladly pass it on. Private-like, to be sure.'

'No . . . yes.' I hesitated. What harm in it? 'If you could thank her for what she did . . . she may like to know we are well and settled. Her name is Violet, Miss Violet Briggs.'

But I remained uneasy about any connection to Derbyshire. And Violet's unexpected letter jolted me. Like someone tweaking an invisible cord bound to my ankles that made me falter and look back over my shoulder instead of leaving me loose to continue moving ahead at a steady pace. Even on this day of August heat, chilly resonances haunted me as I remembered the dark hills and the harsh stone walls of the place that had been my prison.

I walked slowly down the beach reading Violet's letter then, glad to obey her instructions, I tore it to tiny scraps and tossed it into the sea where the pieces slowly scattered on the limpid, easy waves of a summer's tide.

From time to time throughout the year Miss Swann made

an expedition to the market town of Newton Abbot, some ten miles or so distant, and Biddie and I took it in turns to accompany her.

Mrs Greenwood never went on these expeditions. As a young woman, she said, she had once been nearly felled by the flying hooves of a cow run mad from the cattle market to cause havoc among overturned stalls and panic-stricken people. She had refused ever since to revisit the town. 'An uncouth place,' she was wont to say. 'Especially on market day when it is full of riff-raff. I cannot at all see why you must undertake such an uncomfortable and hazardous excursion, Tryphena. After all, Dora must surely appreciate that you have more than enough to do here without gallivanting about the country on errands of mercy. And as to shopping in Newton rather than with tradespeople one knows and trusts in Dawlish, I cannot think there is much advantage save in the matter of choice.'

'If I did not go, Harriet, I should be failing in my duty,' Miss Swann would reply mildly, her main excuse for the day out being to call upon the aged woman who had been her nurse as a child then, in order to offset the cost of the fares from Teignmouth, to spend an hour or two searching out bargains in the market and shops. But even on my first trip with her to Newton Abbot I could sense it meant more to Miss Swann than that. It was an adventure. A day when she could set the routine of Furze House behind her and, freed of all responsibility, indulge enthusiastically in being part of a wider scene. I caught a glimpse then of a different Miss Swann. Someone younger, more lighthearted. A person who – had there been the opportunity, the time, the money – would have rejoiced in travel for its own sake. Who would have gone boldly to seek out new sights, new cities . . . new countries. A person to whom the discomforts and hazards of the journey would have added excitement and thrills rather than distress, and every bend in the road promised a new discovery, a new challenge. No wonder she managed to imbue history and geography lessons with such vitality. She was living them, that was the simple truth. The frustrated explorer in her character taking as much enjoyment from the accounts of voyages and explorations as her pupils.

So, knowing that any day out with Miss Swann was bound to be enjoyable and interesting, I was more than glad to set out with her at six o'clock on the day after I had received Violet's letter.

We walked first to Teignmouth, under a sky as still and tranquil a blue as the cornflowers that grew among the wheat. There we took the boat up the River Teign to the quay at Newton Abbot, this being the most direct and easiest form of transport to the town. On such a glorious day it was a pleasant experience to be out on the river. Once we were away from the harbour and its ships being loaded with clay brought down the Stover Canal from the claybeds inland, the scene was pastoral on every side as, pushed by the incoming tide, the oars and sails of the ferry carried us swiftly upriver. Miss Swann viewed everything with lively curiosity, pointing out landmarks and launching into anecdotes about her childhood of which she was constantly reminded. Today, the sight of a pair of young girls walking sedately hand in hand along the bank brought a nostalgic tale of her older sister who had died of fever when she was eight years old.

'How different life might have been had she lived. Mama never got over her death and succumbed to an ague herself not long afterwards, the house was very sombre after that . . . Ah, but it was completely revitalised when we opened the school and Harriet took the place of the dear sister that I had lost . . .'

Bit by bit – from scraps of Flossie's gossip, from whisperings among the day girls and from Miss Swann's freer-than-usual conversation on these days out – I had pieced together the history of Miss Swann and Mrs Greenwood.

The one the plain, retiring daughter born to middle-aged parents who had devoted her life to their comfort until they died when she was left alone with little more than a too-large house and garden which she loved but would have to sell because her papa's money had gone on doctor's bills and invalid comforts. The other, the too-pretty, too-frivolous only child of a man who, after his wife's death, had found hope and comfort in the strict tenets of an evangelical religious sect. He had seen salvation for his seventeen-year-old daughter (who was inclined to tease him for his newly awakened fervour and was reluctant to cast off the mantle of the established church in which she had been raised) in marriage to an Exmouth man, a member of the same congregation, under whose pious influence the girl would soon learn respectful and responsible habits. Which, to her father's gratification, she did. The absent-minded fondness he had for the child occasionally prodded his conscience into wondering why she had become so thin and wan during this process of reformation, but not for long. There were too many drunken, fornicating sinners in the neighbourhood needing his attention and his prayers. The Lord had called him to preach to these lost souls and it was a call he must follow. Harriet was another man's responsibility now.

That man wore his religion like a weighty burden on his back and could always find a Bible text to justify the harsh authority he had wielded over his wives, the first of whom had escaped by falling from an upstairs window when, it was said, she was walking in her sleep. The second had slipped away during one of her frequent miscarriages and it was rumoured that her face in death wore a contented smile, as it certainly never had done in life. The third wife, Harriet, survived for thirteen years. This was mainly due to her youth, her barrenness and a streak of wilfulness that Mr Greenwood would have been galled to know he had never quite managed to eradicate. Harriet had suffered and waited. Eventually her patience was rewarded. Her husband was felled by a morbid bladder complaint that carried him off within a week of its onset.

The surprisingly substantial inheritance that came to Harriet was some compensation for the years when she had been forced to account for every farthing – with the cold and spiteful wrath of Mr Greenwood likely to descend upon her if she could not. But there was a price for survival which had nothing to do with money. Year by slow year the gaiety, the liveliness, the trust, had been ground out of Harriet Greenwood to be replaced by far more cynical emotions. So when she sat in the office of the lawyer and listened to him advise on ways to invest this money, she felt not relief or gratitude but suspicion, particularly when he assured her that her affairs would be secure in his hands . . . All that was needed was the trifling matter of her signature on these documents and she need no longer trouble her pretty head with complicated financial and legal arrangements which were better left in more capable hands.

He was never to realise that it was the patronising air he always assumed towards female clients that caused her to rise hurriedly to her feet and leave the office, papers unsigned. Mrs Greenwood no longer wished to be beholden to gentlemen who were so very definite in the matter of knowing what was best for her. Experience had taught her that any advantage to be gained was unlikely to be hers. Greatly agitated, she returned to the comfortless house that she had never been able to regard as home and, in order to calm herself, she answered a letter of condolence on her bereavement from Tryphena Swann, whom she remembered as being so sensible and straightforward when they were pupils under the same Dawlish music master and whom, out of nostalgia for those innocent days, she now ventured to suggest might care to visit her in Exmouth.

So the idea of a school was born out of mutual need. An inheritance was satisfactorily invested with the minimum of interference from lawyers, and a much-loved home preserved.

'Such a happy chance, do you not think, Miranda, that we were able to renew our friendship after so long a separation?' Miss Swann said as we clutched our bonnet strings against the tug of the breeze. 'Both of us so worried, not knowing which way to turn – I had been sleepless for weeks – and then the whole matter resolved swiftly and comfortably in the course of one afternoon. I tell you, it seemed like a miracle to me then . . . and, in truth, it still does when I look back over the many contented years we have been blessed with since. Strange, how things turn out, is it not?'

Strange, indeed, the twists of fate as I had cause, myself, to ponder that very afternoon.

The day took its usual pleasant course. We first went to Newton Bushel to call upon Miss Swann's old nurse, Dora. An ancient twig of a woman, near blind now and content to spend her days drowsing in the chimney corner of her granddaughter's cottage. We thankfully unloaded our baskets here, the daughter's eyes glinting as we set on the scrubbed table the brace of whiting, the rich fruit cake, the dozen eggs, the fat bunch of roses and marigolds, a packet of tea, the last pound or two of the Furze House late raspberries . . . for there was little to spare for luxuries from her husband's wage as a jobbing carpenter with granny to feed as well as the ever-growing brood of children.

We sat there for a while and drank tea made with two careful spoonsful out of the packet of new leaves and poured into the best china teacups that were reached down reverently from the topmost shelf of the dresser, and ate a slice of bread and butter. Duty done, we walked briskly in the direction of St Leonard's church and the market.

The business of finding breadths of good quality wool for winter gowns for Biddie and me at the cheapest possible price took up a pleasurable hour or so. Biddie had begged me to persuade Miss Swann away from dull colours. 'Oh, I wish it was my turn to go with her to Newton,' she'd wailed. 'This'll be the first proper new gown I've had in me life and I won't have any say in the choosing of it.'

'I'll do my best, but the material will have to be serviceable,' I pointed out. 'We won't be allowed anything too light or too fancy.'

'But you've got to try, Mirrie! Oh, say that you will! Even if it don't – doesn't – trouble you what you wear on your back so long as you're decent, think of me! Please don't let it be anything mucky brown or dingy grey.'

Biddie was wrong in one particular. I, too, found myself yearning for the prettiest of the materials . . . ivory corded silk, yellow muslin patterned with tiny green leaves, rich red velvet, sumptuous silver brocade. But as these wistful longings stirred, I laughed them away. Even if I had the money to buy such showy materials and lost, entirely, the fear of standing out and being recognised as a runaway apprentice, my indifferent looks and skinny figure would scarcely do them justice. Unlike Biddie, whom I should dearly have liked to indulge. But there was no hope of that so I set my mind to the next best course, of coaxing Miss Swann into choosing the sturdy merino in a shade other than her favourite grey. I persuaded her eventually towards a gentle mossy green, helped by a reduction in price due to the cloth being the last of the bale. Heartened by this bargain, Miss Swann decided that I might choose some velvet ribbon for trimming. For myself I chose a darker, toning shade of green and for Biddie a buttermilk cream that I thought very fetching and hoped that she would, too.

Our baskets grew heavy as we continued our slow perambulation and gathered all the other items on Miss Swann's list. As always when I was in the market I remembered Kit's dreadful experience in Exeter when a thief in the crowd had stolen his purse. Though I carried no money, I guarded my basket well and kept a careful eye on anyone who jostled past us. But it was the breeze that proved the villain that day. Though it was warm and clear still, the breeze grew quite strong that afternoon. One particularly lively gust whirled stinging dust into my eyes. Quite painfully blinded I stumbled against Miss Swann, nearly unbalancing her and sending some of the contents of my basket plummeting to the ground.

I felt the basket taken from me as I groped for my handkerchief and mopped at my streaming eyes.

'Nothing lost, save for a few bilberries spilled out of the

punnet,' a young man's voice said, cheerfully. 'There . . . that's the last packet.'

'Thank you,' Miss Swann said. 'Most kind. Miranda dear, are you recovered? So very painful when one gets grit in one's eyes.'

'Give your nose a good blow,' the young man advised cheerfully. 'That'll shift 'en.'

I did as I was bid, then mopped gingerly at the copious tears that the dust had caused.

'I think . . . yes, I can see again.' The swimmy outline of a sun-browned smiling face came into view. When I could properly focus I saw a stocky, brown-haired young man of perhaps twenty wearing a countryman's smock over moleskin breeches. I put away my handkerchief and made to take my basket from him. He did not immediately let it go, his broad grin fading to be replaced by a frown. His blue eyes regarded me with a puzzling intensity.

'Begging your pardon, miss,' he began, 'but could I ask . . .?'

'Thank you, young man,' Miss Swann interrupted, her large nose twitching as though scenting forwardness on his part. 'Take this for your pains. Come, Miranda, we still have a deal to do.'

But he would not let go of the basket to take the coins Miss Swann offered and said, with dignity, still not taking his eyes off me, 'Ma'am, I'd not take money for what's only a civil courtesy. And I beg no more than a minute of your time. All I want to ask . . . you see, it's not a common name, Miranda, and I knew someone of that name once. It seems to me you've a look, miss, of that little one as she'd be growed up – of her ma as I remember her. And I've wondered often what happened when she was taken off . . .' He stopped, a flush of embarrassment on his cheeks. He let go of the basket handle as though it had suddenly grown hot. 'I . . . I'm sorry, miss. I can see you don't know what I'm talking about. You're not the one. You can't be. 'Twas rumoured she was dead long since.' He stepped back, touched his forehead respectfully. That duck of the head, that almost shy glance under his lashes

. . . once so familiar in the leggy boy he had been, recognisable again in this strapping stranger.

'Jed?' My voice was no more than a thread but it stopped him in his tracks. 'Jed Tozer?'

His jaw dropped.

'Then . . . then . . .'

'It is me, Jed.' I gave a laugh that was more of a sob. 'I am Miranda Brehault.'

We talked of everything in the time that we had. Not long, because Jed must collect his horse and cart and be on his way to the farm where he worked. 'Missus'll be waiting on me getting back with news of the prices I got on the weaner pigs. Mrs Tucker that is. Remember Tucker's farm? I was took on there after you left. When master died last year and missus didn't know which way to turn with only a young daughter and no son to inherit, her grew to rely on me.' He chuckled. 'When grandma insisted on me having book-learning at the dame school I thought it a fine waste of time. But it's come in useful, since, I tell 'ee. Keeps the stock books and the accounts as well as ever master did.'

'Dear Meg. Is she . . .?'

'Didn't last no more than a winter once Crowe put her off,' he said with an abrupt shake of his head. 'She was found a place in the almshouse but her heart and mind was broke, I reckon, once you was sent away and she was turned out of Moondance.'

My own heart was near wrenched in two at this stark piece of news. It was a few moments before I could begin to concentrate on what he was telling me about Theophilus Crowe.

As Jed spoke of him his image rose in my mind in the shape of the ominous black bird of my nightmares. Crowe the predator, the destroyer. I felt no surprise when I learned what he had been about in the years since he had left, only a fatalistic sense of sadness.

It was a tale of profligacy and debauchery. Money flung

about wastefully on all that was showy – ornament and furnishings for the house, the felling of many splendid old trees, the uprooting of shrubs to create a new pleasure garden adorned with heathen statues – this apparently for the delectation of a crowd of raucous friends. They descended on Moondance with their painted women like a plague of rainbow flies settling on the rotting carcase of a once-beautiful creature, indulging in dissipated orgies and drunkenness, with men and women cavorting in the moonlit gardens as naked as the statues that stared down blankly from their moonlit plinths. And when the money was used up and most of the flies had buzzed away to seek livelier attractions, Moondance had fallen back to its slow decay. Soon the servants, expensively hired, were put off one by one. Only the pair of foreigners who had arrived with Crowe remained and he shut himself up, more and more, except for occasional jaunts to Plymouth and Bristol and Exeter. To revive his fortunes at the gaming tables, it was said. Though without much success, apparently. Now he was more likely to be glimpsed pacing his gardens and brooding on his lost fortune, with his fierce heathen manservant, who carried a sharp, curved knife in his belt, on hand to dissuade trespassers from disturbing his silent perambulations.

Jed stopped and cleared his throat at this point, casting an embarrassed look at Miss Swann.

''Tis rumour, of course. Can't rightly say that anyone I talked to 'zackly saw any of the goings on. 'Twas always word that was passed on from another. But I think 'tis true he'd like to catch himself a rich bride, save there's no one within miles who'd let a respectable unmarried daughter or sister anywhere near him. He went sniffing round Farmer Davey's eldest girl. But he got short shrift there.' He gave a dry laugh. 'So I reckon his prospects of reviving the fortune 'tis rumoured he got through are pretty remote.'

After Jed had gone, promising to keep an eye out for us when he was next in Newton, the market lost its savour for me. Miss Swann, ever tactful, did not press me with needless conversation or questions, even though much that she had heard was new to her, for I had never cared to impart more than the briefest details of my early life to the ladies. It was only after we arrived back at Teignmouth and began the walk back along the coast road to Furze House that she said, quietly, 'I have no wish to probe into your private thoughts, my dear, but the meeting with your old friend must have revived many memories of times that are lost and gone for ever. Would it help to speak of them?'

In the sweet-smelling summer dusk, with a huge yellow harvest moon rising above the hills to light our path and cast a silvery trail over the dark, restless sea, the words came easily. I told her of my beautiful mother who had eloped with my father and sailed from India, of her untimely death in childbirth, of my free and happy childhood, my father's increasing restlessness, Aunt Hettie's death after he had left for the East Indies and Meg's devotion to me until the day Theophilus Crowe parted us for ever.

'Oh, if only I could have stayed with Meg,' I burst out. 'If we'd been able to keep together she'd never have given up and died. I know she was old and rheumaticky but Moondance had been her home for so long . . . she could still sew and bake. And I'd have scrubbed floors and washed dishes for the chance to stay at my lovely Moondance. He'd never have needed to know I was there.'

'But it did not happen, Miranda,' Miss Swann said firmly. 'That you must face. There is no comfort in dwelling on the might-have-beens and if-onlies. If there is one clear lesson that I have learned throughout my life it is that one must live for the moment and look forward, not back. Remember the good things – the loving faces from the past – but let go of the rest.' Her gloved hand rested momentarily on my sleeve. Her voice softened. 'I do understand your distress, my dear, but you are young and your life is ahead of you with all its possibilities for happiness. Do not let bitterness establish itself in your heart or your vision will be forever clouded with resentment and discontent.'

I tried to think of a tactful way I could answer without telling a falsehood or giving offence. Her advice was undoubtedly sensible and sound but I had no intention of letting go of the hatred I bore Theophilus Crowe. He was cruel and dissolute. He deserved to be despised for the evil he had done and continued to do. Not least for the degredation he had brought to my beloved home. One day, if there was any justice in the world, I would find a way to drive him from Moondance and reclaim it for my own.

Fortunately, before I could blurt out any of this, Miss Swann was distracted by a man and boy approaching us in the dusk. I recognised them as two of Flossie's five brothers.

'It is that dreadful Matthew Parker,' Miss Swann said under her breath. 'No sooner does the poor girl get her wages than one or other of her profligate family is at the door to relieve her of them.' Aloud she said in a cool voice, 'Good evening, Matthew. Good evening, Saul.'

'Evenin', miss,' the elder one said, raising his hat with one hand and scuffing the ear of the younger lad with the other. 'What do 'ee say, boy?'

Saul gaped at us with little comprehension. 'Evenin',' he said after a minute's thought, his hand wavering to his forelock.

Matthew cuffed his ear again.

'Evenin', *miss*.'

'Evenin', miss,' Saul repeated dully.

'That's better. I'll turn 'ee into a gen'l'man yet.' Matthew gave a loud false laugh, inviting us to share the joke. 'See if I don't.'

Miss Swann remained stony-faced. I tried an encouraging smile on Saul, but there was no response. Whatever intellect or natural cunning had been parcelled out to the rest of the Parkers there had been none to spare for this youngest son. Consequently, the poor lad was the scapegoat for his brothers, the butt of what passed for wit among them and the recipient of impatient kicks and blows to make him do as they wished. Whichever brother was sent by their father for Flossie's wages inevitably had Saul in tow. They all knew Saul was Flossie's weak spot. She might well have taken it into her head to argue the matter of ownership of her wages otherwise. We could not, thankfully, look into the mind of any of the Parkers, but we all knew their reasoning. One glimpse of Saul always made Flossie feel suitably guilty. But even without the convenience of an idiot brother, old man Parker would have found some other way to extract the money from her. And perfectly justified he'd be, they all reasoned, with her no more than an uppity female who needed to learn a bit more respect. Too cocky for her own good, that one, thinking she could go off on her own without so much as a by-your-leave. Still, so long as the shillings came in regular, no harm in letting things be for now . . .

Until she had set her sights on Furze House Flossie had protected and cared for this brother as best she could. ''Twas Ma as made me promise to try an' make somethin' of myself,' she'd whispered to Biddie and me once. 'Afore her died, 'er said I owed it to my real pa and I wasn't to let nothin' stand in my way. Pa wasn't really my pa, see – though he don't know that. Ma said my real pa were a proper 'andsome gent, sent down 'ere on account of his cough. Ma said he wanted to marry 'er – which is more'n Pa ever did – but the cough got worse and he was took off to Exeter, where he died.' She wiped her red eyes. 'Trouble is, I feels that guilty 'bout leaving poor Saul. Every time I sees 'en, he'm quieter than ever and he'll never get no better wi' they great lummocks bawlin' at him.'

I could well believe the tale of Flossie's true parentage though I doubted that marriage had ever been a prospect. From the looks of the rest of the rag-tag offspring and the reputation of the Parker womenfolk, I could fancy that the term 'father' was a very loose description. But at least Flossie's mother had had the guts and the sense – or the desperation – to inspire her daughter to better things.

'Matthew's the best of the bunch,' she had once said, with more hope than certainty. 'So I've begged him to help Saul if he can. He says he'll do his best.'

Evidence for this optimistic view was woefully lacking, though by Parker standards I suppose Matthew might have been considered a little less rough than his brothers. Certainly in appearance. There was a touch of the dandy in him, for sure. Tonight there was a glimpse of a red flannel waistcoat under his grey frieze jacket. A red-patterned neckerchief was knotted jauntily under one ear. With his swarthy colouring and thick-set build he looked handsome enough from a distance. Close to, the coarseness in his blunt features and the slyness in his leering smile sat awkwardly with the ingratiating manner he cultivated. Try as he might to disguise it, he was a loutish Parker to the core.

'I was just sayin' to Saul 'ere,' he said, 'how lucky 'tis for our little sister Floss that 'er's set up so cosy. Our pa's fair tickled pink, I tell 'ee, for 'er was always useless at 'ome, with 'er contrary, ungrateful ways. And no amount o' persuasion ever seemed to improve 'er.'

'Then your father must have used the wrong kind of persuasion,' Miss Swann said, coldly, knowing full well that the fist and the boot were the only two methods likely to have been employed. 'We are very satisfied with her progress. She has proved to be a most conscientious and willing worker. You may tell your father that.'

'Oh, I shall, I shall.' He laughed again, showing big square teeth in the moist red gape of his mouth. A gust of beery breath despoiled the sweet air. I wondered how much of Flossie's hard-earned wages had already been squandered at one or other of Dawlish's taverns. 'He'll be real proud. And 'er tells me her be learning her letters now, an' all.' His shifty black eyes looked me up and down. I tightened my shawl about my shoulders, feeling that perhaps the modest print dress was more revealing of my neck and arms than I had thought. ''Tis you we must thank for that, eh, Miss Miranda?'

'I'm pleased to help,' I said shortly.

He wagged one grubby finger backwards and forwards before my face. 'I'm not so sure 'tis helping, 'zackly. Book-learnin's not for the likes o' Floss Parker, to my mind. Nor to Pa's, I'm thinking. He don't 'old with females addlin' their minds with too much rubbish. Leads 'en to mischief.' He pretended to mull it over, then with a leering wink he said, 'Well, we'll let it ride . . . for now. I can't say fairer than that. Let Pa's mind rest easy until it's a more *fitting* time to remind him of her uppitiness . . . But Pa's is a forgivin' nature. Sooner or later, he's bound to give her a second chance, 'specially as you good ladies give 'er such a fine character. Blood's thicker'n water, after all . . . Oh, yes, he'll forgive her and take her back one of these fine days. Back into the bosom of her family, a-looking after her nearest and dearest as 'tis proper for a young, unwed daughter to be doing.'

Miss Swann's frown deepened but she said nothing more, merely delving in her basket to find the poke of sugared almonds she was taking back for all those left at home. She pressed two into Saul's palm before nodding coolly at Matthew and sweeping me forward. We had scarcely gone half-a-dozen steps before we heard Saul wailing protests.

'Doubtless that wretched child has had to give up his sweetmeats,' Miss Swann said, grimly. 'I should have known better than to bother. No, do not look round, Miranda. Best that we ignore them. A blackguard like Matthew Parker would only be encouraged by our concern. Wretched man! We should have walked right past him and not embarked on any kind of conversation. He always provokes me to indiscretion. I should have said nothing at all encouraging about Flossie. It only gave him the opportunity to remind me that her father has every right to remove her should he be so minded. And that is the worst fate that could be wished upon the girl. Thank heaven, there are the lights of Furze House. I shall be glad to get in and wash off the dust of the journey.'

And to rinse away the unpleasant taint that Matthew Parker left upon the senses. I understood her unspoken thought. I, too, felt as though I had been in contact with something soiled and thoroughly unpleasant.

The candlelit windows of Furze House beckoned us home and I was glad to be back after the long day. All the same, I could not help but pause on the doorstep, my thoughts and my heart involuntarily travelling the rolling miles to the edge of the moor, to where the stones of that other house, painfully dear, glimmered in the light of the harvest moon.

During the night my old nightmare returned in all its horrid clarity, no doubt reawakened by the meeting with Jed. I awoke gasping from the struggle to escape the smothering clutches of the great black bird. Thankfully, I had not disturbed Biddie and the gentle, familiar sound of her breathing went some way to calming my own. But I could not so easily return to sleep with my mind still churning in panic. I eased myself from bed and crept to the window.

The night air, scented with the perfume of the massed stocks in the flower beds below, laid cool fingers on my fevered skin. The moon hung high now in the starlit sky, washing the landscape with silver light and impenetrable black shadow. It was very still, very silent. I leaned from the window, breathing deeply, as if to draw in the essence of the tranquil night. Though I loved this high, airy room, I half wished now that I were not three floors up, under the eaves, but sharing the cramped room behind the scullery where Mrs Hawkins and Flossie slept. From there I could have crept outside easily, walked in the path of the moon, drifted across dew-soaked grass in and out of the sheltering moonshadow . . .

Panic eased. My thoughts lightened, floated airy and nebulous as a drift of mist. Such quiet. Magical in its intensity. Not even the scuffling of a mouse. Whatever creatures were abroad crept soft and secretive along their hidden paths. No smugglers would be about tonight. Moonlight was no friend to those whose covert business needed the cloak of darkness. Emma Rossiter could sleep peacefully for a few nights, knowing that there would be no call on Billy's services.

That other name came sliding into my thoughts alongside his friend Billy's. I did not really want to think about him. I was calm again now and I preferred to remain so.

Will you consider me your friend? – My name is Christian. Kit.

I could not dismiss that so lightly. What sort of friend was I if I barred him from my thoughts? It seemed some kind of betrayal not to pause and breathe a wish that he might be protected from harm. That, wherever he was, asleep or awake, he might be warmed, lifted . . . given hope . . . by the brush of a compassionate thought from someone who wished him well.

A fanciful idea, yet as I thought of Kit the image I had of him changed. For some reason I had been remembering him as he had looked that evening when he had played the violin in the parlour. Intense, concentrated; black lashes shadowing narrowed eyes – lost to us, his audience, as he sought to wrest the soul from the music. But then the image I had of him altered. Was bewilderingly different. I saw him fallen on his back, spreadeagled. Not on the parlour floor. The parlour was gone . . . the violin . . . And his face! The expression blank, unfocused, the lashes heavy, closing . . . but not in sleep. Oh, God . . . not in sleep.

I knew what was happening. Feared it . . . wanted to know, to understand. Was helpless before it . . .

Not dreaming. Not waking. Still alive to the moon, the frozen silver landscape, the black shadows. But the other . . . the other*where* encroaching.

No music now. The roar of flame, of thunder. The colours of nightmare. Crimson on black. Crimson gushing amid tangled curls, sliding in a glossy tide over ashen flesh and spreading into a seeping puddle over the charred planks under his head . . .

Did I scream his name aloud? I think not. Even Biddie could not have slept through that great wailing cry. But he heard it. Kit. The black lashes lifted. I could see the effort it cost him. The narrow gaze focused. His mouth twisted as the pain leaped back at him. There was anger there as he looked at me, as though I had called him back into the confusion, the noise, where he did not wish to be. Anger, yes . . . fear, too. And desperation . . . Then a kind of wonder at what he saw. His lips formed one word: Miranda.

And then it was gone. The vision. Everything.

Only the dying echo of thunder in my head and the frosted moonlight, chill and remote on the empty garden.

'You poor child,' said Miss Swann peering into my face. 'The compresses of eyebright seem to have had no effect at all. You had best call upon Widow Thomas this morning and see what she recommends.'

'Indeed, yes,' said Mrs Greenwood, 'or the other girls will be catching it. You know how pink-eye can spread.' She paused for only a second before adding, with satisfaction, 'I am not at all surprised, however, that you picked up an infection at Newton Abbot market. The heat alone on such a day was enough to draw out all manner of unhealthy miasmas and heaven knows what animal filth was contained in the dust that blew over you. Far better if you had stayed by the sea where we have the advantage of healthy air.'

'It could have happened anywhere in this dry spell,' said Miss Swann mildly. 'Even outside our own gate. Clouds of dust follow every horse or equipage that passes.'

'Ah, but it did not, did it, dear? But then, you never listen to my advice and will go gallivanting off about the country on one of the hottest days of the year . . .'

I toyed with a piece of bread that seemed tasteless this morning and wondered, uneasily, if there was a more sinister reason for my bloodshot eyes. Logical, of course, to blame it on the dust that had blown into them. But logic was nothing to do with looking into a moonlit garden and seeing things that were not there. Perhaps this gritty, painful irritation was punishment for letting myself be lured into believing that I really had been given some sort of vision of Kit in an instant of danger, instead of banishing it as a pure figment of my overheated imagination.

The trouble was, the picture I had seen would not go away. I could not forget it. It was fixed into my mind in all its gory clarity. I had seen Kit desperately wounded, close to death. Illogical or not, I could not dismiss it.

Miss Swann frowned at me when breakfast was over. 'You are exceedingly pale this morning. I know it is not far to Widow Thomas's cottage, but I think Biddy had best go with you in case you turn faint.'

Biddie was less than pleased. With the school closed for the month and discipline considerably relaxed, she had been able to devote a great deal of her time, under Mrs Greenwood's direction, to the creation of the new winter gown.

'I was planning on tacking the bodice together this morning,' she said crossly as we set off. 'Don't know why you need cosseting, I'm sure. Getting soft, that's what. And I hates boring walks with nothing to look at but grass and trees.'

There was another reason for her reluctance to accompany me, as I well knew.

'Own up,' I said, with a grin. 'You're scared Widow Thomas'll put the evil eye on you.'

'Fiddlesticks!'

'You shouldn't listen to Flossie's daft tales. To hear her talk you'd think the poor old soul was in league with the devil himself.'

'All right, clever clogs. How do you know she isn't?'

'She's a harmless old woman. Just because she knows about herbs and keeps a lot of pet animals, people whisper all sorts of silly things. Miss Swann says—'

'She don't know everything.'

'Miss Swann says,' I repeated firmly, 'that if Widow Thomas had been born a man she'd have been respected like a proper doctor. And for all they whisper about her, half the parish goes begging her help whenever they're sick.'

'*Or* they're wanting a love potion or a money charm.' Biddy swished her clean skirts fastidiously away from a pile of fresh horse manure steaming gently in the dusty road. 'So why should they do that if she isn't a witch?'

'Because she sees no reason not to make a copper or two out of their ignorance.'

I was again quoting Miss Swann. To bolster my own confidence as much as Biddie's. I had only seen Widow Thomas close to on the occasions when she had appeared at Furze House to bring fresh honey and collect the used jars. I had seen her from a distance, though, quite a few times, leading her slow old donkey along the road with the pair of grey, padding lurcher dogs at her heels, and had taken care to avoid her. I was not the only one. It was surprising how the road had emptied at her approach and there were few who knowingly would follow where she had walked until someone else, unaware, had trodden in her steps and broken the spell that might bring misfortune.

At first glance she looked like any other poor but respectable old woman. Neatly if shabbily dressed, white hair tucked winter and summer under an ancient sun bonnet that once might have been the shade of violets but was now a dirty grey except for a hint of colour in the deep frill that kept sun or rain from the back of her neck. It was only when she looked directly at you that you felt . . . well, hard to pin down what it was. Strange eyes, that was certain. One a vivid sapphire blue, the other brown. But in that deeply wrinkled, nut-brown face they were youthful and clear. As though a much younger woman lurked under the carapace of age. A woman of strength and confidence. And that odd-coloured, unblinking, *powerful* glance seemed strangely penetrating. As though it could pierce the layers of politeness and pretence and look straight into the heart of the real person to read the truth that was hidden there.

Sensible Miss Swann dismissed tales of witchery with a scornful smile. She treated Widow Thomas as she would any other welcome visitor and insisted we do the same, inviting her into the parlour where one of us would be delegated to pouring tea and handing the plate of cakes. 'I will not have you girls falling into the trap of judging people on suspicion and rumour. You may see for yourself that Widow Thomas is a cultured person fallen on hard times who prefers to maintain her independence in the best way she can rather than suffer the indignity of entering the poorhouse or applying for parish relief. A little eccentric in some ways, but perfectly intelligent and polite.'

And so I saw when it was my turn to wait on her. She sat straight and dignified, endowing her shabby garments with an air of faded gentility. Her voice was low and agreeable and decidedly not of the common class. She smiled warmly when she accepted the tea and buttered scones offered and asked only the most innocent questions about how I enjoyed living in Devon and what subjects I enjoyed best of my schooling. But those odd-coloured eyes, that penetrating, unblinking glance, contradicted the ordinariness of the conversation. I found myself ridiculously unnerved. And now, though I dearly wished to cling to Miss Swann's judgement of Widow Thomas, the closer we got to her cottage, the more I was infected by Biddie's superstitious fear.

We had passed the cottage in the dark on the last lap of our journey to Furze House with Kit. I remembered walking the narrow rutted lane with its towering hedgebanks and seeing the chinks of light emanating from the cottage. By daylight it was even smaller than I had realised, standing on a mere chip of land carved out of a copse of ancient trees. There was a sense of neatness and order about the place. Cob walls newly whitewashed, thatch mossy but sound, the patch of garden bordered by a thorn hedge along the lane, overflowing with flowers and shrubs. Two great ash trees and a massive oak, outposts of the protecting woodland, stood sentinel on the bank by the garden gate where we hovered nervously in the deep green shade cast by their heavy foliage.

I tugged my shawl closer round my shoulders and put out my fingers to the latch. As though at a signal two lean grey shapes slid silently out of the shrubbery and stood, yellow eyes watchful, on the path of sea pebbles and shells that led to the front door.

Biddie squeaked and stepped back. 'I'm not going in with them,' she declared. 'Nasty brutes. I'll stay here. And if you're more than a few minutes, I'm off. I'll wait for you at the end of the lane.'

'I'm sure they're harmless,' I said, without conviction.

'Indeed they are, to friends. Though I could not vouch for their temper if you considered yourself my enemy.'

I jumped. I had not noticed the old woman. She seemed to appear from the bushes with the same silent tread as her dogs. She held the bunched-up skirts of her sacking apron in one hand.

'G-good morning, Mrs Thomas,' I began. 'Miss Swann sent me . . .'

But she was turning away, walking with her slow, smooth stride to where the cottage door stood open. There she paused, glancing back, calling, 'Come in, if you will. I have something urgent to attend to.'

I opened the gate. The dogs did not move, but continued to watch me as I approached. Only when I drew level with them did they stretch out their heads, wet black noses towards me, ears twitched forward, eyes alert. Then, apparently satisfied, they turned once more to watch the gate.

'It's all right, Biddie. They really are friendly,' I said, with more confidence, risking a tentative pat on the rough dry coat of the nearer dog. But a cat chose that moment to glide from under a clump of hollyhocks and stalk, tail up, towards the cottage, and Biddy, who had just ventured on to the pebble path, immediately leaped back and slammed the gate.

'God help us,' she hissed. 'What did I tell you? A black cat! You know what that means, Mirrie. I daresn't . . . Oh, be as quick as you can and take care!'

I followed the cat to the door. On the step it sat down in a shaft of sunlight, licked one paw and commenced to clean its whiskers. I bypassed it with care and had to suppress an almost hysterical giggle when I stepped into the single room of the cottage and saw what awaited me.

Biddie could have had her choice of Widow Thomas's supposed witchy familiars. There were three more cats inside. A tabby lay curled on the cot bed in the corner, a one-eyed ginger tom glared at me from his perch on the back of a chair, another tabby lay on the rag rug before the hearth where a lazy thread of smoke rose from a small fire of logs. And not only cats. On one of the beams in the dim corner a barn owl opened its eyes and jigged its head from side to side as though tetchy at having its sleep interrupted. And on the scrubbed table Widow Thomas had gently spilled out a small hedgehog from her apron and was examining its leg.

'Broken,' she said. 'It will have to be set. Miranda, is it not? I remember you well. I expected you would be here sooner or later. Kindly pass me that basket, child.'

The basket contained clean rags neatly rolled or folded, jars of ointments, and a handful of sturdy twigs. I was too mesmerised by her deft fingers gently straightening the small limb, padding the twig splint with what looked like dried herbs and binding it firmly, to take much note of what she had said. It was only when the hedgehog, which had lain uncurled and seemingly without fear while she attended to it, was placed gently in a hay-lined wicker cage that I thought: *Expected?* But even as my stomach clenched at the dark possibilities the word sent scurrying into my mind, she was carrying the cage out of the back door and beckoning me to follow.

Neat strips and squares of growing herbs and flowers took up most of the small area, with a row of straw bee skeps set to one side. The old donkey was tethered at the edge of the copse and near it was a small enclosure with a stout wooden kennel at one end.

'A badger sleeps himself better in there,' she said. 'Rescued from baiters.' A suspicion of amusement in her low voice. 'It is sometimes an advantage to have a reputation for being, shall we say, *different* when faced with louts intent on evil towards other creatures with whom we share this beautiful earth. Brock is nearly healed. He will be off back to his own kind any night now, unless he is like the young barn owl who has returned to roost in the cottage all summer though the damage inflicted by a boy with a catapult is long since healed. And here are my other patients.'

'Here' was a lean-to against the back wall with more cages standing on a shelf. Some empty, some containing birds in various stages of recovery from injury. She set the new cage alongside the one containing a woodpigeon with a splinted wing.

Intrigued, I could not help but ask where she found them.

'Oh, they arrive,' she said enigmatically. 'Tenderhearted people – children perhaps – leave them at my gate. Sometimes they find their own way. Occasionally I remove them from the jaws of my own cats, but how should I punish them when it is their nature? I see you find it strange, child, that I should nurse these creatures back to health and still keep pet animals whose nature is predatory. Indeed I have more than once cared for a fox cub and released it into the wild, knowing it might well kill and eat one of the other creatures I have sheltered.' The odd-coloured eyes looked directly into mine. She smiled, her face creasing to a welter of wrinkles. 'Well, it is a puzzle that has occupied my mind for many years. All I can say is that I do what I must. The cats themselves were poor mistreated kittens before I took them in and I never had the heart to drown them in a bucket which was the sensible thing to do. Now, shall we attend to what ails you before your foolish friend begins to believe that I have laid some enchantment on you?'

I felt myself blush.

'Oh, she wouldn't . . . that is . . .'

'Indeed she would. However, do not think that I am offended. Why should I be? Is she not right?' There was challenge in that piercing, unblinking gaze. I tried to cling to sensible facts. I was only sent here to seek some medicament for my eyes . . . But the question burned in my mind, came blurting out. 'Why did you say you expected me?'

'Because I was told so by the lady who has befriended you,' she answered promptly, then gave a short bark of laughter. 'Dearie me, child, I believe you are disappointed. Perhaps you would prefer me to speak of spells and magic rites . . . some moonshine tale I might concoct in order to give those like your pretty, foolish friend their pennyworth of thrills.'

'No, of course not,' I said lamely

'It is all perfectly straightforward. I met your kindly Miss Swann two days ago in Dawlish, she being one of the few persons who do not scuttle off like frightened rabbits at my approach. We often discuss matters relating to the health of the household. She told me you were having trouble with your eyes and I suggested that if there was no improvement you might come here to see if I could help you. Simple, is it not?'

'Indeed, ma'am,' I said, shamefaced at having let imagination get the better of me.

'So be it. Let me look at you properly.' She put her hard, earth-ingrained fingers under my chin and turned my face to the sun. 'Hmm. Very fiery. And I see the light bothers you.' She released me abruptly and allowed me to mop my watering eyes with my handkerchief. 'Miss Swann has been preparing eyebright compresses for you, I understand. Continue with those and I think a tonic to encourage the internal system to reject the inflammation might be in order. Also you may bathe your eyes night and morning with a little sea salt dissolved in spring water that has been boiled then allowed to cool.'

In the cottage she moved slowly along the shelves that covered the wall opposite the fireplace, picking out pots and jars and placing them on the table. She took spoonsfuls from some, pinches from others, mixing them carefully in a small canvas pouch. Her hands worked with the same deftness with which she had tended the injured hedgehog, and with a kind of reverence, as though the healing powers of the herbs demanded that she treat them with respect.

'Brew a tisane and take it three times a day,' she said at last, handing me the pouch. 'It should quickly clear the condition and you will soon feel fully restored to health.' There was the hint of mischief in her smile as she added smoothly, 'Of course, with the moon waning it is a good time to cast a spell of banishment on the affliction, should you wish it.'

'I think you tease me, ma'am,' I said, setting down the pennies Miss Swann had given me on the table's edge.

'Do I?' A small pause in which the ginger cat leaped from its perch with a soft thud of velvet paws on the flagged floor and wove itself round the old woman's skirts before coming to butt its scarred and battered head against my boots. 'Perhaps.'

'You admitted it yourself, ma'am.'

'It is true enough that I have found amusement in encouraging people to believe my skills go beyond administering herbs to the sick and needy. Such a reputation has helped to preserve my privacy and protects me against those who would think twice about harming or robbing a witch for fear of the evil eye. But it is also true that I have lived so long alone and close to the earth that I have grown to understand and respect the swelling and ebbing of the invisible tides that govern nature . . . the sun and its seasons . . . the moon.' Her voice was soft. 'I have learned from experience the most favourable time of the moon to sow the seeds of herbs so that they will flourish strongly; the best time to harvest them so that nothing of their healing effect is lost. So tell me this, child. Who is to say if the same powerful moon that governs seed and harvest, the visible tides of the sea and the hidden salt tide of women's blood, does not influence emotions, feelings, wishes?'

Knife-sharp in my mind. Silver light, black shadows. A stillness that heard the smallest breath, the faintest whisper of a compassionate thought stirring in the mind of someone who leaned from a window, entranced in the beauty of the night and the moon. And she had heard. Answered with a tormenting vision . . .

No! I must not think of it! Could not bear to think of it.

I leaned against the table, my legs trembling, eyes closing against a sudden stinging and watering as though I was still out of doors where the sunlight made them uncomfortable.

With an effort I said, 'I must be off . . . Biddie is waiting.' I turned blindly towards the door, groping once more for my handkerchief.

I took but one step before my hands were caught and held.

I made some shaky attempt to free myself, but her grip was

surprisingly strong. I had an instant of dismay; another when I almost laughed at the ridiculous idea that I fancied myself restrained when I was young and agile and could thrust aside such an old bag of bones with no trouble at all; then a third in which I felt a curious resignation steal over me. For there was, I realised, comfort in that touch. A steady warmth in her firm yet gentle grasp that dispelled the chill that had momentarily touched me. As she continued to hold my hands, and as I allowed myself to relax in her grip, it seemed that whatever remaining fear I had of her was dispelled too.

I remembered how the little hedgehog had lain so trustingly still while she tended it, as if it knew she would heal its hurt. For all that I was half a head taller than the old woman, I seemed to feel myself as small and vulnerable and insignificant as that little creature. And as helpless.

'You are afraid, child,' she said, softly. 'But not now of me, I think.'

I looked into those odd-coloured eyes, piercing still, yet in their intensity so very steady and reassuring.

'No,' I whispered. 'I think I've never been truly afraid of you. Not like Biddie. Just of . . . of the things . . . the other things . . . that you seemed to know of . . . that scare me.'

'I thought so,' she said calmly. 'I felt it from the first. You are blessed with the sight.'

'Blessed!' I burst out. 'How can it be a blessing?'

'I have always considered it a gift. Something to be treasured.'

'Then . . . then you have it too?'

'Indeed.'

'And it doesn't frighten you?'

'Perhaps just a little when I was a child, but my grandmother who had the second sight also and who taught me much of what I know about healing plants, showed me how to use the gift wisely. You see, when people come to me with their aches and pains, I often sense the source of their trouble before they have begun to stammer out their stories. Sometimes it is frustrating, true, because I know the cramps in the belly or the painful shoulders are merely physical expressions of a greater hurt about which I can do nothing. But how can I tell a woman to leave her drunken husband when she would starve in the streets if she did? Or find work for a desperate man put off from his labour and not knowing which way to turn in order to feed his family? But even there, such healing powers that I have can be turned to advantage, however slight. I give them herbs to soothe and strengthen the troubled mind which may enable the sufferer to think more clearly about the problem and perhaps see a way to ease it.'

'But it isn't like that for me,' I said. 'Nothing so helpful. And I never know when these . . . these feelings – pictures – will come. And they are hateful!'

'And something happened recently that troubles you?'

I hesitated. It was difficult because I had never in my life spoken of what I saw and felt when these disturbing visions appeared. Yet it struck me that for the first time ever I *wanted* to tell someone. Someone who would understand and not condemn.

So I began. I told her everything, dredging up from memory even things I had consciously forgotten. Like the time when I was no more than three and had tearfully followed my favourite stable cat all day, fearful to let it out of my sight because I knew some awful fate hung over it, though I was too little to explain it to Meg who had merely scolded me for whining. The very next night the cat fell foul of a rabbit snare and was strangled. Again, some weeks after my mother died, I had woken tearful after some unhappy dream, to find her standing by my bed. I had drifted to sleep again, comforted by her gentle touch as she stroked my hair. But I was old enough then to keep it to myself. Aunt Hettie would have been shocked and affronted. She had never been reconciled to her brother marrying this delicate foreign woman rather than some sturdy local girl who would breed strong sons to secure the Brehault line. She would certainly not countenance any evidence of one of Mama's unfortunate traits manifesting itself in her daughter. Then there was Papa who would be distressed, and even dear Meg might look at me strangely. It was not worth the risk of upsetting those I loved.

'The habit of secrecy began then,' I said with a deep sigh. 'It has been bottled up for so long . . . I can't tell you the relief of being able to speak freely of these . . . these moments of knowing.'

'And not all of them unpleasant, though you call them so.'

I nodded slowly. 'Fear blinded me. I thought there was some badness – strangeness – in me that I must avoid dwelling on.'

'Yet you found comfort in your mother's presence. And when you saw the little child you had befriended at the mill, she was smiling . . . happy . . . as though to reassure you she was now beyond suffering.'

'I suppose so,' I said, with reluctance. 'But I still don't want these things to happen to me. I don't want to be different and see things that aren't there and have people avoiding me because of it.'

'Or turn into an eccentric old woman living in the woods with her cats and her herbs.' Widow Thomas laughed and released my hands. 'No fear of that, child. I chose my own path. You will choose yours.'

'I meant no offence, ma'am,' I said hurriedly. 'But I would not wish to live as you do.'

'Nor could there possibly be any need of it,' she said, with a firmness that denied argument. 'You see, I never wanted people and possessions crowding about me, demanding my attention. I was born to privilege but I turned my back on all that meant when I was scarcely older than you and ran off with a penniless young woodsman working on my father's Dorset estate. He was solitary, too. Happy to earn his living as a bodger, coppicing trees and turning chair legs, working alone, as I worked alone with my plants and my animals. We both loved the living presence of the woods. It is there that I feel him closest still, though he has been dead for half my lifetime.'

'I'm sorry,' I said awkwardly.

'What is there to be sorry about? We had more joy in the short time granted to us than many a one has in a lifetime.' She was brisk now, sweeping me to the door. 'You have taken up enough of my time. I will walk you to the gate. And if you ask me what you should do with this gift you have been given, then all I can tell you is to accept it, use it for good if that is possible, and do not be afraid.'

'Easy to say,' I said with a sigh as we walked down the pebble path to where the dogs still waited. 'But I don't know if I can.'

The dogs stretched themselves at our approach, wagging feathery tails, thrusting black wet noses into our hands.

'Then think of it as an extra sharp sense, such as these dogs have.' She ran her fingers over a grey muzzle. 'They do not pine and grizzle because their ears are alert to sounds beyond our perception and their noses pick up a thousand more scents than our own. Who knows? Perhaps such abilities were once commonplace among our long-ago ancestors who worshipped gods we have long forgotten and revered the spirits living in the earth and the hills and the great forest trees.' She lifted bony shoulders under the shabby layers of garments. 'I have talked enough . . . too much. It wearies me. Be off with you, now. No, wait. One more word.'

She was looking beyond the gate, frowning, to where Biddie thought herself concealed in the shadows but was betrayed by a flicker of light against her print skirt.

'That one,' she said, flatly. 'She needs to be watched. She is too pretty and excitable for her own good. Take care she keeps good company for she is lacking in discrimination.' Her smile was suddenly mischievous, dispelling that edge of something deeper, darker, hovering at our backs. 'But do not look so set back at the passing observation of an old woman who has learned much that she has preferred to forget of human nature over the years.' Then she said in a louder, carrying voice, with a wink at me, 'You see how I border my garden with a thorn hedge, and oak and ash are close by? It is well known that such trees provide sure protection against witches, yet I feel no fear of them at all. Strange, is it not?'

She closed the gate after me and turned away back to the cottage without another word. Only then did Biddie dart out of the shadows and drag me off down the lane.

'You were an *age*,' she squealed. 'What were you doing? What did she say about the trees? Oh, that's only to deceive us, mark my words! But thank heaven you're safe. I walked down to the road twice – I was near out of my head with mithering about you. Did you get your medicine? Did she put a charm on it? And how can you be so . . . so *calm*? I'd be all of a lather after . . .'

'After what?' I said somewhat loftily. 'I told you there was nothing to be afraid of. It's just as Miss Swann said. Widow Thomas is merely an old lady who is clever at doctoring people – and animals. I watched her splint the leg of a hedgehog. And she has an injured badger there. And birds. That was what we were looking at. That was why I was so long.'

But there was so much more that could not be spoken of. So very much more.

My bloodshot eyes were clear within a week. And, as they cleared, it seemed I became easier in my mind about the other things that troubled me. I found that I could think of the strange vision of Kit without fear, though it made no more sense than before. For some reason I had been granted an image of him injured in battle. But if there was any purpose in it, any message, it remained hidden from me. And presently, as the comfortable routine of the days reasserted itself, the gory picture began to fade from my mind and was replaced by pleasanter, more engrossing matters.

I plunged once more into my studies, enjoyed the errands about the district and, after the autumn's southerly gales and the exceptional tides, the excitement of beachcombing walks along the sands. The great seas flung all manner of curious flotsam along the tide line and we were not the only ones to poke among it for whatever treasures the sea had yielded.

Poor people gathered a bounty of driftwood for their fires and farmers brought carts to gather the mounds of seaweed to spread on their fields. Sometimes ship's timbers and the sodden remnants of their cargo washed in and were quickly squirrelled away by prudent townsfolk. A crate of sodden oranges would be picked over to find a few that were edible, a bale of fleeces salvaged from the rollers and borne home in triumph. Occasionally the remnants of a lost contraband cargo were dragged from the sea bed and thrown up on the beach. No profit for a beacomber, though, in the barnacled remnants of brandy casks which still trailed the ropes that had strung them together when they had been weighted and thrown overboard for retrieval at a time that had never come. Occasionally there were reports of real treasure . . . gold coins, pewter dishes, once a strange twisted necklace of woven gold wire, that were said to come from some ancient wreck in Lyme Bay.

'Keep your eyes skinned, girls,' Miss Swann would say, head down into the wind. 'I shall expect each of you to fetch back at least one interesting item so that we may examine and write about it later.'

'Interesting?' Biddie would grumble. 'What's interesting about a lot of old rubbish? The only interesting thing that'll happen if we stay out in this cold is that we'll catch our deaths. Seems Mrs Greenwood's the only one with any sense. *She* doesn't stand any nonsense about exercise and fresh air. There she is left all warm and cosy by the fire. I've a mind to plead a belly ache and stay behind with her next time we're supposed to go fossicking in a half-gale.'

Biddie got her wish sooner than she expected. Mrs Greenwood, for all that she derided outdoor pursuits as being detrimental to health, was the one to fall sick that December of a cold on her chest accompanied by a debilitating ague.

A distracted Miss Swann called on me to help with the younger pupils. This was something which delighted me – and not only because I felt this was one small way in which I could repay Miss Swann for her many kindnesses. I loved school work so much myself that to help to educate the little ones and pass on all that I had learned since coming to Furze House was a privilege rather than a chore.

'Rather you than me,' said Biddie cheerfully one day, swishing past from the kitchen with a prettily set tray of coddled eggs and slivers of bread and butter to tempt the invalid's appetite.

'Mrs Greenwood no better, then?' I said.

'Not so's you'd notice, thank the Lord,' she said, grinning. 'I've nearly finished altering that old pelisse of hers she gave me. Wait till you see me in church next Sunday. Knock your eyes out, I will.'

With Miss Swann fully occupied during school hours, Biddie had snatched the opportunity to help attend and amuse Mrs Greenwood. So dedicated was she in these duties that she skilfully managed to escape the schoolroom altogether and instead sat most of the day blissfully enjoying her two favourite occupations – gossiping and sewing.

'And is there anyone else you are thinking to impress on Sunday?' I asked innocently. 'A lordship or even a princeling you've spotted among the visitors?'

She tossed her red curls. 'You can laugh, Miranda Brehault, but you just wait. One of these days, when you're a dried-up old maid who knows nothing but book-learning, you'll be sorry you didn't learn to make the best of yourself when you had the chance. You wait and see!'

She went giggling up the stairs. *Too pretty, too excitable*, Widow Thomas had said. She might have added high-spirited, irrepressible and self-willed, as Biddie surely was. Not such bad traits any of them, I was inclined to think. Indeed those latter qualities had done much to see her through the years of hardship at Crossbank, and would probably serve her well in whatever future she made for herself. *Make sure she keeps good company*. I smiled to myself. Little chance of anything else so long as we stayed at Furze House and, to my great relief, it seemed that our benefactor, Mrs Loveridge, was content for us to remain at least over the winter. She had said as much when she sent the last remittance for our keep.

Unless some suitable position presents itself, I am willing to provide for them for a few months longer. In this way, at least, I can feel that I am making a Stand against Exploitation, whereas my efforts at Crossbank are of small account and the needs of Commerce prevail against the Charity of a Tender Heart. My own Sorry and Weakened State at present tends to give me Dreary thoughts about my Usefulness in this direction.

Poor Mrs Loveridge. I felt so sad for her. Her first baby, joyfully anticipated, had died a few days after his difficult and prolonged birth in October. She had spent several weeks recuperating in Harrogate, her doctor having great faith in the spa waters there. The town, apparently, was not to her taste.

It was so bitter cold, with an East Wind that brought a good fall of snow on two occasions, and the house where we lodged so full of Draughts I was half-perishing with Shivers if I moved a foot from the fire. If only the doctor had been favourable towards the Waters of Bath or Cheltenham, I know I should have been far more Comfortable there, being so much further South and the Nearness to my dear Home County of Devonshire a great comfort also. I dearly Hope one day when my Health is improved and I am relieved of my present Obligations, I might persuade Mr Loveridge to take a Tour of the West Country so that I might revisit the Scenes of a Happy Childhood.

Her 'present Obligations' were to do with her step-daughter's forthcoming marriage. For Biddie and me, spring would bring the unwelcome prospect of finding work and moving on from Furze House. For Ida Loveridge, I thought sourly, it meant that she would merely pass from being a spoiled and cosseted daughter, to being a spoiled and cosseted wife. She had landed herself a fine catch, the son of a rich Manchester cotton merchant. There was to be a grand wedding with five hundred guests invited to a sumptuous wedding breakfast. Afterwards, the young couple were to embark on an extended tour of Italy, returning later in the year to the house presently being built for them on the airy, rural heights of Cheetham Hill, a district increasingly favoured for its proximity to the thriving heart of Manchester – no more than two or three miles distant – yet far enough away to avoid the noxious fumes and smoke emanating from the mills and manufacturies. There, presumably, she would live the rest of her life in the same self-centred, selfish way she had always done with never a thought in her empty head for anyone whose labour provided all the comforts she took for granted.

For many days after that letter arrived, I found my thoughts turning to Crossbank Mill, with all the conflicting emotions that aroused. Uppermost was thankfulness that I had escaped and gratitude to those who had helped me. There was scorn towards Ida Loveridge and her ilk and a fearful bitterness towards her father. Though Mrs Loveridge had made some small improvements to conditions there – and perhaps the knowledge that someone had their interest and welfare at heart might be some comfort to the apprentices – their lot could never be anything less than unpleasant. It was a while before I could shake off the feeling of guilt because I was blessedly free and so many were not, nor had any possibility of it.

Mrs Greenwood continued to ail all that winter. Widow Thomas was called upon several times to visit her, but despite the infusions of coltsfood and aniseed that brought temporary relief, the inhalations of thyme and eucalyptus and the twice-daily glasses of Miss Swann's own particular tonic remedy – nutmeg, ginger and rosemary steeped in Madeira wine – her persistent, wheezy cough remained and she herself was low and dispirited. She grew increasingly sharp and bad-tempered, especially after school reopened in February. Every sound irritated her and she frequently retired to her room, exhausted. I caught most of her scoldings. Biddie, on the other hand, seemed to have acquired the knack of soothing her. 'Nothing to it,' she would grin. 'All I have to do is agree with everything she says, talk about things we both like – sewing and fashions and such – and be ready to run up and downstairs with tasty tit-bits and any snippets of gossip I might have heard in the kitchen or from the girls.'

For myself I was relieved when Mrs Greenwood was forced to retire to her bedchamber. Grown tolerant towards Biddy she might be, but I seemed always to be the particular target of her peevish carping and Miss Swann's calm defence of me whenever she thought her friend's criticism undeserved, only served to inflame her the more.

'We must make allowances. She has been a martyr to her nerves for many years,' Miss Swann said to me, after one such peevish episode. Then, with a sigh, 'She was such a bright, happy-go-lucky girl. How sad it is that . . . unhappy circumstances may change a person so.' This reference was her delicate way of referring to her friend's miserable marriage. 'You see, being unable to shake off this illness is worrying her more than she will admit. Her mother died of a consumption, and she is fearful that it may take hold of her also, though Widow Thomas's opinion gives us leave to hope that this is not so. I trust that with plenty of rest and good food to build up her strength, she will begin to look up. At least she has not been submitted to the blood-letting and fearful emetics the doctor prescribed for my father when he succumbed to a similar bronchitic episode. I believe the treatment so weakened him that it precipitated his death.' Her kind smile softened the sternness of her strong, plain face. 'And we have one heartening event to come out of Harriet's illness. You, Miranda, have proved invaluable to me in the schoolroom. You have the trust and liking of those younger ones I have placed in your care and I can give you no higher praise than to say you have the makings of a most competent teacher. When the time comes I shall have no hesitation in recommending you for a position as governess.'

But, miraculously, the time did not come. Mrs Greenwood did begin to improve in health though it was clear as spring advanced that she would not easily regain her former robustness. The bones of her small, pointed face stood out more sharply than ever and the hint of rouge on her cheekbones only served to emphasise the hollows underneath and the fine dry network of wrinkles that had spread across her skin. As cool, sharp spring advanced it became clear that she was unable to cope as she once had done with the day-to-day schoolwork. She grew more and more sharp-tempered. Minor misbehaviour on the part of the pupils that would once have earned a mild rebuke, now set her into fierce rages which set the culprit weeping. It took Miss Swann all her tact to smooth over these episodes, though one irate mama removed her daughter from the school the very next day and another sought an interview in which she threatened to do the same if her precious Joan was not treated more gently.

'I know Rose was particularly vexing,' I heard Miss Swann say, wearily. 'But we cannot afford to lose too many pupils this way. Mamas do gossip among themselves and the slightest thing may be blown up out of all proportion. It is so bad for the reputation of the school.'

'That is all you think about!' Mrs Greenwood cried, unfairly. 'You do not care two pins that I was cheeked abominably by that . . . that chit of a grocer's daughter! And as to the suggestion that we take on four more boarders, I am astounded that you should give the idea a moment's consideration when we are pressed for space as it is.'

'My dear, it would take very little rearrangement. We have done it before, remember – and the family is a wealthy, well-respected one. Friends of the MacBrides. The fees will more than compensate for the loss of Rose Jarvis. The parents return to their sugar plantation in Barbados shortly and wish for an immediate answer.'

'My head aches at the thought of all the work – the responsibility – involved in taking on these girls.'

'Ah, but I have an idea . . .'

And that idea, presented the following day, was that Biddie and I should stay on at Furze House, no longer as pupils but as paid employees. We would both help with the boarders: Biddie would be a general help to Mrs Greenwood and I should assist with the running of the school.

Chapter Five

Beyond our small domestic concerns, events in the wider world coloured the background to our days. Miss Swann followed the progress of the French war minutely, reading and re-reading the despatches as they appeared in the newspaper and relaying events to the school. She tried to encourage the girls to appreciate the broader issues of the conflict, but there were few who were interested in treaties or the effects of the war upon international trade and the reasons for America's and Britain's being at loggerheads. Of course, if Bonaparte's ordering of blockades to the continental ports was reflected in the extortionate price of British bread or caused men to be laid off from their work – or if, indeed, one of the wildfire rumours of invasion flared up – they were quick to alarm or indignation because these things related directly to their own lives. The excitement of having army and naval officers on leave in the town set many a girlish heart a-flutter. But the girls had little notion of the harsh realities these dashing uniforms represented or the price to be paid by the ordinary soldier and seaman in times of war.

Miss Swann's reminder of the human cost – of the men killed and injured in battle, the towns and villages reduced to rubble, people left starving because their crops and animals had been destroyed – brought easy tears, easily forgotten. It was all too remote from their everyday lives. It was impossible for these sheltered, comfortably off girls to make the imaginative leap that would link heroic victories at Aboukir or Trafalgar or Vitoria – all so very thrilling – with the straggle of half-drunk, noisy beggars who lurched and hobbled down the

Exeter Road one morning and proceeded to make a nuisance of themselves by displaying festering wounds and waving amputated stumps of limbs about in order to solicit alms. One lady fainted right away at the sight and had to be carried into a haberdasher's shop to recover. Several other respectable persons suffered the indignity of the gang congregating under their windows to sing bawdy songs and refusing to move until pennies were thrown down to them. It was not to be tolerated! That evening they were driven away by a band of burly men armed with staves and small boys throwing stones, one of whom was sent to warn us to lock our doors and windows as the villains were now staggering up from the town in the direction of Teignmouth.

'They'm fearful sights!' he cried, eyes sparkling with excitement. 'Slit your throat for a ha'penny, I'll be bound.'

Mrs Greenwood immediately retreated to the safety of her bedchamber from where she could view the road from behind the curtains. The rest of us left our supper unfinished and hovered at the parlour window until the first of the rag-tag bunch came into view.

They passed the front gate slowly in ones and twos, heads down into the fine drizzle. There was little evidence of murderous intent in this limping, shuffling procession. The remnants of once-bright military uniforms hung on shoulders that seemed bowed more by suffering than any weight of villainy. The last to pass were two blind men led by another with a black eye patch visible under a wide-brimmed hat. It was at this point that we heard the bolts being drawn on the front door. The next minute Miss Swann was striding to the gate, tying the remnants of our supper – a slab of Cheddar cheese, half a loaf, a wedge of apple pie – into a table napkin. The man with the eye patch turned as she called and we shuddered at the sight of the raw red scar that ran from one ear to the other. Half his lip and nose were gone and the skin was so puckered that his face was drawn to a permanent and repulsive grimace.

Miss Swann did not flinch. She looked straight at the man,

pressed the bundle upon him, dropped coins into his palm. The grotesque head under the wide-brimmed hat bent for a moment as he contemplated what she had given him. Then, with immense dignity, he drew himself up straight and saluted her, military fashion.

Despite the drizzle Miss Swann stood at the gate for a few moments until they had gone out of sight. When she came indoors drizzle beaded her head and shoulders like pearly tears. All she said quietly was, 'That such men should be obliged to live as they do. It puts us all to shame.'

We none of us spoke much for the rest of that evening. Even the little ones were subdued. The horror of war had briefly touched us and against that our quiet pursuits seemed infinitely more precious for their very ordinariness.

The long-drawn out war came to an end in June 1815. Truly the end. Not the false armistice when Bonaparte had been confined to Elba and had escaped once more to raise his armies. Now his destination was the far-off British island of St Helena where he would live out his days in exile. When word flew about the district at the end of July that the seventy-four-gun *HMS Bellerophon*, the famous Trafalgar veteran known more commonly as 'Billy Ruffian', was at anchor in Torbay with Bonaparte aboard, a press of little boats from Dawlish and Teignmouth made an unexpected profit from bearing sightseers round the coast to Berry Head in hopes of a glimpse of the monster himself. Those who did glimpse him were a touch disappointed. 'He is but an insignificant little fellow in a green coat,' one was heard to say in surprise. Those young people who had grown up under the threat wielded by many an exasperated mother or nursemaid, that if they did not behave Old Boney would get them, were even more taken aback that the ogre of their dreams was now seen to be human, and not a very impressive-looking human at that.

Delight in the thrilling victory at Waterloo that sparked off all manner of celebrations and effigy-burning bonfires, became muted among more sober-minded people when news filtered through of the carnage on the battlefield, particularly among the defeated French who were said to have lost more than twenty-five thousand men. Even less pleasant was the grim knowledge that many of the injured had lingered for hours – days – and died where they fell before help could get to them. Some had been heartlessly finished off by ghoulish thieves intent on removing what booty they could scavenge.

'At least Master Kit's out o' that lot,' Flossie declared, stacking our after-dinner coffee cups on her tray in the parlour on the afternoon Miss Swann finished recounting these terrible facts. 'Savin' he'm still in the land o' the living, o' course.'

'I do not recall asking for your opinion, Flossie,' Mrs Greenwood said with a look of pained exasperation.

'No, ma'am. Sorry, ma'am,' Flossie said, unabashed. 'And ma'am, Mrs Hawkins asked partic'ler if 'ee'll give her your opinion on the currant pudding you just ate at dinner. 'Tis a new receipt an' her thinks 'tis a bit heavy on nutmeg.'

She whisked away, eager and energetic as ever. We were all deeply thankful that her father had not so far seen fit to summon her home. Perhaps he had grown used to a dependable and regular income, small though it was. Especially since his two eldest sons were no longer available to ply their usual trade of horse-dealing. They were at present aboard the *Leviathan* hulk at Portsmouth awaiting transportation to Van Dieman's land where they would spend seven years on account of picking pockets at a contest between fighting dogs. The youngest, Saul, was fit only for gathering cockles on the Teign sandbanks at low tide – and even then he was as likely to fill his basket with empty shells or bits of driftwood as with good cockles that the Parker women could usefully hawk about the streets. The remaining two, Matthew and Dan, earned a little here and there as rat catchers with the aid of Dan's two flea-bitten terriers, or netting songbirds for sale to an Exeter dealer. That they engaged in more profitable activities, less widely advertised, was certain. They were inclined to absent themselves for days or a week or two at a time – to Plymouth, Exeter, even so far as Bristol, it was rumoured – and return well pleased with themselves, Matthew always with some dandyish addition to his clothes, Dan usually rolling drunk, both lavish with wagers at the local cockpits for a while afterwards and disinclined to stir themselves catching rats or luring much-prized bullfinches into their nets until their pockets were empty once again.

I guessed that Matthew Parker was far more skilful at the petty thieving that had been his brothers' downfall. He had the inbred cunning necessary to keep himself and his gin-swilling brother out of trouble. He would not make the mistake of fouling his own patch. He was prepared to go further afield in search of prey and would take care to be well on his way home before suspicion fell on him. More's the pity. I had a profound dislike of him and often wished he had been caught and sentenced with his brothers to a good long term in Australia.

Biddie had once laughed at the way I shuddered whenever I saw him.

'I can't help it,' I had said. 'There's something in him that reminds me horribly of old man Hatcher. The slimy way he looks at you. Ugh! Makes my skin crawl.'

'He's not *that* bad, for heaven's sake. He's certainly not a filthy, greasy old man.' Her eyes glinted wickedly. 'Quite well set up, really.'

'Oh, Biddie,' I said, shocked. 'You mustn't encourage him. Please.'

She giggled. 'Your face! It's a picture! 'Course I wouldn't. I've got bigger fish to fry . . . and don't look at me like that.' She tossed her red curls. 'I know what I'm about.'

'I hope you do!'

'You're jealous,' she teased. 'Just because I have admirers practically throwing themselves at my feet.'

'Hah! Who'd want a kiss from Myrtle Watts's spotty brother?'

'A girl's got to practise,' she said blithely. 'Besides, he brings me bits of ribbon from his father's shop . . .'

'But why sneak off to meet Farmer Woodruff's lad? A six-foot lump without a brain in his head.'

'Because *he's* got a friend who's thick with the footman at that grand new house on East Cliff. He's promised to sneak me in to have a look round. It's like a palace, they say. Don't know who I might come across there, do I?'

'Some sprig of the gentry who'll be so dazzled he'll fall on his knees and propose on the spot? You're hopeless.' I laughed and gave her a hug. 'You'll get into no end of trouble if you're caught. Just take care, that's all.'

She hugged me back. 'I shall. Anyroad, it'll have to be when the family's out. And even if the worst happened, I reckon I could soon sweet talk my way out of it if a handsome gentleman did catch me dallying in his parlour.'

'I daresay. But suppose it's his sour-faced mama? You'd have a job then!' We both dissolved to giggles at the thought, but after a moment I said, seriously, because it bothered me, 'But you will promise not to have anything to do with Matthew Parker?'

She shrugged. 'You are a fuss pot. I've told you. He doesn't interest me at all. Why should I *want* to get mixed up with him? Just because I'm friendly with Flossie doesn't mean I've got to like her brothers. Poor Floss despairs of the lot of them.'

'I know. It's hard when you're trying to live a decent life and you've got a feckless bunch like that hanging on your coat-tails.'

Flossie. She seemed hardly to have changed at all since we first glimpsed her through the Furze House window, though she was all of sixteen now. If she had grown these last years it was hardly discernible. She was still as skinny as a blade of grass, though Mrs Hawkins was always chuckling at the amount she ate. 'Her eats enough to satisfy a carthorse! Where 'er puts it all, I don't know.' Flossie's one great flaw – in Mrs Greenwood's opinion at least – was that she had never mastered the art of moving silently and discreetly about her duties. In consequence she never thought twice about adding her opinion to any conversation, to Mrs Greenwood's chagrin and Miss Swann's amusement. 'Her comments might be unfortunate at times, but she means no offence by them,' Miss Swann said firmly. 'We are blessed that she has turned out so competent and willing and good-tempered. I, for one, am deeply grateful that we do not have to contend with churlish behaviour or laziness.'

But today there was nothing to amuse Miss Swann or any of us in Flossie's blunt words. Rather, they sent a little ripple of shock around the room. *If he'm still in the land of the living.* She had expressed what we had not yet dared to voice aloud: the possibility that Kit had not survived the conflict.

'Nearly three years since he went,' Biddie ventured, looking up from the pink ribbon trimming she was stitching on to her summer bonnet. 'You'd have thought we'd have heard something by now.'

'Indeed, indeed,' said Mrs Greenwood dolefully.

'We must try not to be pessimistic,' said Miss Swann. She adjusted her eyeglasses more firmly on her nose. 'No news may very well mean good news.'

'To cling to false hope, Tryphena, is foolish,' said Mrs Greenwood. She was lying back in her chair, eyes closed, wafting her face with a paper fan. 'I prefer to look facts in the face. There have been as many lost at sea, I am sure, as ever fell on land.'

Such cold, cold words. I felt the touch of them stirring the hairs on the back of my neck, stilling my hand over the paper so that I narrowly missed marring my careful writing with a blot.

'It is not unknown for sailors to return after several years at sea,' Miss Swann said. But there was the hint of a sigh in her voice that spoke of sadly wavering hope.

Though the windows were open back and front there was a breathless quality to the August afternoon. Even the voices of the five little girls out in the garden sounded muted as though the heat was dulling their play.

'I do believe we shall have a thunderstorm,' Mrs Greenwood said. 'It will clear the air, of course, but I do so dread the noise. My head aches abominably as it is. Perhaps, Bridget, you would be kind enough to run upstairs and fetch my bottle of lavender water. I find it is the only thing that gives me cooling relief.'

Mrs Greenwood had slipped into the role of semi-invalid with the greatest ease. Ever since her bad bout of bronchitis and my appointment as Miss Swann's assistant, she had gradually relinquished most of her school duties, now choosing only to give lessons on the forte-piano in the parlour to a few carefully selected girls whose papas were willing to pay a higher fee for her exclusive attention. The rest of the time she commandeered the ever-willing Biddie to entertain her with gossip or a hand of cards or to run up and downstairs with possets and comforts. Theoretically, she took a turn supervising the boarders out of school hours, but more and more that duty fell to Biddie or me. Not that either of us minded. The mothering of little girls, who might well have been orphaned for all they saw of their parents, was something we could both carry out with understanding. Besides which, we felt that whatever we did would barely compensate for the kindness we had been shown at Furze House. Not least in the matter of the salary we were now paid. Small though it was, ten pounds a year each, paid in quarterly increments, it gave us a tremendous sense of independence, of being truly valued. We both, though, had very different ideas about spending it.

Biddie's quarterly fifty shillings burned her fingers until it was gone. I put mine carefully aside so that I could draw out the enjoyment of the occasional luxury I allowed myself – usually a new book to set alongside *The Lake of Killarney* on the table in our bedchamber. I had six small volumes now, besides the one Violet Briggs had given me. But once it had been a pen cutter – plainer than Miss Swann's ivory-cased one but just as efficient on the goose quills Farmer Woodruff gave us. Another time a pretty glass ink pot with a hinged brass lid. A perfect waste of good money, in Biddie's opinion, who was perplexed that I did not wish to indulge in fripperies for personal decoration, as she did.

It was hard to explain. There was a quality so reassuring – so *lasting* – about these small items. They spoke to me of a future in which they might be enjoyed – used – over and over again. I could still be taking pleasure from the touch, the feel, the look of them when I was eighty as I did now, when I was almost eighteen. It was the continuity they represented. The sense of permanence. I loved them for that. However restless and unsettled my life should turn out, these things, I knew, would not change. Though I had not heard from Violet Briggs since Billy brought word two years since that Mrs Turpin had died of an apoplexy and the inn was taken over by Wesleyans who were providing prayer and plain food for travellers, rather than girls and gambling for Buxton dandies, I still thought of her with gratitude whenever I picked up *The Lake of Killarney* to re-read.

The rest of my salary I portioned out for the necessities we must now be responsible for such as new boots and clothes. I had now, thankfully, finished growing and had filled out very little, so my few dresses needed nothing more than letting out here and there and darning or patching where necessary. The sturdy boots Mrs Loveridge's largesse had provided cost no more than a shilling or two to be repaired and I was fortunate that I was able to replace my light summer shoes with a pair the cobbler had left on his hands after the death of one of his customers. So I saved what I could, for I knew exactly what I planned to do with it. And very soon. Excitement stirred in me whenever I thought about it: I should take a trip to Moondance.

For a long time I had struggled to contain the hunger to see my home. Now, with the means to do it, and the growing confidence that the secure years at Furze House had given me, that hunger had grown to a pressing need. I had enough to cover the fare and lodging somewhere near for a night or two. All I should like now was Miss Swann's blessing. I closed my mind to thoughts of disapproval. She was the most considerate and sensible of women. Surely she would understand? But she had once told me to look forward not back and perhaps it was uncertainty about her reaction that had so far stopped me from broaching the subject. For if she did oppose me, I should find it very sad to lose anything of the respect and affection that lay between us.

My self-appointed task was done. I gave a sigh of relief as I wrote the last word and cleaned my pen on the neatly bound penwiper Biddie had made for me out of a scrap of black velvet.

'Finished, dear?' Miss Swann asked. 'May I see?'

'That is the last,' I said, handing her one of the handbills I had made out.

'"Mr William Rossiter,"' she read aloud, '"respectfully begs to inform previous purchasers of his elegant CARVED WOODEN ANIMALS and BIRDS that a new selection may be viewed at the address below. If any lady or gentleman should wish a private viewing Mr Rossiter is willing to wait upon them at a convenient time, entirely without obligation."

'"To persons new to the town, these ornamental carvings have been the subject of much favourable comment by residents and visitors alike. They constitute a charming token of a visit to Dawlish and are conveniently sized to blend with any tasteful arrangement of ornament in the fashionable drawing room. Prices from One Shilling."'

I laughed. 'I have taken a little licence for I daresay if any carvings have fallen into the hands of visitors it is quite by accident. But we are residents, are we not, and we think them very fine, so that is not stretching licence too far.'

Miss Swann nodded. 'It is excellent, Miranda. I am sure Billy will approve.'

'I had prodigious arguments with him over the wording, leave alone the amount of persuasion needed to allow me to draw up the handbills.' I stacked them into a neat pile. 'He is too modest for his own good. But Emma was greatly taken with the idea of advertising in this fashion. As for the prices, left to himself he would sooner give his carvings away – as he very nearly did when his brother used to take them to Newton for him and began to sell them in job lots to that rascal of a shopkeeper.'

'Indeed,' said Miss Swann stoutly. 'When you pointed them out in the shop window I could hardly believe my eyes. How much had Billy received for them?'

'Fourpence each.'

'And there was not one priced under half-a-crown! Not to mention that large and very fine heron at seven and sixpence!'

'Well, we'll see if these bills drum up some decent business, without any sort of middleman. Though I reckon if Billy is called upon to visit anyone with his wares, Emma had better go with him or he will be bound to offer them more cheaply than we have agreed. She's far more practical and businesslike.' I stood up and stretched my cramped, inky fingers for I had been writing all afternoon. 'If you will excuse me, I will make haste and deliver them before he has chance to change his mind.'

'I'll help you, if you like,' Biddie said quickly. Then with a glance at Mrs Greenwood, 'At least, if there's nothing else for the moment . . .'

'Nothing I cannot cope with, dear,' said Miss Swann before Mrs Greenwood could answer. 'Run along both of you and keep an eye on the weather'

'So what is the attraction in Dawlish today?' I asked Biddie as we walked down the hill. 'Not delivering handbills, that's for sure.'

'Perhaps I fancied a little exercise,' she said airily.

'You? Never. Perhaps I should rephrase my question. *Who*'s the attraction?'

She tried to look innocent and failed. 'I do intend to help. Honest. After all, I do have certain *connections* in East Cliff.'

'Ah, I see. The footman in that big house who sneaked you in for a look round.'

She giggled. 'You should see him in his livery. So handsome and with such fine manners. Won't it please you if I can persuade him to take a handbill and pass it on to his mistress?'

'It depends what form this persuasion takes,' I said dryly.

'Oh, don't be so stuffy! If I allow him to hold my hand for a minute or even snatch a kiss by way of payment, what's the harm?' Her eyes sparkled under the brim of the straw bonnet she had fetchingly adorned with a length of yellow ribbon to match the muslin of her last summer's gown which she had now altered and tucked and trimmed to seem entirely new. 'If you'd take your nose out of your books sometimes, Mirrie, and listen to the gossip among the girls, you'd know that the allowing of such liberties is quite commonplace among their older sisters and friends.'

'You're a tease and a flirt, Bridget Riley,' I said, shaking my head.

'Why not?' She was quite irrepressible. 'It's such *fun*.'

She went off laughing in search of her handsome footman and I turned to my less exciting – but certainly more efficient way – of ensuring the handbills were brought to the attention of potential customers. I knew many people in the town now, from the parents of our pupils to tradespeople and genteel acquaintances of Miss Swann and Mrs Greenwood. In no time at all I had disposed of the handbills to those who had properties rented out to visitors or who let out rooms, pleased that everyone promised to bring the notice to the attention of their tenants.

My final call was upon the Rossiters. Emma was alone in the cottage with the children, the two older ones playing on the doorstep, the new baby occupying the cradle in the corner.

'All delivered,' I said as I carefully stepped over a pre-tend tea party of flower-petal food arranged on pebbles and sycamore-leaf plates. 'I saved just one which I thought you might put in the window.'

I read it out to Emma and she listened attentively. 'You'm lettered it just as we agreed,' she said. 'And you priced 'en one shillin'?'

'*From* one shilling, remember. Try to get at least a florin or half-a-crown for the bigger pieces. They are worth every penny. And anyone who comes to look is sure to admire the way you've set everything out.'

'Looks 'andsome, Miss Miranda, though I says it myself.' She stood back proudly to review her handiwork.

Billy had knocked together a makeshift table which was placed under the window where it could be seen by anyone passing. Emma had covered it with a sheet and set the carvings around a handful of marigolds set in an old cracked mug. Arranged as they were, in a good light, it was possible to appreciate Billy's sure touch and countryman's eye for detail. The impression of quick, darting movement in his favourite model, the perky wren. The swirl of hair on a rabbit's side as though the wind ruffled it. The predatory tilt of a kestrel's head . . .

There were a good many carvings – too many, Billy would have said. His ulcerated leg had laid him up for much of the summer and there had been many empty hours to fill. Emma's relief that he had become too slow and incapacitated to be sent out on deliveries for Captain Luscombe had soon turned to anxiety. Their small savings were quickly swallowed up and though relatives – little better off themselves – did what they could and Emma took any rough cleaning work available, the spectre of the poorhouse hung perilously close. I had managed to sell one or two carvings to a stallholder on Newton Abbot market who was more scrupulous in his dealings than the greedy shopkeeper, but what little profit I had gained for Billy he immediately counteracted by pressing on me two of his pieces, one for me, one for the Furze House parlour.

''Tis small thanks for the many kindnesses we'm been given,' he said gruffly. 'So I'll thank 'ee, maid – Miss Miranda – to take 'en with my blessing.' He grinned shyly. 'You'm a quiet mouse, so I thought that'd suit 'ee – and the cutty for they good ladies, if you please.'

So the perky little wren now adorned the Furze House parlour mantelshelf and the mouse, finely detailed even down to his whiskers, stood with my other treasures. And though I felt a little guilty about it, I knew better than to refuse a gift that was offered with such gentle sincerity.

'So where is Billy?' I asked now.

'Hobbled off down the shore with his fishin' line.' Emma frowned. 'If he brings 'ome somethin' for supper it brightens 'im up. He'm shamed about all this, see.' She gestured at the carvings. 'He don't think 'tis proper work for a man.'

'But he's so talented,' I protested. 'He should be proud of what he does.'

'To him 'tis only by way o' being an idle pastime. It don't bring a proper man's wage, do it? He puts a good face on things, my Billy, but it cuts 'im deep that he'm not providin' for his family as he should . . . And now his leg's on the mend, I'm afeard he'll take up with Captain Luscombe again.' She looked at me with wide, anxious eyes. 'Trade's busier than ever since they Frenchies opened up the Channel ports last year. Word is, the Captain's making a mint o' money now he'm able to trade wi' Roscoff again.' She sighed. 'The thought of Billy doin' all that journeying up and down the country fair upsets me. Widow Thomas says 'tis only rest and careful poulticin' with marigold and comfrey an' such, as can keep his leg sound. Gallivantin' over the country'll only set 'im back where he was – desperate with pain and scarcely able to put his foot to the floor.'

As I followed the brook sliding to the shore between its green sheep-nibbled banks, I thought of how Emma's bright face was beginning to show the careworn look that was the mark of all women too poor ever to feel secure. She was no more than one and twenty, yet strain was already beginning to etch frown lines in her forehead and turn down the corners of a mouth that had once been so quick to smile. I hoped desperately, for all their sakes, that Billy might find some easy, regular work soon.

Biddie and I had arranged to meet near the lower bridge across the stream, but she was not in sight. I looked anxiously at the sky. Thunder growled distantly. Gulls floated like scraps of white paper against the dense purple-grey clouds that had now swallowed up all the summer blue. The red of the cliffs, the greens of the fields on the hills above the town, had taken on a strident, lurid quality. It had gone very still. Not a breeze stirred the glassy pewter of the sea's surface. Strollers were beginning to scatter for shelter. I was thankful when at last I saw Biddie coming down the road. I watched her approach with some impatience.

Biddie rarely hurried. She was drifting along now in her usual slow way, careful to avoid sharp stones that might damage the thin soles of her shoes and holding her skirts lightly with one hand to prevent them becoming soiled by the pink dust that fluffed up from the road surface at every step. She seemed not to realise that the more she dawdled, the greater the likelihood that we should get a drenching from the imminent storm. What a wailing about ruined clothes there would be then! And just look at her now, the silly ha'porth . . . Well aware of the knot of idling men congregated in front of the Public Rooms, she released her skirts so that the daffodil yellow perfection of her dress could be properly seen and tilted her head in that coquettish way she had, not looking directly at them but sliding her glance sideways so as not to miss anything of their appreciative looks. Her expression was innocence itself, an innocence born of the knowledge of her own devastating prettiness, her romantic day-dreams and the simplicity of her trust in the promise of those dreams. An innocence that was betrayed by the slow languor of her walk which expressed an altogether different, deeper sensuality – something so much a part of her, so natural, that she was quite unconscious of it. And something that added profoundly – perhaps dangerously – to her attraction in the eyes of men.

Dangerous?

Depending on my mood, I was either amused by the effect Biddie had on the opposite sex or made impatient. It was only recently that I had felt the unworthy and unexpected pangs of something very like envy at the way my friend drew every male eye. This was something new to me and decidedly bewildering when I had taken such care – such satisfaction –

in keeping myself ordinary and unremarked. At first for fear of recognition as a runaway. Then, as that became of secondary importance, feeling no urge whatsoever to bother myself with primping and preening and discussing whether a flounce here or a bow there would improve a bodice or a skirt. For heaven's sake, why should I want to be like Biddie? I had spent the last three years improving my mind. That was more important to me than anything else . . .

Dangerous.

The word reverberated in my head a second before I saw one of the men step away from the others, lean towards Biddie and say something.

Matthew Parker.

My stomach knotted. I took a step towards her, urgency propelling me to run across the bridge and drag her away, but at that moment a huge gust of wind, forerunner of the storm, whipped in from the sea and blustered up the combe, sweeping me off balance and almost taking the bonnet from my head. One of the men lost his hat and ran after it over the lawns. The others, grinning, moved off. Only Matthew Parker remained to watch Biddie as she crossed the bridge. Only he was there to observe how the yellow muslin moulded itself to rounded limbs and hips and the full swell of young breasts as the wind dragged at the daffodil dress. I had heard scandalous tales of women in society who damped their petticoats so that they clung to the skin. This in order that the light muslins of their dresses should offer little impediment to a viewing of the contours of the body beneath. In that instant Biddie, unknowingly, was as near-naked as any of those lubricious women who knowingly flaunted their bodies to any lewd or shocked eye.

Matthew Parker saw. Matthew Parker laughed and called some comment that the wind whisked away.

And I wished I had been a man and could have knocked him down and kicked him where he lay and ground that leer from his face with my heel . . .

The wind dropped as suddenly as it had arisen. Then Biddie

was beside me, breathless, retying the loosened strings of her bonnet, giggling, 'God a-mighty, I thought I'd have been blown into the stream.'

I took her arm, shook it. She blinked at me in surprise.

'What did he say?' I demanded. 'What did Matthew Parker say to you?'

'Him? Nothing much. Passed the time of day, that's all.' She tugged her arm away. 'What's up with you?'

'You promised you wouldn't encourage him!'

'I only said good afternoon,' she protested. 'What's the harm in being polite?'

What was the harm? I took a trembling breath. It was difficult to speak of the panic that had consumed me. I knew what it was, but that troubling 'other' sense had lain dormant for a long time and I had forgotten its effects . . . *Trust your feelings . . . do not be afraid.* Widow Thomas's words came back so strongly that she might have been whispering them in my ear.

I was surprised that my voice sounded so calm and reasonable when I managed to say, 'Matthew Parker's the sort of man who'd take even an everyday politeness as encouragement. You'd have been better ignoring him completely. I hope you will do in future.'

'Yes, Miss Swann, no, Miss Swann,' Biddie mimicked. 'Honestly, Mirrie, you get more like her every day.'

'I take that as a compliment.'

'I didn't mean it as such . . . leastways, I know *you* think the sun shines out of her arse but what is she but a dried-up old maid? That's how you'll end up if you don't watch out.' Then, her sense of fairness overcoming her flash of temper: 'Oh, I didn't mean it like that. She's good-hearted. God knows, we've both got reason to be grateful to both the old dears. But that doesn't mean we can't have ideas of our own.'

'So long as they're . . . sensible ideas,' I said coolly, striving not to think of my own fantasies about Moondance and Theophilus Crowe.

'Dammit, Mirrie! What's sensible got to do with anything?'

Her green eyes flashed dangerously. 'I don't want us to fall out, but don't be always on at me about things you know – or care – nothing about or we shall. Understand?'

I looked at her, my friend, and for an instant she was a stranger. A beautiful, wilful, unknowable stranger. No longer a person to be coaxed or chivvied or persuaded to do anything against her will. Then the stranger vanished, became the Biddie I knew, her mouth curling into its ready smile, her tone reproachful and teasing, 'Don't you want to know how I got on up at East Cliff?'

Nothing more to be done. I could not make her listen. I could only watch and wait and guard her as best I could.

'Yes,' I said quietly. 'Yes, I'm sorry. Of course I do,' I said. 'I daresay I was . . . over anxious. On account of the storm. Tell me as we walk.' I took her arm, more gently this time, urging her to hurry up the road as the dazzling flicker of summer lightning snapped round us like the white fangs of a pack of hunting dogs.

The first huge drops were splattering down as we burst into Furze House, breathless and laughing. We took off our bonnets and were tidying our hair at the hall mirror when Flossie whisked into the hall, eyes wide, to say in an awed whisper, 'There's a visitor a-waitin' for 'ee. You'm best hurry. 'Er's been waitin' this half-hour – a Mrs Lascelles.'

Biddie and I looked at each other. We knew nobody of that name.

'Mrs Greenwood said you'm to go straight in.' Flossie gave Biddie a none-too-gentle push in the direction of the parlour door. ''Er's gentry! From Exeter. As fine a lady as I ever did see a-strolling in the town. Quicksticks.'

That it was something important and of a private nature was evident. The bottle of Madeira, usually reserved for visits of the well-to-do parents of our boarders or for special occasions like Christmas, stood at Miss Swann's elbow on its silver tray with an accompanying plate of water-thin biscuits. The five young boarders who would normally have been called to wait upon the visitor as a way of instructing them in the art of polite entertaining, had evidently been despatched to the schoolroom. I could hear the patter of footsteps and the faint sound of chatter overhead.

The visitor inclined her head in acknowledgement as we made our curtsies, the rim of the bonnet momentarily shadowing her face. One elegant hand lay on the arm of the chair. The hand was clothed in a glove of the finest cream kid. A fall of creamy lace adorned the bodice of a rich silk gown the colour of ripe apricots. On her head a matching silk bonnet decorated with cream and brown ribbons and a large feather which curled gracefully around the brim from which a knot of shiny blonde curls emerged. I could almost feel Biddie taking frantic note of all the fashionable details of this expensive attire before this elegant vision raised her head and spoke. It was the tone of the sharp, clear voice that snapped me back three years though her speech had lost all but the faintest trace of its north-country origins.

'Good afternoon, Miranda, Bridget. Do you remember me? I am Mrs Lascelles. I was Miss Briggs.'

Biddie's jaw dropped. I was rendered quite speechless. Violet Briggs?

'I see that you do,' she said dryly. 'And I think you find me somewhat changed in appearance from when I was forced by circumstances to find work as a companion to the late Mrs Turpin, under whose roof you took shelter when you were, shall we say, in need of protection.'

Companion! That was a new name for it.

'And the change in you is remarkable.' She looked us both up and down, her fine eyebrows raised. 'I find it hard to believe you were ever in such straits as when I last saw you . . . But there is no need to look apprehensive. My visit is made from the most amiable of motives. I have already had a most instructive conversation with Mrs Greenwood and Miss Swann. Perhaps you would care to seat yourselves and we may continue.'

A searing flash of lightning followed by an enormous clap

of thunder made us all jump. Beyond the back window the lurid darkness and the drumming rain made it impossible to see anything beyond the wildly thrashing bushes growing close to the house.

'I chose a poor day to call,' Violet said. 'I am afraid I shall have to beg your hospitality until the rain stops.'

'Of course,' said Miss Swann gruffly.

'Oh, you must certainly not attempt to leave before the storm is over,' Mrs Greenwood fluttered. The presence of the fashionable visitor seemed to have had a miraculous effect on her headache and invalidish languor.

Violet smiled the cool, clever smile I remembered well. 'I was tempted by the prospect of a pleasant walk after the drive from Exeter or I should have come to the door in my carriage. Still, I am not one to overtax my horses. They have the long drive home to face this evening.'

My carriage. Well, well.

'You . . . you are staying in Exeter?' I ventured.

'I live there and have done for more than a year. My late husband had connections in the town. I must explain. Two years ago I married. Sadly, my husband was taken from me barely three months later after an accident on the hunting field.'

'So very sad,' Mrs Greenwood murmured.

Or convenient.

'Indeed,' Violet said. Her blue, intense gaze went from Biddie to me. I recognised the warning. Accept this as the truth. This is how it must be. Take care what you say. 'My husband was very fond of Devonshire and only days before he died we had been making plans to spend a few weeks in Exeter before journeying to Plymouth and taking passage to Italy for the winter. Alas, that was not to be.' A faint shrug, an almost imperceptible sigh to convey a grief too deep for mere words. Beautifully executed. 'It was something of a pilgrimage in honour of his memory that brought me to Exeter. And I found it so congenial a place and the people there displaying such refinement and quiet amiability that I decided I could do worse than make your gracious county town my home.'

I could not resist the question.

'How did you find us, Miss . . . Mrs Lascelles?' I asked innocently.

'It was not too difficult. I believe it was the gentleman who was your escort, Mr Warrener, who mentioned your destination as a school in Dawlish. Such a charming and talented young man, as I recall. I have been greatly saddened this afternoon to hear what has happened to him. It was a small matter to put about enquiries as to the schools in the district.' How smoothly the half-truth slid from her tongue. 'You are perhaps also wondering why I took the trouble to seek you out?'

'That did cross my mind, ma'am,' I said gravely.

'I have a small interest in works of a charitable nature.' A modest gesture with one kid-gloved hand. 'There are many lonely hours to fill, d'you see, when one is placed as I am. But I have always found satisfaction in turning my mind to the welfare of those deserving of assistance among the poor and destitute. Retaining, as I did, a curiosity to see how you had fared . . . well, I had quite made up my mind that if I discovered you in any kind of distress I should do my best to help you. But I now see that any anxiety I had on your behalf was quite misplaced.'

'Was it not kind of Mrs Lascelles to take such trouble?' Mrs Greenwood said.

'We're both very grateful,' Biddie replied, recovering her speech, though she still looked a trifle dazed.

I feared she might say something out of turn, so I said hastily, 'Indeed we are, ma'am.' I smiled at Miss Swann. 'We truly fell among friends.'

'That is all I wished to hear,' Violet said. 'I shall return to Exeter greatly relieved in my mind. Ah, thank you, Miss Swann, just half a glass more if you please, and yes, I should indeed like another of those delicious biscuits. Your cook has a very light hand.'

The conversation fell to general matters, in the course of which Violet managed to mention her fine house in Bedford Circus and her acquaintance with several titled persons whom she encountered at meetings of the charitable committees on which she served.

Mrs Greenwood was deeply impressed. Even Miss Swann, whose instincts were keener and whose judgements more thoughtful, seemed thoroughly taken in. And why not? There was nothing in Violet's performance to merit any doubt. I was intrigued. How much was lies and how much truth? Was she really a rich widow? *I have plans*. I remembered her saying that. Clever, manipulative Violet. Those plans had obviously come to a ripe fruition. I longed to catch a minute alone with her to find out more, but my hopes of that were dashed when, once the rain had stopped, she asked if her maid, Wilkins, could be summoned. Of course there would have to be a maid! No lady of quality and careful of her reputation would wander about a strange town unaccompanied. Wilkins turned out to be a smiling, neat, middle-aged woman who had been consigned to the kitchen with Mrs Hawkins and Flossie and now appeared bearing a large umbrella and a light silk shawl which she draped carefully round her mistress's shoulders before they ventured into the damp air. But there was to be one more surprise before she left.

'How very pleasantly I have spent the afternoon,' Violet said, smoothing down the apricot silk of her skirt. Then, with a sighing glance at Miss Swann and Mrs Greenwood, 'In truth, I find myself a touch envious of your little establishment. Of course, I am exceedingly comfortable in Exeter and am admirably looked after by devoted servants – but when one is widowed and has not the blessing of any other family in the world, well, to be sure, it comes to me how very fortunate you are to have agreeable young people constantly about you.' A hesitation, then, more briskly, 'Which brings me to mention a matter I have been mulling over while I have been enjoying your hospitality. I find both Miranda and Bridget a great credit to the care and affection they have received here.'

A gracious, approving glance at both ladies. 'However, it does come to me that I might be in a position to give some assistance in introducing them to a wider sphere of society. With your permission, I should like to invite both girls to spend a few days with me in Exeter.'

'That is most gracious of you, Mrs Lascelles,' said Mrs Greenwood. 'So very kind . . .'

'Kind? No, no, not on my part, I assure you. It is these young ladies who will display kindness by accepting my invitation, for it would divert me exceedingly to show them some of the charms of the town and accompany them to a concert or arrange some entertainment to which other young people might be invited. Miss Swann? Would that be agreeable to you?'

Miss Swann, never to be rushed over any important matter, considered for what seemed to be a very long moment. Then she nodded slowly. 'I have no objection if Miranda and Bridget wish to avail themselves of your generous offer.'

'Oh, yes, Miss Swann,' Bridget burst out, green eyes sparking with excitement.

'And you, Miranda?'

'Thank you,' I said. 'I should like it very much.'

'Then I shall be in touch shortly,' said Violet.

Two days later her invitation arrived written on smooth, expensive paper. A week later Miranda and I took the morning coach from Dawlish to Exeter where we were met by Violet's coachman and escorted to Bedford Circus where we should spend the final ten days of August.

'Husband?' Violet kicked off her satin slippers and sank back into the lacy pillows on her bed. She threw back her head and laughed uproariously. 'I was his *mistress* – so-called, though he barely had strength to raise his voice, leave alone anything else! He was close on eighty, with a sanctimonious old wife and a brace of sour old-maid daughters. All I had to do was submit to his fumblings and try to rouse that part of him which had not known life for twenty years. To no avail whatsoever, I may add. If I had been virgin when our brief but rewarding partnership began, I should still have been virgin at the end of it.'

We had washed off the dust of our journey in adjoining bedchambers – each twice the size of the one we occupied at Furze House – dined in the formal elegance of the mahogany and crimson dining chamber, drunk tea afterwards in a blue-and-white drawing room set about with slender gilt chairs and a pair of matching settees upholstered with striped blue silk. Violet had then escorted us on a tour of the rest of the house. We peered wonderstruck into a library and an adjoining room with card tables, and on the upper floor the two bedchambers beyond the ones we occupied. And all the while Violet did not once relax her guard. She played the role of gracious mistress of this fine establishment to perfection, having cautioned us sharply the first moment we had been shown in to her on our arrival to say nothing out of place in front of the servants.

At last she had shown us into her own bedroom and closed the door.

'*Now* you may ask the hundred questions you are burning to ask,' she said. She turned the quelling gaze of the old Violet on to us. 'But before you begin, let me warn you here and now that if you betray me by one word, even by accident, to anyone – I repeat, *anyone* – then I shall pack you off back where you came from.' A small pause in which her hard blue eyes shone with the glitter of a small ferocious animal. 'Not only that, but if I am found out, then you are found out, too. Do you understand me?'

We did. But, stung by her tone, I could not help replying huffily, 'We're well versed in discretion. Though I find myself surprised that you bothered to look us up at all if you're convinced we're about to announce to the world that here is Violet Briggs who once earned her keep as a whore.'

She raised her eyebrows. Then smiled, looking not in the least put out.

'That's more like it. I had feared the old dames had turned you prim as well as dowdy. And by God, girl, we shall have to do something drastic with your appearance before you are seen in public with the fashionable Mrs Lascelles. At least you, Biddie Riley, show some pride in yourself, even if the result is overblown to the point of vulgarity.'

'*Mrs* Lascelles?' I interrupted. 'Who, then, was this unsuspecting creature you settled on to be your husband?'

That was when she sank to the comfort of the bed, gestured us to draw up two chairs beside her and laughed away any idea that she had been married.

She had known Vincent, she said, as long as she had been at The Plough.

'He escorted his wife and daughters from his Lancashire estates to take the Buxton waters twice a year, in spring and autumn, and in order to escape being closeted with them in lodgings, he spent most of the time riding about the countryside on the pretext of collecting rock specimens for his geological collection. One day he called at The Plough for refreshment. By accident, he claimed, and I have no reason to doubt him for he was not of the set which patronised such places for the diversions on offer, or had ever been so. He was a country squire of plain tastes and faithful inclinations. Until he met me.' She stared up at the yellow pattern of flowers strewn across the white quilted canopy above the bed, her expression momentarily remote, whether to hide sadness or satisfaction it was hard to tell. 'My looks reminded, him, you see, of a girl he had known when he was young and should have married had she not died of a brain fever.'

'And he fell in love with you because of that?' Biddie breathed. 'How romantical, even if he was so old.'

'Love? Lust more like – and less for me than for his lost youth, the ugly old fool,' she said, without heat. 'Aye, ugly. He was bald as an egg, with the sad looks of an aged bloodhound. The other girls were glad he always picked me. Their preference was for young men with pretty faces and pleasing bodies. They hadn't the wit to see that he was more of a gentleman than most who claim the name nor did they guess how easily I earned my money . . . Half the time he did no more than hold my hand while he talked of the girl who died and the hopes that died with her. Sometimes he had me pretend that I was this Pamela and we were on our wedding night – and even then he was almost too overcome to touch me.'

'He must have adored her,' I said.

'Then more fool he to be besotted by a dream.' She sighed. 'The reality would probably have proved very different. The saintly Pamela might have turned out a shrew or cuckolded him with his best friend or bankrupted him for love of gaming. Or something equally human and understandable.' She waved her hand impatiently. 'What do I care about her? Nothing, save that I was able to use my likeness to this paragon to good advantage after Mrs Turpin turned up her toes. She fell dead of an overstrained heart one morning in October. By then, she was dropsical and scarcely able to waddle from bed to table, though perfectly able to give orders and keep a tight hold on the purse strings. God strewth, I was practically run ragged keeping the place going and the customers happy, for I was the only one she trusted to do everything properly. And little I got but promises that she'd see me right one day for all the extra work I'd done.' Her face creased in to a complacent smile. 'Once she'd gone, though, I made damned sure I got my reward. She'd never been one to let her hard-earned money into the hands of bankers. I knew the exact place under the floorboards of her room where she kept it.'

'You stole her money?'

'Stole? Goddammit, if anyone had earned it, I had! Should I have left it for a stranger to find? Should I have turned it over to lawyers to get their greedy fingers on? There was a will of sorts among her papers, a fair amount of gold jewellery which she saw as a solid investment, some good china and silver . . . I touched none of that. And I could have done. Cleared the place of everything valuable and disappeared before she was cold. But I didn't. I saw her decently buried, the lawyers who dealt with the lease informed, the other girls and the servants paid what they were due and only then did I take my leave quietly before whatever cousins Mrs Turpin had left turned up to squabble over the spoils. She had seen none of them for years. They did not give a fig for her.'

'But you did?' I said softly.

Violet paused. 'She was cunning, unscrupulous and greedy but she could have moments of generosity and she dealt fairly enough with her girls so long as they were considered an attraction at The Plough. I suppose . . . I suppose she was the nearest thing to a parent I ever knew.' She gave a wry shake of her head. 'The old girl had a measure of respect for me, though I do not flatter myself it would have made any difference had she not become ill. She would have put me off as ruthlessly as she did the others when she considered the fresh bloom of youth had begun to fade. But she grew to rely on me more and more and in that final year we became . . . well, not friends exactly. Allies, shall we say, in a common cause.'

'What about the old gentleman?' Biddie said. 'How did you take up with him afterwards?'

'Vincent had been due to leave Buxton with his family to return to his estate just to the north of Manchester. He was distressed at the thought that he should no longer be able to see me, so I struck a bargain with him. I should not have done it had I not had the means to be independent. But though I had watched and worked and practised to better myself, if my greater ambition was to be achieved, I had a great deal more to learn. I asked him to find me lodgings at a rent I could afford somewhere convenient to us both where he could visit me at any time. I promised I should be faithful entirely to him. In return I asked only that he find someone to teach me the manners and etiquette demanded of a lady in society.'

'And he did?'

'He was a man of his word. I was a woman of mine. He found me suitable rooms in a modest terrace with my own door which opened to an entry alongside the high wall of a brewery where a visitor might come and go without being observed. On three afternoons a week a genteel widow fallen on hard times came to give me instruction or sometimes we would walk out in the fashionable parts of Manchester, or go to the theatre, in order that I might observe how ladies conducted themselves in public places. As often as he could, Vincent rode the five miles into Manchester to visit me. I believe in those few months we gave each other a deal of contentment. If he had not fallen from his horse . . . well, it is speculation to say I should have stayed all this while. But I would have given him a year, at least. Before I moved on.'

'To further this ambition of yours?' I said.

'Ah, ambition.' She looked slowly round the bedroom with its elegant rosewood furniture and sunny yellow upholstery. 'I have achieved it. I wanted to be . . . respectable. I wanted to eradicate every trace of my past and reinvent myself as a person who could be acknowledged and accepted by polite society as one of their own. Now I have exactly what I wished for. But as I once heard or read somewhere, it is as well to be careful what one wishes for lest it is granted.'

'Aren't you happy, then?' I asked, puzzled.

'Happy? Let me tell you of the retired colonels and admirals and nabobs and their strait-laced wives and dutiful daughters who make up the circles to which I have gained entry. One must be polite to them, support their views and their charities and their card parties and soirées if one wishes to establish oneself in the role one has chosen for oneself. Which, in my case, is the comfortably off young widow of an elderly country squire, who spent her childhood quietly, in rural Staffordshire, with an elderly aunt. There have even been a brace of widowers and one or two hopeful, well-bred sprigs of impoverished families who have come sniffing round with a view to establishing themselves as suitors. Diverting them provided some little entertainment, for I have no intention of ever again making myself beholden to any man or woman. Also, my decorous behaviour and devotion to my late husband's memory has increased regard for me among the Exeter matrons. I am someone to be trusted to be firm but kind with a calf-sick son or a husband with a straying eye.' Her smile was cynical. 'So I have what I have sought for so long . . .'

'But?'

'But . . . I had not expected to be quite so *bored*.' She swung herself off the bed and spread her arms wide. 'I have all this, yet cannot be satisfied. Is it not sad that I am reduced to inviting two runaway brats for a visit in order to furnish myself with a little excitement?'

Biddie giggled. 'You're joshing us, Miss Vi . . . Mrs Lascelles.'

She shrugged. 'Perhaps it is my nature never to be satisfied. I cannot remember a time in my twenty-four years when I have not been striving to better myself.' She walked to the window and looked down into the road below. 'Now I have reached a plateau of attainment and, like the prospect I look out upon here each day, I find it a little too bland for my taste.'

'Well, I don't care what reasons you have for asking us here,' Biddie said stoutly, 'I'm glad you did. And if I'd have come across Mrs Turpin's money, I'd have bought a house just like this. It must be the nicest one in the town.'

'Not by a long chalk,' Violet said. 'But suitable enough for a widow living alone . . . And let me assure you, Mrs Turpin's hoard did not buy this house.' She still stared down into the road, her voice level and unemotional as she said, 'It was a lawyer who brought me news of Vincent's accident. He advised me that his client had left instructions to ensure that I was cared for. Mr Piggot – for that was his name, Vincent Alexander Lascelles Piggot – wanted me to have a house anywhere I wished. Arrangements would be put in hand, discreetly, through an agent upon my settling upon a location. Money had already been invested on my behalf, the proceeds of which would allow the establishment to be comfortably maintained and I need never be in want again.' She broke off, said with the faintest of tremors in her voice, quickly stilled, 'I . . . I had never, never expected anything of the kind. And I could not thank him. That was the worst of it.'

I went to her and put my hand on her arm.

'You thank him by remembering him with gratitude and affection. Which is, surely, what he would have wished more than anything else?'

'Yes. Yes, I know.' A small silence, then she straightened her shoulders, shrugged off my hand and in a different voice said, briskly, 'I chose Exeter because Mrs Turpin was always dreaming of coming back here. She began her life in service as a scullery maid in Heavitree. Her memories were painted in such glorious colours that I thought it sounded a veritable paradise. It seemed as good a place as any to make a fresh start. And I had the example to encourage me of a pair of starveling runaways who had from all accounts prospered well enough in the county.' She swung round and said, 'But come, the pair of you, now you must tell me what you would wish out of a visit to Exeter. I shall enjoy spending a little of Mrs Turpin's hoard on such entertainment as will please you. Bridget?'

'Oh, I'd love to see the grand shops and the fashions.' She grinned impishly. 'A handsome duke or a fine young officer to dance attendance wouldn't come amiss, either.'

'Hah! The first request is easily granted. But a good family and comfortable fortune are what count among Exeter society, my girl. As you are possessed of neither, you had best divest yourself of hopes on that account. Now you, Miranda. How would you care to spend your time here?'

'All I wish is to visit my old home in the country, which will be easier to do from Exeter than Dawlish,' I said confidently. 'And I shan't put upon your charity to do it, thank you all the same. I have the means. I shall be away no more than two or three days.'

'Will you, indeed?' she said, in surprise. 'Where is this old home of yours?'

'On the edge of Dartmoor. Ashburton is the nearest town.'

'Mirrie's family were gentry,' Biddie put in, grinning. 'Perhaps she's the one you could find a husband for.'

'It's none of your business, Biddie Riley!'

'She doesn't like talking about it. Can't see why myself. If

I'd been born in a big house and my pa had been a "Sir", I'd boast about it every day . . .'

'What is there to boast about?' I said, unable to keep the bitter edge from my voice. 'The baronetcy died with my father . . . the house belongs to someone else.'

'May I ask then, why you wish to go back?' Violet enquired in her clear, cool voice. 'Out of nostalgia, perhaps? Will that not be upsetting?'

I hesitated. 'Perhaps. But I still know that it is something I want to do more than anything in the world.'

'Good. I admire a sense of purpose.' She smiled brilliantly. 'And what do you propose to do when you get there? Ring the bell and invite yourself to tea?'

'No!' Then, less vehemently, 'No. I . . . I just want to . . . look and remember.'

'So, you intend to skulk in the bushes and brood on the past. How very Gothic.'

'It was the purchaser of the house who sent me to Crossbank,' I said steadily. 'I've no desire to see him lording it over my father's estate.'

'I'm not surprised.' Violet's eyes glinted. 'No fun to be got in presenting yourself looking as you do, all frumpish and dowdy. At best you would be ordered to the servants' entrance, at worst driven off as a vagrant!'

Biddie giggled. I said, incensed, 'Keep your nose out of my affairs, Violet Briggs. How I choose to look and what I choose to do is no concern of . . .'

'Much the best if you returned as a young lady of fashion,' she said, as though I had not spoken. 'Oh, yes, that would be most satisfying.' She prowled round me. 'How old were you when you were put to the mill? You see, he would have no idea who you were . . . and you have good bones and despite your height you do not stoop. We should have to do something with your hair. Wilkins has great skill. Yes, I like the idea better and better.' She completed her circuit and stood in front of me once more. 'Well?' she demanded. 'Would it suit you if we all drove up to the moor on a little excursion? Three young ladies indulging in the popular pastime of viewing notable estates? That is the likeliest ploy to get us entry into . . . what is the place called? Moondance? Very fanciful. From my experience, a shilling to a gardener will secure us the grounds. Half a guinea to the housekeeper will get us inside if the family is not at home. If it is, then such a respectable and vivacious little party might still be invited in . . .'

'There's no housekeeper,' I said through gritted teeth. 'And I don't need any help.'

'If you won't indulge yourself,' said Violet, 'then indulge me.' She linked her hand through my arm. 'Here was I, wilting from boredom, and you have presented me with a perfect little intrigue. Think of it! What fun we shall have if we meet this villain who cast you off! We shall gull him into believing us innocent explorers of the sylvan scene . . . charm him . . . ply him with questions about the house and the previous owners . . . then at an appropriate moment you may announce yourself! The return of the rightful heiress to confront the wicked interloper! Why, it is as good as any melodrama I saw performed upon the stage in all the time I have been in Exeter.'

'Save that I'm not an heiress,' I said flatly. 'And there is little point in confronting someone who has a perfect right to be where he is.'

'Don't be such a killjoy! I won't have it. Come now, you must find *some* amusement in the idea?'

Not so much amusement. More a growing sense that Violet's idea, minus the more melodramatic elements, had a certain merit worth careful consideration. On the few occasions I had met Jed in Newton Abbot he had told me that Theophilus Crowe seldom left his house these days. His gambling forays had become infrequent and there was no more talk of scandal-making visitors. Sightings of him were rare, except from a distance when he was to be seen strolling about the grounds. His foreign manservant was reported to be fierce in guarding his privacy. Would he be, I wondered, a match for Violet? I found the thought interesting.

'No need to decide this instant,' Violet declared. 'We shall go for a little stroll while you think about it. Northernhay Gardens perhaps – and I shall pray we do not meet anyone to whom I must introduce you while you still look such country bumpkins. Biddie, I shall find you a plain silk shawl to cover that excess of frills. The bonnet you came in is tolerable.' A sigh. 'I suppose, Miranda, that weathered straw of yours is your only one. Well, I daresay anything better would show up your gown for the shabby thing it is. At least the shawl is good quality, if a little faded. I will send word right away to my dressmaker to attend us this evening.'

As I was to discover in the following days, having Violet in charge of us was like being swept along by a small, energetic whirlwind. And truth to tell, the novelty of the experience after the quiet routine of Furze House was something I began to find, to my surprise, both invigorating and pleasurable.

The dressmaker, a quiet efficient woman, attended us with one of her apprentices. She brought pattern books and a few fashion papers, which we were allowed the briefest glimpse of before Violet took them over and fell to an earnest discussion with Mrs Chadwick who whipped about us with the measuring tape while the apprentice marked the inches into a book. They ignored Biddie's attempts to give her opinion on what she wanted. I did not bother even to try. I wanted the embarrassing experience of being discussed as though I were deaf, blind and mute over as quickly as possible.

Two days later Mrs Chadwick returned to fit the dresses and stayed to make the final adjustments. I was aghast to find that we had not one but two gowns each, one for day and one for evening. And then there were the gloves and bonnets and slippers . . .

'But the expense,' I wailed. I could think of a dozen ways the outlay could have been less frivolously used. Especially since the result – on me at least – was bound to be disappointing. 'Oh, Violet, you're so kind, but . . .'

'But nothing,' she said crisply. 'Sit still, do! How can

Wilkins attend to your hair while you fidget and pull faces? We are late enough as it is. I had intended to be at the milliner's by now and Biddie has been ready and waiting this half-hour.'

Biddie revelled in every moment of the mornings we spent shopping with Violet. We were fawned upon exceedingly by shopkeepers to whom the displaying of half their stock before the elegant Mrs Lascelles was an honour and a pleasure. I felt nervously that we put these poor people to a deal of unnecessary trouble, as we so often walked out without making a purchase.

'It has been amusing to learn the ways of those born to privilege,' said Violet in a satisfied voice as we were bowed effusively out of a haberdasher's, leaving a rainbow of rejected ribbons on the counter. 'Half the battle of being accepted as a person of quality, d'you see, is confidence and a manner that expects impeccable service and intends to get it. A lesson you could both usefully remember, girls. Now I think we shall just have time to walk to Southernhay and see the exhibition of paintings that has been the subject of most scathing comments by several persons who believe themselves to have great judgement in these matters. Let us see what we ignoramuses make of it.'

I was prepared to be bored. My own feeble attempts at drawing and painting had given me no pleasure. The paintings hung on the walls of Furze House – darkly varnished portraits of Miss Swann's ancestors and a quantity of Mrs Greenwood's careful and insipid watercolours – had never encouraged me to give them more than a fleeting glance. Biddie's interest in art was purely that of someone who had discovered that a graceful young lady occupied at a drawing board made a more attractive picture than the daub she was attempting. It was a surprise to us both to find the exhibition quite definitely different from anything we knew of.

Insipid was a word one would certainly not have attached to the paintings of Mr Greville Grant. At first I could not even make out what some of them were about. Observed too closely there was such a streaming, mingling confusion of colour it was hard to make anything of them. Yet when one moved away and glanced back the colour took on shape and form in the most dramatic and arresting fashion. The ruined buttresses of an ancient abbey standing black and stark against the palest lemons and pinks of a dawn sky. Wind-twisted trees and the bent figure of a man struggling against a storm of blown snow. A wild grey sea merging with cascading sheets of rain and one single ray of watery sunlight picking out a boat with torn sails about to be dashed on rocks. Even the few more formal pictures seemed to have something to make one pause and reflect. The one I liked least – a still life, portrayed almost with an intention to shock, of a hunter's booty of assorted dead and exceedingly bloody wild creatures hanging from a butcher's slab – had a hint of humour in the form of a floppy-eared, eccentrically shaped mongrel dog sneaking off with a woodpigeon in its jaws.

'A pity we couldn't borrow the thieving dog to remove a certain moulting cock pheasant,' I whispered to Biddie before we moved on to examine several small watercolour sketches. 'I believe it would be the greatest relief to all at Furze House . . . Oh, do look, Biddie. That must be a view of the cathedral from the other side of the Exe. The clouds look exactly as they would on a March day when the wind is sweeping them along.'

But Biddie was staring back down the room. She nudged me. 'That's the same dog, I'd swear it.' We both looked again at the still life then back to the dog which was prancing around several people engaged in conversation, one of them a fair, somewhat rumpled-looking man of perhaps five-and-twenty in a grey coat that seemed overlarge on his slight frame. 'I suppose it belongs to the artist.'

As we looked there was a ripple of laughter from the group at which the dog gave a bounce of excitement, its disproportionately long tail thrashing energetically against the emerald skirts of a florid lady who fastidiously stepped to one side.

'Sir, I would beg you to restrain your animal,' she said in carrying tones.

'My apologies, ma'am,' said the fair-haired gentleman. 'It is his good nature that makes him forget his manners. Here, Gyp. To heel, sir!' The dog leaped to his side where it squatted on its haunches and gazed up adoringly into its master's face. The ridiculous tail continued to fan slowly backwards and forwards across the polished floorboards.

'That must be him – the painter – then,' Biddie whispered. 'Handsome, isn't he?'

I thought him agreeable-looking rather than handsome, his quite ordinary features enlivened only by expressive eyebrows and a mouth that looked quick to smile.

'Offer the lady your paw, you thoughtless brute,' he said sternly. The dog obediently did so, but the offended lady was already moving in the direction of the door, booming to her mousy companion that she did not care to stay where uncouth beasts were loose and in any event the pictures were not to her taste. 'They do not have the nicety of elegance that I should require in my drawing room,' floated back to us as she exited.

The gentleman gave a comical grimace and bent to stroke the dog's ears. 'I have learned from experience that one cannot please everybody, but I hope she does not air her views too forcibly to her friends or I shall be sadly lacking in patrons.'

'You may be assured we shall recommend the exhibition to *our* friends, Mr Grant,' said a young lady in pink gauze, with a hint of laughter in her voice. 'We find your paintings perfectly . . . fascinating, do we not, Papa?'

'Perfectly, my dear,' her father said, he also seeming to struggle with ill-contained amusement. 'Now come along or we shall be late for our next engagement.'

With a smiling glance the girl left with her family and for a moment the rumpled Mr Grant looked a touch more rumpled. Something to do with the set of his shoulders, which sagged in a somewhat forlorn fashion now he was alone and thought himself unobserved. Then he straightened himself, seeming to sigh when he regarded a brace of gentlemen giving the pictures mere perfunctory glances as they strolled round deep in conversation and several ladies who were whispering behind their hands as they peered mystified at the man in the blizzard. He brightened when he saw Violet, a little ahead of us, studying intently a picture in which black and orange predominated. She scarcely had time to transfer her gaze to the small card with details of the painting beside the frame, before man and dog had bounded up the room to her side.

'If I may, ma'am,' he said with a deep bow. 'The picture is of an ironworks at night, painted when I was on a tour of the manufacturing districts of the Midlands.'

'You are the artist?'

Another respectful bow. 'Your servant, ma'am. Greville Grant. And the painting above is . . .'

'Is the one I should certainly like to purchase. About this other . . . I am less sure.'

Surprise expressed itself in his eyebrows which disappeared under the strands of straight fair hair that flopped over his high forehead. He swallowed. Then said, hastily, 'I congratulate you on your discerning taste, ma'am.'

'My *unusual* taste,' said Violet dryly. 'Judging by that dog of yours, Mr Grant, it seems you have an affinity with the eccentric. The subjects – not to say the execution – of many of your pictures don't appear to be consistent with a desire to please the purchasing public.'

'Well, ma'am, I wouldn't quite say that,' he began uncertainly.

'Would you not? Then you have sold a good many of your works?'

He shuffled his feet. 'The watercolour sketches of Exeter have proved popular.' Then, as she fixed him with her quelling eye, he said, in a crestfallen voice, 'I have sold two of those in the week.'

'And that is all?'

He nodded, shrugged, said hopefully, 'But perhaps you have changed my luck, ma'am.'

Violet's expression indicated she thought that highly doubtful but she did not press the point any further. She made arrangements for the painting to be delivered. She was precise about the day and the time on which it was to be brought. 'You will bring it in person, will you not, Mr Grant? I should like your opinion of the best place to hang it . . . and if by then you have not sold its companion-piece of the ironworks, you may fetch that also and I will give it further consideration.'

'It will be my pleasure, ma'am,' he said fervently.

The dog, evidently attuned to its master's mood, began an ecstatic dance about him, with excited leaps in our direction that caused its scrabbling claws to clatter and slip on the floorboards. At the end of one such leap it slid across the floor to land at my feet. I laughed and bent to stroke it, whereupon it sprang upwards, knocked my bonnet askew and dealt me a great lick across my chin.

Mr Grant was in a lather of mortification. 'He means only to be amiable . . . get down, Gyp! Your gown . . . your bonnet . . . Oh, dear . . .'

'No harm done,' I said firmly, setting my bonnet straight and smoothing down the skirt of my new dress. 'Please don't scold your dog. He is a very fetching animal, I must say. Who could possibly be cross with a creature of such comical proportions?'

'It is very ungallant of you, sir, to go about discommoding charming young ladies,' Mr Grant said sternly, then looked at me with a glance that lingered. And with such a genuinely approving light in his eye that I was suddenly at a loss for words.

It was a novel experience to be regarded so appreciatively. I found it quite unnerving. Though the looking glass that morning had reflected back a shockingly flattering image, until this minute I had not truly believed it.

The dress was of rose pink muslin with a tucked bodice and a trim of darker silk ribbon. The lines had been kept very simple which served to emphasise the quality and the elegant drape of the material. I realised how cleverly Mrs Chadwick had cut and sewn the gown, while Violet's choice of a colour, that I had thought much too delicate, was perfect. The soft tint against my skin was a revelation. It seemed to bring out a rich, creamy quality to my complexion that I certainly had not known it possessed. My unfortunate straight hair which defied any attempt at curl had not daunted Wilkins. Indeed, when it was washed and rinsed with rosemary water and given the lightest application of her special pomade that smelled deliciously of rose-petals, she had waxed ecstatic.

''Tis a pity, miss, 'ee couldn't leave it loose and straight. I never did see such a glossy colour. Like a blackbird's wing.'

Bequeathed to me by my mother, I thought, remembering with a pang how I had loved to watch her clever fingers coiling that heavy blue-black silk into a smooth knot into which she would twine a single rosebud, or a spray of jasmine. Odd how the memory so long forgotten came back to me as Wilkins twisted and pinned my own tresses.

'I shan't use curling tongs on it, miss,' she went on firmly. 'Curls wouldn't last five minutes. Straight hair looks best when 'tis managed more simply than is fashionable at present. I shall part it in the centre, so, then loop it up at the sides – not scraped back like you had it, but softer . . . If you watch me carefully, miss, you can see where to pin it and bring the weight up and to the back – the ribbon can be twisted through the knot like so and the ends left to fall from a bow – there! Quite simple and very becoming, if I might say so . . . in fact, 'tis a shame to have to cover it with a bonnet but if you're careful you won't disarrange it.'

And now here was a gentleman whose warm brown eyes were silently expressing an enthusiasm equal to Wilkins's, and though his glance moved on to encompass Biddie in the same appreciative glow (she had thought her own blue gown somewhat austere, though to my mind its plainness was a perfect foil for her striking looks) I felt the stir of a curious kind of elation. Quite ridiculous, I scolded myself, to be flattered for the way I looked rather than for the person I was. Nevertheless, the glow stayed with me, to be thought about and deliciously revived whenever I felt myself overshadowed by Biddie's more flamboyant prettiness.

Mr Grant duly presented himself at Bedford Circus with his paintings and his dog who was immediately banished to the kitchens with stern orders from Violet to the housemaid to keep him there until Mr Grant should leave. The dining chamber was eventually chosen as the right place for the painting to be hung.

'Opposite the place I usually sit,' Violet decided.

'A most suitable choice. It will catch the light there,' said Mr Grant. 'And the dramatic content of the picture will be enhanced by the formal setting.'

Mr Grant was not to know that aesthetic considerations had nothing to do with why Violet wished it to be placed where she would see it every day. Nor that she had made that decision long before he had arrived. Nor that the painting had not been bought for any pleasurable reason.

'It will be a reminder of everything that I have escaped from,' she had said. 'And should I get too blasé about what I have accomplished, then I will only have to look at that abominable scene and give thanks to whatever guardian angel has overseen my progress so far.'

The painting, in oils, was of a group of bottle kilns harshly outlined against a lowering sky with a terrace of sooty houses huddled in the rutted road beside them. Dim candlelight spilled from the small windows, the frail glow serving to emphasise the pall of smoke that endeavoured to blot out what little natural light could filter from the grey sky. There was a powerful sense of hopelessness about it. It was not at all a comfortable picture.

'It was outside a potbank very like that one I was first made to tout for custom as a whore by the man who protected the woman who took me in after my grandmother died,' Violet remarked in a flat expressionless voice as we left the exhibition. Then in her usual crisp tones, she said, 'I cannot like the subjects Mr Grant chooses, nor am I any sort of authority on art, but if the picture I have bought manages to arouse such strong feelings in one who grew up in those surroundings . . . well, I daresay he must have a talent of sorts.' She paused, thoughtfully. 'I think he deserves encouragement.'

What form that encouragement was about to take became clear the afternoon he called. Violet, apparently, was still in two minds about the picture of the ironworks. 'Oh, dear, you will think me a very foolish female,' she said, looking no such thing, 'but I am still not sure. Perhaps you will take some refreshment with us while I decide.'

But she did not seem to be thinking very hard about it as we drank tea and watched Mr Grant struggling not to wolf down too quickly a quantity of fruit scones and seed cake. She seemed more interested in finding out as much as she could about him. I thought there seemed a kind of desperation in his over-optimistic answers to Violet's questions.

'I studied for two years in London under Mr William Payne, who is also a native of Devonshire and was always very flattering about my – my originality of style, though of course I have developed it more successfully since . . . Yes, I was born in Honiton, ma'am, where my father is a gamekeeper on an estate. He made considerable sacrifices to have me educated and to encourage such talent as I have, and any day now I expect to be able to repay some of the debt I owe him . . . Oh, indeed, ma'am, I have exhibited several times to – to great advantage . . . Next year I am hopeful of Bath where society looks favourably on what is new and original.'

'But this year, the people of Exeter do not,' said Violet. 'And in the meantime that ill-behaved animal of yours appears to feed better than you do, Mr Grant. Is that not so?'

He opened his mouth as though to protest. Then, meeting Violet's uncompromising gaze, closed it, thought for a moment and said in a very different, quiet, voice, 'All I can say, Mrs Lascelles, is that I had rather go hungry than betray my principles. I feel very deeply about my work and whatever emotions colour my interpretation of the scenes I paint, they are true and honest ones. As is my wish to express the qualities of darkness and light in the way that I see them, not as laid down in some rule book that must be slavishly followed by those whose vision is limited to conventional attitudes.'

Violet smiled. 'Thank you for your honesty, Mr Grant. I fancied that must be the case. Let me be equally frank. I shall not buy your ironworks painting – no, don't look so crestfallen. I should, though, like to borrow it for the evening – and perhaps one of a more rural scene – the ruined abbey, perhaps? It has a certain brooding and romantic aspect. Perhaps you would be so kind as to fetch it here before seven, say . . . I make no promises, mind, but I should like to try a little experiment in *persuasion* among persons who might not normally cast a second glance at your pictures. Are you prepared to trust me? Good. Then allow me to pour you another dish of tea . . . and pray do finish the scones.'

Afterwards, when Mr Grant had bowed himself out, I looked at her curiously. 'So? What are you proposing to do, Violet?'

She laughed. 'Provide myself with a little amusement.'

'Don't you mean to help Mr Grant, then?' Biddie put in somewhat anxiously.

'Of course, if it is possible. But to be frank, I think the pleasure for me will be in the game itself.'

'What game?' asked Biddie, frowning.

'Oh, turning the tables on several persons who have tended to patronise poor, widowed Mrs Lascelles or annoyed her with their pompous views. One or two of whom will be among the company I have invited this evening for cards and supper,' Violet said. 'But why should you trouble yourself on his account, my dear? He has nothing to lose and everything to gain.'

'I wasn't worried in the least,' Biddie said, her cheeks reddening. 'I just felt a bit sorry for him.'

'To be sure,' said Violet easily. 'Well, I shall do my best to ensure Mr Greville Grant does not continue to starve artistically in his garret.'

'But how?' I insisted. 'You said yourself these were not people who would normally be interested in his paintings.'

'There's more than one way to kill a cat,' Violet said. And proceeded to prove it that evening.

'Mrs Lascelles . . . you have worked a miracle! Three of my biggest paintings sold in the course of the day . . . and the possibility of two others. Enough to cover the hire of my room and buy paint and canvas to last the winter.'

'And to restock your larder, I hope, Mr Grant,' said Violet, dryly. 'I should not at all appreciate having my work on your behalf go to waste because you had allowed yourself to fade into a decline.'

Mr Grant had called at an awkward moment when Violet and I were waiting in the drawing room for Biddie – inevitably the last to be ready – to join us. We were to attend a concert of sacred music at the Cathedral and were already cutting it rather fine.

He stood in the drawing room with his hat in his hand, reminding me – thin and bony under his over-large grey coat – of a dishevelled heron about to take flight. But looking so pleased with himself and the world, so bursting with gratitude, that I could see even Violet had not the heart to be sharp with his unfortunate timing.

'A Colonel Bonynge bought the two most expensive paintings,' he said with awe. 'Eighteen guineas, the pair! To think they will be on display in one of the finest new houses in the town. Such a compliment! He said he had been impressed by the pictures you had shown him here. Oh, I could wish I had heard you, ma'am, so that I might learn how to be so persuasive. But there again, I should perhaps be accused of being over-blown with conceit in my own prowess if I tried it.'

Violet smiled, with the look of a small cat that has made off with a prize mouse. 'Exactly. A third party may be fulsome in praise of another's talent without giving offence. Which it has been my pleasure to do. I am gratified it achieved some success.'

I was glad she did not go into any more detail. I feared Mr

Grant's spirits might have been deflated somewhat had he realised that Colonel Bonynge's interest had nothing to do with an appreciation of fine art.

Half-a-dozen couples and a brace of unmarried daughters had been invited for cards and supper and it was not until we were finishing a hearty cold collation in the dining chamber at close to eleven o'clock that Violet mentioned her purchase and invited general opinion on the other two pictures.

'Of course, they may not be to your taste. I have to say that they are scarcely the kind of thing I should normally have looked upon with any favour. However, placed as I am without the benefit of my dear husband to protect and advise me . . . well, I am in no position to refuse sound financial advice when it is presented to me.' Her glance appealed in a charmingly helpless way to the gentlemen seated round the table. 'One should not allow sentiment to interfere with business, I am told. More wine, Colonel? And your glass is empty, Mr Cutler.' Then she politely turned her head to the elderly gentleman on her left and took up the threads of a conversation they had been having about some new plantings in Northernhay Gardens.

'An excellent claret,' the Colonel said gruffly, swallowing down another half-glass.

'Excellent,' echoed Mr Cutler, a prosperous solicitor, among whose clients were many landed families in the district. His long nose twitched as though it caught the hint of something interesting in the air. At the first lull in the conversation he leaned forward. 'And this – this advice, you were given, Mrs Lascelles?' he queried in a casual voice.

Violet frowned as though trying to recollect what they had been talking about earlier. 'Oh, about the paintings,' she said, vaguely, as though it was a subject of little importance. 'One does feel quite conscience-stricken that the artist himself seems to be the one who profits least from his efforts. Still, when he is more widely known – at present it is just a select band of connoisseurs who are appreciative of the growing value of his work – he will be able to command far greater sums.' An airy wave of her hand, an insouciant lift of the shoulders. 'I daresay a Greville Grant will be beyond my pocket when that not too distant day comes but that is when I shall feel the benefit of having purchased at a favourable time. Even if the paintings are perhaps a touch . . . well, unusual for my taste at present, I shall be able to dispose of them advantageously in a year or two.'

'Can't say I've ever heard the name,' the Colonel growled, frowning.

'You will, be sure of it,' Violet said in a very definite voice, and tapping her fan playfully on his arm by way of emphasis. Then, raising her voice a little, 'If everyone is finished, shall we retire to the drawing room? Miss Bonynge, I believe you are to favour us with a song.'

While Mildred Bonynge warbled through three songs in an uncertain soprano, Mr Cutler, who had contrived to place himself next to Violet, bent to whisper once or twice in her ear. And later, as carriages arrived and wraps and hats were brought, he and the Colonel managed to disappear into the dining chamber for a moment and emerged nodding sagely and looking not a little pleased with themselves.

'Philistines, the pair of them,' said Violet coldly when they had gone. 'And greedy. I've come across their sort before. They know the cost of everything but the value of nothing. They wouldn't know a decent painting if it jumped off the wall and hit them in the eye. But if Mr Grant profits from their ignorance and avarice, then I shall feel very satisfied at having gulled them.' She laughed. 'It will be interesting to see what happens in the coming days. Rumour has a way of spreading itself. A whisper here, a word there . . . How amusing if the little seed I have sown flourishes and bears a healthy harvest for Mr Grant to reap.'

Now it was clear that there were at least some signs that the seeds had rooted.

'So, you will keep me informed of what happens in the coming week, Mr Grant?' Violet said with an impatient glance at the door. 'You must excuse us, we are on the point of leaving once Miss Riley honours us with her presence. Oh, and tomorrow we are to go away for three days exploring the delights of Dartmoor. Perhaps you might call when we are returned . . . join us for supper. Ah, at last, Bridget! I'd near given up on you. Now where did I put my reticule?'

A flurry at the door. Mr Grant departing. Bridget entering. He standing back to allow her through.

'I'm so sorry, Miss Riley.' A half-bow.

'My fault entirely, Mr Grant.' A flustered laugh.

Then a pause in which he stood as if transfixed. Staring, staring at Biddie in a gown the colour of newly broken beech leaves, her hair glowing in a vivid aureole of curls and ribbons around her face. And Biddie equally still and wide-eyed, with such a shy and smiling glow about her that I felt a wash of sheer pleasure and pride in her beauty when I remembered the ragged, deprived urchin she had once been I wanted to share my pleasure with Violet, who remembered too, but she had turned away to take her reticule from the table where she had put it down and the moment slipped away.

As did Mr Grant. Bowing, his gaze never leaving her, he retreated reluctantly through the doorway, and Biddie watched him go as though caught up with him in some shared dream . . .

Then Violet straightened up and said crisply, 'I shall send you a note, Mr Grant, when we are returned.'

'Tha-thank you, ma'am,' he managed. 'I look forward to it.'

And he was gone.

And everything was normal again. Violet berating Biddie for keeping us waiting, sweeping us out into the warm evening air for the short walk to the Cathedral.

I think that the concert was entirely wasted on Biddie. From the dreamy look on her face her thoughts were far more satisfying than any rendition of Bach or Handel. And I had the amused conviction that Mr Greville Grant might perhaps be in something of the same state.

Well, well, well . . .

But I had my own difficulties in concentrating on the music, for all that it thundered so richly through the great nave, reverberating round the massive pillars and soaring up into the magnificence of the fan vaulting above our heads. Tomorrow we should leave on a journey that would take us to Moondance. And now that the time was so close it seemed that every nerve of my body was alive to what the next days would bring.

Chapter Six

From the tumbled grey rocks that crowned the tor we looked down the long slope to the road where the carriage waited.

To Biddie and Violet it was just another scenic spot to add to the many we had paused to enjoy during the day's tour out of Ashburton. I heard them, faintly, pointing out landmarks, talking of the grandeur of the vista, exclaiming at the strength of the breeze now that there was nothing to shelter us from its keen bite.

I had no ears to listen, no voice to speak. All I could feel was pain – the great, deep hurt that made me want to curl over and hug myself against the assault of the memories that came at me like arrows.

All was familiar. The folds of the hills, the dark wedges of woodland and the little stone-walled fields on the lower, more fertile valleys. I knew how many village roofs and chimney pots could be spied a mile off where the road dipped down and disappeared from view among the purple swathes of heather, and where to look to catch a glimpse of the river . . .

All around and below me grey moorstone boulders protruded like the bones of ancient monsters from the mottled skin of turf and whin and furze, each one seeming to speak of the times I had played among them. Occasionally with Jed, mostly solitary at my childish games and never caring if I was alone for there was nothing here to fear and Meg would come calling and scolding to the gates to halloo me down when it was time for dinner or bed.

No Meg now. Dead and buried in St Mark's churchyard not a hundred yards from the almshouse in the village where she had spent her last days. No Meg now to call me home.

I almost seemed to see her standing down there beside the gates that were neglected even in Papa's time, and rusting still. Powerful iron gates to complement the boundary wall of grey moorstone. Great slabs and boulders of granite, prised from the ground and hauled by sweating men and horses centuries ago to be laid in rough symmetry around the captive acres. Now the wall itself was almost lost under the burden of the plants that had rooted and flourished in its interstices; deeply shadowed by the trees within its bounds that hung heavy branches over the road.

Beyond the boundary wall, the mounded trees reached to the grassy spaces by the lake. Green now, but in January speckled white with snowdrops. Then, as the seasons turned, wild daffodils would jostle for space beside primroses and violets. Swathes of bluebells would spread from the woodland and, as they faded and died, foxgloves would raise their pink spires. All of which I would gather in great bunches for Aunt Hettie to set about the house.

I let my gaze drift to the lake itself, its surface crisped to little wavelets in the brisk breeze, and there, above it . . .

I closed my eyes, opened them. Still there. I was not dreaming. I was really here.

Moondance.

The house was so close to the lake that it seemed, from this distance, the water lapped at its walls. An illusion. The house stood on rising ground and there was – had been once – a stretch of lawn and shrubbery running down to the lake, and a stone seat where Aunt Hettie and Mama had liked to sit on a summer evening to watch for Papa riding back after exercising Rajah.

So many summers ago. And today, the lake and house, cupped in the green valley, looking no different than they had ever done, in the dusty yellow August light. Yet soon, if all went according to Violet's plan, I should be able to see the damage Theophilus Crowe's reign at Moondance had wreaked. I wondered if I could bear it.

'Come, Miranda,' Violet said, shivering. 'We shall catch our deaths up here.'

They went ahead of me, carefully finding footholds on the smooth, sheep-bitten grass and holding their skirts well away from the furze bushes. My own feet seemed to find their way down the slope as though they recognised an invisible path.

'Thank goodness we are out of that wind,' Violet said as we crossed the carriage way. 'Splendid views, I suppose, but I think I have lost whatever appetite I had for desolate places. My years at The Plough – which I often felt was built in the draughtiest spot in Derbyshire – set me against too much intimacy with open country. It is best left to sheep, in my opinion.'

'But it isn't desolate here,' I said. 'It's . . . it's . . .' Home, I wanted to say. But couldn't. Because it no longer was. 'It's . . . peaceful and beautiful,' I said with a catch in my throat.

'I should hate it.' Biddie pulled the mulberry silk shawl borrowed from Violet about her shoulders with a shudder. 'It's worse than Furze House and that seems lonely enough on winter nights when the wind's howling. Give me town anytime . . . well, are we going in?' she said, with a yearning glance at the carriage. 'The big gate's chained and padlocked,' she added hopefully.

'Not this side gate, though,' said Violet, testing it. It creaked open on protesting hinges. 'And no gatekeeper to stop us. The lodge is a ruin.'

It had already been derelict in my day. Visitors were rare. The carriage and horses, hardly ever used, had been finally sold after Mama died. Little need for the grand gates to have a permanent attendant. The smaller one, never locked, allowed passage for horses or walkers.

The gravel drive was full of weeds. Again, no difference. The scrunch of our feet sounded loud and intrusive. I stepped on to the grass, walked a little way. This was the place where the first Northfield bride had been lifted down from her horse in the moonlight . . . there was where she had stood against the leafless trees, hating it, fearful of her marriage . . . loving someone else. I was certain of it, yet how could I be? Oh, I knew the legend of the bride who had first named the house, but to imagine – to dream – of how she felt? The Northfield name had died out near on a century ago, when my Brehault ancestor, knighted for his privateering activities on behalf of the Crown, had married the only surviving Northfield daughter. But perhaps some legacy of blood still coursed, however thinly, in my own veins, linking me to that far-off bride. Those self-same trees had been here when I was a child. Three massive oaks. Only one left now, hollowed with age, more ivy than foliage on its meagre branches. The others were roughly sawn stumps. *He* had done that. The interloper. The destroyer.

There was anger now with the pain.

'A charming aspect, indeed,' said Violet, in a loud voice, slipping into the role of a passing tourist lured into the grounds. I followed the direction of her gaze and saw an odd colourful figure approaching. 'The lake, the house . . . delightfully picturesque. I am sure we might be allowed a closer inspection. Ah, here is someone to whom we might put an enquiry. Tell me, is your master in residence? Or your mistress—?'

The small, brown, elderly man had come soft-footed from the trees. He had a blue cloth wound about his head and wore a loose shirt. A brilliantly patterned blue and white cloth was draped round his waist covering his legs down to his shins. His ankles and splayed brown feet were bare. His shiny black eyes regarded us without expression.

This must be the foreign manservant Jed had told me of.

'Your master? Is he at home?' Violet repeated.

The man bowed. 'Who ask, *mem*?'

Violet reached into her reticule and dropped coins into his palm. 'Be so good as to inform your master that Mrs Lascelles of Exeter and two friends wish to view the grounds.'

The coins disappeared swiftly into a fold of the blue cloth. Another bow. '*Tuan* not wish people disturb. Please to go, *mem*.'

For all his lack of inches the man looked as though he was possessed of a wiry strength and determination. I could see why the villagers feared to cross him. Leaving aside the moor-dweller's engrained distrust of any incomer, the man's very foreignness and manner of dressing were enough to make them wary of him. His fierce guardianship of his master's privacy was notorious, Jed had told me. Tradesmen, whether from the village or Ashburton, were always ordered to leave their goods by the derelict lodge from where the servant took them to the house on a handcart. I could see now how his quiet but somehow threatening manner would only serve to reinforce whatever rumour sprang up out of the inevitable grumblings and gossip. There was no one, man, woman or child, Jed said, who cared to venture to set a rabbit snare or a bird trap in the woods at Moondance these days or sneak in to steal kindling or fruit. The man had an evil eye and who knew what curses in his heathen tongue he might lay on a trespasser . . .

'Please to go,' the manservant repeated.

'We shall take a circular route round the lake,' Violet said as though she had not heard him. 'We do not need to follow the carriage drive to the house. I see that this path leads to the footbridge across the stream down there. Quite charming! You may advise your master that we intend to spend no more time than necessary to complete our tour. I am sure he could not possible deny us the privilege of enjoying the tranquillity of his delightful demesne. Come, Bridget, Miranda.'

She was stepping out briskly as she spoke and the little man made as though to go after her. 'Please, *mem* . . .' he began, but she waved him away with an imperious gesture of a white-gloved hand. He scowled at Bridget and me as we began to follow her. 'Master not like,' he said. 'I fetch master. He tell you.' He turned on his heel and made off back into the woods.

Violet was already at the little clapper bridge across the stream by the time Biddie and I caught up with her, Biddie torn between giggles and fright.

'Fancy a man wearing a skirt,' she said. 'Oh, Violet, what do you suppose his master will do? We shouldn't really be here. We could have waited in the carriage and let Mirrie come in on her own . . .'

'What? And miss all the fun? Nonsense.'

'Fun?' I stared at Violet, anger and then pain curdling in my stomach. I wished desperately that I was alone. I wished that I hadn't agreed to Violet's stupid scheme. I wanted silence and to have time to be with my thoughts, with my memories. On my own I might have been able to slip in unobserved. Climb the wall, perhaps. Sit quietly in the woods. Or even have stayed out on the tor content to look, to be close . . . not standing out here in the open, unprotected, vulnerable. 'I should never have agreed to do this. Perhaps it would be best if we all left now. Before he . . . that man . . . finds us.'

Violet's hand was on my arm. 'Too late, Miranda,' she said quietly. 'He's coming with his servant.'

I squeezed my eyes shut, not wanting to look. 'No! Please. We'll go back to the carriage.' The nightmare. I was ten years old. The great black bird was coming to snatch me up in its claws and smother me under its black wings.

Anger and pain and *fear* . . .

Violet's fingers bit into the flesh of my arm. 'Hold up, you fool.' Her voice sharp, peremptory. 'Open your eyes. Face him. It is the only way.'

'I . . . I can't.'

'Bollocks to that,' she said crudely. 'Remember who you are. Your father was a brave adventurer! Your mother too – braver perhaps for what she did. Leaving her family, her country, to elope for love. An unreliable emotion at best. Do you want to shame their memory? For God's sake, what can this . . . this man Crowe do to you now?'

Somehow . . . somehow the sick feeling ebbed. I lifted my head, managed to say through dry lips, 'Don't say who I am. Promise me?'

Then, slowly, I turned to look at Theophilus Crowe as he

hurried across the grass towards us with the foreign man at his heels.

I heard nothing for that first few moments for the thundering of blood in my head. I saw Violet's lips moving, I saw Biddie's apprehensive expression and the foreign man's broad impassive features. I saw Theophilus Crowe bowing stiffly, frowning, shaking his head.

Violet's voice faded in, '. . . how very splendid to be able to live in such an idyllic spot, sir. You cannot imagine how we city-dwellers envy those with country seats to retreat to. Exeter can be so unpleasantly stuffy in the height of summer and the offensive odours even in some of the better thoroughfares are quite unbearable.' She inhaled deeply, allowing her lashes to fall as though caught up in some ecstasy of sensation. 'Such good air. How very different from Bedford Circus. If you are acquainted with that area of Exeter, sir, then you will know I have nothing to complain of in the comfort of my house or the convenience of its situation to the many amenities Exeter has to offer. But one cannot deny that towns breed dust and noise. Whilst here –' another deep breath '– all is peace and harmony and the air as good as a glass of sparkling wine. Such a disappointment if you do not allow us to crown our splendid day with the final experience of exploring your estate. We thought ourselves so lucky to have discovered this truly charming little gem . . .'

She raised her lashes to look at him fully with a convincing air of feminine helplessness, yet she allowed her silk shawl to slide just a little from her shoulders and her gloved hand to rearrange it more comfortably. That same hand strayed innocently across the bodice of her fashionable summer gown so that he could not but be aware of the smooth curve of her white skin as it swelled to the topmost curve of her breasts. All her years of experience with men, the knowledge of their masculine instincts, was in that gesture, that look, had he but known it. But there was no way that he could have done. He merely saw a lady of quality – a very gracious and pretty one, with an admirable figure – gracefully acknowledging his own male authority, but so very appealing in her wish not to be denied this small concession.

'Madam, I . . .' A hesitation. Then, perhaps sensing that the speediest way to rid himself of her was not to stand here arguing, he said a touch irritably, 'Very well. If you insist.'

'Mr Crowe, I cannot tell you how grateful I am. And my young friends will be so pleased. Are you not, my dears?' His glance moving to Biddie, to me.

From somewhere my voice came calm and clear. 'Indeed, yes. Perhaps, sir, you would be so kind as to point out the places where it would benefit us to pause and look at a particular aspect of your grounds. Or some interesting botanical feature.'

I had a hysterical desire to laugh now that I allowed myself to study him properly. Was this really the the giant who had stalked my nightmares? This man of no more than average size – scarcely an inch taller than I was – and dressed in leather breeches with a disreputable jacket pulled roughly, as though in haste, over a flannel shirt. He was hatless. Sawdust and woodchips clung to the mane of straight hair tied into a rough queue. No longer the black that I remembered, but streaked heavily with grey. I recollected him – a child's-eye view of all adults – as old. Now I could see he must have come to Moondance a man in his prime, for he was no more than forty today. A long chin, a mouth set into the downturned lines of dissatisfaction – or was it disappointment? Or maybe neither of these but rather a harassed impatience at being interrupted at his labours and being caught, hatless, in such rough attire in the presence of three fashionable young ladies.

'Botanical features?' he repeated. He regarded me with the look of one who took questioner and question with the utmost seriousness. 'There are new plantings of willow at the other end of the lake where it tends to become boggy, and if you care to look to your left when you reach the lower bridge you will see the topiary garden. But it will not be at its best for a year or two yet. As to the arboretum on the far side of the house, well, twenty years . . . fifty . . . and you may begin to appreciate its value. The plantings to give shelter from the worst of the winds are growing well. At this height above sea level one has to take extra care.'

Topiary garden? Arboretum? What was this havoc he was wreaking on Moondance?

'You seem to have been extraordinarily busy, sir,' I said sharply. 'Not least in sawing down trees. I noticed not far from the gate two ancient specimens had been removed. Oaks, I presume, as one still remains.'

'Unfortunately one blew down in a gale two winters ago and, falling as it did, made the other unsafe. We shall plant new sapling oaks near there this winter. Grown from acorns gathered from those very trees.' For the first time his long face creased to the beginnings of a smile. 'There is much satisfaction in such continuity, do you not think?

'Oh . . . certainly,' I said, taken aback.

'The woodland itself has been much neglected by the previous owner. I have only this year begun to clear out the dead wood in order to assess what may be saved and improved and what needs to be got rid of. We have logs and to spare for firing, at present, but I plan in time to coppice a section of trees in order to ensure future fuel supplies in an economical manner.' He broke off. Another stiff little bow. 'Forgive me, I'm sure you did not wish a dissertation on the subject of woodland management.'

'Oh, I am sure my young friend has been quite fascinated,' Violet said. 'As I am myself.'

'I will not keep you from your walk,' he said curtly.

'Could you not spare the time to walk with us, Mr Crowe?' Violet said. She clasped her hands as though suddenly taken by this splendid idea. 'I should dearly like to hear more of your plans for these charming grounds . . . and perhaps a little of the history of the house, which is clearly ancient. Ah, if stones could speak! What stories these ancient piles would tell then.'

'Most of it best forgotten, Mrs Lascelles,' he said. 'For

myself I prefer to look forward, not back, and to deal with growing things not lifeless objects.'

And no wonder he doesn't care to look into his past, I thought bitterly. The wickedness of despatching a small helpless child to a life of slavery must surely test his conscience, even one so hardened by debauchery and corruption.

'Then I beg that you will walk just a little way, sir,' said Violet, 'and describe how you envisage the gardens will look in fifty years' time.'

He hesitated. Then eagerness to speak about what was evidently – and disconcertingly – a passion with him, overcame his reluctance to prolong the interview. He nodded. 'Very well. If you cross the bridge and turn on to the path by the lake you will see that I have introduced a yellow water lily, *Nuphar lutea*, and removed a great number of the old white lilies which had choked up much of this shallower part. I have left the reed beds untouched. I like the natural grace and movement of reeds and see no reason to interfere with nature if the effect is pleasing . . .'

He went ahead with Violet, leaving Biddie and me to trail behind. I listened to snatches of their conversation with resentment. How dare he! How dare he make all these alterations – so-called improvements – to what had been beautiful in its own right! How dare he accuse Papa of neglect! Yet all the while I was aware of a disconcerting – and growing – sense of unfairness in my judgement. Papa *had* taken little interest in the management of the estate. He had preferred to direct his energies, and what remained of his fortune, to his adventures in exploration of distant lands. The beauty I remembered *had* been created by that very neglect – grasses left long and unkempt for a child to romp through in unthinking play. Shrubs choked with strangling growths of old man's beard or growing together in tangled masses to create an illusion of health in the upper layers while the lower stems grew twisted and leafless from lack of light. I had crawled through the gloomy tunnels made by those arid stems and believed them to be the mysterious highways of fairies and elves. Had thought myself very fortunate to have such secret labyrinths to explore. But were they not another symptom of the creeping dereliction that was overtaking Moondance? The woods themselves were full of death as much as life. Branches, whole trees, left to rot where they fell and living trees crammed together, growing weedy and tall in the fight for light and air . . .

No! I would not think so disloyally! But as I looked at what Theophilus Crowe had already done and was creating, a reluctant admiration was forced upon me.

There were ornamental ducks on the lake now among the wild mallard and grebe and waterhens. A pair of small new grassy islands sprouted sapling trees on their mounded tops. They would make safe havens out of the way of the foxes and badgers that had always been wont to make inroads on roosting or nesting birds. I saw with a pang of nostalgia that the stone seat where Mama and Aunt Hettie had liked to sit of an evening was still there, but a scented arbour of roses and lavender bushes had been created around it with an arch overhead through which a young wistaria was twining. I allowed, reluctantly, that it looked far more inviting than it ever had. Everywhere there were similar signs of regeneration, of a more ordered and harmonious kind of beauty being created out of the chaos that the gardens had become.

The path lay between the lake and the west side of the house which stood on the raised ground to our left as we walked.

'It's bigger than I expected,' Biddie whispered, round-eyed, and then as if it really struck home for the first time, 'God almighty . . . to be sent from this to a place like Crossbank.' She reached for my hand and squeezed my fingers in a gesture both sympathetic and comforting. 'I was used to a rough life. Even the Clerkenwell poor looked down on us. Low Irish they said we were, fit only to live like pigs in our own muck. And what chance did we have to do anything other? Even the workhouse seemed an improvement on the cellar I'd lived in with my ma. Crossbank was horrible, true, but you . . . I think

I'd have given up and died if I'd come from here and the life you must have had.'

Violet saved me from having to answer, strangled as I was by the great lump that choked my throat. It was not only Biddie's words that brought the surge of emotion, it had been building steadily all the time we walked. But Violet turned and cried, 'Keep up, my dears. Mr Crowe has kindly offered to show us the formal gardens.' And by the time we turned off the lake path I had my emotions once more under control.

The door on the south face of the house, Aunt Hettie had told me, had once given access to a bowling green and skittle alley in the level and sheltered space formed by the back of the stables on one side and the wall of the kitchen garden on the other. In my day it had been nothing more than a repository for all manner of clutter and rubbish falling to rust and decay amid banks of nettles. The transformation was astonishing.

The windows on this side of the house now faced down a green walk lined either side with yew bushes, small as yet, that were in the process of being clipped and shaped into the forms of animals. And here were the marble figures Jed had told me about, the ones that the villagers had deplored as a sign of the debauchery that Theophilus Crowe had wrought upon Moondance. I looked at them in astonishment. They were quite, quite beautiful. Pagan figures, I supposed, of nymphs or goddesses clad in clinging drapery, and small naked cherubs, but there was such delicacy about them, particularly in the faces – grave, smiling or mischievous – that it seemed wrong to associate them with the rakehell orgies and naked midnight frolics that had scandalised the village.

'I was in Plymouth to collect several specimens of ornamental plum which a ship from China had brought for me when I saw these figures,' Theophilus Crowe was saying, with satisfaction. 'They were one small and insignificant part of a privateer's booty from a French ship out of the Mediterranean. Quite ancient statuary, they said, dug out of some ruined city in the desert sands of Northern Africa. I bid for them at auction and got them for a song. I knew exactly the place that would accommodate them to best advantage for I had just cleared and grassed this area.'

'And quite splendid it is,' said Violet. 'And through there?' she queried, indicating the stone arch at the end of the topiary garden.

'Nothing as yet, but I am considering another small enclosed garden, formal in manner. Come through. You see the ground is level here also, if somewhat exposed, but I think I may plant windbreaks on all sides save to the south. There will be seating . . . perhaps a rose garden where one may rest and view the arboretum.'

We followed the line of his pointing finger. The sparse scatter of sapling trees was spread up the hill, fanning out as far as the trees that marked the boundary wall.

'It takes imagination to visualise how it will be,' he said gravely. 'Each tree is placed carefully, according to its girth and height at maturity, and also taking into account the colour of its foliage, whether it is coniferous or deciduous and so on. I shall be adding to my collection as and when I receive specimens. I spent some years travelling abroad and have acquaintances among sea captains who have promised to fetch back anything unusual that they come across. In time, too, I hope to repair and extend the glasshouse in the kitchen garden in order to raise orchids. I came across many fascinating kinds when I was in the East.'

'It is all very exciting,' Violet murmured. 'You are a man of vision, indeed, sir. I feel very privileged to have had this glimpse of what you are achieving.' A teasing laugh. 'But I have the feeling that when word spreads of what you are doing here, your manservant will have to drum up reinforcements in order to keep out the many ladies and gentlemen who will wish to view your gardens.'

'I have no objection, Mrs Lascelles, to serious-minded persons taking an interest in my endeavour,' he said gruffly. 'But I have been bedevilled at times by the other sort – those whose object is to desecrate and destroy. The ignorant trespasser may unwittingly do untold damage tramping where he should not. I do not fear being solitary. Sooner that than see the work of weeks or months destroyed in minutes. As has happened.' A thin smile. 'There is an advantage in having a Malay servant, even if he does take his protective duties more seriously than perhaps is strictly necessary. Ahmed has a fearsome reputation among the rustics. He has a fine mastery of Malay oaths which frighten them simply because they do not understand the language. I find it politic to foster the myth that he has ringed the property with evil charms that will bring misfortune down on anyone who disobeys him and intrudes on my privacy.'

'Dear me, Mr Crowe,' Violet said, in mock alarm. 'I trust we have not laid ourselves open to being bewitched.'

'You are perfectly safe, madam. Witchery works only on those who believe it. In this case small boys out for devilment and those who would poach my wildfowl or the songbirds which give me so much pleasure.'

'So, Mr Crowe, it is with some reluctance that we must take our leave,' Violet said with a sigh. 'We have taken up far too much of your time already. Besides which, we have had a tiring day, if a deeply satisfying one observing Dartmoor's wild scenery. Indeed my throat is quite parched on account of all the walking we have done. Perhaps I might beg a cup of water. I noticed the well near the house . . .'

'Of course . . . er, that is . . .' He was awkward now, deserted by the authority that had characterised him while he talked of the garden, the civilities of everyday intercourse perhaps little used and therefore needing to be thought about carefully. 'If . . . if you would care to step inside I will fetch . . . or my housekeeper. No, better. I . . . I take a dish of tea about this time. You would be welcome to join me.' Looking quite bashful as he proposed it.

'How very civil of you, sir.'

'This way . . . this way.' He bustled us to the door, thrust it open. The same plain heavy oak that was characteristic of all the outside doors. Unpretentious and sturdy. I followed the others, lingering, absorbing this moment when I stepped from the light of the August afternoon to the dimness within. Pausing to inhale the remembered odour of woodsmoke and candlegrease, old timber and stone. The scent of childhood. Inside, the corridor that had once seemed so high and wide, seemed to press close on either side. This was not the formal entrance with its wide hall and double staircase rising to a gallery on the upper floor, but it was the most familiar because it led to the suite of rooms which were used because this part of the house, the southern wing, was the warmest and sunniest and least affected by the damp that pervaded the rest of Moondance. Here were Papa's library, the south parlour and the wainscoted dining chamber, with the arms of Queen Elizabeth in faded colours on a boss in the plastered ceiling under which we had eaten meals grown chilly from the distance they had to be fetched from the kitchen in the north wing.

And if I had expected the new broom to have swept cleanly through all this, I was swiftly disabused. Lozenges of dusty light fell through the small-paned windows of the parlour on to the familiar faded carpet, on the pair of worn chintz-covered settees, Aunt Hettie's sewing chair, Mama's éscritoire . . . But Jed had told me how everything had been changed, I thought wildly. Everything bought new . . .

'I live simply these days,' Theophilus Crowe said, reaching for the bell pull that hung by the slabs of moorstone that formed the fireplace. 'I had illusions, when I first came, of opening up the house.'

'A very ancient and gracious house,' said Violet.

'To be sure, and worthy of restoration. In time perhaps. I made a start when I first came on the more formal rooms,' a shrug, 'but having been so long abroad and often solitary . . . well, these few rooms are comfortable enough for a bachelor. I deluded myself once that I should like to live grandly, but a taste of it was enough to persuade me that there was more satisfaction to be found in following the dictates of one's nature and interests.'

Liar, I thought. *Liar*. Showing himself as this man of simple tastes when everyone knew of his dissolute behaviour. This *gentleman* was so despised and distrusted in the county that no decent family would allow an unmarried daughter near him.

'Pray do be seated. Ah, Rokiah, we shall require tea.' The elderly woman with the swarthy foreign looks of her husband, the manservant, was wearing a piece of cloth patterned in red and orange draped around her hips with a silky overbodice in yellow, heavily embroidered with silver flowers and a filmy scarf lying loosely over her grey-streaked hair, which was coiled and knotted low on the back of her neck. In the faded confines of the parlour she glowed like some exotic bird. Her master repeated the request in her own language and she padded out, her bare brown feet making scarcely a sound.

I did not sit when the others did but went to the window and looked out as though to admire the view of the lake. But I scarcely saw it. I was listening to the conversation behind me. Violet's voice delicately and cleverly slipping questions into the polite small talk. *His* hateful voice answering and a picture forming of a young man born and brought up in Plymouth, the son of a sea captain who drowned, and who made off after his widowed mother died to seek his fortune in the East Indies, taking any clerking position in the rich private trading houses of Penang and Malacca in order to finance his exploratory expeditions to the interior. 'It was in Malacca that I met the man who had inherited this house,' he said. 'Sir Anthony Brehault.'

The name dropped like a stone into my heart. I closed my eyes, my hands reaching to grip the cool stone of the window ledge.

He sighed. 'We struck up an instant fellowship. Two young men, far from home. Both full of the spirit of adventure that has characterised Devonshire men through the centuries.'

'And did you have adventures, sir?'

'More than enough,' he said dryly. 'As with many a man, the siren call of gold was impossible to ignore.'

'Gold, sir? How thrilling! And did you find it?'

'Small amounts had been mined for many years in the

foothills of Mount Ophir but Sir Anthony had word of the discovery of a rich new seam near to Geminchi.' Another sigh. 'No one can say we did not go with our eyes open. We knew the tribes in the interior were fierce and warlike. Few Europeans ever ventured beyond Malacca territory and even our porters were terrified once we were beyond the safety of the borders. This is not to mention the normal hazards of travelling through tropical forest . . . Tormenting insects and leeches, sweltering heat and violent rainstorms, crocodile-infested rivers and predatory tigers . . .'

'Goodness gracious, Mr Crowe, it is a wonder you lived to tell the tale.'

'Indeed it was by sheer fluke that I survived. Sir Anthony, alas, was not so lucky. He had become very ill with a fever just after most of our porters deserted camp and when we eventually reached our destination it was to find others were there before us. Namely one giant of a Norwegian who was prepared to drive off any competition and had a cut-throat gang of brigands on hand, prepared to defend his interests . . . ah, here is the tea. Thank you, Rokiah. Mrs Lascelles, would you oblige me by pouring? And, please, let us turn to more cheerful subjects . . . I cannot think how I came to indulge myself with such morbid recollections. All water under the bridge and best forgotten. It is so long since I was in Exeter, perhaps you would be kind enough to tell me what is new and of interest there at the moment.'

'Do drag yourself from the view, Mirrie, and join us,' Violet called to me. 'As to being morbid, Mr Crowe, I found your tale perfectly enthralling. Now, Mirrie dear, seat yourself next to Bridget.'

But I did not sit. I stopped by Mr Crowe where he hovered by the low table politely waiting to pass teacups.

'You cannot leave us in suspense,' I said softly. 'What did happen to . . . to your friend. And to you, sir?'

His glance met mine, slid away. There was something furtive in his eyes, I thought, but he said, with a dismissive shrug: 'Oh, I had the luck of the devil. I escaped by a fluke when a local tribe of Malays attacked the small camp the Norwegian had set up. I had managed, you see, to persuade him that we posed no threat to his mining activities. Sir Anthony by then was delirious and racked by convulsive spasms, and I begged that we be given shelter until he was fit for me to take him back to Malacca. So the Norwegian allowed me to nurse my friend with the aid of one of the camp women. There were several rough attap – palm-thatch – huts on the site. In the night we were attacked, the huts set ablaze, the women carried off. As to the men . . . well, suffice to say that by morning I was the only one left alive. In the mêlée I . . . I had blundered out into the darkness and cast myself down into a hollow overgrown with ferns and bamboo. By some miracle the invaders did not find me and I would swear that they ran past not an inch from my head.'

'And . . . Sir Anthony?'

'There was nothing left of the hut where we had slept but smouldering embers.' His long face was sombre. 'My . . . my only consolation – if it is a consolation – is that he was too ill to have known anything of it. And I fear even if we had not been so cruelly set upon, he would scarcely have lasted another day. I dared not even linger to bury the men who had escaped the flames, lest the savages return. I made my way back . . . surviving somehow . . . a pitiful, half-starved wreck when I made my way to my lodgings where Rokiah and Ahmed, who had been my cook and houseboy all the time I had lived in Malacca, found me and nursed me back to health.'

'And you returned here? To your friend's house?

'The shock of what I had seen . . . the loss of my friend . . . I had become disillusioned with adventure. I decided to return to England, and of course to bring word of Sir Anthony's death to whatever relatives were left. I knew of a sister and a daughter but I found Miss Brehault had predeceased her brother and the house was put up for sale by the bank which had foreclosed on the mortgage. It seemed . . . fate that I should be looking for such a place to settle and put down roots.' A short bark of laughter. 'In a quite literal sense.'

Violet, smiling in appreciation of the pun, said lightly, 'And the daughter?'

'The daughter, Miranda . . .' He hesitated, frowning. 'I . . . I made what I believed at the time to be adequate arrangements for her to be looked after but am led to believe she, too, died soon after. A sad case. She had been left to run wild after her aunt died, in the charge of a decrepit old nurse so bent and crippled with rheumatism that the kindest solution was to find the woman a place in the almshouse where she could live out her days in peace.'

'Instead of which, Mr Crowe,' I breathed, 'she never stopped grieving for the child who had been snatched from her care, nor for being put off from the place that was her home.'

'What more was I to do? I did what I thought best . . .' He stopped, stared at me. 'You know of her?'

'I do indeed.' I let the silence grow, then I said, very softly, 'Look hard at me, Mr Theophilus Crowe. Do you see any likeness to that child you despatched so summarily from Moondance that September day? Or indeed to the man you claim as your friend? Yes, you may look shocked. I daresay you did not expect to see me ever again. You washed your hands of me, didn't you? Your so-called friendship had little value when it came to inconvenient dependants.'

Astonishment was quickly erased by an urgent need to defend himself. 'It was not like that . . . you must not think for one moment . . .'

'That you did not intend me to be apprenticed in a cotton mill that used and exploited little children in the most inhuman and degrading manner?'

'No! Well . . . yes, but it was not quite . . .'

'And while you lived fatly in *my* home, even . . . even,' I choked, 'with my aunt's – my mother's – things about you . . .' I gestured round the room.

'These bits of furniture? Good God, I saved them – bought

them and other things – from the creditors – tradesmen – who were crawling about the place when I arrived, demanding compensation for what your family owed.'

'While you lived fatly,' I insisted, 'and introduced debauched company into my beloved home – and you need not bother to conceal what happened with fresh lies, because I know about the wild parties and the dissolute behaviour. I was beaten and half starved and forced to work up to eighteen hours a day, year in, year out. It was only with the help of friends that I was able to remove myself from that dreadful place. *Real* friends, not the sort who claim friendship but whose actions betray them as something very different.'

I saw the strange, haunted expression that I had noticed before leap into his eyes, his face, but in the passion of my anger and hatred I scarcely registered it.

'Those five years that I spent in purgatory I lay upon your conscience, sir. Five years of unnecessary suffering that could have been avoided had you taken the slightest trouble to concern yourself with the true needs and wishes of that helpless child who was obliged to cast herself upon your mercy and understanding. Mercy! You do not know the meaning of the word! Nor anything of the gentler tenets of human understanding. Otherwise you would have listened to Meg when she begged you not to separate us – yes, I heard her weeping. She echoed my own tears as I was carried off.'

'But you do not understand . . . it was meant for the best. I thought his scheme respectable . . . that you would have schooling, be cared for and taught a useful trade . . . Oh, a difficult parting, but better a short, clean cut rather than a prolonged, more painful one.' He stopped short, his long face suddenly darkening, as though my anger had begun to fire his own. 'I would remind you, Miss Brehault, that you came uninvited into *my* estate, *my* house. Not yours. It was never yours, for all you choose to pretend otherwise. It had even ceased to be your father's well before he died when the bank foreclosed on his debt. Not that he would have cared even if he had known. He had little love for this place. Perhaps there was precious little for you either. Bear that in mind when you strike out at someone who tried to offer what seemed a practical solution at the time, even if the outcome was unfortunate. Your father never mentioned you more than once or twice and then almost as though you were part of a past life he preferred to forget and had already put behind him.'

'I will not listen to your lies!' But even as I protested I knew the cold truth of it. It was my mother he had loved. Once she had gone there was nothing to hold my father here. Whatever affection he had nurtured for me had not been strong enough to keep him.

'Your father never meant to return. He said the house was full of bad memories and he had sooner let it rot than torment himself with thoughts of what might have been had his wife and sons not died. So, Miss Brehault, even had I not come along and done what I believed to be my best by you – though it turns out I was hasty and misguided – you would probably have ended up in the poorhouse or some foundling home, and who is to say you might not have finished worse off than you did?' He looked me scornfully up and down. 'You have fallen on your feet, it seems to me, for all that you moan about past hardships. Look at you! The picture of fashion.'

'But this gown . . . you must not think . . . that is, I am not rich, sir.'

His scornful look deepened. 'Then you are Anthony Brehault's daughter through and through. He was a man whose pride never allowed him to admit that his finances were in a worse case than mine, which as a mere clerk were never lavish and had to be eked out economically. He never stinted himself and lived permanently beyond his means. As many a poor tradesman found to his cost. At least I can hold my head up in that regard, Miss Brehault. No debt of mine has ever gone unpaid.'

'How dare you insult my father! And I am not in debt . . .'

'I speak the truth. Make no mistake, he was my friend, but that did not blind me to his weaknesses. I tolerated them, as he tolerated mine. Which is what friends do. Nobody is perfect. I do not claim to be. But I am not the monster you seem to think me, Miss Brehault, any more than your father was the sainted being you probably imagine him to have been. Now, I would be obliged if you would leave my parlour – *my* parlour – and my property.'

He had turned the tables on me. I was on the defensive now and needed to attack. Make the enemy run before the force of my words. But words would not come. *He had little love for this place . . . precious little for you . . .* The phrases rang in my head, drowning all the fire of my rage in a cold, dampening flood.

'Miranda dear,' said Violet in a lazy, amused voice, 'you might have allowed us to drink our tea before you set about revealing yourself to Mr Crowe. Those little cakes look most inviting . . . but there it is. Needs must when the devil drives.' She rose gracefully. 'It was most kind of you to invite us in, sir. It is unfortunate that we must take our leave so precipitately.'

'I suppose you were part of this charade, madam.' His lips were a tight line. 'Shame on you to abuse my hospitality so! If yours has been an example of Exeter manners then, devil or not, I am glad not to be part of the fashionable scene.'

Violet smiled and dipped her head as though in receipt of a compliment. She swept to the door. 'Pray do not bother to see us out. Come, girls, we have outstayed our welcome.'

Biddie hurried after her. I went more slowly. Stopped. Something – some instinct – made me look down at the small piece of furniture against which my skirts brushed. I remembered it as standing in the window corner; now it was near the door. Mama's éscritoire. I touched it, suddenly and sharply aware of a breath of cool air swirling in from the corridor. I swung round and looked at Theophilus Crowe standing with his head thrust forward, eyes sparking still with anger. The words were in my ear, then on my lips before I had time to consider them. As though a voice, a remembered voice, soft and feminine, whispered close to me: *Ask him, my darling . . . ask him now.*

'For a man who was a mere clerk, you live very well now, sir. I wonder how that is?' My voice was very cold, very sharp. 'You pay your debts, you say. But with what may I ask?' Then, the thought sliding clear and strong into my mind, I said slowly, 'You have a secret, don't you, Mr Crowe? Something . . . something happened that you don't care to remember too closely. Was it something to do with my father?'

'Get out! Get out! Before I have you thrown out!'

His face was suffused with rage. But the last thing I saw as I turned my back on him and walked with as much dignity as I could muster into the corrider, was the flare of that haunted, almost desperate, look in his eyes. And I knew I was right.

That night I dreamed of my mother. It was dawn, a misty morning, and I was standing in the shadow of the three oak trees at Moondance watching her as she came towards me, smiling, waving, along the lake path. I felt great joy and anticipation which quickly turned to alarm as the mist thickened to an impenetrable fog. I called to her but the fog blanketed all sound. Then an irritable voice, Violet's, said, 'Bear up. No use looking back. I like someone with purpose.' But when I turned, it was not Violet but the first desolate Northfield bride mounted on a gaudily caparisoned horse, and on another horse Kit Warrener with a bloodied face from the gash in his head and staring at me strangely. Then the fog was gone and I was alone, standing by the stumps of the felled oaks, and my mother's voice whispering, 'Be sure, my lamb, that you judge wisely . . .'

I awoke with tears slithering down my cheeks. For the loss of my mother, for Moondance, for that unhappy bride, for Kit . . . And a good deal of it for myself. I snuffled self-pityingly into the sheet for a long time. I was glad of the racket outside of a coach arriving, though Violet snoring softly in the other bed, and Biddie a slumped mound beside me, slept as deep and sound as if the inn would have to fall about their ears before they would rouse.

By the time the horses were changed and the coach had clattered off into the night I was calmer and my thoughts drifted to Moondance and the painful events of the afternoon. It was all so different from my expectations. The gardens altered – for the better, I had to confess – and little sign of the debauched Theophilus Crowe that rumour had painted. The evil ogre of my dreams had shrunk to a very ordinary human being. That very humanity enlisted something that was dangerously near to sympathy in my mind. His evident devotion to beautifying Moondance's gardens, his assurances that, however mistakenly, he had tried to do his best for me, seemed to protest against the hatred I had felt for so long. But I had no intention of letting any such weakness dilute my feelings towards him. I remembered, grimly, that haunted look on Theophilus Crowe's face. There was some mystery to do with my father's death, I was sure. Something that hateful man was covering up. And I should dearly like to find out what it was.

That was the thought that teased me time and again over the next three days, our last in Exeter. Violet and Biddie were both glad to be back in the bustle of the town. Biddie's face was all smiles as the carriage jogged us back to Bedford Circus. Violet sighed with pleasure as she walked into the house, ordered lemonade and biscuits by way of refreshment after the hot, dusty drive, and as we settled ourselves in the drawing room, began to delve among the letters the maid brought in.

'I think we might accept this invitation to a soirée at Colonel and Mrs Bonynge's house. I don't promise it will be the liveliest way to spend your last evening, but we shall find some amusement in pretending surprise at his acumen in purchasing Mr Grant's paintings . . . speaking of whom, here is a note from that very gentleman.' She smiled. 'More paintings sold and he is positively awash with gratitude. Oh, and here is a letter addressed to you both.'

It was from Miss Swann, in answer to the one we – or rather I – had written, Biddie's effort being but three scribbled lines on the end of mine. Miss Swann wrote in a lively manner of the day-to-day activities at Furze House. The only sober note was struck by news that Mr Loveridge had suffered an accident at the mill.

> *No sooner had Caroline returned from a visit to her step-daughter and the new baby, when Mr Loveridge was crushed against a wall by a runaway horse and cart in the mill yard and has suffered injuries to his head and back which have rendered him bedfast and the physician unable to predict how and when or even if he may be restored to full health. How unfortunate for such an accident to happen just as the difficult years for Mr Loveridge, occasioned by the war with America which interrupted the supplies of raw cotton, were behind him and the prospect of peaceful trade with the Continental countries promised a new era of prosperity. Poor Caroline will be out of her mind with distress and worry.*

I doubted that. Caroline, it seemed to me, might well see a helpless and dependent invalid for a husband as a very satisfactory state of affairs. Since the unfortunate loss of her first – and only – child, she had increasingly found excuses to be absent from Crossbank. Distressed nerves seemed to be the prime reason for the doctor's ordering her to Harrogate or Buxton to take the waters. A very convenient symptom, I thought dryly, which a strong-minded and manipulative young woman might use to her own advantage. Then there was Ida Loveridge who, since her marriage, had borne two children in quick succession, and had provided a good excuse for Caroline to be absent for weeks at a time in Manchester.

'Poor Mr Loveridge, my heart bleeds for him,' said Biddie sarcastically. 'I hope they send Ma Hatcher up to the house to nurse him. She'll soon have him back to work, even if he's half-dead on his feet.'

I shuddered. 'Don't remind me.'

'So, I must now write to accept the Bonynges' invitation,' said Violet who had been only half listening as I read out Miss

Swann's letter. 'And I shall send word to Mr Grant to come to supper tomorrow, as I promised, on condition he leaves that unfortunate animal behind. I trust that is agreeable to you, girls?'

'Oh, yes,' said Biddie, a little too fervently, then blushed and looked so confused that I said quickly, 'It will give us chance to wear our pretty new evening gowns, for we shan't have much occasion to wear them in Dawlish, shall we, Biddie?' And Violet gave a little scoffing laugh and said, 'Ah, the old pussycats have you in bed by nine, do they? You must take care not to be entrapped by such a wickedly high lifestyle. Lord knows what by-ways of sin it might lead you to.' By which time Biddie had recovered herself, though her colour remained a little high and often when I looked at her the rest of the day it was to catch her staring dreamily into space and smiling at nothing at all.

Supper with Mr Grant was a lightearted and jolly occasion. He bowed his way in, as untidy and amiable as ever, and bearing an enormous sheaf of yellow roses for Violet and a nosegay of white rosebuds each for Biddie and me.

'You will never grow rich if you spend your money as soon as you get it,' Violet scolded, but her eyes were bright with pleasure at such a gallant and poetic gesture, which seemed to set the tone for the evening. Mr Grant had a comical way of telling a story which had us in gales of laughter. His accounts of life among the artistic elements he had encountered in his travels were recited with the dramatic touches he brought to his paintings. Snippets of scandal about well-known painters added a touch of spice to his good-humoured anecdotes. He even had a tale to tell about the distinguished portrait painter and first President of the Royal Academy, Sir Joshua Reynolds. He had a sister who, apparently, had shown early promise to equal his own, but had first been obliged to look after their ageing parents in Plymouth before becoming housekeeper to Sir Joshua himself.

'I heard that he refused to give her any instruction though she begged it of him.' He shook his head. 'So the world will never know what she might have achieved had she not been kept down, as he seemed to think proper. Which seems to me the greatest shame.'

'Ah, that is the lot of the female if she is without means and subject to any male person,' said Violet.

'If I had a talented sister, I would consider it shameful to impose my will on her in such a way,' he said heatedly.

'Or even your wife, should you marry?'

'Particularly my wife,' he retorted. 'I consider marriage an equal partnership, not a matter of the male dominating the female.' Then, unable to be serious for long, he grinned and said, 'Though I cannot imagine any woman fool enough ever to take on a man of no fixed income and with a future at best uncertain – even with your generous help, Mrs Lascelles – with at worst destitution and bread and water in a debtors' prison being a serious possibility.'

Amid the laughter as we left the dining table and repaired to the drawing room, his glance slid – as though he could not help it – towards Biddie, who had scarcely taken her eyes off him all through supper. With Violet preceding us, he deftly manoeuvred himself alongside Biddie as we crossed the hall and swiftly drew up a chair beside her when she settled on the sofa with the nosegay of white roses in her lap. There were many moments during the rest of the evening when they exchanged smiles. Though there was little chance to speak privately, I noticed that once or twice he leaned towards her and whispered some comment, and once his hand brushed her arm just below the puffed sleeve of the light green gown and her lids swept down as though the lingering touch roused some emotion that she could not bear anyone else to see.

As midnight approached and our guest rose to take his leave, Violet said, 'Thank you for your very good company, Mr Grant. It is an age since I laughed so much. The company of artists is clearly more congenial than that of retired colonels.' She frowned thoughtfully. 'It has occurred to me once or twice this evening that there may be other persons among the artists, writers and musicians of this town who would welcome the chance to meet in comfortable circumstances. No chance of being bored in such company, I think.'

'Bored?' Mr Grant said, laughing. 'Not unless you would be bored by arguments and displays of temperament from those whose genius does not allow them to behave as circumspectly as ordinary mortals.'

'Better and better,' said Violet. 'Yes, I find the idea . . . tempting. Do you suppose it would be possible?' She was musing half to herself, her eyes glinting. 'Once it was known . . . word of mouth, rather than open invitations – though one would be more formal with visiting celebrities like Madame Catalini, whose voice so thrilled the Exeter Music Festival, or leading actors from the theatre, or eminent literary personages – then it might become something of a draw. Oh, it would not be so grand as the London salons . . . but in a small, provincial way, Mrs Lascelles's house in Bedford Circus might provide a more intimate, though no less stimulating attraction on one or two afternoons or evenings in the week.' She tapped Mr Grant playfully on the shoulder with her fan. 'You shall help me spread the word.'

'My pleasure, Mrs Lascelles,' he said with a sweeping bow. 'It would be but a small return for all you have done for me.'

We walked with him into the hall where the sleepy maid awaited to hand him his hat. He turned as he reached the open front door as though struck by a sudden thought. 'But I am forgetting,' he said. 'I hope to be making a sketching trip to the southern coast probably – er – next month. If I should be in Dawlish . . .'

'Oh, but you must call on us,' Biddie said quickly. 'At Furze House, on the coast road to Teignmouth. I . . . that is, we would be very pleased to see you. Wouldn't we, Miranda?'

'Yes, indeed,' I murmured.

'Then perhaps I may write and let you know when I may be calling.'

'That would be best, most certainly,' said Biddie.

The two beamed at each other as though they had achieved some private understanding. As perhaps they had in those brief moments when they had whispered together and his touch had lingered on her arm. I felt myself wanting to smile with them. For all Biddie's dreams of a rich and grand young suitor, here she was with stars in her eyes for an impoverished painter of unfashionable pictures. It was rather sweet and touching.

Violet did not think so, though. She had caught that look between the two of them and seemed suddenly taken aback. As though this was something she had not realised . . . had overlooked and found unpalatable. There was an instant when the vivacity died from her face, taking the usual sharp confidence from it, and she looked less pretty, a little gaunt . . . even for a second or two vulnerable, like a child from whom the prospect of a treat has been snatched.

'To bed with the pair of you,' she said, tartly, turning back into the drawing room after the maid had closed and bolted the front door. Ordering her off, too. 'I will put out the candles down here.'

The drawing-room door made a loud slam behind her as we went upstairs. Biddie, not noticing, drifted up as though she were already asleep and dreaming; I plodded behind somewhat wearily. Feeling a little sad on Violet's behalf. Poor Violet. She was always so adamant that she never wished to be beholden to any man and perhaps she had never meant to be. Yet she had clearly been more captivated by Mr Greville Grant's amiable charm than I – or perhaps even she – had realised.

I had thought Violet cool and impervious to any feelings beyond those of the practical and clear-seeing kind. How strange, I thought in my innocence, that attraction – love – should be so sly and insidious as to entangle hard-headed Violet almost without her being aware of it. But then I had not the experience to know that love is the most wayward and incomprehensible of emotions. It strikes where and when it pleases and all the commonsense and determination in the world will not deflect its sensuous and painful arrows.

One odd event happened before we left for Dawlish.

On our last day, Biddie and I went out to find small gifts to take back for our friends in Furze House. As we came out of Bedford Circus, I saw a man whisk away round the corner. In a very great hurry, but I thought no more about it. I was feeling rich because I still had the money I had saved from my salary, Violet having refused my offer to pay anything towards the trip to Moondance. We had already decided on a pretty ribbon for each of the little girls in residence and a pair of white gloves for Flossie. Mrs Hawkins would have some of her favourite mint toffees. We were undecided whether Mrs Greenwood would prefer a silk-embroidered handkerchief sachet or a small piece of lace with which to make a collar. In the end I drifted off towards the large bookshop and left Biddie to make the final choice, arranging to meet her by the Guildhall in half-an-hour. The pleasure of choosing three books all at once tempted me far more than haberdasher's fripperies. I should buy one for Violet as a thank you gift, one for Miss Swann and one for myself. Such luxury! I was debating in my mind if Miss Swann would prefer a copy of a book from a favourite author or something adventurously new, when from the corner of my eye I thought I caught a glimpse, in the shifting crowd in the High Street, of . . . I stopped. Stared. No. It could not possibly have been. I was seeing things.

The half-hour slipped away on flying minutes. With my three purchases I walked briskly out of the shop and came to a halt. It was Theophilus Crowe! He was standing in front of me, blocking my way, raising his hat.

'Miss Brehault,' he said. 'Forgive me. I . . . I had to speak.'

'I think we said quite enough two days ago, Mr Crowe,' I said coldly. 'Kindly let me pass.'

'Please hear me out. I have been in two minds. Whether it

was best to forget – to let you forget – or whether I should try to make up a little for . . . for my . . . for past mistakes.' His long face was creased into lines of strain, his eyes were shadowed, as though from lack of sleep. He was formally dressed today in a dark blue coat under which a paler waistcoat showed, his stock high and crisply white. He looked very much the prosperous man of property. No longer the earthy labourer we had found the other day. 'I went to Bedford Circus, meaning to find Mrs Lascelles's house, but then I saw you . . . and, in truth, I played the coward's role and retreated . . . and I still do not know if I am doing right to approach you.'

'You followed me!'

'In order to say, Miss Brehault, that sometime I should wish – like – to request a more . . . more constructive interview than that which we had the other day. I believe . . . I believe neither of us was thinking clearly. I realise now the emotional upheaval it must have been for you – to return to your old home – and with such bitter thoughts about me. The shock of knowing you were alive when I supposed you dead set me off balance also.'

'And why should I not have bitter thoughts?' I said. 'Do you not warrant them, sir?'

'D'you see? You are set on despising me! Yet I would wish you to hear the full account of what happened after I returned to England. Just as I should wish to hear more of your side of the story.'

I bit back the harsh retort that was my instant reaction. Perhaps it would be best to be more circumspect. No point in cutting off my nose to spite my face. After all I wanted to find as much as I could about my father in the years we had been separated. Who else was there to ask other than the man who claimed to be his friend? And there again, if we talked I might get some hint as to why Mr Theophilus Crowe was haunted by guilt to do with Papa's death.

'What did you intend?' I asked warily.

'That we arrange to meet here. In Exeter. On neutral ground. Perhaps I might bespeak a room at a respectable inn where we could be quiet – naturally you would arrange to be accompanied. I would not wish to compromise you in any way. A discreet friend . . . a maid perhaps.'

'I don't live in Exeter, Mr Crowe. Nor am I the fashionable butterfly you seem to think I have become. This gown you commented on so sourly was a gift from Mrs Lascelles. You would see me very differently if you could observe me in my place of employment, to which I must return tomorrow.'

He looked abashed. 'Hasty words on both sides, eh, Miss Brehault? All the more reason to set things straight between us. Do you travel far? Might I visit you there?'

'Dawlish,' I said, and hesitated. 'But I think I should prefer neutral ground, as you suggest. Mrs Lascelles has kindly invited me back to Exeter in January. We could meet here then.'

His face fell. My instinctive, illogical reaction was that I did not want him in Dawlish, however strong my curiosity to learn about my father. I could not bear his presence – with its inevitable links to Crossbank – to disturb and sully the quiet, peaceful order of my life there. Better he kept his distance . . . Yet a cautionary voice warned that by January he might have changed his mind. Whatever trouble his conscience was giving him now, the passing months might soothe him back to his previous unconcern and I should never get to the bottom of the mystery.

I said, reluctantly, 'Very well. If you wish to come to Dawlish, then I will see what I can arrange.'

'So be it! Where do you suggest we meet?'

'I will be able to see you only when it is convenient to my employers.'

'Will you write to me then? And where should I address my reply?'

When I told him, he said awkwardly, 'You have means to pay the post boy for the receipt of letters? I would not wish my writing to you to be any sort of imposition . . .'

'Your concern is touching, sir,' I said dryly. 'If a little late in the day. I assure you I shall not be bankrupted by the arrival of the post boy.'

The ghost of a smile touched his face. He raised his hat. 'I am glad to hear it. Till next we meet then, Miss Brehault.'

I watched him go, then went to join Biddie.

We left Exeter on a day as hot as any that summer. I hugged Violet and gave her the book I had bought. 'I hope you'll enjoy it. It is just a small thank you for all your kindness and generosity.'

'I'm sorry to be going,' Biddie sighed. 'It's all been such fun. It'll seem so quiet in Dawlish after Exeter.'

'Not *so* quiet, surely?' said Violet tartly. 'Not if a certain gentlemen of our acquaintance arrives on the scene.' She waved an impatient hand. 'Oh, don't pretend innocence. Enjoy yourselves and don't allow him too many liberties – or is that a contradiction in terms?' Her laugh was a mite forced. 'Just remember he is an artist and artists often have passionate temperaments and unconventional views on matters of the heart and marriage. So take care he does not sweet-talk you into allowing him too much licence if it is a ring and respectability you are after. Now what is this you have given me? Silly girls, I do not expect you to waste your money on me.' She opened the book and smiled. 'Ah, Miss Austen's latest offering. I take back what I said. I give you leave to be profligate with your pennies if you bring me gifts like this. Now, be off with you. Don't make yourselves late.'

'We have plenty of time,' Biddie said, fanning herself with her hand. 'Goodness, it's even hot indoors this morning.'

'Far too hot to hurry,' Violet said. 'Thank goodness I need do nothing today save sit and make plans for my salon, after which I shall put my feet up and enjoy *Mansfield Park*, without having to worry my head about entertaining you pair of rustic maidens. It is very pleasant when guests arrive but even pleasanter when they leave, I may tell you. But don't fret yourselves. By January I shall have forgotten all the disturbance you have caused to my well-ordered life and will welcome you back with open arms. Now, off you go. I envy you not one jot your dusty journey to Dawlish. My regards to the old pussycats!'

For all her mocking words, it seemed to me there was something wistful in her face as she shooed us out. My last thought was that she looked lonely and rather small and lost in the elegance of her drawing room. But I knew that, however much she regretted our departure, nothing in the world would have made Violet Briggs admit to such weakness. Any feelings of loneliness would be accepted, dismissed, and she would turn her mind briskly to other things. I daresay that was how she would treat whatever hopes or desires she had harboured towards Greville Grant. I admired her for that. And for not casting any shadow of jealousy or resentment over Biddie.

I thought, as we left the house, that for an adventuress, an ex-whore living day by day under false colours and wholly engaged in hoodwinking the society she courted, there was a very great deal to be liked and respected about Violet Briggs.

The coachman carried our bags the short journey to the New London Inn. I rather wished we had outside seats on such a day, though Biddie was thrilled, as she had been on the journey from Dawlish, to be seated inside like proper gentry. Violet had been very generous to us. As our bags were taken up and we prepared to climb inside I was nearly knocked over by a lolloping hound that threw a cloud of dust over me from its wildly scrabbling paws.

'Ah, Mr Grant,' I said. 'I thought you would not be far behind your all-too-friendly beast.'

'Down, Gyp!' he commanded, uselessly. 'Dear me, I thought I was too late.' He mopped his face with his handkerchief and pressed a flat package into Biddie's hands. 'Just a little something I thought you might like as a keepsake of your visit to Exeter. For both of you, of course.' Then, seeming to lose his voice, he continued to beam at Biddie in a very silly manner. And she at him. Until I was practically forced to haul her inside, from where she continued to wave until the coach turned the corner and Mr Greville Grant was lost to sight.

Biddie unfolded the brown paper reverently, to reveal two pencil sketches. 'He has drawn likenesses of us!' she whispered excitedly. 'Isn't he clever? Oh, he has exactly caught that solemn look you have . . . but I think he has made me too pretty, don't you?'

'Stop fishing for compliments,' I said. 'But certainly, if beauty is in the eye of the beholder, then you may be sure he beholds you as very pretty indeed.'

They were drawn with quick, fluid lines and intended, I thought, to flatter. He had made me far too handsome, though Biddie's portrail was accurate enough. Which was only to be expected, I thought, smothering a chuckle, as he had spent a great deal more time looking at her than at me.

Throughout the journey to Dawlish we were in a lather of sweat and discomfort. The other inside passengers, two old ladies, demanded that the windows be tight shut on account of the quantities of dust billowing inside, so that it grew exceedingly stuffy. The heat combined with the swaying and jolting of the coach caused us both to feel queasy. It was wonderful to get out of the coach at Dawlish and feel and smell the salty breeze, even though it was as warm as the waft from a cooking range. Miss Swann was waiting, her plain face wreathed in smiles, accompanied by the five little boarders who hopped up and down in their haste to tell us that they had just come from the beach where they had been allowed to take off their shoes and stockings and paddle their feet. I cast a somewhat yearning look myself at the limpid water as we walked past the beach. I envied the ladies being trundled down to the water in bathing machines though Miss Swann would have been disapproving to know that I did. Both she and Mrs Greenwood regarded sea bathing for women as something only to be contemplated on medical grounds. The fashionable who indulged themselves out of idle curiosity were condemned as foolish sensation-seekers. 'If the good Lord had meant us to bodily invade the watery element he would have provided us with the scales and gills of a fish,' Mrs Greenwood had cried scornfully. 'Just as he would have given us wings if he had intended us to fly with the birds.' But today I would willingly have joined the bathers, scales and gills or not. Even the squeals of the timorous as they were thrust into the water by strong-armed attendants sounded less alarmed than usual, as though the chill of the water was pleasurable rather than frightening.

But once Biddie and I were back in our familiar bedroom at Furze House we could enjoy the lesser luxury of unbuttoning ourselves from our sticky, crumpled travelling clothes and sponging ourselves down with the fresh water Flossie had put ready.

Biddie regarded her pretty new blue gown with dismay as she laid it on the bed. 'You were right,' she said mournfully. 'I should have travelled in my old dress. I picked up a horrible black mark in the coach – and look how the skirt has crushed.'

'Mrs King will know what to do to get the mark out. She'll soon have it looking like new again,' I said comfortingly, privately feeling more than glad I had travelled in my old print. Now I could bring out the rose pink gown freshly laundered by Violet's washerwoman, and show it off to Miss Swann and Mrs Greenwood in all its perfection. I slipped it on and smoothed my hands over my hair to subdue any stray ends ruffled by wearing my bonnet. Wilkins had brushed and arranged my hair this morning and threaded it with matching ribbons. 'Now watch again what I do, miss,' she had said. 'You're managing a bit better, but you still tend to drag it back too severe. Leave a little softness here . . . and here, like so.'

I should miss Wilkins's ministrations. I should miss, I had to confess, the life of a leisured lady. It had been nice, for a little while, to be so pampered.

Biddie shook out her yellow dress. 'I suppose I'll have to wear this old thing,' she grumbled, 'while you go down looking like lady kiss-me-arse.'

'It's very pretty,' I said, firmly. 'You look well in it.'

'It doesn't look much set against yours.'

Nor did it. It looked what it was, cheap and showy. Something that Violet had noticed from the first but now, set against the subtle colour of mine, and the style and quality of Mrs Chadwick's work, I could not help seeing for myself. Oh, Biddie had fashioned the dress as cleverly as she was able, but in the poor quality of the material – and with Mrs Greenwood's influence very evident in the overburdening of frills – it compared unfavourably with our new gowns.

Still, nothing could dim Biddie's prettiness and I fully expected that there would be more exclamations of admiration over her new hair style – her vibrant locks deftly and ravishingly tamed by Wilkins – than over my appearance.

I was wrong.

There was a small silence as we entered the parlour where the others were assembled.

It was broken by one of the little girls, Nell. 'Is it really you, Miss Brehault?' she said, round-eyed. 'You look *very* pretty.'

I laughed. 'Fine feathers make fine birds. A very clever lady made this dress. Another one did up my hair with ribbons.'

Miss Swann said quietly, 'Do not be so modest, child. I had not realised quite . . . well, just how much you had changed these last months . . . how grown up you had become . . . and quite . . . quite graceful.'

'Oh, come,' I said, still laughing, still misunderstanding. 'I shall have inky fingers and my old print dress on tomorrow and you will have no difficulty in recognising that I am exactly the same as I always was.'

Oddly, it was Mrs Greenwood who made me pause; who said, sourly, because whatever I did at the school she had never properly approved of me, or liked me, as she did Biddie, 'I am glad to hear it. At your age a girl's head is easily turned. I will not have you taking on airs and graces on account of finding yourself the object of a few flattering remarks. It would be most unbecoming.' And I thought, in astonishment, Why, even she thinks I look well, I can see it in her face.

By the time we had eaten dinner and the gifts had been distributed and exclaimed over, we were all feeling drowsy with the languor of the hot afternoon. Despite the open windows there was scarcely a breath of air indoors. Mrs Greenwood was soon snoring gently in her chair, Miss Swann's glasses slid down her nose as her head nodded forward over the copy of *Waverley* I had chosen for her in Exeter. Even the anticipation of enjoying this highly popular work and speculating as to who might be its anonymous author had not been enough to keep her awake. Biddie grimaced and tiptoed out in search, presumably, of Flossie who would be agog for the rest of the Exeter news that she had not gleaned while waiting on table. Presently I, too, wandered outside with my book and found a shady spot by the pond where there was an illusion of coolness.

If ever I had a free half-hour and the weather was good, I liked to sit out here and read. Or dream. The pond had been dug from a boggy patch near the deep stone basin which had been built long ago to trap the underground spring which at that spot bubbled close to the surface. It was a never-failing spring which provided the house with its excellent water. The pond waters were utilised about the garden and Miss Swann liked to see the swarms of toads and frogs that came to spawn there in the spring as she reckoned they, along with the chickens, kept down many of the pests that invaded her plants. Set against the lake at Moondance, the pond was a mere puddle. Yet, sitting here with my book, I could let my imagination drift and pretend I was sitting on the banks of that other lake. Back in my home. Back where I belonged.

The water was clear and still. It was very peaceful. The voices of the children playing in the orchard made the merest ripple of sound. I leaned my back against the old damson tree, the book unopened in my lap, and watched bold turquoise and gold dragonflies darting over the water and frailer blue damselflies shimmering above the water weeds . . .

Did I sleep? I think, perhaps, I did. It seemed part of a dream that the children's voices were suddenly stilled as though interrupted in their play. That there came the sound of footsteps – no, not so much footsteps, as the sense of someone approaching from the direction of the lower garden. Someone who had come in by the wicket gate. Not the milk-lad or the boy with the fish at this time of day. Nor the old gardener, who appeared before breakfast and was gone before dinner.

And why did I believe – know – it was a man? He had not spoken, had he? He had walked soft-footed and slowly up from the gate by the flagged path as though he wished to take his time looking about, savouring everything that was here, that he remembered. The children fell silent when they saw him because he was a stranger to them and they wondered who he was.

But I knew. Even before I opened my eyes and saw him where he had halted, to whip off his hat and say, 'Excuse me, ma'am, I had not realised you were there . . .' Then stopped as I rose to my feet.

We stared at each other wordlessly.

He standing with the full sun striking down on black hair which even when tied back into a sailor's tarred pigtail could not be entirely controlled and sprang into tangled curls about his ears and forehead. He was very brown, very thin, the bones and planes of his face more sharply etched, older than when last I saw him. He wore clothes faded by sea-salt and sun and there was a new, whippy, lean strength about his shoulders and long limbs that spoke of hard physical labour.

I saw all this as I stood in the dappled shade of the damson tree in my elegant pink dress with ribbons in my hair. No longer the skinny waif of his memory but a young woman at whom, for a full minute, he looked without recognition but with a kind of startled, lingering wonder.

It was a moment that even to this day I can conjure in my memory and feel my senses sharpen to everything I saw and felt and heard then. The touch of the warm air on my arms. The faint whirr of a dragonfly's wings. The scent of crushed grass and dried mud. The weight of the bowed branch, heavy with purpling damsons, that touched my shoulder as I took a step forward and held out my hands to him.

'Welcome home,' I said.

And Kit said, huskily, 'Christ, is it really you, Miranda?'

And took my hands and, very slowly, raised them to his lips.

Chapter Seven

'My dear boy, words cannot express what it means to see you once again in our parlour,' said Miss Swann, her fine blue eyes shining with tears. 'Though we have remembered you daily in our prayers, we had begun to fear the worst.'

'*You* might have wavered in hope, dear, but *I* never did,' said Mrs Greenwood, blithely managing to forget that she was the one who generally expressed the gloomiest opinions.

'Does everyone have a full glass?' said Miss Swann. 'Then I shall propose a toast . . .'

I looked round at the smiling faces. Flossie and Mrs Hawkins had been summoned from the kitchen to celebrate this moment. Even the five little girls had been given a glass of watered wine.

I raised my glass with the others, murmured his name, sipped at the wine, feeling strangely detached, almost as though I stood apart and viewed the proceedings from a distance. As though my real self still lingered under the damson tree, my hands imprisoned in his, the touch of his lips against my fingers.

Kit said, with a quiet dignity that belied his rough, faded garments, 'Thank you. It is good to be back for there were times when I never thought I should be. And in return, I raise my glass to all you good people for your warm and generous welcome.'

I believe we were all glad when the emotionally charged moment was broken by Nell – always the most forward – who cried, 'Did you ever meet Old Boney, sir? Did he really have horns and a great black tail like the devil himself? My old nurse said he did. She swore he could see through the walls and knew when I was naughty.'

'No, I never did meet him,' Kit said gravely. 'And though his reputation is very fierce among nursemaids, I know for a fact from those who have had the minding of him since he was made prisoner, that he is an ordinary man, without horns or tail, who gives no thought at all to the misbehaviour of little children.'

'So you see, Nell, it is just as I told you,' I said quickly. 'You needn't worry any more that he is watching you in the dark or hiding behind the washstand waiting to pounce.'

'Most certainly not!' Kit said. 'He is imprisoned on an island hundreds of sea miles from here. I have seen the place myself. A great rock rising in the midst of desolate empty ocean from which there is no chance whatsoever of escaping the eye of his gaolers.'

I smiled my thanks over Nell's head for his understanding. Perhaps now we should have a little more success in persuading Nell out of her bedtime fears. He smiled back and it was nothing at all to do with Nell. I wondered afterwards how so much could be expressed and understood in such a few seconds.

I think we had until then exchanged no more than a dozen words. Even when we were together in the garden the words I knew I should be saying out of politeness seemed irrelevant. He was here. He was whole. That was enough. We had walked up to the house in near silence. Not touching, but the small distance between us seeming to spark with some invisible, exhilarating energy.

I left questions to the others. The children were sent outside to play again, leaving the adults to talk more soberly. Kit answered everything in short, dismissive sentences. It was as though he had determined not to dwell on his experiences, at least not to us. Yes, he had been in despair at first, but he had adjusted in time to the life. He had been in but one battle, when the frigate he served on came under fire from an American ship off the Peninsula. They had been lucky, he said, to escape. He had been injured, as had many men, but recovered. His glance flickered to me and away again and I thought of that still, moonlit night when I had seen him lying bloodied in the thunder and fire of battle. He had been put ashore in Portsmouth, a week since, and arrived only today in Dawlish.

Miss Swann immediately said, 'We are a little pressed for space, Kit dear, but I'm sure . . .'

'Please, you are not to trouble about me,' he assured her. 'I have already found myself lodgings in the town.'

'Ah, then you will want the things that you left. Most of all your violin. It was so fortunate that an honest man found it and passed it to the Rossiters. Emma brought it to us to keep.'

'So you may set about your practise straight off,' said Mrs Greenwood. She pressed her hands together 'How wonderful it will be to hear you play again. You must promise we shall be the first to be granted a recital!'

A pause, in which his face went still and a dreadful bleakness seemed to glimmer in the depths of his deep-set, grey-green eyes. Then it was gone, and he said, half smiling as though it was of little consequence: 'I'm afraid that is out of the question. The injury I spoke of – it was due to cannon fire which felled a spar, fetching it down on top of me. I was caught a glancing blow which knocked me senseless but the wretched yard had not finished with me. It decided to make its final descent on to my left hand.'

He held it up, turned it this way and that. At first glance there looked little wrong with it, save for the near-invisible white striations of healed scars as the light caught them. But when he wriggled his fingers only his thumb and first finger responded. The others remained crooked and rigid.

'Dear heaven,' Miss Swann breathed.

'At least I still have a hand that manages to be reasonably useful,' Kit said. 'And that is entirely due to the surgeon's assistant who prevented the surgeon from chopping off the lot. The surgeon himself swore it was too crushed to be worth saving. Fortunately he had many other patients that day upon whom to display the elegance of his technique with the saw. His assistant, a man of patience and intelligence, decided he might attempt to move the bones back into position and splint the hand.'

Biddie shuddered. 'I can hardly bear to think of it.'

'I was mercifully unconscious for a good deal of the time. The surgeon reckoned it was pure miracle that my hand recovered, but his assistant had such a passion for cleanliness in his work that I have wondered since if that had something to do with it. He constantly plunged his instruments in boiling brine which the loblolly boy kept fresh and heated on a stove, and insisted on washing his hands between patients. A performance which alternately amused and annoyed his superior who seemed to think the amount of ancient gore that clung to his working clothes and instruments was a tribute to his experience. He was constantly bellowing about time being wasted in pernickety practices.' He shrugged. 'Yet I still have my hand – and what's more it healed without festering. Many a sailor who was hacked about by the surgeon did not survive the putrefaction that set in. I was . . . lucky.'

Lucky? But those crippled fingers would never again move strong and supple and sure over the strings of his violin. I could only begin to guess the frustration and despair behind the resignation in his voice.

Deprived of music, my spirit would have shrivelled and died.

That is what he had believed when he ran away from home. What of that spirit now?

He stood up.

'I have taken enough of your time. Perhaps you might allow me to take a few things now from my trunk. I shall borrow a handcart to fetch the rest tomorrow, if that would be convenient?'

'Of course,' said Miss Swann. 'Miranda will show you where . . . No, I was forgetting. It is bound to be dusty amongst the lumber and you have on your new gown. Perhaps I had best ring for Flossie.'

But I was already on my feet.

'I shall stay clear of dust,' I said calmly. I would have risked my dress in a coal cellar to chance this time alone with him, but she was not to know that.

We walked up to the attic floor without speaking. Only on the top landing did we stop and turn to each other, speaking together.

'Kit . . .'

'Miranda . . .'

Then we laughed and I found myself suddenly shy and he, too, seemed for a moment tongue-tied so I began again, saying quickly, before courage deserted me, 'I just wanted to say how . . . how pleased I am that you are back safely.'

Pleased. How weak and dull a word to set against the reality of what I felt.

'And I to be here. But perhaps I am not. Perhaps I am asleep and dreaming. Are you really the Miranda Brehault who was once a child as skinny and frowning and ill favoured as any I did see?'

'Did I frown?'

'Fearsomely.' He paused, said gently, 'But then, you had little reason to smile. And have you learned differently these last years? No, don't answer, it is a foolish question. I have eyes. I can see the difference well enough for myself.'

'They have been good years, Kit,' I said quietly.

He shook his head. 'It was once hard to believe you were the daughter of a baronet. Now I think that is too low a rank. Your father must have been earl at least! Or a duke!'

I laughed. 'I do not always look so fine. You heard Miss Swann say the gown is new.'

'Gown?' He looked genuinely puzzled. 'What I am talking of is nothing to do with gowns and folderols. Oh, I suppose such things as they may help dazzle the eye into overlooking a lack of grace or an indifferent complexion or unfortunate figure – but you have no such imperfection.'

He was searching my face so intently that I felt my colour rise and said, lightly, out of confusion, because I was torn between wanting most desperately for him to continue and embarrassment that I wished him to, 'Well, I have heard that sailors learn a way to charm the girls along with seamanship. Now I see it to be true.'

He hesitated, then as though taking my lead, said equally lightly, 'Ah, the rose may have blossomed, but she wishes it to be known that she bears a thorn or two.'

'Perhaps. Now will you stop your flattery and come along.'

I moved briskly ahead of him along the attic corridor. That was the only way to take charge of myself. To walk away before the urge to reach out and touch him overcame me and all will and reason melted away completely. I reached the door of the farthest attic and wrested it open.

'Your trunk is the corner. You will have to move the old picture frames and those bags.'

I was wholly aware of him as he cleared a path to the corner in that hot little space under the roof tiles. Aware of how his long limbs moved, of the musky masculine smell of his body, of the way the dancing dust motes formed a nimbus round his head whenever he crossed the shaft of late-afternoon sunlight that pierced the small window. Aware, too, of how often he looked at me.

I spoke. Commonplaces. Remarking on the amount of lumber, that most of it had belonged to Miss Swann's parents, that she could not bear to part with it and it could do with a good spring clean. He answered. Commonplaces. 'Yes' and 'No' and 'Certainly'. Filling the stifling air with words. And all the while, underneath the level, sensible manner of our speech, it seemed that a different conversation took place. As though our bodies, our senses, had a way of communicating over which we had no control at all.

He dragged out the trunk, opened the lid and reached inside to fetch out clothes, which he set on one side. Then he brought out the flute in its soft wrapping, and the violin . . .

He sat back on his heels and opened the violin case. He brought out the violin and tucked it under his chin. He allowed his ruined fingers to brush awkwardly across the sagging broken strings then, very slowly, laid the violin back in the case and closed it up.

I said, softly, 'I am sorry, Kit, that circumstances could not be different.'

His expression changed. His voice too. 'Please do not burden me with your sympathy, Miranda. It serves no purpose.'

'What will you do?'

'I shall sell the violin. I need the money.'

'But . . .'

'But what?' His voice was harsh. 'Do you expect some miracle to restore to me the use of my fingers?'

'There could be improvement . . . some treatment. I could ask Widow Thomas . . .'

'Improvement is not enough. I can never play as I did.'

'What about your flute?'

'A tin whistle is more use to me than that. It will be sold.'

'And . . . and will you compose?'

'No!' He slammed down the lid of the trunk and began to drag it across the floor. 'I am done with all that. If I cannot have it all, I do not want any of it.'

Everything had changed suddenly. As though the almost languorous mood that had enfolded us had been snatched away and some invisible barrier now lay between us.

'But you have so much to offer, Kit. You could teach . . .'

'And be reminded constantly of all that might have been? Never.'

'Then how will you live?'

He stood up, eased back his shoulders. Smiled. It was not a comfortable or a companionable expression. 'I have learned other skills this last three years,' he said. 'The proceeds from the sale of the Cremona will buy me a part share in a lugger. The French ports are open to us now. And we – my friends and I – have other contacts. I think we shall make a steady living in the trade.'

I stared at him. 'Free trade, do you mean?'

'Trade,' he repeated. 'That is all that need concern you.'

He bundled his clothes together, tied a string round them.

Put the flute into the inner pocket of his faded jacket. Picked up the violin in his free hand.

I said, quickly, 'Please, Kit. If your plans have anything to do with smuggling, I beg you not to involve Billy. Emma worries herself sick. She hates the trade . . .'

'Billy is his own man,' he said gruffly. Then, more amenably, 'If it eases your conscience I have no plans for Billy. You have been helping them, I hear. Emma sings your praises. She tells me they have had quite a brisk trade this last week in Billy's carvings because of some bills you put about.'

'It worked then.' I felt pleased about that. 'They deserve some good luck for a change. I wish there was more I could do.' I hesitated, struck by an idea. 'As a matter of fact, I did speak to a friend in Exeter about him. Biddie and I have just come back from staying with her. I am to send her a sample or two of his work to see if she can get a better price for him in Exeter. She is a . . . a lady of some influence.'

'Influence, eh? It seems you really have come up in the world if you have such friends.' He frowned. 'Something amuses you.'

I managed to keep my face serious. 'The lady in question is a Mrs Lascelles. She lives in Bedford Circus. Can you remember that?'

'Why?' he asked suspiciously.

'You may already have a purchaser for your violin. No? Then I suggest that if you are determined to get rid of it, you could do worse than approach her. She has an interest in the arts of all kinds. Or rather, those who work in the creative fields of music, painting, literature. She is a very clever person. I'm sure if anyone could help you she could. In fact . . . in fact your name came up in conversation during our stay, as someone who would have been welcomed at one of her artistic salons. But now, well, she may help you in a different way – and perhaps Billy, too, if you could take some of his carvings with you to save me the trouble of sending them.'

He shrugged. 'I suppose I could. I have nothing to lose.'

'Mrs Lascelles, remember.' Now I did smile openly. 'And

when you meet her, please don't call her by the name you once knew her by, or I could not guarantee your safe exit from her house.'

'Why? Who the devil is she?'

So I swore him to secrecy and told him.

I suppose in my heart I was hoping that Violet would perform some miracle of persuasion upon Kit to prevent him from selling his violin and turning his back on his music. In this I was to be disappointed. Kit returned from Exeter without flute or violin and with money in his pocket with which he immediately bought his sixth share in the lugger. It was a new one, being fitted out at yard in Exmouth. Even if I had had the chance to speak to Kit I would not have cared to enquire too deeply into the manner of this fitting out. There were a myriad dodges that could turn a respectable craft into one suitable for illicit activities, from false keels to hollow bilges and spars. I had little doubt that the *Phoebe-Jane* was undergoing an alteration of this sort and that Kit's dedication to the new venture was because of his expectations of large profits. Not only in what they might take out of France, but what they might take in. Until the boat was launched he and his friends were busy searching out a suitable cargo of woollen goods, cotton stockings and sewing needles which would find a ready sale across the channel.

In a last vain hope of finding something with which to lure Kit back to his music, I called upon Widow Thomas as soon as I could and poured out the tale of the damaged hand. She questioned me closely about the injury and then said, gently, 'If the fingers have healed so stiff and crooked, then I fear there is little I can do now to restore the old flexibility of movement. Of course, I could make up an oil to be massaged regularly into the hand, which might ease some of the stiffness. And if rheumatic pain sets in, as often happens when bones are broken – and such a-many fragile bones in the hand – then I could find something to relieve the pain.'

We were seated at her worktable. As soon as I had walked

in she had looked at me hard, waved me to a stool and set about preparing a tisane. I knew her well enough by now to trust that the brew would be pleasant and comforting. I rarely came to consult her professional services on my own account, for thankfully I kept in good health. Usually I was sent by the ladies to explain what ailments were affecting the children and request her advice. Or, without any excuse for it was always a pleasure to me, I would pay her a social call. But she always seemed to sense when I was feeling the griping pangs that heralded the onset of my courses, or a headache from poring over my books too long, or a meal that sat too heavily on my stomach. Whatever she gave me usually relieved the discomfort. Today, even though I felt in the rudest of health, she seemed to believe I still had need of one of her herbal brews.

'Just a little something to warm you through while we talk,' she said comfortably. 'Such a damp, cool day after the heat we have had can sometimes be unsettling to the system. Even the dogs prefer to be indoors.'

The lurchers were sprawled before the hearth, their rough grey coats steaming gently in the heat and infusing the herb-scented air with a decidedly canine whiff. The owl drowsed on his beam. The cats were draped about the room in somnolent attitudes. Outside, the rain came down in a steady drizzle. Inside, I felt cocooned in warmth and peace.

'So there is nothing useful we can do for Kit,' I said sadly.

'Very little. Even if he would allow it.'

I sighed. 'Such a waste.'

'Nothing is wasted in nature, Miranda. Whether it be a dead leaf falling from a withered tree or knowledge painfully gathered. The one will eventually give new heart to the earth, the other may have uses that may not be immediately apparent, but in time may prove worthwhile.'

I clasped my hands about the coarse earthenware beaker. I felt as useless to help him as one of the tiny specks of leaf that had escaped the muslin sieve and now hung suspended in the clear golden liquid of the tisane.

'Do not fret, child,' she said gently. 'You have done what you could. He must work out the bitterness that is in him in whatever way feels best. You will not divert him from his path if it is meant to be.'

'But I am frightened where that path will take him. There is so much danger in what he is doing. He could find some safe occupation if he really tried. Even if he cannot play, he could teach music. I tried to tell him that but he would not listen. The navy has turned him hard and pigheaded.'

She laughed softly. 'Ah, child. You would bind him close with loving wishes but those ties could easily turn to weighty fetters that would chafe him beyond endurance if he was kept against his will. Better to let him go now and hope he finds his own way back to you.'

I looked up sharply. Her smile was enigmatic.

'You forget that heartsick maidens come frequently to my door wanting charms to bring the reluctant lover to heel or to make the wayward one give up his philandering. I know the signs, Miranda.'

Had she then seen in me what I had observed in Biddie? If so, I was humiliated. I had watched my friend in the grip of infatuation and thought how silly she looked. All cow-eyes and adoration at the very mention of his name. I refused to be like that.

Yet for an instant, under the damson tree . . . for an hour in the parlour and half that time again in the hot, dusty attic, I had succumbed to the shock of that seductive, bone-weakening sensation and would have cared not one jot how foolish I looked. I had given myself utterly to the waking dream of knowing, without any doubt at all, that this was right and meant to be. And perhaps had always known from that time when I had heard his voice speak my name on the steps of Crossbank Grange. It was only afterwards that cold reason interposed itself between the dream and reality. I had *thought* his look, his words, the way he had kissed my hands, meant that he too had been as deeply affected. I had *believed* – during that wakeful night that followed and the day afterwards when the school reopened and I had the utmost difficulty in concentrating on my duties – that fired by the same heady emotion that consumed me, he would burn to see me again. I had been so sure he would search me out as soon as he could.

How wrong I was. When the school day finished I had to learn from Flossie that Master Kit had brought his handcart and taken away his trunk while we had been occupied in the schoolroom. No word. No message. Nothing. A day or two later, I had found some excuse to go into Dawlish and learned from Emma that Kit was in Exeter. It was from Emma, too, that I discovered that he had sold his violin, hired a horse and gone off about his business of bespeaking a cargo for the *Phoebe-Jane*.

So now I was here in Widow Thomas's cottage and up to this moment I had pretended to myself that my visit to her was made solely from the highest of motives: a wish to help Kit. But I realised I had not been entirely honest with myself. I had wanted – needed – that miraculous potion in order to give myself a good excuse for arranging to meet him. Perhaps had even visualised his admiration and gratitude; the way he would listen gravely to what I had to say and agree that it was foolish to turn his back on God-given talent and he would immediately dissociate himself from the free trading. My spirits, which had been buoyed up by this hope, now spiralled down to my boots. I drew pride about me in a vain attempt at dignified protest.

'You cannot think I came in search of a love-charm,' I said, stiffly, ignoring the treacherous inner voice that whispered of a miraculous healing potion with which I might lure him to speak to me. 'I am not a . . . a silly maidservant or fisher-girl.'

'No, child. Just a young woman feeling love's painful darts for the first time. Princess or pauper, the condition is likely to strike without warning or concession to station in life. Comfort yourself that few escape and most survive the experience.' She leaned across the table and took my hand. I felt the hardness of her strong fingers, the warmth that seemed to seep under my skin and into my blood, to flow in a steady tide. 'Give him time to come round to acknowledging what he feels,' she said. 'Give yourself time. You are so very young—' She broke off, a frown causing all the myriad fine wrinkles of her sun-browned face to seem more deeply etched. Her grip on my fingers tightened.

Something disturbed one of the dogs by the hearth. It suddenly lifted its head and looked at us, its eyes glinting yellow as a log slipped and sent up a spurt of flame that twisted and flared in a gust of wind blowing down the chimney. Mrs Thomas dropped my hands as abruptly as she had taken them.

'You had best be on your way, Miranda,' she said. Her voice, calm as ever, surprised me. I had expected . . . what had I expected? In that moment I sensed, like the dog perhaps . . . *something* . . . some chill. More than the spiralling of the draught along the flagstones and a flurry of rain against the small window. *Something*. Yet all she said was, 'The wind is getting up and the drizzle will soon be a downpour. Off you go and you will be back home before the worst of it.'

I pulled up the hood of Mrs Swann's unbecoming but enveloping cloak, which was always hung on the peg in the hall for anyone at Furze House to borrow on inclement days, and went to the door. The dog which had wakened stretched itself and came to me. I scratched its rough ears and it leaned its long head against my thigh, as though in acknowledgement that we had shared the same disquiet.

Disquiet?

Did I sense it even then? Did I catch the flicker of Widow Thomas's intuitive thought? Or was it merely the wind throwing a spiteful handful of rain in my face as I lifted the latch and opened the door? Whatever it was caused me to shudder under the weight of the heavy serge cloak.

'Summer is over,' she said quietly, standing close. 'And winter will be a long, desperate season if I read the signs a-right. Travel safely, child. My blessings, such as they are worth, go with you.'

She was still standing watching me when I stepped out into the puddled mud of the lane and turned to wave goodbye. Then I bent my head into the rain and wind and hurried home.

Contrary to Widow Thomas's prediction, summer had not quite had its last fling. As September died, the days mellowed once more and Biddie was in an ecstacy of excitement about Mr Greville Grant's impending visit. He was to spend three weeks sketching and painting along the south coast, starting in Torbay. I had a strong suspicion that he would find inspiration particularly compelling in the environs of Furze House.

I, too, was distracted by the prospect of a visitor, though my thoughts were less enthusiastic than Biddie's. My interview with Theophilus Crowe was looming and I was still not at all sure that I was right in inviting him to Dawlish, especially as Miss Swann insisted that the interview should take place at Furze House.

'Dawlish is too small a place for a stranger to go unnoticed,' she said after I had confided in her. 'By meeting in any public place you would become the subject of wagging tongues, however discreetly we went about it. No, best that he should come here which would not be remarked upon. Shall we say on a Saturday afternoon after Mrs Greenwood has finished her music lessons? Then you may be comfortable in the parlour without any disturbance.' She sighed. 'I do understand, dear, the motives behind your visit to your old home, but I still think it was unwise. Dredging up old sorrows never did any good to my way of thinking. You are quite sure this second meeting with Mr Crowe is necessary?'

I nodded slowly. 'I would truly like to learn what he knows of my father's last years.' And to probe a little deeper into whatever he was keeping to himself about Papa's death, though I thought it wiser to say nothing of that. 'He was, after all, the last person to see him alive.'

'Well, if you think it will not be too upsetting . . .'

Oh, it would be upsetting, no doubt about that, especially

when I had to listen to his excuses for despatching me to Crossbank. But that would have to be endured. I should so much have liked to talk to Jed before Theophilus Crowe arrived in order to ask him what he remembered about the time when I had been taken away. What had been said. What he had noticed. Anything that would help me to discern when Theophilus Crowe was distorting the truth to put himself in a good light. Unfortunately, it had been Biddie's turn to go to Newton Abbot with Miss Swann on her last visit and though I had primed her with questions, Jed had been too full of the news of his own forthcoming marriage to Mrs Tucker's daughter to take much notice. I was delighted he would now have a real stake in the farm. He would be able to put into practice all the new ideas he was burning to try. But none of that helped me to be more sure of my footing when it came to any argument with Mr Crowe.

Mr Grant arrived and filled my expectations to the letter. He had spent only three days sampling the artistic delights of Torbay before pressing on eastwards. I believe he had scarcely time to throw down his bags in the rooms he took in Teignmouth before he was out again and with his ridiculous dog was on the way to Furze House. Once he was introduced to Miss Swann and Mrs Greenwood and invited to join us for tea, he immediately informed us that he thought the estuary of the Teign peculiarly rich in the scenic aspects which most appealed to him, 'I find that great cliff called The Ness on the Shaldon side fascinating. When I crossed the river this morning and looked back it made a most dramatic sight, rising blood red in the morning light from a bank of fog which lay over the sea. I have already made sketches . . . I shall hope to see a stormy day while I am here, with clouds racing overhead and some small fishing boat struggling to make for the safety of harbour amid a welter of waves crashing over the treacherous sandbanks. Ah, what a picture that would make.'

'Singularly uncomfortable for the fishermen,' I remarked. 'Can you not be pleased like the rest of us we have fine autumn weather, and use your imagination for the storm, Mr Grant?'

Biddie shot me a dark look at this gentle ribbing of her beloved. But he only grinned. 'Ah, but when one strives for authenticity in a work there is nothing to compare with experiencing the elements and observing from that experience how they wreak their havoc on man and nature.'

Mrs Greenwood nodded sagely.

'So true. When one has artistic inclinations one understands that well. Observation of details is so important.' She waved one lace-mittened hand towards the wall above the mantelshelf and inclined her head in the same direction, to make sure he did not miss the tepid watercolours displayed there. 'Of course, the masculine character is best suited to stronger themes, such as the storm you mention. Feminine sensibilities are much more inclined to gentler subjects.'

'This is your work, ma'am?' he said, taking the hint with grave politeness. 'Quite . . . charming. I see you prefer still life to landscape. Those pears, well, they look perfectly . . . edible. And I instantly recognise the pheasant as the one under the glass there. Such feathers!'

The ambiguity of Mr Grant's words, spoken as they were in such a kindly way, were entirely lost on Mrs Greenwood. Afterwards when he and Biddie had escaped into the garden in search of Gyp who had been taken off by the girls to play in the orchard, she said, with satisfaction, 'What a very pleasant young man. I do hope he will take the opportunity to call again while he is in the district.'

Try and stop him, I thought sourly.

'Do you suppose,' she went on, 'he could be persuaded to give a short demonstration of his sketching techniques to the senior girls one morning?'

Nothing so certain. He would leap at any excuse for a visit to Furze House. Aloud, I said, a trifle brusquely. 'You can but ask, Mrs Greenwood.'

It was Miss Swann who frowned and said, 'He seems

amiable enough. What do you think of him, Miranda?' And I knew she had caught my sour mood and believed I had taken against Mr Grant. I was instantly sorry. It was nothing to do with him except that his presence here, ardently in pursuit of Biddie, pointed up the hopelessness of my own yearning for someone who did not care a fig for me.

'I like him very well,' I said, managing a warm smile. And sighed inwardly because I knew that after each of Mr Greville Grant's meetings with Biddie, I should have related to me in bed each night every detail of what he'd said and how he'd looked and what she believed he was thinking about her . . . And I was so deeply, deeply envious that for Biddie, love should run so smooth and easy a course, while I was destined to have nothing but heartache.

So I thought. But then I had not known what the dying months of the year would bring when I should regret every one of my shallow and ignorant opinions.

Flossie was in a subdued mood after her brother Matthew called the following Friday for her wages. For once, he had not brought along young Saul.

'He'm poorly, ma'am,' she had said to Miss Swann after breakfast on the Saturday. 'He'm taken badly with pains in his belly. Matt do say 'tis on account of stuffin' himself with new bread. But I dunno. He'm had somethin' of the sort on and off before and got over it wi' resting and being looked after, but I don't know if he'm getting much attention these days. If perhaps, ma'am, I might take my half day early and make sure he'm all right . . .'

'Of course, Flossie, go as soon as you have cleared breakfast,' Miss Swann said, adding with a note of caution induced from her knowledge of the Parkers, 'if you are quite sure you are needed and it is not that Matthew was alarming you unnecessarily?'

'Oh, no, ma'am,' Flossie said. 'He'm proper worried or he wouldn't have said nothing. Oh, thank 'ee, ma'am, I'll go soon as I've washed up.'

If Matthew Parker had been worried when he'd called yesterday there had been little sign of it. He'd swaggered in through the back gate, his hat tipped back on his head, thumbs hooked into his jacket pockets, the scarlet slash of his waistcoat visible between the undone buttons.

'Good afternoon, to you, Miss Riley, Miss Brehault,' he said, sweeping off his hat. ''Tis a fair day for the time o' year.' The politeness of his words was overset by the insolence of his leering smile. ''Tis a fine crop of apples you got there. Need a hand, do 'ee, moving the ladder or such?'

'Thank you, no,' I said crisply. 'We have all the help we need.'

'You can take these baskets to the kitchen, if you like,' said Biddie carelessly. 'Save me a journey. Here.' She thrust the baskets at him and turned back quickly to the foot of the ladder, calling, 'Are you all right, Mr Grant?' She watched anxiously as he slowly backed down from where he had been hidden from view among the topmost branches, giving a little squeal as his coat snagged and nearly unbalanced him. When he was safely on the ground she fussed about him, brushing leaves from his coat while he grinned at her, and said, 'I thought I had been lured here to demonstrate to little girls how to draw fruit, not pick it.'

'Ah, but you accepted an invitation to dinner afterwards, so you must take the consequences.'

They were far too absorbed in their laughing, teasing banter to notice that Matthew Parker had not moved. The leering expression he always assumed when talking to a woman altered as he watched the pair of them – became one of such chilling calculation and malevolence that I hastily stepped forward to draw his attention, making up some remark about Mrs Hawkins needing the apples. Immediately, he reverted to his usual air of insolent mock-servility and moved away. But the distasteful memory of that look seemed to have left in the air a lingering sense of evil to sully the gentle enjoyment of the afternoon. I was glad that we went indoors ourselves shortly after that and did not have to encounter him again as he made off with Flossie's wages.

Flossie and I left the house at the same time that Saturday morning. Her face was drawn and pale as she hurried off in the direction of Teignmouth carrying the Furze House complement of little treats which were always so generously dispensed to those in need – a jar of Mrs Hawkins's calves' foot jelly, another of chicken broth and a twist of tea. I hoped fervently that poor Saul would be allowed the benefit of them and that Flossie might have some time alone with him without the interference of her horrible brothers.

I walked quickly in the opposite direction. With this afternoon's interview hanging over me I had felt too restless to stay quietly indoors. I had volunteered to change Miss Swann's book at the circulating library and to call for a pair of Mrs Greenwood's shoes that had been left at the cobbler's for re-soling.

I did my errands and retraced my steps down Pleasant Row. For once, my thoughts were occupied with the coming interview and not with keeping a lookout for Kit. It was October now, over a month since his homecoming, and I had not clapped eyes on him once since then. I believe I had begun to despair that I ever should. Or even, now, that I wished to. What good would it do? He clearly did not care for me. I was only opening myself to more heartache if I continued this silly mooning over what could not be.

The raw-boned piebald horse was almost up to me before I realised who the rider was. He was in the faded, salt-stained clothes he had worn the day he had come to Furze House and his hat was pulled down over his half-closed eyes as though to shade them from the bright, cool sunlight. A ruffianly swathe of black stubble shadowed his chin. He had the look of a man exhausted to the point where he could scarcely keep awake and who was relying on the horse's sense of direction to get him home safely.

If he had been alert perhaps he would not have reacted as he did. But extreme exhaustion makes a mockery of self-will, strips a person of all pretence and guile. He regarded me sleepily through red-rimmed eyes and without comprehension for an instant, as I made to stand aside and let him pass. Then, as recognition dawned on his dulled senses, he smiled. And it was a smile of such gentleness, such genuine delight in seeing me, that I could not but return it. It was as though the weeks of separation had never been. My imaginings that had rendered him cold and heartless and uncaring were instantly swept aside by a flood of pure, bone-melting desire.

He reined in and I reached for the bridle and held on, as much to steady myself as the horse. Yet the words I spoke were so light and ordinary I wondered how I could achieve such control when my blood throbbed as loud as the waves bursting on the shore.

'Goodness, what a state you are in. You look as though you've been sleeping in a hedge.'

'A hedge?' he said with a prodigious yawn. 'Would that I could have had the luxury for the last two nights and days.' He leaned low over the neck of the horse and trapped my hand under his. '*Phoebe-Jane*'s maiden voyage was everything we could have wished,' he said quietly. 'I helped crew her this once, though I shall be shore-bound in future. She's as fast as we could have hoped and we sold our cargo in St Malo at an excellent profit.'

'And the return cargo?

He grinned, his teeth flashing white against the blackness of his stubbled chin. 'You heard nothing? Then we were successful indeed.'

'What do you mean?'

'Only that the wind being right, we used the little cove that lies under the cliff nearest to Furze House.'

'But half the steps are gone. Have been for years, Miss Swann says. She never lets us try to scramble down there.'

'*Were* gone,' Kit said. 'There have been some improvements put in hand in recent weeks . . . Then we carried the goods up the lane that runs by Furze House, just as it was used in Miss

Swann's father's day. Perhaps the shade of the old gentleman was keeping guard on us, for everything favoured the quick and safe despatch of the goods.'

'Miss Swann's *father*?'

'He was a venturer – one who backs the business with hard cash – for many years. At one time the Furze House linhay was used to store goods. Miss Swann has never said anything about him?'

I shook my head in amazement. 'If she ever mentions the trade it is with disapproval.'

'Quite likely. I daresay she prefers not to dwell on it. From what I gather the fortune he made was gradually wiped out in a series of disasters. Boats lost at sea or caught, confiscated and cut up by the Revenue . . . sad. His later years were unfortunately dogged by debt.'

'Let that be a warning to you, Kit Warrener,' I said sternly, then out of love and desperation, I released the bridle and forced his hand up, turning my own so that I gripped his fingers and with all the urgency I could muster, said, 'Please, Kit. You have been lucky this time, but everything could so easily turn to disaster. I fear for you so. Can you not get out of the business before it is too late?'

Very gently he disentangled his fingers from mine, yet his glance was not cold or forbidding. Just deeply, deeply sad under the tiredness. 'It is already too late, Miranda,' he said softly. 'It has been too late since I found myself on my back with a gash in my head and my hand pinned by a fallen beam. I believe I was meant to die then. I *wanted* to die when I realised . . . But instead I saw – I dreamed – that you were there. It was so real I felt I could have touched you . . . and you called me back.'

'Oh, God, Kit,' I whispered. 'I had the same . . . the same dream. I saw you injured . . . I thought you were dying and I was so afraid, so desperate to give you strength . . . Then you opened your eyes . . .'

My voice trailed off and we stared at each other in mutual shock.

Then very slowly he raised his left hand and looked down at it.

'I came back to the knowledge that I should never play again, Miranda. And I am not sure why I should have been spared when I must suffer that loss for the rest of my life. But live with it I must . . . and a poor depleted existence it sometimes seems.' His long dark lashes lifted again. He looked at me. 'I try my best to forget what might have been, but I cannot . . . that is the worst of it. Poor Miranda. Such eyes . . . they haunt my sleep . . . but best you forget me . . .'

His chin sank down to his breast; his eyes, near-closed, were red-rimmed slits. A weary jerk of his heels set the horse in motion. It was some time before I could brace myself to walk away in the opposite direction.

Theophilus Crowe bowed over Miss Swann's hand. 'How good of you, ma'am, to allow me the privilege of meeting Miss Brehault in your home.'

'You are welcome, sir,' Miss Swann said. 'You will be perfectly private in here and I have made sure you will not be disturbed. I shall occupy myself quietly while you talk.'

We had rearranged the furniture a little, placing two chairs facing each other with a low table between in the front window and moving a large maidenhair fern in a heavy pot to screen Miss Swann where she now seated herself at the other end of the room. Flossie had set a jug of raspberry cordial, glasses and a plate of biscuits on the table. Poor Flossie was looking worse than when she had gone out this morning. White-faced, her eyes swollen with crying. Though young Saul had not been as desperately ill as she had feared, the visit to her family had evidently been horribly upsetting, though – quite unlike her usual openness – she would not be drawn as to what had happened. I hoped to heaven that her father had not been demanding she give up her work and move back to the squalour of the Parker hovels.

'So, Miss Brehault, here we are,' Mr Crowe said.

He was smoothly groomed, not a strand of his silver-streaked hair out of place. Black coat and trousers, dove-grey waistcoat, crisp white stock. His hands resting on his knees. Broad hands. Practical hands, I thought, but beautifully clean today, the nails cut short and smooth. The hands of the clerk he once was, not of a man who worked as a labourer on his own estates. I noticed one nail unconsciously nagging at an unevenness in the cloth of his trousers. It was the only hint that there might be a certain nervousness under the tight control in which he held himself.

'May I suggest that you begin by explaining what happened to you after you were taken off by the mill agent that day?' he said.

He made no comment all the time I was speaking. I related my story as briefly as I could, striving to be honest in every particular, yet allowing room for his imagination to fill in the gaps that even now I did not care to dwell on.

When I finished his long-jawed face was solemn. He stayed silent for a few moments while he poured cordial from the jug into the two glasses and set one down at my side of the table. He raised his own glass and drank it down. I wondered if he wished it were brandy to give him courage.

'I can understand why you hold such bitterness towards me,' he began. 'Had I known – had I not been so wrapped up in my own affairs – I should have not acted so . . . so cavalierly.' He stared down into the empty glass as though searching for the answer in the pink dregs of the cordial. 'You see, I was too full of excitement to notice anything beyond the fact that I had bought the house and the land for a song and they were mine to do exactly what I wished with. If I am honest – I have forced myself to be since our last meeting and what I have discovered about myself as I was then has not given me much pleasure – all I wished to do was sweep out everything that was a reminder of those who had gone before. I was the new owner. I would cherish this forgotten, neglected estate. Bring new life to it. I did not want old servants telling me how wonderful the Brehaults were or a Brehault daughter looking at me as you looked at me, despising and condemning me because I was not your father returning to claim his house and his child.'

'If you had been kinder . . .'

'Would it have made such a difference? To you I should always have been the interloper. No, it was best, I thought, that you made your life elsewhere and had no chance to become the thorn in my side that I sensed you might very well turn out to be. Young as you were, you had much of your father's manner about you. That sense of self-worth, of natural, inborn certainty of your own importance, so that even if you had not two ha'pennies to rub together you felt compelled to act as though the world must bow to your superior heritage.'

I looked at him in disbelief. 'You saw that in a child of *ten*, Mr Crowe?'

'Indeed, yes, Miss Brehault. Instantly. Had I not had two years of being patronised by your papa because of my humble origins? What is more I was a person who boasted about his drowned, sea-captain father but who actually had no knowledge of who his father was – which information I unfortunately let slip when grown maudlin over a few too many glasses of strong brandy one night. Your papa never allowed me to forget that, Miss Brehault, even though he had some admiration for the way I had pulled myself up by my bootstraps. So you may begin to glimpse why I did not want you nearby, reminding me of all that I had left behind. I was lord of the manor now. Me, Theo Crowe, natural child of a Saltash milliner. I wanted nothing to sully that triumph.'

'You . . . you did not like my father,' I whispered.

'Strangely enough I did like him. He could be good company. I think he liked me as well as he liked anyone, though he saw me more as someone who could be of use to him rather than a true friend of his own standing. I was young and vigorous in health and with no tiresome attachments to hold me back from devoting myself to his enterprises.'

'You never married?'

'I married when I was in Penang. The widow of a fellow

clerk who died suddenly. It was not a success. My wife left me for another man, seeing in him a chance to return to England. She died on the voyage home, as so many did, of the morbid recurring fever that plagues so many Europeans in the tropical latitudes. The same, I believe, that killed your father and which I was lucky to escape – except in its mildest form – all the time I was in the East.'

Into the silence came the crackling of the fire, the scratch of Miss Swann's pen as she wrote to Caroline Loveridge commiserating on the declining health of her sorely injured husband, the squalling of a gull on the roof. Real sounds. Not the unreality of these strange distortions of the truth. Papa, myself, seen as proud and patronising . . . But surely my own defiant attitude had been understandable? I had hated him on sight. What more could he have expected when he told me I was not to be allowed to stay at Moondance?

Ah, but what of the time *before*? Before I knew that he was going to send me away? Had I been pleasant to him then? He had made two visits. The first occasion had been to tell us about Papa's death and to look over the estate with a view to purchase. The second was when he brought the agent who had taken me to Crossbank and I had cried and screamed not to be parted from Meg. But that first visit was a fainter memory, overlaid and overpowered by the greater, more painful one. I recollected now that I had been dragged indoors from the garden by Meg, made to wash my face and tidy my hair and remember my manners. I had resented all of it. Resented this stranger, this bearer of bad news . . . But it was more than that. How could I deny that I had a strong, proud thread in my make up? It was true. Aunt Hettie, after all, had spoken constantly of our inheritance, fed my imagination with the legends of our ancestors, rapped my knuckles if I spoke in the local dialect. I was a Brehault with Northfield blood and therefore different from everyone else we knew. Better, superior . . . And after she had died I wove my own tales of how my wonderful papa would return in triumph. My brave, powerful, handsome papa. I found my hands gripped tightly together as I faced the reality in Mr Crowe's words. Papa had turned out to have feet of clay. Seen by others as patronising . . . a cheat who ran up bills he knew he was unable to meet. Who scarcely gave a thought to his neglected daughter left alone, but for a nursemaid, in his decaying house. The same daughter who had frowned at the stranger in the same haughty way as her papa.

All the same, there could still be no justification for what Theophilus Crowe had done to me. I said, slowly, 'If I was proud – or it was merely you thought me proud, sir – then you chose a cruel way to bring me down.'

'I would not have chosen it had I known the end result.' His words fell heavy and sad between us. 'It was the lawyer's clerk in Exeter who, when I enquired about a school or an orphanage for you, urged me to speak to his cousin who was the agent recruiting labour for the mills in the north. Such a tale they spun between them,' he went on bitterly. 'You would be well looked after, educated and given a decent trade which would stand you in good stead in later life. God forgive me, but I thought the discipline would do you good after so long running wild.' He shook his head. 'It must have been eighteen months later that I spoke to a young man walking with his family to Plymouth in order to seek passage to America where they had hope of a better life. A poor, undersized, creature he was. He told me a sorry tale about the mill where he had spent his childhood and youth and I immediately put about enquiries as to where you had been sent, contacting the agent through his cousin and intending to go north and see for myself that you were well placed and comfortable. But word came back that there was no trace of a Miranda Brehault. Dead, they presumed.'

'They thought my name too fancy,' I said through dry lips. 'I was registered as Mary Bray at Crossbank.'

'If I had found you in such circumstances as you describe, I would not have let you remain. Will you believe that, Miss Brehault? And if you doubt that I did enquire after you, I will give you the name of the lawyer's clerk.'

'No. I . . . I take your word, sir.' I took a deep breath. By arbitrarily changing my name Mr Loveridge had effectively cut me off from rescue. It was a thought almost too bitter to be borne. I wrenched my thoughts from it, said, instead, 'May we speak a little of Moondance?' When he nodded, I went on carefully, 'It puzzles me that you profess to have such affectionate and protective feelings for the place, yet within a year, as I understand it, you had invited in a rowdy crowd and turned yourself into an object of gossip and scandal.'

He grimaced. 'I make no excuses. I was a fool. You see, I had never had entrée to society. My status precluded it. I was always an observer, on the outside, no matter how I schooled myself in the manners of my so-called betters. Even in the East such boundaries still held good. I was, to those whose opinion mattered, a threadbare clerk, without influential connections, barely clinging to the fringes of acceptability. The person they asked to dinner or card parties only if the numbers needed to be made up. I wanted – needed, perhaps – to change all that once I had the means and opportunity. To make society sit up and take notice. To prove to myself I was as good as any of them.' He gave a cynical laugh. 'Except that I went about it in exactly the low-bred fashion that would have made your father look down his patrician nose. I had spent all my life saving, scrimping, eking out what I had. I had a need to be lavish, to be reckless, and that is what I did. I threw my money about openly which is a ploy, I discovered, when I came to my senses, that inevitably attracts parasites.' He shrugged. 'It lasted six months – nine months at the most, this . . . this wild phase. Until one morning I awoke and knew with certainty that it must end.'

'What happened?' I prompted after a moment.

He hesitated, then said slowly, as though the memory was painful: 'I had invited guests to Moondance as I had done once or twice before. I had thought these people devilish good sorts. So lively and amusing and daring. Until one night, everything got out of hand. Liveliness turned to vindictiveness, daring turned to lewdness – and I saw them for what they really were. Shallow, selfish, pleasure-seekers whose only concern was discovering fresh amusements to divert their jaded senses. That night they ran riot. Through the house, through the grounds . . . I had then just cleared and lawned the area which was to become the topiary garden and had the statues set out so that I might judge if there needed to be any rearrangement before they were permanently set into position.' He broke off, said curtly, 'I need not go into details. Enough to say that the work of months was overset in a night. When I looked at the . . . the destruction these so-called friends had wrought in their drunken revels, I knew that I had no choice but to dissociate myself from them. I wanted to create something of beauty, that would be lasting. I did not wish to become the sort of mindless creature who lived only for the pleasures of the moment uncaring of who was offended or distressed or scandalised.'

I said, bluntly, 'If I might take that a little further, sir. You say you gave up your outrageous friends, but gossip still has you down as a gambler who goes off from time to time in order to revitalise his fortunes at the tables. It also declares you to be in search of a marriageable heiress for the same reason, though it is said no decent families would associate themselves with you.'

He was not offended. Indeed, rather to my surprise, he smiled with genuine amusement. A smile that made him look younger, livelier, than the sober image he presented.

'I had a lucky escape with the one heiress by whom I was somewhat dazzled. She was the daughter of a serge merchant I was introduced to at an assembly in Exeter. A pretty little thing. Fortunately – though I did not think so at the time – my suit was dismissed once my ex-friends set off spiteful rumours about me. You may take your pick of my character from those rumours, Miss Brehault. Diseased rake, penniless fortune hunter, a would-be bigamist with a wife and children left behind in the East Indies – I believe that was the one that frightened off the serge merchant – reckless gambler, and probably a deal more that never came to my ears. I was angry for a while, particularly over my lost chances with Delia. But I soon realised she would never have been happy incarcerated in the country where *I* was content, and away from balls and assemblies and all the things that made *her* happy. We would have made each other miserable within months.'

'And the farmer's daughter?'

'You are very well informed, Miss Brehault,' he said gravely.

'I have made it my business to be, Mr Crowe,' I said with equal gravity.

'All I can say is that she was a jolly country girl with whom I passed the time of day once or twice in the lane and before I knew it, I had her father at my door, shaking his fist and telling me he would not stand for the likes of a degenerate such as myself sniffing round his daughter when she was spoken for by a respectable lad.' Another smile, a somewhat weary one. 'I believe it was after that incident I decided the only way to preserve my dignity and peace of mind was to have as little as possible to do with those who lived round about. This time I allowed rumour to work for me, not against me. If they choose to believe in curses and witches, that is their business. If they think I prop up my sagging fortunes at the gaming table and associate with dissolutes, let them.' He looked me straight in the eye. 'My fortunes are perfectly healthy though I do occasionally have a flutter at the tables or the races. Even a recluse such as I have become sometimes longs for company other than trees. And before you ask, Miss Brehault, for I see the question burning to be spoken, I will tell you that I gained my fortune because I was the only one who survived the attack at Geminchi.'

His face drew into hard, set lines as he spoke. His voice was harsh. 'I knew, you see, where the Norwegian kept his cache of gold. It was buried and the site guarded day and night. It was not discovered by our attackers. So once that terrible night was over, I grubbed it up and loaded my pack with all that was there. Which I daresay makes me a thief of sorts, though I have searched my conscience and cannot think of anyone else who could lay title to it. The Norwegian had no kin, that was for sure. Careful investment of the proceeds – I had used my intelligence to glean all that there was to know about setting money to make money while working in the merchant houses – gives me the assurance of a comfortable income. The rest you know.'

His glance slid towards Miss Swann as she rose from her seat, lit a taper at the fire and returned to her writing table to soften the wax and seal her letter.

I did not take my eyes off him. For the whole of the interview I had felt that he was being honest, as he saw it. I was, in fact, quite shaken to find that I did believe him. Even the story about making off with the gold that had founded his fortune had the ring of truth. So why did I *still* believe that he was withholding something about the time of my father's death? As if fear – or guilt – held him back. Was it, perhaps, that having achieved what he set out to do – convince me that he did not have horns and a tail but was a man possessed of human frailties and weaknesses and decencies – he feared to shed light on some incident that would shatter my frail beginnings of trust in his word?

When his glance came back to me he was already beginning to push back his chair, signalling his departure. It was too late to say anything more.

'Thank you for your time, Miss Brehault,' he said. 'I am truly indebted to you for allowing me to clear the air. And to you, Miss Swann,' he added, raising his voice a little.

She left her desk and came across to us.

'You leave Dawlish now, Mr Crowe?' she enquired politely.

'Tomorrow, ma'am. I have bespoken a room for the night at the New Inn. I had sooner ride by daylight when there is no moon.'

No moon. The lugger was doubtless on her way across the Channel again. But at least *Phoebe-Jane*'s first cargo was ashore and Kit safe for a night or two. Oh, my dearest, dearest Kit . . . whose feelings for me were shadowed by his own despair that he must live without his music. Whose dream of me urging him to live, when he wanted nothing more but to be left to die, must haunt him whenever he looked at me.

'. . . I daresay I shall have a walk around Dawlish before I leave tomorrow,' Mr Crowe was saying. 'I have an overwhelming curiosity as to what is growing in other people's gardens, I fear. I often come across an unusual shrub or tree during my perambulations and find that people are most generous with cuttings or information as to where I might acquire seedlings.' He laughed. 'Forgive me, ma'am, but I did notice a particularly fine dwarf Michaelmas daisy in your front garden. It is such a brilliant shade of blue compared to the pale sort that I have growing at Moondance that I wondered if I might beg a slipping . . .'

'Of course, of course – and I have some rather colourful pink asters that I could spare. Have you time to take a turn round the back garden?'

By the time Mr Crowe left he had a substantial parcel of cuttings and rooted clumps of plants from the Furze House garden and Miss Swann had the promise that he would send her one or two interesting specimens of his own to see how they did in the softer, saltier air of the coast.

We also had an invitation to visit Moondance.

He spoke almost diffidently, clearing his throat, glancing at me as though unsure how I would take his offer. 'If it would give you pleasure, Miss Brehault, I would welcome you to Moondance. And you, Miss Swann, of course,' he added hastily. 'Indeed, if you thought – if it was possible – in the spring perhaps – I have expectations of a good show of camellias next year, now they are well established . . .' His voice trailed off. 'It . . . it was just a suggestion. Some reparation for . . . well, I realise you may find it too painful, Miss Brehault. It was clumsy of me to think you could do anything but reject the idea out of hand.'

'Thank you, Mr Crowe,' I said quietly. 'But I do not reject the idea at all. May I give it some thought?'

I watched him go with his bundle of plants. Then I sat

quietly in the parlour for a while, and lost myself in a dream of wandering in the gardens of Moondance as they would look in the spring.

We had not quite seen the last of Mr Crowe. When we were walking to church the following morning we saw him strolling on the banks alongside the Dawlish Water. He raised his hat and bowed. And when I looked back he was still there, watching us go. He seemed to me to be a somewhat lost and lonely figure standing solitary in the breezy sunlight, and I felt compelled, when I was on my knees in church, to wish him well on his journey home.

Mr Grant was to return to Exeter at the end of the week in order to prepare for an exhibition in Plymouth to be held in December, which had come about due to the modest success of his Exeter exhibition. Biddie tended to a great deal of sighing and doleful looks as the time drew on.

'It's gone so fast! Only three days left,' she moaned, as she sat before the mirror one night, winding her turbulent red hair into rag curlers. 'Oh, how can I bear to be apart from him until January! We've had so little time together.'

'You've seen him nearly every day, for heaven's sake,' I said, climbing into bed. 'And he'll be sending you love notes twice a week no doubt until you meet him again.'

'But if only we could have had more time together! Trying to get five minutes alone with him is nearly impossible. The old girls have eyes like hawks.'

'It strikes me,' I said dryly, 'that you have managed more than five minutes alone with him on several occasions. Twice I noticed you managed to disappear for half an hour when he was in the back lane sketching the linhay. Then there was the afternoon you were supposed to be walking into Dawlish to match some sewing cotton which you mysteriously did not manage to do – though I have since seen something suspiciously like the shade you were after in the haberdasher's. Where did you actually go to?'

She knotted the last rag curler and giggled. 'Oh, just for a little walk on the cliffs,' she said airily. Then, sighing, 'But you see, Mirrie, when you fall in love with someone you want to be with him every minute of every day. You'll understand when it happens to you.'

I knew well enough. Though there was nothing at all I could do about it when the person concerned preferred to keep his distance.

'Oh, come to bed,' I said grouchily. 'I daresay he'll be on the doorstep soon enough.'

He did call the next day, on his way to the Warren. There was a brisk south-easterly blowing under a lowering sky and he thought he should take advantage of the weather to capture the mood of that desolate spit of sand when under assault by pounding waves. If conditions proved favourable he would then go on to Starcross to paint the view of Exmouth across the estuary and perhaps take lodging for one night at an inn there. But, he promised, with a lingering glance at Biddie, he would be at Furze House early the following morning in order to take the final painting class.

'By ten at the latest,' Mrs Greenwood cried. 'The girls are benefiting so much from your expert tuition.'

Biddie was doleful for most of that wild, gloomy day. It was only before supper that she seemed to brighten considerably, but I was absorbed in reading and marking essays on 'Autumn Weather' which I had set the junior girls and did not take a great deal of notice save to be vaguely glad that she had cheered up.

It was not until we had climbed the stairs to bed that I realised there was about her an air of tightly controlled excitement. Only when we were alone did she burst out, 'Oh, Mirrie, he's come back and I'm going out to meet him.'

I frowned at her uncomprehendingly. 'What do you mean?'

'Mr Grant – Greville! Oh, I hoped he'd find a way for us to meet alone again before he left! And he has! He sent a message with Flossie. He's waiting for me in the lane. I knew it! I knew he'd ask me to marry him before he left. This'll be his chance.'

She was kicking off her slippers, gathering her outdoor boots as she spoke. 'I'll creep downstairs and put my boots on in the kitchen. Flossie's leaving the scullery door unbolted. Mrs Hawkins won't hear anything. She's always dead asleep and snoring as soon as supper's cleared.'

'But . . . but you can't go out at this time of night!'

'It's scarcely half-past nine! Think of the hours we kept in Exeter. Folks like Greville don't think it's late.' She whipped her cloak round her shoulders. 'I'd have put my best gown on if I'd known. A girl should look her best when she's being proposed to. Still, he'll perhaps not notice . . . though he's bound to have a lantern. Does my hair look all right?' She flew to the mirror, tweaked a curl or two in place, pinched her cheeks though there was little need of it for her face glowed pink with the excitement of it all. 'It'll have to do. Do you think the old girls will be settled yet?'

'Biddie, I really don't think . . .'

'Oh, I can't wait a minute longer. I'll have to take a chance. Wish me luck!'

Then she was at the door, opening it softly . . . and she was gone.

I stood stock still, bewildered from the suddenness of it. Shocked a little, I suppose, that Mr Grant could dream up such a scheme. I had guessed they had been meeting secretly but this was different – after dark, on a wild, windy night . . . there was something not right about it. Something unpleasant . . .

I went cold.

Flossie. Flossie was the key. How had Mr Grant managed to speak to her without anyone knowing? Without Mrs Hawkins, at least, seeing him if he'd come to the kitchen. Mrs Hawkins would have sent him away with a flea in his ear at the very suggestion of anything underhand. And Flossie would never go out alone even to the privy after dark. Especially on a wild night like this. She was too scared of what lurked in the darkness. She and Mrs Hawkins always made the last trip of the day there together. Which meant that this was no last-minute arrangement. It had been planned much earlier . . .

I was out of the door and down the stairs, uncaring if I made a noise to rouse the ladies or not. Into the kitchen passage, pushing open the kitchen door. Silent. Dark save for the dull glow of the banked-down fire. Across to the scullery where the flicker of a candle held in a wavering hand sent black shadows scudding wildly across the ceiling.

'Flossie!'

She stood there in her nightgown, white-faced, shivering.

'Oh, miss . . . I didn't want . . .'

'What?' I had her by the shoulders, shaking her. 'What have you done, Flossie?'

'Oh, 'tis him, miss . . . Matt – he made me! Said he'd send my Saul to a fearful place where he'd be kept chained up if I didn't do as 'e asked. I couldn't rest . . . it was wrong what I did . . . I meant to stop 'er, but 'er's gone . . .'

'God in Heaven! Is it Matthew out there?'

Her white, stricken face told the whole sick story. My mind went blank for a minute. What could I do? What could I do? We were a houseful of women . . . There was no time to run for help.

I flew back into the kitchen, grabbed the poker and the long brass toasting fork. Ran to the scullery and thrust the fork into Flossie's cold hand, tore the candle holder from her and threw it in the sink, grabbed her arm.

'If anything's happened to Biddie, Flossie Parker, I'll cut out your liver and lights personally,' I hissed. 'Now run with me. Run!'

Stumbling, cursing, I half dragged her down the path, uncaring that she was barefoot. I felt every stone through my own thin indoor slippers – but there was no pain. I was too desperate to get to Biddie before . . . before . . .

We were almost at the wicket gate when I heard her voice. A scream, instantly muffled. Then the rumble of men's voices – two men. One swearing, the other laughing. Two of them. Two grown men to tackle.

'Twist 'er arms back, you lummock.' That was Matthew. The one who laughed.

''Er bit me!' Dan, the other brother. I was sure of it.

''Er'll not bite now. There! That's tight. Can't make a noise now, can 'ee, maid? 'Tis the best way for a woman to be. Silent and obedient – and on 'er back for preference . . . Now, let's see a bit more of 'ee, eh?'

The sound of cloth ripping. Flossie whimpered. My fingers bit into her arm as I shook it to quieten her. We crept to the gate and peered through.

There was a lanthorn placed on the ground, the candle within casting a frail glow on the dark figures moving against the hedgebank. All I could see of Biddie was a flash of white as she kicked against the black bulk of Matthew Parker. His hand went out and gripped the flailing leg.

'Still full o' aggravation? Well, we'll soon make 'ee think twice about that.' A raised arm, the dull thud of a fist striking bone. 'That'll learn 'ee to turn your nose up at Matthew Parker in favour o' some fancy man from Exeter. An' now there's a bit more learnin' you gotta have. From me first. Then my brother Dan 'ere. We'll show 'ee what proper men are made of . . .'

I whispered urgently in Flossie's ear: 'When we run, make as much noise as you can . . . you go for Dan.' Then we flung open the gate and with a great whooping and screeching, ran into the lane.

Surprise was our friend.

Dan bellowed with shock as Flossie ran the toasting fork into his buttocks. He hopped backwards, kicking the lanthorn so that it flared to brilliance as I beat and beat at Matthew Parker's shoulders with the poker. When he swivelled round, raising his arms to protect his head, I lunged for the part of him that hung exposed through his open breeches. The scream he made as he doubled over clawing at his groin was satisfying in the extreme.

While he crouched, moaning and temporarily helpless, I grabbed at Biddie, pulling down her skirts, tugging at the scarf tied round her mouth. Hauling her to her feet from where she had been thrown down against the grass of the bank. She crumpled against me, her weight making me stagger, and I saw Matthew Parker begin to straighten up.

'Get back to the house, Flossie,' I yelled. 'Get help!'

The candle died. In the sudden darkness I began to drag Biddie to the gate, horribly aware that Matthew Parker could pounce at any minute . . .

Then it was over.

Dan Parker cried, 'I'm off. Someone's coming.' His boots scrabbled away up the lane.

And on the other side of the garden wall, Miss Swann's voice, firm and commanding, 'Who's there? What's going on?'

'Miss Swann,' I cried. 'Quickly!'

There was candlelight again, flickering towards the arch of the wicket gate.

'Bleedin' bitches . . .' Matthew Parker's voice held all the venom of his evil nature. 'You'll pay for this. And you, Flossie Parker.'

'Leave her alone!' I was amazed at the strength in my voice. 'And your poor brother Saul, too, you . . . you disgusting, foul blackguard. I'll see you punished for this.'

'And tell me,' he hissed, 'who'd believe the word of a hussy like that . . . that red-haired bitch? 'Er led me on. Flauntin' 'erself. 'Er's a right whore, that one . . . wantin' it, she was. A-beggin' for it . . .'

He ran then, disappearing into the inky blackness of the night, and I found that I was trembling like a leaf and my heart was thumping so loud it could probably be heard down in the town.

We got Biddie back inside, removed her torn dress, sponged her down, put her to bed. She was silent the whole time and shuddering – great convulsive shudders – as though taken with an ague. There was a dark red patch on her temple and round her eye that would be a livid bruise tomorrow, scratches and welts on her arms and legs. We had got there in time, saved her from the worst physical violation. But what violation had been done to her emotions, her spirit? I wondered, as we helped her to sip a little warm milk and brandy, and made her comfortable against the pillows. Wherever the cheerful, giggly, bright-eyed Biddie was, it was not here in this bed. This staring, silent, bewildered red-haired creature looked as if she would never smile again.

When eventually the house settled down I snuffed the candle and crept into bed beside her. I thought she was sleeping but her cold little paw crept out and fastened on mine.

'You won't tell him, Mirrie, will you?' she whispered. 'Greville . . . I couldn't bear for him to know. I want nobody to know . . . they'll think it was me. Leading him on. I didn't. Honest. I just . . . I just talked to him, that's all. Once or twice.'

'It's wicked that he should get away with what he did! But if it's what you want . . . And we have already spoken about it – Miss Swann and Mrs Greenwood and I. Said that it would perhaps be best if we said you'd had an accident – a fall in the dark. Flossie and Mrs Hawkins won't say anything. The children mercifully slept through it all.'

'Why did Flossie do it? I thought . . . I thought she was my friend.'

I told her, then went on, 'She is very ashamed and upset. She insisted she would leave in the morning but Miss Swann said there was no need. She was only acting to protect her poor brother. Mrs Hawkins is grown very fond of her. She will talk her round when she is calmer.'

Biddie thought of this for a while.

'I feel . . . I feel so dirty. Not like when I was at Crossbank and never washed properly from one month to the next. Different. As though I . . . I can feel his hands on me still, smell him on me . . . and it won't wash off. Ever.' She gave a convulsive sob. 'Oh, God, Mirrie, will he come back? Matthew Parker. What will I do if I see him?

I put my arms round her. 'He won't,' I said. 'Not if he

knows what's good for him. He won't dare show his face round here again!'

I was less convinced than I sounded, but it was true that we saw neither hide nor hair of Matthew Parker or his brother Dan again. We heard, months later, that they had gone off to Plymouth. Rich pickings there, someone said, for the brothers were seen finely dressed in Dock with fancy women on their arms. Not long after that they were caught removing silver from the parlour of a fine house in Manamead. It was likely they would both have joined their brothers in Australia had not Matthew Parker's temper got the better of him. But he badly injured a footman who got in his way and was sentenced to be hanged.

But that was for the future, and they did not immediately go to Plymouth. Matthew Parker was not one to let a houseful of women have the last word. Three nights after the attack on Biddie, someone put a flaming brand through the parlour window.

It would never be proved who did it, but we all knew that Matthew Parker had taken his final revenge on Furze House.

Chapter Eight

Biddie did not see Mr Grant again before he left for Exeter. And though she sat up in bed weeping over the little note he had written to accompany the bunch of yellow chrysanthemums he had brought to Furze House when he learned of her 'accident', I had the feeling that perhaps it was a relief to her that she did not have to face him yet. For once she was content to be cocooned safely in the attic bedroom, with nothing demanded of her except that she rest and get well. With us, her loving friends, who knew what had happened, there was no necessity to talk if she did not wish to, or to put on any sort of brave façade. We cosseted her, laid compresses of arnica and witch hazel on her bruises, coaxed her to eat, and slowly, slowly, the haunted expression began to ease from her face. We allowed her to come to terms with what had happened in her own time, and gradually she did.

Oddly enough it was Mrs Greenwood who seemed to bring most comfort to Biddie. She would take up her sewing and sit with her, as Biddie had used to do when Mrs Greenwood herself had been ill with her bronchitic chest. And when she left, Biddie was always able to sleep without starting awake at the slightest noise. Or manage a mouthful or two of chicken or bread-and-milk. I thought at the time it was perhaps Mrs Greenwood's capacity for chattering on about nothing very much that eased Biddie's mind. But a long time afterwards when I asked her about it she said, simply, 'Mrs Greenwood understood how I felt. She had suffered violence for many years.' And I remembered, then, the young, pretty, lively girl who had learned obedience at the hands of a strict husband.

Perhaps Mrs Greenwood had always favoured Biddie because she saw in her something of the girl she had once been. I found that thought sobering. Oh, I had known the facts of Mrs Greenwood's history, but I had never been able, quite, to appreciate what she must have gone through to turn that lively girl into the woman she had become. Ever after that I did my best to reconsider and think more kindly towards her, whenever I was inclined to feel impatient or dismiss her as a silly, tiresome woman.

Flossie, too, cut a pitiful figure that week. She was racked with guilt about her part in the affair. 'I wouldn't have done what Matt wanted, honest, miss,' she snuffled, 'save that 'e swore to me if I didn't do as 'e said, 'twould be the worse for Saul. There's terrible places, he said, where they put people like Saul. Where they chains 'en up in filthy pits and folks go an' throw muck at 'en and laugh an' jeer. Oh, I couldn't abide it, miss . . . an' I'm that worried he'm still sick, and I daresn't go and see for fear I meet Matt . . .'

'Perhaps your father . . .'

'He'm useless!' Flossie wailed. 'He'm half the time drunk and the rest asleep.'

I felt for her distress, but there was little I could do – that any of us could do – at present to relieve it. We were too busy keeping the school functioning in its normal smooth and efficient way, in caring for our invalid, in trying to put the events of that horrible night behind us. That was what we told each other. In truth, of course, we none of us could bear the thought of facing up to any of the Parkers, least of all Matthew. And if we were ashamed of our cowardice, we kept it to ourselves.

At least, for Flossie, there was to be some consolation in knowing that she saved us from disaster on the night of the fire. She was the one who heard the sound of breaking glass sometime before midnight, roused Mrs Hawkins and alerted the house. And while we got Biddie and the children down the back stairs and out into the garden, she aided Mrs Hawkins in smothering the flames with wet cloths. When I ran indoors again, Flossie was beating out the last smouldering patch on the carpet. Mrs Hawkins, red-faced and panting, crying, ''Tis naught but the curtains and blinds is gone . . . and a bit o' they carpet. If it hadn't been for Flossie, here, we'd all have been cinders by mornin', I reckon.'

We got the children and Biddie quickly back to bed. Then, while the ladies attended to the burned fingers Mrs Hawkins and Flossie had acquired, I pulled on Miss Swann's old cloak and went outside again to fasten the storm shutters over the broken glass of the window.

It was then I saw the ominous glare down at the bottom of the garden. The linhay! There were dark figures moving against the glow . . . and now I heard someone pounding up the path towards me. My hand flew to my throat. Oh, God, not Matthew Parker . . .

'Miranda, quick. We need buckets – saucepans, anything to carry water!'

It was no time to be questioning what Kit was doing here in the middle of the night. Nor the other men who formed a chain from the pond, to throw buckets of water over the now blazing thatch and the surrounding hedges to stop the fire spreading. Not that I needed to ask. And certainly the ladies, with cloaks and shawls covering their night attire standing huddled together, with Flossie and Mrs Hawkins trying to comfort them, were too grateful, too shocked, even to begin to wonder why so many men had arrived fortuitously on the scene.

But there was little that they could do save contain the fire. It had too good a hold. There could be nothing left in that inferno. It must all be gone. The chickens, the winter stores of fruit and potatoes, the garden implements. Even the tack belonging to the horses old Mr Swann had kept when the linhay was used partly as a stable.

I stood under the leafless damson tree and watched the last of the thatch fall in with a great flare of sparks into the night sky. I grieved for the poor, gentle, innocent hens which I had always so much liked to look after . . . I could never bear to watch when Mrs Hawkins wrung the neck of those selected for the pot. If they had been my chickens I daresay they would have been allowed to die of old age. And now . . .

As if he knew what I was thinking, Kit was suddenly at my side, putting his arms round me, holding me close, saying softly, 'It was all tinder dry. It went up like a torch. Anything in there . . . well, it would have been a quick end.'

I leaned against him with a tired sigh. He smelled of smoke and sweat. I could hear the thump of his heart and feel his hand twisting in my hair. I wanted to stay like this forever. Comforted. Protected. Not wanting to think . . .

'The fire's dying now,' he said. 'It will burn itself out by morning. I'll leave a couple of men to stand guard in case it flares up again.'

'You can't stay, I know.' My voice was muffled against his shoulder. 'But I wish you would.'

'If it were possible . . .'

'You would stay?'

'No!' His tone was harsh.

'I miss you, Kit,' I whispered.

He knew what I meant. I could feel it in the sudden tensing of his body.

'Dammit, woman, why do I have to be tormented like this?' He sounded angry and there was nothing gentle in the way his fingers tightened on my hair, tipping back my head. 'Christ, Miranda, I don't want to think about you and I can't bloody well stop myself. But I will, I must!' He jolted me closer, bent his head and began, roughly, to kiss me, as though he were someone intending to get an unwanted task over with in all possible haste. Perhaps to prove to himself that he could kiss me and leave me and that would be an end to whatever problem I presented.

But it was not like that at all.

Not after the first few seconds when our teeth clashed and the stubble on his chin uncomfortably raked my skin and I wasn't quite sure how I should hold myself or respond because this was nothing like any kiss I had ever experienced. This was no friendly peck on the cheek or lips in greeting or farewell, which was all I knew.

This was . . .

Five seconds. Ten.

Not rough or uncomfortable any more. And no problem whatsoever about what I should do with my arms and hands. They acted in a very satisfactory manner, apparently of their own volition, fastening themselves behind his head, fingers twining into the short curling hair where the tarred pigtail had been cut off. All that I can say about the rest of me is that it . . . melted. There is no other term for it. Such a warm, soft, boneless melting . . . I wanted it to go on forever. Probably it did, for I had no notion of time. Nor, apparently, did Kit for I reckoned one of his men had shouted his name several times before he acknowledged it. I had, vaguely, been aware someone wanted him. But it was of no interest . . . It belonged to that other world beyond the two of us. Where a thin drizzle was beginning to fall and there was a burning barn and there were irritating people demanding our attention . . .

Then, suddenly, it was all over. He reached up behind his neck and unfastened my hands. Pushed me away. What he said then was very strange. No word of love, or tenderness. No goodbye, even. His voice was low and steady and expressionless. 'Miranda, will you give a message to Miss Swann and Mrs Greenwood? Tell them that I had word today that my cousin Caroline's husband has died.'

And that was it. He was gone. A black sillhouette against the glow of the fire. Mingling with the other dark, moving shapes. Away about his illicit business.

I stood there dazed. Still lapped by the warmth of love and desire. Beginning to rouse to the cold truth that he had left me. And that the message he had given me had a meaning that I did not wish to think about at the moment.

'Miranda dear, come in out of the rain.' Miss Swann's voice. Yes, it was raining. I moved from under the tree and held out my hand. The fine drops dripped into my palm like chilly tears.

I followed the others back into the house.

By daylight the barn was a sorry sight. The walls still stood, but the timbers of the roof were fallen in and lay black and smouldering in a deep bed of wet ash, for the drizzle had thankfully turned to heavy rain to douse the last of the flames. But, as the news spread, the many kindnesses shown to those in need by the ladies of Furze House were now reciprocated. Farmer Woodruff sent a sack of potatoes and an offer of a couple of his men to clear the debris. Others promised to help raise new roof timbers, a new door. Someone else would give a dozen pullets and lend a coop to house them. Garden forks, a spade, a rake, were donated by kindly people who suddenly found that they had a surplus of these implements. Billy limped up to the house with half-a-dozen whiting, part of his payment for helping draw in the seine nets on the beach and a posy of autumn leaves that May had picked. Widow Thomas called with two fat jars of honey and a variety of soothing herbal remedies. Flossie was so glad to have the pain of her blisters eased by the St John's Wort lotion that Widow Thomas smoothed on her fingers, that she gathered her courage to ask advice on the belly ache that affected her brother Saul. She was astounded to silence when the old lady said she would call on him and see for herself what the boy needed.

'Are you sure, Mrs Thomas?' I asked her later. 'They are such a rough lot.'

She smiled. 'Who better? Even Matt Parker would think twice before offering violence to a known witch.'

I thought: She knows. Or guesses. Perhaps other people guessed, too. A barn mysteriously ablaze . . . though there was always a risk where hay or straw was kept and someone who had been careless with a lantern or candle might be too feared to own up. But a new window having to be put in at the house and damage to curtains and carpet reported by the glazier? Could that be coincidence? Those no-good brothers of the Parker girl who worked up to Furze House could never be trusted. The Good Lord only knew what they got up to when the drink was on Dan, or Matt had a spite against someone. They'd very conveniently cleared off on one of their jaunts, so nobody could question them. There again, all manner of vagrants and beggars were about the countryside these days, folks looking for work or penniless and sent back to become a drain on their own parishes or put off from the army or navy now the war was finished. It made you wonder what the world was coming to when decent people could not sleep in their beds at nights for worrying if some varmint was going to damage their property . . .

But nobody said anything directly. The ladies maintained a dignified silence. Presently, the firing of the Furze House barn slid back in to memory, overlaid by newer gossip.

For instance, the matter of Widow Thomas taking in that idiot lad of the Parkers'. More than one person had seen them coming from Teignmouth. And a proper weird sight they made. Him lolling, limp as a badly stuffed doll, on the back of the donkey, her striding out in her raggy clothes like a black old crow. Mind, best speak in whispers about it, for you never knew how much came to her ears, being, you know, as she is – and be sure to make the sign against the evil eye while you do . . .

The rumour was true. 'I could not leave him there to die in filth and neglect,' she said. 'No more than I could leave a hurt beast or bird to be tormented. Whether I can do much for what ails him, remains to be seen. The inflammation he has in his guts is settling, but I have come across the condition before and understand its nature. He may go for years with the pain flaring and passing off. But sometimes a poison sets in that becomes morbid. We shall see.'

'But what will you do when he is better?'

'I shall look after him. He will be no more trouble than any other lost creature. Indeed, he may learn to be useful. There is a spark there that might be encouraged. He is gentle with the animals and they with him. I shall fetch him to visit his sister when he is fit and you may tell her that there will be no more demands on her from the man who claims to be her father.' She smiled. 'Where man's law does not frighten him, an old woman's hints of a different kind of justice may have a salutary effect. Flossie is free of him. As to her brothers,' her odd-coloured eyes took on the distant look that I knew meant she was not looking on anything I could see, 'I fancy they will not be back.'

By early-December the linhay was as good as it ever had been – better, in fact. Limewashed inside and out, a stout new door and a sturdy yellow thatch laid over the new roof beams. Inside there were perches for the hens and nest boxes and a partition to keep the chickens from scratching round among the stored fruit and vegetables. It was a triumphant occasion when we could shut the hens into their new home for the night.

'It is as though that dreadful time had never been,' said Miss Swann, with satisfaction.

But for Biddie nothing was quite the same. She recovered physically, was as pretty and bright as ever, but I felt some spark had gone out of her. A carefree innocence that would never again be recaptured. That made her a little wary of the admiring glances she had once accepted without question as her due. Less easy in her mind. She talked happily still of Greville Grant, of the success of his exhibition in Plymouth, of what they would say to each other once they met again in Exeter, but increasingly with a kind of desperation, as if the excitement of being so wildly in love was beginning to elude her and she was clinging to it with increasingly weakened fingers. It was no help that Mr Grant – clever as he was with a paint brush – was no great shakes as a letter writer. His notes were infrequent and scrappy though, truth to tell, Biddie's were little better. She spent more time chewing the end of the quill and mopping up blots than actually writing and the end result was no more than a few stilted lines. Distance, it seemed, did not lend enchantment to their courtship.

It did, however, to mine.

Courtship? It was all in my head. I had no idea at all if it was in Kit's mind. He came often to help with the repairing of the barn but whenever it was my turn to take the jug of cider and pasties to the men, his greeting would be polite, guarded, and he would barely pause to take a mouthful or two before he was back at work. But I dreamed. Oh, how I dreamed. Unable to stop myself. Not wanting to, if I was honest. For in my dreams there were no barriers, no awkward words or situations. We lived, we loved, we were happy. And if I dreamed hard enough, then one day it might all be possible . . .

Until then, though, there were the humdrum days to get through and the worrying nights when I knew he would be shifting cargo from the *Phoebe-Jane* and shepherding his men and his goods about the dark lanes. Though I looked through the bedroom window often enough, I never caught any glimpse of them and knew that tide and wind – and the need to vary the locations where they dropped the cargo – meant they might use any one of several places between the Exe and the Teign. I relied on Emma for news of him. His lodgings were in the next street and he was often at their cottage of an evening. I was deeply grateful – Emma, too – that he had discouraged Billy from becoming involved with his band of freetraders.

'He'm dead set against Billy makin' his leg worse. He'll not even let him stand look-out. Says 't'wouldn't be fair, for if there was trouble Billy couldn't dodge about like anyone with two good legs. I mean, look at last week. Master Kit's lot 'ad a bit of a set to wi' some of Cap'n Luscombe's men who was about the same business – and there were a few sore heads and limping legs in town next day, I can tell 'ee. As Master Kit said, my Billy would have come off badly in a set to such as that. Oh, aye. He'm talked to Billy proper sensible. He says to him that he'm blessed wi' a talent above the ordinary and 'tis fitting 'e should use it as though it was a proper trade and be glad he has his two good hands to do the work. Which give my Billy cause to think, for he values Master Kit's opinion and he knowed 'ow badly 'e feels about not being able to play his fiddle any more. So he puts in a good many hours now at his carving without so much pining about going to sea.

'Oh, Miss Miranda, I can't tell 'ee how grateful I am to 'ee and that Mrs Lascelles. Master Kit, 'e brung us back more'n three pounds last time he was to Exeter. And 'er sent down a few good pieces of yew wood and an order for a matching pair o' hawks for someone who 'as such things on what they calls a family crest. 'Er says, come spring, 'er'll have Billy up to town and let him meet other folks in the same line o' trade, that'd be able to give 'im some more learnin' about the carvin' and that.'

Violet's salons, after a small, tentative start, were apparently now flourishing.

> *When you come in January you will have much more interesting Company to entertain you than Colonel Bonynge and his Set. You must prepare yourselves for Dancing Lessons for we shall attend at least one Assembly. I have set Mrs Chadwick to making suitable gowns for you, to the measurements she took in August. She can make any final adjustments when you are here. I have bespoken seats for you on the Exeter coach on the 2nd and trust the weather stays clement for the journey. I hear the Master of Crossbank Mill is gone to his Maker. Few tears will be shed on that account, I'm thinking. I will tell all news when I see you.*

Violet's rare letters were always short and to the point.

Biddie was less excited than I expected about the dancing lessons. 'I'm not sure Greville does dance,' she said, frowning.

'Well, he might not be at the assembly at all!' I pointed out. 'Violet may be intending to introduce you to other young men – maybe some sprig of the gentry, who will want to partner you for every dance. Think of it, you might be swept off your feet and forget all about Mr Grant.'

But where once she would have giggled and invented a story

to cap that one, now she merely smiled and said, 'I'd sooner Greville was my partner. Now are you going to read all night? Do put out the candle soon. It keeps me awake.' She turned over, hunching away from me. But long after the candle was snuffed, she was still tossing and turning restlessly as though sleep was a long time coming.

That same night I lay awake in the darkness and thought of Kit continuing to visit Violet. He was often up in Exeter, Emma said, regularly delivering Billy's carvings when he needed to take *Phoebe-Jane*'s cargo of tea, brandy and tobacco to the contact there and to negotiate in the town for the woollen goods that were so popular across the Channel. I thought, wistfully, that when we were in Exeter I should perhaps have a better chance of meeting him and hoped Violet might ask him to supper as she had done Mr Grant.

My thoughts drifted to Christmas. Soon it would be here. A gentle season of simple celebration and quiet enjoyment. When the last pupil had left on Christmas Eve we would go into the lane to gather evergreens and mistletoe to form into a kissing bunch. Later, the carol singers would come, shuffling their boots awkwardly on the step, their voices more or less in tune depending on how many glasses of hot punch or mulled ale they had already consumed at other houses. Then there was church on Christmas morning, the fine goose Mrs Hawkins would roast for dinner, the exchange of small gifts . . . This would be our fourth Christmas at Furze House, but somehow this year I could not feel the same pleasurable anticipation as I usually did and as I lay there thinking about it I could not understand why. I had no expectation of seeing Kit, of course, and there was the exciting New Year trip to Exeter overshadowing it . . . but it was more than that. Something was casting a cloud over the celebration and I wondered, sleepily, if it was the impending visit of Caroline Loveridge.

When I looked at everything clear-eyed and sensibly, I knew there was nothing to fret about. Mr Loveridge was dead and his widow was in the process of selling the mill and the house. It was Caroline's wish to move back to Devonshire. Miss Groom, having nowhere else to go, would accompany her. If all went well they would be in Teignmouth a few days before Christmas. They were to rent a villa recommended by an acquaintance who had spent the previous winter nursing a consumptive daughter in what she termed a 'pretty and convenient house in a new terrace where one might walk to the Den within a few minutes and so gain every advantage of the ozone-laden air'. They would then spend the winter months examining properties in the district for a permanent residence. What could be wrong with any of that?

Nothing. It was true that there was a small, locked-away part of me that cowered from any connection to Crossbank. That shrank from meeting Miss Groom who would see in Miranda Brehault the Mary Bray who had behaved disgracefully when she was honoured by being invited to take tea at Crossbank Grange, and to cap it all had run off, taking another girl with her. Runaway apprentices! What a shocking example to others in her situation. People like her should not be allowed to get away unpunished, however long it took to rout them out.

Oh, yes, there was that. But that could be faced, overcome. After all, if she took it into her head to do anything about it, Miss Groom would have Caroline to answer to.

Caroline Loveridge.

I shivered. Lying snug in the feather mattress with good blankets and a fat quilt over me, I felt the cold run down my neck, my spine, my limbs.

It was her shadow that lay long and dark and threatening over the Christmas festivities. Over more than that. Over me. Over Kit.

I looked into that shadowy darkness and tried to see why, but everything was so fragmented. A snatch of conversation on a sunny terrace where a teaparty was in progress . . . a few lines on a letter that were not for my eyes: *I cling to the memory of the promises we renewed . . . I live for the day when I shall hear you say them to me again . . .* Kit saying,

'Tell them I had word today that my cousin Caroline's husband has died.'

A message for Mrs Greenwood and Miss Swann? Or a message for me?

Miss Swann had felt it her duty to inform Caroline immediately he had arrived in Dawlish of her cousin's safe return, phrasing it carefully, though Mr Loveridge, by then a helpless, bedfast invalid, was beyond interest in anything except the next dose of the laudanam that took away his pain. Caroline had written by return, expressing her delight, enclosing a note to be passed on to Kit. Miss Swann had delivered it to his landlady herself. Presumably their correspondence had continued. No let or hindrance now, with Mr Loveridge past worrying about communication between the cousins which would most certainly jeopardise his wife's chances of inheriting her uncle's fortune.

'Tell them that I had word today . . .'

Kit had been the first to know. As though the minute her husband had gone, Caroline had dashed off the news to her cousin.

The ladies had not heard for another twenty-four hours. A short formal note. The kind of note one would address to a whole list of persons who must of necessity be informed of a death in the house. Not a dashed-off letter to someone to whom the news was important.

I remembered the other letters, secret from her husband, which she had sent Kit before he went away. How they had always cast him down into some private misery . . .

The key was there, but I could not turn it. And even if I could – or wanted to – I knew that whatever was revealed when the key turned and the lid lifted on the things that were hidden, it would not be to my advantage. Like the contents of Pandora's box, once released they would be hurtful, unhappy things. When I eventually slept I did not have happy dreams.

The weeks running up to Christmas were very wet and raw.

There was so much rain, sometimes sleet, that the small lanes quickly turned to squelching red quagmires. Even the good roads became deeply rutted with every passing carriage or cart. The holes gouged by hooves quickly filled with water and pedestrians clung to the grass verges where the going was easier and their boots did not accumulate clumps of heavy mud.

The watery air seemed to breed infection. There was certainly a great deal of illness about, not least influenza, which though not lasting more than a few days caused a sudden onset of shivering and aches in head and limbs that could only be relieved by taking to one's bed. Half the school went down with it and we worried that Mrs Greenwood would catch it and it would affect her weak chest. But she was one of the few who did not succumb, possibly due to the fact that once the contagion began she retreated to her room to apply eucalyptus oil to her chest at regular intervals and burn lumps of camphor on a shovel to discourage unhealthy miasmas from entering her bedchamber. It was Miss Swann who had to be persuaded to her bed, just as I was rather shakily back on my feet. Then Biddie was taken and two of our boarders. The household was in such a fragile state by this time with Flossie, who remained unflaggingly healthy, run ragged trying to wait on everyone, that it was decided to close the school early.

'It wants but a week to Christmas when we should have closed until February anyway,' Miss Swann croaked, still grey-faced and lacking in energy to do anything but huddle to the parlour fire. 'Besides which attendance has been so poor, I think it was best that we did not to try to keep going for the sake of those few who did turn up.'

'I quite agree,' I said fervently, for it had been a struggle for me these last days to manage lessons for half-a-dozen girls where normally I could have comfortably organised all the school. 'Now let me get you something to drink. Would you prefer hot lemon or a spoonful of beef broth? Then I will go upstairs and see if Biddie is awake and look in on the little girls. Nell is being very good reading to her poorly sisters and

Mrs Hawkins is giving the others their dinner in the kitchen.' Meals had become somewhat moveable, makeshift feasts this week with so many sufferers living on slops or not eating at all. 'We have one consolation anyway,' I said to cheer her up. 'Our appetites should have improved by the time Mrs Hawkins is ready to roast the goose for Christmas dinner.'

To which she gave a wan, disbelieving smile and pulled the shawl more tightly around her shoulders.

I was in the kitchen attending to the making of various brews that had been ordered – including a cup of broth for Mrs Greenwood who had called to Nell on her way downstairs that she could starve in her room for all the attention anyone gave her – when there was a hammering at the scullery door.

It was Emma. When Flossie brought her in she sighed with relief to see me. 'Oh, you'm all right, thank goodness. I'd heard all the folks to Furze House was poorly. I'd thought to find you bedfast. 'Tis Master Kit, see. We'm all sorely worried, he'm that bad wi' this ague. I just been to fetch out Widow Thomas . . .'

'How bad?' I said, my voice sounding strange and reedy.

'He'm out of his head wi' fever an' his breathin's that hard an' painful . . . an' he's kept callin' out your name, Miss Miranda. I thought, perhaps, if 'twas you could spare the time to come down, 'twould ease him, though 'tis rainin' fearful hard and you'm a peaky look about 'ee . . .'

'I'll come.'

Forget everything. Forget the drinks for the invalids upstairs. Let Flossie deal with those. A quick word with Miss Swann. Pull on the sturdy bad-weather cloak. Heaviest boots and take the big black umbrella Miss Swann crept out of the parlour to remind me of. And run as best we could. Hopping over the puddles, slithering in mud on the steep descent into Dawlish. And Emma's voice in my ear, breathless with the hurry.

'He started bad some days back, but they'd a cargo come two nights since – and they 'ad to fetch 'en in at the Warren. They'd a terrible soaking. 'Twas the nag got him back so far as Sam'l Snell's stable, 'im as hires hosses, and Mrs Rudd said

– that's where 'e lodges – 'er didn't know how 'e made his way 'ome from there, though it's no more'n a street away. Fell in a dead faint on the step, 'bout six o'clock in the morning, it'd be, and 'er had to call in two men passin' on their way to work to get him inside and into his bed . . .'

Take the turning into the town, the Dawlish Water running full and brown between the sodden banks. Rain pounding on the umbrella and dripping on to my boots. Up to the mill, turn right over the bridge . . . Kit . . . Kit . . .

'Yer 'tis, Miss Miranda. Go right in, we'm expected.'

Inside the low thatched cottage a plump, grey-haired, worried-looking woman in a white apron, taking my cloak and umbrella.

'I'm that thankful to see 'ee, Em . . . What about the widow woman? He'm through 'ere, miss . . . I hopes 'er don't delay, for I'm afeard he'm worsening.'

Their anxious voices fading as I walk into the small back room, ducking my head in the low doorway. Very clean and sparse. His travelling trunk in one corner. A chest of drawers on the far side of the narrow bed. A chair this side, with knitting needles and a grey half-knitted sock set down on it, as though Mrs Rudd had dropped them there when she heard us come in.

The rasp of his quick, shallow breathing seemed to set up a terrible, reciprocal pain in my own chest. I felt myself to be choking. Wanting to breathe for him. Deeply and steadily. The breath of life. The skin of his forehead was burning dry under my cold fingers. His head moved restlessly as I touched him and he gave a short hard cough which obviously pained him for he frowned and winced and muttered something incomprehensible. His face on the white pillow looked all bones. Greyish skin stretched tight over them with a hard red flush on each cheek. The narrow eyes with their heavy black lashes, sunk into dark, bruised pits.

I had once, in a waking dream, seen him lying injured, perhaps dying, and tried to will him back to life. I daresay it was nothing to do with my desperate calling of his name, but just that it was not meant that he should die at that time. Perhaps it was merely that his strong constitution had pulled him through, or some far greater power than mine that had decided the time was not ripe to call Christian Warrener's soul from the world. Whatever the cause he had not been grateful for it. Now I wondered if I had the right to interfere . . .

But only for a moment.

If there was life, there was hope. The bitterness in him would soften, grow less sharp. He would turn again to his music, find an outlet for all that suppressed creativity – in composing, teaching . . . something. I sank to my knees beside the bed, cradled his face in my hands, pressed the lightest of kisses on his dry, rough lips. 'You will get better, Kit Warrener,' I whispered. 'You can't die. I won't let you. You are too dear to me. I love you.'

'Miranda?' His eyes flickered open. They were fever-bright, without comprehension.

'I'm here, my love.'

'I can't find her. Do you hear? Miranda . . . the ship leaves on the morning's tide . . . where is she? Is she lost?' His hoarse voice sank to an unintelligible mutter.

A flurry of voices, a door banging. Then Widow Thomas was bending over the bed, staring down at him. She put her hand on his forehead, moved it down to the pulse that beat in his neck. Then she drew the curious cone-shaped horn funnel from her basket that I had seen her use on Mrs Greenwood. She laid one end on his chest and put her ear to the other. When she straightened up her expression was solemn.

'We have hard work ahead of us, my dear,' she said quietly. 'Now this is what we must do . . .'

Minutes and hours slipped and ran together, became days and nights. By day I never left him. At night Billy would come, or Emma, or other neighbours, turn and turn about when I went home to wash, to change, to snatch a few hours' exhausted sleep.

Miss Swann croaked, 'Dear girl, if I were only better . . . but I would be a hindrance like this.'

Biddie said, green eyes huge in her pale face, 'Don't fret about us. Do your best for him.'

Mrs Greenwood said, seemingly sparked with new energy, 'He has my prayers. I shall go downstairs today and organise the household. It is grown disgracefully slack.'

Poultices of flaxseed sprinkled with mustard, laid across his chest and round his ribs where it hurt most when he breathed. More pillows to prop him up the better to let him breathe. Support his head and encourage him to sip the infusion of garlic, hyssop and comfrey root and other mysterious ingredients that Widow Thomas brewed freshly several times a day. Replace the hot brick wrapped in flannel at his feet. Sponge his face and hands with warm water, change his nightshirts. Billy – his kind friend – gently pushing me out of the room when it came time to deal with chamber pots and slop buckets. . . . And all the time suppress that frantic sensation that nothing we do is making any improvement. We must keep on. We must hope.

But the fever burned him with its dry fire. Delirium racked him. Causing him to cry out and fling himself violently about the bed. Sometimes he was at sea, sometimes riding a horse that he could not control. Sometimes he called my name but he never heard when I answered.

In serious cases of inflammation of the lungs, where life hung in the balance, Widow Thomas said, the crisis tended to occur on odd-numbered days. Three or five or seven or nine. Then the fever would break and the congestion loosen. And if it did not . . .

The third day passed with no change except the sense that he was weakening. The fourth. The fifth. Widow Thomas came that afternoon and stayed. The light outside turned to dusk, then December darkness. I felt suspended in timelessness. Waiting. Waiting . . . Sometimes I reached out and smoothed the dark tangle of his hair, traced the white line of the scar that curved up above his eye . . . At some point Billy looked in and went away. Mrs Rudd fetched in small glasses of elderberry cordial. 'Something in it to give 'ee heart,' she said, and I choked as I drank it. I wondered if the brandy with which she had laced it had been brought in by *Phoebe-Jane*, and found myself swearing under my breath that Kit had ever mixed himself up in the trade that had brought him to this. I think I was still cursing silently as I nodded off. I awoke with a jerk, my head sunk at an uncomfortable angle. I had lost a few minutes, I thought, but it must have been much longer. Then I realised the difference.

'Oh, God, why didn't you wake me?' I wailed.

He lay there still as death. His face carved in marble, no breath that I could hear . . . While I had been asleep, he had, he had . . . Then, miraculously, his heavy lashes lifted and there was recognition in them. I saw his lips move as he struggled to speak. I took his hand, lifted it to my cheek. He smiled and I said, 'Hush, my dear. You must rest. We will talk when you are well again.' Then I tucked his hand under the covers and watched him slide into sleep. Restful, calm sleep. I could see that now.

Widow Thomas said, quietly, 'The crisis is come and gone. In a few hours, he will wake and be himself again.'

I was still sitting staring at him, scarcely able to believe it was true, when I heard voices at the door. Billy was saying, 'He'm mortal ill, p'raps 'ee'd better wait, ma'am, while I see . . .'

'I think not.' I knew that voice, those cool, clear, tones. 'I am his cousin. Kindly let me pass.'

I turned my head slowly.

Rich black silk rustled as she took the few paces across the floor to the foot of the bed. The flame of the candle set on the chest of drawers bent and flared as the draught caught it, sending her shadow whirling about the room.

'My poor, dear Kit,' she said softly. 'How is he?'

I could not speak. It was Widow Thomas who answered quietly, 'I believe he is over the worst.'

Caroline Loveridge looked at me then. Under the rim of her black bonnet, her features seemed more finely drawn than I remembered, though it gave her distinction. The narrow, deep-set eyes were the same. Kit's eyes. Though the expression in them was different. So sharp and cold and clever. Chilling me.

'Can this really be Miranda? Of course it is, I see it now. I came straight from Furze House when they told me.' She moved round the bed, placed her hand on my shoulder. 'I have heard how devotedly you have nursed my cousin. My grateful thanks for all you have done. You look exhausted, child. Go home to your bed. I will see to everything now.'

It was true, I was exhausted. Quite suddenly and overpoweringly. My body seemed too heavy to rise from the chair and how on earth should I find the energy to walk home?

But Widow Thomas was on her feet.

'I will walk back with you, Miranda. There is little more that I can do tonight. All he needs now is to be left to sleep.'

At the door I looked back into the room. She was leaning towards him, as I had done so often, stretching out her hand to touch his forehead. Then I turned away and let Widow Thomas lead me home.

I slept the clock round and nobody disturbed me. When I woke, Biddie was standing over me with a laden tray.

'You're not to move until everything's gone,' she said sternly. 'You've scarcely eaten a thing this week.'

She sat with me while I ate. Chivvying me to finish my egg, eat a second piece of toast. 'You've got to get your strength back for Exeter,' she said. 'Violet won't be pleased if you turn up looking so pale and thin.'

'I'm not sure I should go,' I said, leaning back on the pillows. 'Kit will need looking after for a while yet.'

'But there's plenty of others to do that!' She jumped up from the bed and walked to the window. Not looking at me. 'He doesn't need you in particular to nurse him. Miss Swann's better now. She'll keep an eye on him.' A hesitation, then, 'I know that you . . . you like him, Mirrie.'

I sighed. 'More than that, Biddie.'

'Does he feel the same about you?'

'Sometimes I think – I know – that he does.'

'It's best to be sure.' Her voice was so sad that I put down the cup of chocolate, threw back the covers and went to her.

'What is it, Biddie? What's the matter? Are you worried about Mr Grant . . . Greville? What has happened?'

There was a long silence before she said, 'I am expecting his baby.'

'Oh, no! Oh, Biddie, love.' I put my arms around her, hugged her close. 'Does he know? Will he marry you? If he doesn't he'll have me to answer to!'

She gave a shaky laugh. 'I have little fear that he won't.'

'Then it doesn't matter! We can arrange something . . . when we get to Exeter, Violet will see to it all. You know she will.' I hugged her. 'Well, it's not so bad then, is it? You're not the first to go to the altar with a child expected and you certainly won't be the last. There's no need to look so worried.' I thought to josh her out of her sadness. 'How did I not know? I thought you had your courses as normal.'

'I pretended they came when yours did, and put my clean cloths with yours in the soaking bucket. They soon took up the red stain. You didn't notice. I don't suppose Mrs King did when she came to boil them . . . No, it's not Greville, Mirrie, it's me.' Her eyes filled with tears which overflowed and slid gently down her cheeks as she talked in that same, dead little voice. 'I felt so sure, I was so happy with him. But it's all gone. All that feeling. I thought it was love, but I think now it wasn't. Just . . . just infatuation. I don't care if I never see him again. But now . . .' She laid her hand on her belly. 'Now I must for the sake of this baby. We only did it the twice. For that I shall be tied to him for life.'

'When you see Greville again, it might be different. You'll love him as you did before. Perhaps it's what happened with . . . with Matt Parker that's set you feeling like this.'

'Maybe. Everything was such fun . . . so exciting before.'

'There you are then! You're not over the shock of it yet! You'll forget about it in time.'

But I heard the hollowness in my own words. The violence of that night had altered Biddie. Caused a difference in her perception of men, of herself. That clarity of vision had encompassed her emotions. Made her reassess what she felt about Greville Grant. Love and infatuation. How easily the two might be confused . . .

'You didn't mean what you said? About not going to Exeter?' Her tear-stained face turned anxiously towards me. 'I . . . I can't bear to go through with it on my own. Oh, Violet's all right. But you're my proper friend, Mirrie. I need you there.'

'Then of course I'll go,' I said quietly.

And she was right about one thing. Painfully, shockingly right. Kit had no more need of me. When I arrived at his lodgings later that morning, it was to find Mrs Rudd vigorously turning out his room.

Caroline Loveridge had arrived in her carriage an hour before and taken him off to complete his recuperation in her house in Teignmouth.

We made the best of Christmas for the sake of the little girls. Miss Swann still looking wan and languid. Biddie subdued. Myself going round smiling, talking, laughing to cover the emptiness within. Miss Groom came to visit on Boxing Day, walking up from Teignmouth. She had accompanied Caroline to Furze House the night of Kit's crisis and been left there while Caroline took the carriage to Dawlish and the reunion with her cousin. The ladies – Mrs Greenwood in particular – had taken to her and she to them.

'There is little I can do to help,' she said, accepting a second cup of tea as we sat in the parlour. 'Caroline has her cousin under the care of Teignmouth's finest physician with two good nurses in constant attendance. Which leaves me quite free to enjoy the salubrious air of this charming district. Such a difference from Derbyshire, which I always found rather bleak after living in Hertfordshire as I did in my youth. Indeed, I shall not pine in the least for Crossbank Grange.' She looked across to Biddie and me. 'Caroline took me into her confidence early on about her part in your escape from the mill. I have to say at first I did not think it at all suitable that she should involve herself in such an impulsive way, however well meant the intention. But we had such long interesting talks about the necessity for improving the lot of the apprentices in accordance with modern philanthropic principles that I found myself quite swayed to her point of view.'

I could imagine it. Clever Caroline, making an ally of Miss Groom. Turning unpromising material to her advantage.

'I should not have liked her to make a habit of allowing apprentices to run off whenever they wished,' she said with something of her old prim air, 'but I did see sense in ensuring that they were kept healthy, in mind and body, in order that they could work to the best advantage of all concerned. Which is what we set about doing. Why, by the time Mr Loveridge suffered his unfortunate accident, the children were having butcher's meat twice a week, and the apprentice house had been much improved. Cleaned and limewashed and the children suffered to be bathed once a fortnight – which was by no means a popular move – and a small infirmary set up. What with that and the curate persuaded by means of a small retainer to supervise regular lessons for the boys so that Caroline and myself could attend more comfortably to the teaching of the girls – I daresay the Crossbank apprentices were better off than any others in the county! And I have heard that the new owners, being of the Quaker persuasion, intend to make even more improvements. I should not be surprised if they put off the Hatchers – *she* was amenable enough, but neither Caroline nor I could abide *him*, though Charles thought him an excellent overseer. However, he is fond of his drink and the new owners are set against anything of that sort, so we shall see.'

The change in her was astonishing. Where was the mousy, downtrodden Miss Groom of memory? Her mourning black was fashionable and of good quality. Her bonnet of the latest shape with black silk roses nodding under the brim. When we were at Crossbank I had thought her elderly. Now she seemed a great deal younger. Certainly not as old as Miss Swann and Mrs Greenwood. There was a brightness about her that had certainly not been apparent before. And not hard to discover the reason. It was Dear Caroline this and Generous Caroline that. The second Mrs Loveridge had evidently set herself to eradicate the influence the first Mrs Loveridge had laid upon the timorous spirit of the dependent cousin.

She called again the day before we left for Exeter. Biddie and I had been busy at our packing and had not realised we had a visitor. I had gone downstairs in search of a book I had left in the parlour and which I wanted to take with me. Hearing Miss Groom's voice within, I paused at the door. I had every intention of retreating. I daresay we should have to come down to take tea in a while but there was a limit to how long I could bear to sit with Caroline Loveridge's wonderful character being extolled in every sentence. Then I heard Miss Groom say clearly, 'Kit is still very weak, of course, but he improves every day. It is wonderful how patient Caroline is with him.'

That was a crumb of comfort for my poor starved heart. He was mending, thank God. I did not wish to hear how Caroline was taking part in that process. I turned away. And then I heard it. Heard the key turn in Pandora's box.

'Oh, it is such a wonderfully romantic story. I tell you this in the strictest confidence, but Caroline has confided in me that she and Kit are to be married as soon as he is fully recovered.'

'Married?' Mrs Greenwood's voice. 'How very exciting. Will it be here?'

'But she is still in mourning.' Miss Swann, more cautiously.

'Dear Caroline feels there is little point in waiting another year when they have been separated for so long.' A fulsome sigh. 'She thinks spring will be the best time. I do so agree. After all, they will only be fulfilling a promise they made to each other when they were still living in her uncle's house in London. Had Kit not been obliged to leave home when his father was so unkind to him, and Caroline wed by the time he returned, they would have married as soon as he came of age. Eloped, if necessary. Of course, he did return when he was twenty-one, but he was unfortunately just too late . . .'

I broke away and ran upstairs. I knew exactly what I wished to do now. What other course was open to me? To stay here living for scraps of news? Always to be reminded of where he was and with whom? Somehow I finished my packing calmly. I was glad I did not have many personal possessions, but there were enough books to weigh down my bags considerably. I did not go down for tea when Flossie came to tell us we had company. I pleaded a sick headache. And later after supper, when Biddie was seeing the little ones to their beds, I had a quiet word with Miss Swann and Mrs Greenwood, telling them what I had heard, what I had decided and why. I left them both looking a little shaken, a little sad. I felt stricken myself. But it was the only way.

The next morning before we left, I took a turn round the garden just as it was growing light. The sky was brightening to lacklustre sunshine. Miss Swann was already out, hoeing around the two small camellia bushes Mr Crowe had sent in exchange for the cuttings he had taken to Moondance.

'They seem to have taken no harm from the transplanting,' she said, pleased. 'Look at the fat buds on this one. Mr Crowe said they would flower early. Are you ready for off, Miranda? I shall get my cloak.'

'No, please. We can manage the bags between us. It is a long walk back up the hill and you are not properly well yet.'

She began to protest, then fell silent.

I cleared my throat and said, 'You will give him – Kit – my . . . my good wishes when you see him? I hope he will be happy.'

Miss Swann drew her handkerchief from her apron pocket and blew her nose before she said, quietly, 'I shall, Miranda. Dear me . . . so sudden. Yet I do understand. Sometimes a clean break . . . I have become used to partings over the years, but some are more painful than others.' She paused to gather

her thoughts and said, more briskly, 'And one thing that may ease your mind a little when you are gone. I have made up my mind to speak to him about his involvement with the free traders.'

'You know?'

'I have always known. Even from the time when he was mixed up with Captain Luscombe's band. I thought it best not to interfere. Men will not listen to what they do not wish to hear. But now I think it has gone far enough and I hear whispers that with the French war being over, there are naval cutters to spare to go about the business of intercepting cargoes. I think things will tighten up on land and sea and there will be far more danger than there is at present.'

'Perhaps it is Caroline you should persuade,' I said bitterly. 'She seems to have most influence.'

'I sometimes think it is the women who are left behind who suffer most,' she said sadly. I knew she was thinking of her father's misfortunes and I regretted my sharp answer. If Caroline could turn Kit from the smuggling, then I sincerely hoped that she would.

'Though I understand your reasons for leaving,' she went on, 'I should like you to know there will always be a place here for you if you ever need it.'

'Shall you manage?'

She smiled. 'Oh, yes. We managed before, did we not? Harriet has some notion that Miss Groom might favour being asked to give us an hour or two. And we can always take on one of the brighter girls to train up as an assistant. That is not to say we shall not miss you. And we shall write to each other.'

'Whatever happens, I shall never, never forget what you did and these happy years.'

I kissed her soft cheek and turned away quickly before I should disgrace myself with tears. Then I went back into the house to say goodbye to the others.

We were halfway down the hill into Dawlish when we saw

Widow Thomas striding towards us, the lurchers at her heels, a basket over her arm, her old faded sunbonnet incongruous on this January day.

'So you are away,' she said without preamble. 'It is for the best, I think.'

Then she turned her odd-coloured gaze on to me. For a second there was such an intensity in her eyes that it was almost painful.

'I shall think of you, child. There are decisions still to be made. You will know when the time comes to make the right choice.'

She said nothing more but left us to continue our walk down the hill to await the Exeter coach.

Biddie and Mr Greville Grant were married before January was out. A day of hard frost and a bitter east wind that threw spiteful flakes of fine snow at us as we came out of the church. A simple ceremony with just Violet and myself to represent the bride and a friend of Mr Grant's to stand for him.

Mr Grant, with two succesful exhibitions behind him and a number of good commissions in hand, was able to rent a house in St Sidwell's in a newish terrace. It had the benefit of a large back room facing north, which he set about turning into a studio, and there were two good bedchambers besides and a decent parlour and kitchen. Biddie flung herself into the role of new bride with enthusiasm. The purchasing of furniture, the choosing of materials for curtains and cushions, the sewing of tablecloths. She was teasingly affectionate with Mr Grant and he was clearly besotted with her. Only occasionally, when we were quiet together and she was tired, did I see the shadow in her eyes. But as the days drew on even that did not appear so often or seem so dark as it had been.

In April Mr Grant was to have his exhibition in Bath. By then, Biddie was growing a little too cumbersome to fancy the long journey by coach. Instead, she came with Violet to visit me at Moondance.

* * *

I had fully intended once I was back in Exeter to advertise for a position as governess. It was Violet who delayed me.

'Oh, not yet, Miranda. Not until the end of the month, or it will upset all my plans. You really are the most thoughtless pair . . . And you are more than thoughtless, Biddie, you are a fool! To be breeding without the benefit of a ring on your finger! I did warn you, remember? And it was all quite unnecessary, I may say, for if you had come to me first I should have instructed you how to conduct yourself so as not to get in that plight. But there again, I must take some of the blame for not realising passionate temperaments will have their way. Still, what's done's done and we must make the best of it. I suppose we must get you engaged straight off. But at least your belly is still decently flat and the gowns I have ordered will not need much adjustment . . . Oh, yes, I insist we shall go to an assembly or two still. The dancing master will come every morning this week to teach you the rudiments.'

Although I had not expected to enjoy myself in the least, I discovered that learning to dance was the greatest fun. I picked up the steps far more quickly than Biddie and at the assembly, even if I stumbled occasionally or had to be propelled by my partner to the correct position in the set when I took a wrong turn, it could be passed off with a good-humoured apology. Mr Grant did dance if – a little unfortunately – in the manner of his dog. All bounds and eagerness and flailing feet. Biddie danced mostly with him, as was proper for a girl newly engaged, and only a turn or two with the likes of soberly married gentlemen such as Colonel Bonynge.

I, on the other hand, scarcely had time to fix a face to a name before I was whirled off by one or other of Violet's less weighty acquaintances whom I had met in her drawing room. Her salons seemed to have attracted a considerable number of young, struggling artists, an actor or two, and three poets, one of whom declared himself madly in love with me the third time I met him and wrote me a rather bad poem dedicated to 'MB, in the hope that her radiant orb will alight with favour on her most devoted admirer'.

'I'm afraid my radiant orb is singularly unattracted to Mr Rudyard,' I said to Violet. 'In fact it overlooks him most of the time since he scarcely comes up to my shoulder.'

'Which gives him the most wonderful acquaintance with your bosom,' said Violet dryly. 'I rather fancy his real interests lie in that direction.'

'For radiant orb read bosom?'

'Precisely.'

We laughed a great deal in those weeks. I gave myself completely to the pleasures of the moment. Why not? New gowns, new acquaintances, a flirtation or two, dancing, cards, growing to accept compliments as my due. It was easy. I did not need to think, or worry or plan. There were only a few difficult moments.

When Violet said, 'Sad about Kit Warrener's injury. I got him a good price for his fiddle.' Or, 'I am sorry Kit does not come any more with the tea and the brandy. I get charged more by the man who delivers it now.' Or, 'What is this Caroline Loveridge like?'

Then just before Biddie's wedding a letter arrived from Miss Swann:

> *You will be interested to hear of a most dreadful battle occurring between the customs men and the freetraders. It is believed that Captain Luscombe informed an officer about the* Phoebe-Jane*'s expected rendezvous with a tea clipper some miles off Dartmouth. The lugger, with a full load of tea aboard, was duly confiscated by a Revenue cutter and at the same time an ambush was laid at the Warren where the men were waiting to bring it ashore. But the officers were spotted and the ambush foiled. However, Captain Luscombe's gang, thinking the customs men were employed elsewhere, were taking in a shipment at Holcombe, when they were seen by the officers riding back to Teignmouth. There was considerable fighting and injury and many men*

wounded and taken prisoner. Captain Luscombe himself has been closely questioned, some of his men turning traitor. It has given Kit leave to think. He has been in a considerably more thoughtful frame of mind during his convalescence. I do not suppose he would wish to tie what funds he has in another ship. The Phoebe-Jane *is now destined to be cut up and a loss to all who invested in her . . .*

Violet was the only one to be disappointed.

'I made a nice little profit on the surplus brandy I sold. No matter. Something else will crop up, I daresay . . . Oh, here is another letter for you hiding under mine.'

It was from Theophilus Crowe. He had been in touch with Miss Swann and had heard that I had left Dawlish for good. He had a proposition to put to me which might be of interest. He would be in Exeter next Thursday and would call at Bedford Circus if it was convenient at three o'clock.

I wrote back – out of curiosity more than anything – and asked him to call.

The house was quiet without Biddie. And the prospect of a visit from Mr Crowe seemed to cast a sobering influence over my mood. Or rather, I suppose, I was tiring a little of the round of somewhat thoughtless pleasure and beginning to turn my mind to more practical matters. Such as finding myself some useful, paying occupation. Violet, carelessly, said I could stay as long as I wished, but it was not what I wanted. I sighed. I seemed destined to wish for things I could not have. Moondance. Kit Warrener. Other people had a greater claim on both. Now I felt aimless, adrift. My life without purpose . . .

Mr Crowe appeared promptly and was shown into the drawing room, looking a little awkward when he saw Violet, who laughed and said, 'I think we were a little at sixes and sevens last time we met, sir. Perhaps we should start again and pretend I never went to Moondance.'

It was about Moondance that he had come. He did not prevaricate in any way and I found myself grateful for his directness. He had come, he said, to offer me a position in his house.

'I have tried, Miss Brehault, two methods of living since I came to England,' he said frankly. 'Both outrageous in their way and neither giving me full satisfaction. I prefer, if anything, the life of a recluse but even that has begun to pall of late. I feel that having swung between two extremes I now wish to attempt the middle road. I intend to live fairly modestly still, but with a little more openness to plain society. I shall begin again on the refurbishment of the house, as well as continuing my work on the gardens, which as you know is my first love. This time I shall be more practical, opening up rooms one by one and employing one or two reliable servants, which the house needs as Rokiah and Ahmed have expressed a wish to return to their native land. The winters are very bad for them, so this is an opportunity for me to begin afresh.

'The house also needs the supervision of someone who cares for it. Someone who will supervise the work there – which truth to tell does not interest me very much. Someone like yourself, Miss Brehault. When I heard you would probably be looking for a position, I thought it a most fortuitous coincidence. I should not expect you to answer straight off for I realise the position of housekeeper perhaps does not have quite the same status as that of governess or teacher. And knowing my . . . er . . . background and comparing it to your own, well, such a reversal of fortunes might set you against the idea also.'

'You wish me to be housekeeper at Moondance?'

'As I say, I shall not hurry your decision. Shall we say a week?'

'Indeed not, Mr Crowe.'

His long face fell.

'Ah, I had my doubts.'

'Did you? I did not. I will accept your offer gladly, Mr Crowe. Now, when would you expect me to take up my duties?'

* * *

So it was that in April Violet and Biddie came to visit me, at Mr Crowe's invitation. By then, with the aid of the new parlourmaid, Freda, and a sturdy woman who came by the day from the village, I had cleared and refurbished two good rooms in the south wing where they could be comfortable. Rokiah and Ahmed had already left. I had hired a cook and a kitchen maid and Mr Crowe had taken on a pair of young brothers from the village to train to his methods in the garden. Once it was known that the Malays had gone and that Miss Brehault, the last of the old family who had been thought dead, was in residence, there was no lack of applicants in search of work at Moondance.

The weather turned glorious the week that Violet and Biddie were with me and even they, with no great love for open spaces, could appreciate the splendour of the garden when everything was bursting to fresh, green life, the grass thick with spring flowers and the dark-leafed camellias full of fat pink and white blossom. Miss Swann had so much wanted to see them, but she could not be spared from the school just yet. But she would come in August – and Mrs Greenwood if she could be persuaded – and I looked forward immensely to that.

Biddie, Violet and I sat often in the little rose arbour, chatting and sewing. Biddie seemed drowned in contentment, talked often and lovingly of her husband and seemed to have achieved a measure of serenity that boded well for her future. They were very admiring of what I had achieved so far in the house and of the little room – Aunt Hettie's old room – that I had taken over in the south wing. I had made it very comfortable and Mr Crowe had given me Mama's old éscritoire as a gift. As I sat up in my little eyrie, writing my letters or reading, I often had the fancy that I was not alone. That I heard the swish of Mama's skirts, caught the faint fragrance of the jasmine scent she wore. They were sounds and scents that gave me the greatest sense of peace.

On the April afternoon after Biddie and Violet had left

and the house was quiet again, I walked round the lake to my favourite spot and sat in the sunshine as I had often dreamed of doing. How very fortunate I was that after all this time I was back here in the place I loved best, caring for it, working for it.

It had been a pleasant week with my friends, but in a way I was glad to be alone again with my thoughts. There was a deal to think about. I had not told Violet or Biddie that Mr Crowe had asked me to marry him. Very gravely and formally.

'Not yet, Miranda. In a year, perhaps. More if you should think it necessary. I want you to think about it carefully. I have grown fond of you. I would hope in that time you would grow fond of me. I do not speak of love, my dear, but I think we could make a good partnership.'

Fond. Yes, I had already grown fond of him. And remained so, even when I heard the truth about my father's death. I had to ask him. And he had been honest with me.

'It is an episode I am ashamed of,' he said with a sigh. 'You see, I did not escape in the uproar of the attack. I was already well away from the huts when it happened. I had left your father to his fate. He was dying, I could see that. I was thinking only to save my own skin, because I did not trust the Norwegian. So that night I had already decided to leave, steal the Norwegian's cache of gold and make off back to Malacca. The young native woman who was caring for him watched me go. I will never forget the look in her eyes. They seemed to spark "traitor" in the lamplight.' He took a deep breath. 'I killed a man that night. The ruffian who guarded the gold. I put my hand over his mouth and my knife in his back. Then I dug up the cache and made off. I was no more than a few yards along the track when I heard the screaming and saw the flames go up.' He stopped, then said in a flat, expressionless voice: 'So there you have it. I abandoned your father and killed a man and I have never spoken of it before, nor shall again.'

I sat in silence for a while.

'I am grateful for your honesty.'

Unexpectedly, I began to cry. Perhaps they were tears that had been building up for a long time. Tears for my father, tears for Kit, tears for lost hopes . . . tears of relief that there was a purpose to my life again, a new beginning. Perhaps even a tear or two for Mr Crowe, who was not a man without conscience, after all, even though he had deserted my father and killed a man out of desperation and greed.

He comforted me awkwardly. Patting my arm, handing me his handkerchief.

'I am so sorry for upsetting you,' he said when at last my weeping subsided.

'It was not your fault,' I said. 'It was many things. And best got rid of.'

So now I sat among the daffodils with my book in my hands and looked at the sparkling ripples running across the surface of the lake. I did not know how I should decide, or how I should feel a year hence, but I was content to wait. Content to live in and help to restore my beloved home to the beauty it deserved.

The ripples on the water seemed for a moment to blur and shift. And as I looked I heard someone calling my name.

For a moment I went cold, with the certainty that it was one of those moments of knowing that I had never quite managed to accept. I knew that voice. Knew it so well. But the call came, louder, more urgently. And it was real.

The book dropped from my fingers. Somehow I got to my feet. I turned and saw him coming across the grass, starting to run.

I did not move. Could not. Within a yard of me he stopped dead.

'Miranda,' he said. 'I could not go away without seeing you.'

He was far too thin, I thought. Too pale. And, oh, to hear him say my name in that way, with such longing.

'Go away?' I said, faintly. 'I . . . I had thought you married by now and living in Torquay. Miss Swann said March . . .'

He shook his head. 'It was a childhood dream. We are no

longer children. Caroline . . . I would have made her very unhappy. I had to make her see that. It was . . . difficult. I have had a lot of time to think while I was ill.'

'Where . . .' I swallowed. 'Where will you go? What will you do?'

He shrugged. 'Away. I . . . I need to find my music again. Somehow. To find myself.' He held up his damaged hand. 'I once said if I could not have it all, I did not want any of it. Now I know I was wrong.' He looked into my eyes. 'About many things.'

I reached out and took his damaged hand in mine. Slowly I raised it to my cheek.

'I remember – was it a dream? – when I was ill. Seeing you, feeling your touch, your kiss.'

'It was no dream,' I said softly.

He drew me close.

We stood together a long time. Heart beating against heart. Then he released me. 'Will you wait, Miranda? Do I have any right to ask?'

'Oh, yes,' I said softly. 'On both counts.'

He smiled. 'You have brought me back from death twice. Now I know why.'

'Take care. I do not have an infinite capacity for restoring you to health.'

'You do, Miranda, you do.'

I stood a long time watching him go, then I picked up my book and went back into the house.

Epilogue

One morning in the summer of 1818 a grey-haired gentleman riding a hired nag came up to the gates of Moondance. He dismounted and led his horse through the small gate and paused to look at the lodge which seemed newly rebuilt though apparently not yet occupied. He walked the horse along the raked gravel, then turned across the grass to where he remembered a clump of oak trees had once stood, though there was now only one of the large old trees left. A brace of new saplings, he saw, had been planted a little way from the stumps of the two that had been cut down. And there was the house, amid its green lawns and mounded trees, with the silvery sweep of the lake at its feet. Just as it had stood through the centuries.

He was not sure whether he should have come. It had been impulse. Company business had brought him to London, the first time he had been to England for more than fifteen years. It was extraordinary, the tale he had heard from the innkeeper in Ashburton: that Theo Crowe now owned Moondance.

Aminah had always said Theo had escaped before they had been set upon that night at Geminchi, though he had no recollection of it. No recollection of anything until he had eventually recovered under Aminah's tender care. It was her father who had led the attack, to rescue his daughter from the devils who had taken her. Aminah, a princess among her own rich and powerful people, whom he had married and who had given him three fine sons.

He had once had a daughter, too. Perhaps it was conscience that had pricked him when he was on his home ground again, though he no longer thought of England as home. That was the lush, green tropical land where his knowledge of and respect for the native tribes had enabled him to create a special role for himself. A go-between in negotiation and diplomacy that had done much to ease the tension between the people to whom he was bonded by respect and marriage and the powerful East India Company.

A very satisfactory life that he had no wish to change.

For two pins he would ride off now. He could see for himself that everything prospered here. But there again, he might find out where Miranda was now. Look her up. Married to a music teacher, the innkeeper had said, an incomer of only three years' standing who would not have recognised Sir Anthony Brehault, with or without his white hair and sun-browned skin. She had been housekeeper here for some time. Now she lived the other side of the moor somewhere.

Was it right to dig up old memories? He thought about it for a moment. Thought about Theo. Thought about his daughter. Why not? After all, he had come so far out of his way it would be foolish not to complete what he had set out to do.

He swung himself back into the saddle and turned the horse for Moondance.